Dedication

To my grandson Ketan, who is very kind and helpful, and achieves excellent results when he competes at swimming competitions in which he has won bronze, silver and gold medals

ABB

Please renew or return items by the date
shown on your receipt

www.hertsdirect.org/libraries

Renewals and enquiries: 0300 123 4049
Textphone for hearing or 0300 123 4041
speech impaired users:

L32

written permission of both the copyright owner
and the publisher of this book.

52 380 270 2

Chapter One

Helen Whitley frowned at her reflection in the full-length mirror of her luxurious bedchamber in her brother-in-law's rented house. Pringle, her middle-aged dresser, bent to tweak one of the frills above the hem of the new, cream gown into place, and Helen sighed with pleasure at the sight of soft silk that flowed from beneath her breasts.

Once more, she scrutinised the low-cut bodice, ornamented with tiny seed pearls. Although, in her own opinion, she was too tall for beauty, she was the epitome of a well-dressed young lady ready to attend a ball.

The expression in the green eyes, gazing at her from the mirror, softened. Soon her brother-in-law's comrade in arms, Major, Viscount Langley, would arrive in Brussels and propose marriage to her. She would accept and insist they loved each other too dearly to delay their wedding. Afterward, she would be free from her brother-in-law's charity, which, to be just, the gallant Major Tarrant never seemed to begrudge.

Another long sigh escaped Helen when she coaxed a pomaded curl into place on her forehead. Perhaps she was an ungrateful wretch

5

to find it so difficult to be dependent on her older sister, Georgianne, and her husband. After all, through marriage to Tarrant, their cousin-in-law, Georgianne saved her and their younger sister Barbara from their mother, who imbibed excessive amounts of alcohol and wine.

Helen shuddered at the memory of Mother whipping Georgianne with a riding crop.

After the viscount and Tarrant rescued her, Langley made it obvious he had fallen in love with her.

"Miss?"

Her head filled with thoughts of Langley, Helen allowed Pringle to enfold her in a rose-pink velvet cloak which would keep her warm on her way to the ball with Georgianne and Cousin Tarrant. Once, she looked forward to entering society. Now she was part of it, her enjoyment was diminished by Langley's absence. The evening would be perfect if he were present. She longed for the day when they would be husband and wife.

Chapter Two

Hertfordshire
12th March, 1815

Major, Lord Langley rode toward his ancestral home, Longwood Place, for the first time in five years or more. He frowned. Ruts and weeds marred the drive. Small saplings and brambles sprouted beneath the plane trees on either side of the once magnificent approach.

Troubled, he guided his horse through a pair of tall wrought iron gates. At first sight of the lawns sweeping up to the house, he caught his breath. They should have been scythed. They looked more like meadows than green swards which befitted a nobleman's estate. Although his father, the earl, rarely visited the property due to an irrational dislike of it, he should maintain the house and grounds.

Langley dismounted in the forecourt. He looped his horse's bridle around one of a pair of grimy urns devoid of plants. What could be amiss? He ascended the broad steps. Before he applied the knocker, a footman admitted him.

"Send for a groom. Tell him to walk my horse until he has cooled, and then water and feed him."

Immaculate in a black coat and trousers, every white hair on his head in place, Chivers, the butler, stepped toward him. "Welcome home, my lord." His faded blue eyes shone with obvious pleasure.

Langley smiled. He had sent advance notice of his arrival, so no doubt Chivers had been waiting for him.

His quick gaze around the oak-panelled hall confirmed his conviction something was wrong. The oak panels needed to be polished and the red damask curtains were faded.

No matter. Soon he would bring his bride, Helen, daughter of the late Major Whitley, who gave his life fighting against Napoleon's soldiers in the Iberian Peninsula, to Longwood Place. Helen would help Mamma set all to rights. A vision of his intended bride, tall and shapely, with a wealth of chestnut-brown hair, filled his mind. Yes, she was young, eighteen to his twenty-eight years, but with an aura of calm which suited him after so many battles during which he saw friends killed or maimed. Now, curse it, Napoleon had escaped from Elba. Langley did not doubt he and his best friend, Helen's brother-in-law, must fight again. If he had not been granted a brief furlough, he would be in Brussels with their hussar regiment, The Glory Boys, part of the army of occupation.

Chivers cleared his throat. "My lord, the earl awaits you in the library. The countess is in the morning room with your older sisters."

"My brothers?"

"My lord, have you forgotten Mister Julian is at Oxford and Master Giles is at Eton."

"Yes, how remiss of me."

Chivers inclined his head. "May I take your hat?"

Langley handed the man his hat, to which his valet had attached an officer's cockade. He indicated his dusty boots. "I cannot join the earl until I have mended my appearance. My man will arrive soon with my baggage."

Chivers cleared his throat. "The earl left instructions for you to join him when you arrived."

Langley pointed at the dusty chandelier. "Have the cobwebs removed."

"Yes, my lord, I apologise. There are too few servants to do all the work."

"I am sorry to hear that." It would not be proper to question his father's butler. "Chivers," he added.

"My lord?"

"You need not continually address me as my lord. Major will suffice."

"Yes, my…I mean Major."

Langley strode to the library.

Inside the large room, ornamented with marble busts and a handsome globe, he inclined his head toward his tall thin father, whose hair, once black, was now white.

The earl looked up from a table piled with papers. "So, you are home, my boy, soon to embark for Brussels. Supposed you were back in England for good, when you sold your last army commission."

"Rupes and I could not desert Wellington, now that it is certain he must invade France to put a stop to Napoleon's pretensions."

"Rupes? Oh, you mean Major Tarrant, who married a nobody. Mind you, the Major is only a baronet's son so he is of little consequence."

What would his father say when he informed him he intended to marry Helen? "May I be seated, sir?" He did not wait for permission to sit on a wing-chair opposite the desk. "How is Mamma?"

"In a sad-to-do."

"Why?"

"Problems, my boy, vile ones. If this damned palsy were cured, I would make good my losses in London where my luck would be sure to change."

Langley caught his breath. "Cards?"

"Yes." The earl looked down at his tremulous hands with disgust. "Lady Luck did not favour me. Now my hands are too unsteady for me to play. I am done up, my boy. Forced to dismiss half the indoor servants, gardeners and grooms. My confounded man of business says I must retrench even further." Papa waved a document at him. "Longwood is mortgaged."

"The house in Brighton?"

"Lost it on the turn of an accursed card."

"The manor in Hertfordshire which you prefer to here?"

"Sold to pay my most pressing debts. Why else would I be in this damned mausoleum?"

No wonder his mother was in a 'sad-to-do'. Langley pressed his lips into a thin line, a habit acquired in the army when he wanted to check his anger.

"Well, you know your duty, my boy." Papa reached for the brandy bottle. "Pity you did not marry Amelia Carstairs. Rumour says she will inherit her grandmother's fortune. You must marry another heiress."

"Impossible!" he exclaimed, furious at the idea of marriage to meet his father's gambling debts. "I shall marry Rupes's sister-in-law."

"What! An almost penniless girl?"

Langley nodded.

Papa's cheeks became an alarming shade of scarlet. "I forbid it."

"With all due respect, sir, you cannot. I don't need your permission to wed. Moreover, I have sufficient funds to support myself and a wife."

"Enough to provide for your mother and sisters when I am dead and buried?"

"Once it becomes known you are almost bankrupt, my marriage prospects will be negligible."

"Are you a numbskull?"

No, he was not.

The earl thumped his fist on the desk. The goose quill fell from the inkpot onto a sheaf of papers, spattering ink over them. "Plenty of rich merchants would be pleased if one of their daughters married you in exchange for a title and a fine estate." Papa's blue-tinged lips tightened.

"Longwood is no longer a fine estate."

"Bah, money would restore it. With regard to your marriage, there is a fellow, a manufacturer called Mister Tomlinson, who made a fortune. He would be glad to have you for a son-in-law."

Langley stood. With difficulty he refrained from upbraiding his father for recklessness. He strode to the pair of tall windows, which overlooked the grounds at the rear of the house. More unkempt lawns stretched toward a stand of trees in front of a high brick wall. If only the grass still resembled a tranquil sea as it did during his grandfather's lifetime.

He could not understand the earl's aversion to Longwood Place. Once it was a centre of political power and now—

Papa's voice broke into his thoughts. "We must lose no time, my boy."

In spite of his inner wrath, he did not remind the earl he was no longer a boy.

"You shall meet Miss Tomlinson before you embark for Brussels. Two or three days later you may propose marriage to her. We shall find some pretext or other for you to wed her before your departure for the Low Countries."

"Miss Tomlinson might reject my proposal."

"Nonsense!"

Langley turned slowly. Perhaps Papa exaggerated. Maybe his situation was better than he claimed. His man of business in charge of the family's affairs might be able to offer another solution.

The notion of wedding anyone other than Helen disgusted him. Yet, one thing his papa said was true. He knew his duty.

"What have you to say, Langley?"

"That there is much to consider, sir."

This morning he set out from London to inform his parents he would wed Helen. Now, he stood in a library that smelled stale. The windows should be opened to admit fresh air and sunlight. The sights and unpleasant odours all around him tarnished the happy news he had intended to share.

"Excuse me, sir; I must wash and change before I greet Mamma and my sisters." Without waiting for permission, he left the room.

"My lord." Chivers caught him off guard.

The old man must have been waiting outside the library, curious to know what he and Papa spoke of.

"Her ladyship ordered me to have the green bedroom prepared for you instead of your old room near the nursery. Your valet is unpacking your baggage. Shall I have hot water sent up for you to wash and shave?"

Langley nodded.

Some thirty minutes later, dressed in his uniform, he went to join the countess and two of his sisters, eighteen-year-old Charlotte and fifteen-year-old Margaret.

He opened the morning room door quietly. For a few moments, he stood at the threshold observing them. The three fair-haired ladies— her ladyship gowned in pale green silk and his sisters in sprigged muslin—made a charming picture.

Mamma looked up from her embroidery. "Langley, my dear son, how fine you look. Your uniform becomes you. But you are as dark-skinned as a gypsy."

"The effect of sun and harsh weather, Mamma."

Margaret stood quickly, spilling a basket of embroidery silks from her lap onto the floor. "You are here!"

"So you see."

His lively sister flung herself into his arms, almost knocking the breath from his body. He frowned, surprised because he had imagined she might be shy. After all, he had spent many years on campaign with only two brief furloughs. During the last year, since his return to England, he had seen little of her.

"I am glad. Now you are here, Papa will stop raging and Mamma will stop crying. Of course, you will agree," Margaret gabbled.

"To what?"

"To marrying the vulgar manufacturer's daughter so we can have some new gowns and Charlotte can have a London season."

Across the top of her head, Langley looked into Charlotte's calm grey eyes. What did she think of the proposed match to a woman of inferior birth, who would be looked down on by the ton? "You look well, Charlotte."

"Thank you. It is good to see you, although I fear your home-coming is a sorry one."

"You will marry Miss Tomlinson, won't you, Langley?" Mamma asked. "Although it was not quite to my liking, I obeyed my dear Papa when he ordered me to marry your father."

Langley pitied his mother but could not repress a surge of resentment. Why should he wed to rescue his family from financial disaster?

Mamma pressed a small bottle of smelling salts to her nose before continuing. "Thank goodness your older sisters are married." She sighed. "What is to become of my poor Charlotte, Margaret and your little sisters? I don't know. I doubt they will have dowries to match those of their older sisters." Her hands fluttered. "Those wicked men who robbed your father at cards are—"

"Mamma," Charlotte interrupted, "they did not rob him. Papa nearly bankrupted himself at the gaming tables. It is unfair to expect Langley to marry only to restore Papa's squandered fortune."

The countess sank back against the chaise longue. "Langley, I am all heart. Charlotte is not."

"To the contrary, Mamma," Charlotte said, her voice cool, "I have too much heart to wish my brother to be sacrificed to vulgar Mister Tomlinson's elephant of a daughter."

"A reducing diet will much improve her," the countess murmured, "and I don't doubt I might grow fond of her in time."

"Will you marry her?" Margaret asked. "Her father is nice. He has lots of money. I told him I wanted a parrot more than anything else. After his previous visit, he sent me a grey one in a gilded cage."

Even if she was too young to understand the full implications of such a marriage, Margaret shared his parents' selfishness.

Mamma wafted her fan to and fro. "A dreadful, squawking bird with a...a shocking vocabulary. Of course we cannot be rid of it for fear of offending Mister Tomlinson when he visits us today."

Today! His parents wasted no time. With difficulty he managed not to scowl.

Chivers entered the morning room. "Some wine, my lord?"

Langley nodded, grateful for the timely interruption.

"Cook regrets your favourite, salmon, is not available to fortify you before the dinner hour. She enquires whether you would care to partake of lamb sandwiches."

"Yes, I would. I have not eaten since I left London. Please thank her."

Charlotte stood. "Chivers, there is no need to serve my brother in the dining room. You may bring a tray to the blue parlour." She crossed the parquet floor and held Langley's arm. "No need to disturb yourself, Mamma. Margaret, stay here in case our mother requires anything. Come, Langley."

Chapter Three

13th March, 1815

Langley stood aside to allow Charlotte to precede him into the parlour. A quick glance around the room revealed pale blue wallpaper with encroaching mould, and chipped white paintwork. Heavy-hearted, he gestured to a pair of chairs on either side of a sash window.

He sat opposite Charlotte. "Grandfather would not have tolerated such decay."

"Would he not? I rarely saw him, and don't remember much about him. I was only five years-old when he died."

"A pity, he was a magnificent old man— not a gambler like our spendthrift father. He never neglected the house and estate. He valued the orchards, the wood from the forest, farmland and fish from the lake. The good Lord alone knows why Papa has never liked the property."

Charlotte opened her mouth to speak. She refrained when Chivers ushered in a footman.

Solid silver cutlery, china painted with fanciful bucolic scenes, sandwiches and a bowl of pickled walnuts were put on the table between their chairs.

A second footman placed a tray loaded with a decanter of wine and some glasses on a high table which stood against the wall.

"Some wine, my lord?" Chivers asked.

Langley nodded.

While the butler served him, Langley noticed a darn on one of Charlotte's puff sleeves. Disgraceful for her to wear a shabby gown!

"Some wine, Lady Charlotte?"

"No thank you, Chivers. That will be all."

With stately tread, the butler led his underlings out of the room.

What, Langley wondered, should he say to this sister, eleven years his junior? To gain time, he tasted a lamb sandwich. "Delicious! It is far superior to most of our army food while on the march." He sipped some wine. "By the way, I appreciated the many letters you sent me over the years. They were a breath of England. When I read them, I imagined my homeland while I bivouacked in flea-ridden quarters."

"At first my governess insisted I should write to you. When I grew older, I enjoyed doing so and looked forward to your replies. Thank you for the presents you sent me."

"Think nothing of it. I enjoyed choosing them. Now, please tell me what you know about our father's affairs."

Anger flashed in Charlotte's eyes. "I hesitate to mention something you would hear elsewhere. Father lost so heavily at Whites' that…that…he suggested staking my hand in marriage on the turn of a card."

"What!" Langley nearly choked.

Charlotte's cheeks blossomed scarlet. "Oh, nothing came of it. The Duke of Midland

19

intervened. I don't know precisely what ensued, other than Papa did not make the wager."

Enraged, Langley walked back and forth across the parlour.

"Please don't disturb yourself, Langley. Palsy keeps Papa from the card tables, so he is counting on your marriage to Miss Tomlinson to restore the family fortune."

Langley sank back onto his chair. He gazed out of the window, and across the drive around the side of the house, which led to the stables and beyond them to fertile Hertfordshire farmland. He pressed his lips together. Last year, at the end of the war in the Iberian Peninsula, the heiress, Amelia Carstairs, tricked him into proposing marriage by leading him onto a balcony during a ball. First, she claimed she needed air, next, she pretended to faint so he had caught hold of her. Amelia's grandmother, with a score of others, had followed them. In order to save the young lady's reputation upon being discovered with her in his arms, he was obliged to propose marriage, although he wanted to marry Helen. Fortunately, the engagement ended by mutual consent. In love with Helen, he could not marry anyone else.

"Charlotte, please tell me what you know about Miss Tomlinson."

"I am scarcely acquainted with her."

"After meeting her you must have formed some impression."

Charlotte's large grey eyes stared into his. "Well, you heard Mamma say a reducing diet would greatly improve her. Even so, she is not ill-looking."

"Margaret said the father is vulgar, so I suppose the woman's manners are common."

"You are too harsh. Although Mister Tomlinson is somewhat crude and ill-at-ease in a nobleman's mansion, the lady is gently bred. She attended The Beeches, a young ladies' school with an excellent reputation."

Langley rebuked himself for his reference to Miss Tomlinson as a young woman instead of a young lady. "Her mother?"

"She died during Miss Tomlinson's infancy. From something Mister Tomlinson said, I think her ancestry was superior to his."

Langley restrained a sigh. He hoped the earl's financial affairs were better than they seemed.

"Langley, there is no need to despair. I don't dislike Miss Tomlinson. I think she is either shy or extremely reserved. She is well-educated and seems to share our older sister's passion for gardening. Indeed, much to the head gardener's astonishment, Miss Tomlinson offered excellent advice concerning the vegetable garden. Apart from this, I can only tell you she has pleasing manners."

Memories of Helen filled his head. Why he had fallen in love with a young lady barely out of the schoolroom remained a mystery. He believed he would be faithful to her until he died. Her natural calm would steady him. He wanted to confide in her, be her husband and share her bed. Langley swallowed hard. It seemed he would not be in a position to ask his love to wed him when he reached Brussels. Of course, he could not have expected her to tie the knot while he was in danger of being maimed or killed during the inevitable invasion of France and confrontation with Napoleon. Yet the knowledge she would have been his wife if he survived would have sustained him.

"Langley, will you marry Miss Tomlinson?"

He shook his head, turning his attention to Charlotte. "My dear sister, whatever happens in the future, I have sufficient funds to bear the cost of a London Season for you."

Charlotte's lashes fluttered. "You are too generous, but what would Papa say?"

Langley wanted to reply he did not give a tinker's curse for whatever the earl might say. He choked back the disrespectful words concerning their spendthrift parent.

* * * *

Attired in his black and scarlet dress uniform, Langley went to the drawing room to join his family and the Tomlinsons, before they dined.

He entered the room too quietly for them to notice his presence. Mamma sat next to an excessively plump young lady gowned in white, and ablaze with diamonds more suited to a matron than an unmarried girl. He could not see

22

her face, for she gazed down at the carpet as though nothing could be of more interest. His mamma said something. The young woman, whom he presumed to be Miss Tomlinson, nodded, her thick brown hair glowing in the candlelight.

Opposite Mamma, deep in conversation with her, sat a man of ample proportions, garbed in a dark blue velvet coat and breeches, white stockings and a waistcoat embroidered in gold thread and garish colours.

Langley suppressed a desire to flee. "My lord, my lady." He inclined his head toward his parents.

The guest, who must be Mister Tomlinson, stood. He guffawed with obvious delight. "No need to stand on ceremony, Lord Langley, for judging by your uniform that's who you are." The man winked at him. "After all, we will soon be on the best imaginable of terms."

Langley quenched his first instinct to snub the presumptuous man. Good manners did not allow him to be rude to a guest in his father's house.

With extravagant gestures, Mister Tomlinson indicated the faded straw-coloured brocade upholstery and shabby carpet. "I'll soon set all to rights."

Langley stepped back to avoid the manufacturer nudging him in the ribs. Across the room he caught sight of Charlotte, seated at right angles to Mamma, her eyes filled with amusement.

"A glass of wine, my lord?" Chivers asked Langley, his face impassive.

"Of course the lad will have one," Mister Tomlinson said.

"Father," a small, reproachful voice spoke. "You have not yet been introduced to the gentleman."

"No need, no need, he knows who I am."

Papa stood, elegant in a perfectly cut corbeau-coloured coat and breeches, a white waistcoat, white silk stockings, and a cravat cunningly arranged in the style named 'The Oriental'. "Miss Tomlinson, may I present my eldest son, Viscount Langley. Langley, I have the honour to introduce you to Miss Tomlinson."

Langley hoped his disapproval of the profusion of fussy trimmings at the lady's ample bosom did not reveal itself on his face when she glanced at him for a second or two.

Miss Tomlinson looked down, giving no time for more than a glimpse of a pair of hazel eyes and slightly sun-kissed complexion, something most ladies went to great lengths to avoid. What was her Christian name? Her age? Nineteen, twenty or a little older? Regardless of Mister Tomlinson's plans, did she want to marry him?

"My lords, ladies and gentlemen, dinner is served," Chivers announced.

They stood. Mamma placed her gloved hand on Mister Tomlinson's arm.

The earl committed a breach of etiquette by accompanying Charlotte. No doubt Papa was determined to make sure he missed no opportunity to become acquainted with Miss Tomlinson. He offered his arm to the young lady.

Still conscious that Papa should have escorted his guest to the dining room table, Langley sought to set the young lady at ease. "Miss Tomlinson, my sister, Lady Charlotte, tells me you are interested in horticulture."

Despite the anxious expression in her large hazel eyes and colour flaming in her cheeks, she nodded.

What agitated her? "I apologize if I am mistaken." He led her down the high-ceilinged corridor, past oil paintings of his ancestors. Among them was a picture of the Longwood hunt, its men dressed in hunting pink and mounted on fine horses surrounded by a pack of hounds.

The hand on his arm quivered.

"Is my sister mistaken?"

"Yes, I enjoy gardening, but I beg you not to mention it. My father does not think it is a proper occupation for a lady."

"I see," he said, although he did not. His mamma devoted much time to her rose garden. His eldest sister, the mother of several offspring, enjoyed cultivating her flowers and herbs with the help of a gardener. Indeed, while he served overseas she enclosed sprigs of dried lavender, rosemary, thyme and other fragrant dried herbs with her letters.

He led Miss Tomlinson into the large dining room, the table decorated with a centrepiece of early daffodils and laid with silver and fine china.

Langley guided her to her seat on his father's right. He took his place between her and his mother, who sat at the foot of the table with Mister Tomlinson on her right. This necessitated Charlotte having to sit between their father and the manufacturer.

A footman served chicken soup. Papa picked up his spoon. Before he could taste it, Mister Tomlinson spoke. "My lord! Grace!"

"Grace?" the earl said. "There is no one present called 'Grace'."

"My lord!" Mister Tomlinson repeated. "I refer to thanking the Lord for our meal."

"No need to thank me." Papa's mind was obviously elsewhere. "I have an excellent cook."

A half-strangled sound escaped Charlotte, who buried her face in her linen napkin.

Mister Tomlinson's face reddened. "Don't mock me, my lord. Remember the commandment 'thou shalt not take the Lord's name in vain.'"

"I think," Langley began, careful not to allow his amusement over his papa's obtuseness to reveal itself, "Mister Tomlinson wishes to thank not you, sir, but the Lord our God."

"Why did he not say so instead of rambling on while my soup becomes cold? What does he take me for, a damned bishop or a mealy-mouthed parson?"

Charlotte removed the napkin from her face. "Heavenly Father, we thank you for the food we are about to eat. Amen."

His face brick red, Mister Tomlinson picked up his soup spoon. "Well, Lord Langley, what do you think of my girl?" he asked presumably mollified by the brief Grace. "You needn't worry in case she'll waste away if she becomes sick; she's enough substance to her not to miss a few pounds or more."

Charlotte seemed to choke. Speechless, Mamma stared at Mister Tomlinson. Miss Tomlinson's cheeks flushed rose-red. "Father," she murmured.

Langley pitied the young lady's embarrassment. "I am sure your daughter is all that is agreeable."

Silence filled the dining room. Turbot in white sauce garnished with parsley, lobster, a fish stew, and sundry other dishes replaced the soup tureen.

Conversation resumed. The meal progressed until the ladies withdrew, leaving the gentlemen to enjoy their port. Papa, still annoyed by the request to say Grace, drank no more than a single glass before he retired.

"Pass the port, Langley. There's a good lad," the manufacturer said. "Can't deny I'm pleased with the chance to have a private word with you. Provided you treat my girl right; you'll never find me ungenerous. Bless you, I can solve your pa's financial problems and set you up for life. There's no need to delay the wedding. My girl knows it's my ambition for her to be a titled lady and mistress of a great estate." He eyed the tarnished gold tassels which trimmed the royal blue curtains. "At least, with my money, Longwood Place shall be great again."

Torn between affront and amusement, Langley opened his mouth to respond. Before he could do so, the fond father spoke. "No need to thank me, lad. It's a privilege to shackle my girl to a hero. Oh yes, I know how often you were mentioned in dispatches. Mind you, I don't think much of your pa, but I've nothing but respect for you."

"Why? You have only just met me."

Mister Tomlinson's brown eyes widened. "Upon my word, you don't think I'd marry my girl off without investigating her husband-to-be? I know more about you than you can imagine. I have decided you should marry my daughter before your furlough ends." His forehead puckered. "Don't be surprised if she seems reluctant to enter the parson's noose so fast, my girl is a little shy."

Instead of giving in to his immediate reaction at the idea of wedding a virgin who would submit to her fate on the altar of matrimony, Langley gulped some port before he spoke. "Mister Tomlinson, there is much for me to mull over before I consider marriage. I might be seriously wounded, lose a limb or die. To wed Miss Tomlinson now would be dishonourable. She might be widowed in a few months."

The manufacturer thumped his fist on the table so hard that his glass wobbled and the nuts in a bowl rattled. "She might not. No, no, I've decided you're the husband for her, so there's no need to delay." He guzzled some port. "By the grace of Almighty God, you'll survive. If you don't, my daughter might have your child to console her. You may be sure I'd take good care of it."

Unbearable to think of any son or daughter of his being raised by this blunt man, unversed in the ways of polite society. "We have pursued this matter far enough."

"Well, well, my lord, I see you think I am a rough person." He grinned. "Don't forget I'm a shrewd one. It's only a question of time before your pa's bankrupted. Where will you and your family be when his creditors are banging on the door? What will you do?"

"My plans are uncertain. The entail could be broken."

Mister Tomlinson laughed. "You're prepared to lose your inheritance?"

Langley considered the pleasures of riding on his ancestral land, fishing and hunting. No, damn it, he would not give it up. With careful management of the income from tenant farmers and elsewhere, the house and huge estate could be gradually restored to its former glory.

"Given you something to consider lad, haven't I?"

"Indeed, you have." He drank the remainder of his port. "It is time to join the ladies." Langley put the crystal glass on the table with exaggerated care. "Come to the drawing room where the countess will preside over the tea tray."

During the short walk along a corridor, Langley considered the unbelievable truth. His father expected him to marry the ill-bred manufacturer's daughter instead of Helen.

By birth, he and Helen were unequal, but she was a lady, born and bred. Moreover, he looked forward to their marriage strengthening his relationship with her brother-in-law, his closest friend. He looked back to the days when he and Rupes first went to Eton and then to Oxford, before they joined the same regiment. Comrades-in-arms, they fought for over ten years with few furloughs. Best man at Rupes's wedding to Georgianne—whom he considered an honorary sister—he knew Rupes and Georgianne were aware of his love for Helen. What would they think of him if he did not propose? Before he could decide whether or not he should explain his situation to them, a footman opened the drawing room door. Langley gestured to Mister Tomlinson to precede him.

They sat on chairs opposite the ladies. Chivers brought the tea tray, which he placed on a low table in front of Mamma. Relieved, because she neither suggested they entertain themselves with music nor that they play cards, Langley relaxed a little.

"You may go, Chivers." Mamma picked up the teapot. "Charlotte, dearest, please pass the cups?"

Langley stared at the heavy silver tea service. How much was it worth?

He must save the property. Surely there were enough treasures in Longwood Place to pay Father's creditors. If there were not, the London house and the hunting lodge could be sold. Of course, this could not be accomplished without Father's approval. His jaw tightened. He sighed. So few days before he must embark for Brussels, but first he would speak with the bailiff and the steward, then consult Father's man of business in London.

"What do you think, Langley?" Mamma asked.

He turned his attention to her. "I beg your pardon."

"I referred to Mister Tomlinson's suggestion." Mamma drew her Paisley shawl a little closer around her shoulders.

"I don't know what to say," he said, suspicious of any suggestion the manufacturer might have made.

Charlotte laughed. "Langley, confess you were wool gathering. Mister Tomlinson said he prefers 'piping hot food' to cold food and suggested the dining room should be nearer the kitchen."

Langley considered the conveyance of meals up the servants' stairs, through the door on the first floor and along the corridor to the dining room. Nothing remained hot. He turned his attention to Mister Tomlinson. "A sensible solution if my parents agree to the change."

"Some more tea, Mister Tomlinson?" Mamma asked.

"I don't mind if you pour me another cup, Missus."

"My lady!" Langley exclaimed, rigid with outrage. "Mister Tomlinson you will address my mother by her title."

The manufacturer cheeks turned red as a rooster's wattle. "Will I? It seems I—"

"Don't lose your temper, Father," Miss Tomlinson intervened in a low voice. Her hand shook. A little tea spilled into the saucer.

Her parent subsided like a punctured pig's bladder which poor children used in place of a ball. "Yes, well, lad, I don't think worse of you for taking your ma's—"

"Father!" Miss Tomlinson looked down, seeming surprised by her temerity.

"For taking her ladyship's part," the manufacturer said hastily.

Mamma stood. "Some more tea, anyone? No? Then I suggest it is time to retire. Come, Charlotte."

Langley hurried to open the door for his mother and sister.

In the hall, the countess glanced at Mister Tomlinson. "Although your dinner was too cold, I hope you will find nothing lacking in your bedchamber. Charlotte, your arm, if you please, I need your support. I am overset. Perhaps I need my sal volatile."

"For goodness sake, Mamma, you don't need your smelling salts." Charlotte frowned. "Mister Tomlinson is quite right. We would enjoy hot food."

At the bottom of the broad flight of oak stairs, a footman handed each of them a candlestick to light their way to the second floor.

On the landing, Langley kissed his mother's cheek. "Goodnight, Mamma."

She dabbed her eyes with a dainty handkerchief. "Langley, I am much moved. You have rarely kissed me since you were a small child."

He looked fondly at her. "After I went to Eton, I have seldom been at home to do so." He smiled at Charlotte. "Goodnight. I hope you will sleep well"

"Thank you." She kissed him on the cheek. "Goodnight,"

Langley eyed the manufacturer. He tolerated it when addressed as 'lad'. He would not put up with the least incivility to his mother, however unintentional it might be. "Mister Tomlinson, Miss Tomlinson."

He strode down the corridor to his bedchamber, glad to be momentarily free of his cares.

"My lord," said his man, who came forward to help remove his tight-fitting coat. "I've unpacked. Are you going to ride before breakfast tomorrow?"

"Yes."

"Very good, my lord."

"Dawkins?"

"My lord?"

He handed the man his waistcoat. "You weary me."

"I am sorry, my lord," the slender, wiry young man said, not sounding the least apologetic.

"I don't care to stand on ceremony. 'Major' instead of 'my lord' will suffice."

Dawkins's dark eyes gleamed. Perhaps he was thinking of the adventures they experienced when he served in the Iberian Peninsula. "Thank you, Major."

Langley unfastened the last button of his shirt, removed the garment and gave it to Dawkins.

The enlisted soldier, who acted as his valet, passed him his nightshirt. Langley resisted the temptation to ask him what the other servants said about the Tomlinsons. It would not proper to discuss his parents' guests with an underling, even trustworthy Dawkins.

Langley settled himself in the four poster bed. "Much better than most of the billets in Spain. You, Dawkins?"

"Quite comfortable, thank you, Major. Will that be all?"

"Yes, thank you."

Fatigued by the long, eventful day, Langley closed his eyes. Sleep deserted him. He could not still his mind. He found the prospect of marrying anyone other than Helen repugnant. Langley punched his pillow. Due to his father's circumstances he found no alternative to marrying a lady with a substantial dowry. He stared into darkness as oppressive as his thoughts. Tomorrow, he must discuss the possibility of auctioning silver plates, fine china, oil paintings and other treasures with Papa. On the following day, he would go to London to talk to Papa's man of business. His plan of action brought some relief.

14th March, 1815

When Langley woke, his rumpled quilt, which had almost slipped to the floor, bore testament to his restless night.

A ride would set him to rights. He pulled the bed curtains apart sufficiently to get out of bed. His feet bare, he crossed the parquet floor to the window and yanked open the curtains. Last night, dusk's red sky forecast good weather. The frost-spangled grass, beyond the gravelled path beneath the window, lured him.

He would enjoy a ride in the crisp morning air beneath a sun shining from a clear blue sky. No need for Dawkins, he could dress himself.

Despite his efforts to leave the house without being observed, when he unbolted the front door, the sound woke the footman on duty, who sat in a wing chair upholstered in leather.

"My lord." The man rubbed his sleepy eyes. Before he had time to stand, Langley hastened down the front steps.

He strode across weed-strewn gravel. What time was it in Brussels? He wondered if Helen slept, her luxuriant hair plaited. He must stop dwelling on her. Striding down the path which divided two knot gardens, surrounded by over-grown box hedges, he passed through a gate in the high brick wall and entered the kitchen garden, beyond which were the stables. To his surprise, he saw Miss Tomlinson bent over a bed of rhubarb. He cleared his throat to make her aware of his presence.

Miss Tomlinson straightened. Hand at her throat, eyes wide in obvious surprise, she stared at him.

Conscious he had not shaved, Langley bowed. "Good morning. A beautiful day, is it not? Did it tempt you to take the air?"

The lady curtsied. For several moments, she seemed reluctant to speak. It seemed Charlotte was right. Miss Tomlinson was shy.

"Yes, it is a nice day. Up north I am accustomed to being up at dawn. At this time of day, it is as peaceful in our garden as it is here."

She indicated the bed of rhubarb. "I am admiring the new growth. You must have an abundant supply. Does the countess make use of its curative properties?"

Langley noticed her shyness evaporated while she spoke of the subject which interested her.

"My herbal informs me the leaves are poisonous, but the roots and stalks are efficacious when used for digestive problems," Miss Tomlinson continued. "I dose my father with it when he suffers from gripes after indulging in too much rich food."

His lips twitched. Langley could not imagine Mamma concerning herself with the medicinal properties of rhubarb. He could imagine her horror if Miss Tomlinson mentioned digestive problems and gripes.

Aware of Miss Tomlinson's eyes, more green than brown in the clear light, and regarding him anxiously, he spoke. "Your father is fortunate to have so able a daughter,"

He must go. If her father discovered them without anyone else present, he would expect him to make an immediate proposal of marriage. Langley wondered if Dawkins mentioned he would ride early in the morning. If so, through servants' chitter-chatter Mister Tomlinson might have found out and instructed his daughter to waylay him.

Why, Langley asked himself, was he the unfortunate victim of the manufacturer's determination to see his daughter settled in life?

Well, he would not be snared. He swished his riding crop against his boot. "Miss Tomlinson, I presume I shall see you later at the breakfast table." He marched away at a brisk pace down the mossy brick path between the vegetable beds.

"My lord?"

Good manners dictated he should not ignore a lady. He turned around. "Yes."

His irritation must have shown, for Miss Tomlinson blushed. She retreated into shyness by shaking her head, before hurrying toward the house. Poor girl, the situation must be no less uncomfortable for her than for him. He pressed his lips together. No one could force a grown man to marry. More than likely, after he went to Brussels, he would never again meet the manufacturer's daughter.

* * * *

Langley returned to his bedchamber, invigorated by his early morning ride in countryside not ravaged by Napoleon's troops. When the victorious English army entered France, its citizens, accustomed to soldiers grabbing whatever they wanted, were impressed when those in Wellington's army paid for food, drink and other commodities.

With Dawkin's assistance, Langley shaved in preparation to meet the demands of the day, but first he needed to eat.

He made his way to the breakfast room where Charlotte sat alone at a circular table, a cup of steaming coffee on her right.

"Good morning, Charlotte."

"Good morning, Langley. I hope you slept well, although I doubt it because you have so much to consider."

Langley went to the side table laden with silver dishes. He piled a plate with steak, kidneys, ham, eggs and two slices of freshly-baked bread.

"You are hungry."

"I rose early to ride across our land." His mouth watered as he looked at his plate.

"It is fortunate I ordered breakfast to be served at nine o'clock instead of ten."

"To escape from Papa and his guests?"

"It will not affect their comfort. Breakfast is served until eleven. Shall I pour some coffee for you?"

"Yes, please."

He cut a bite-sized morsel of steak.

"So," his sister put a full cup of coffee on his right, "what are you going to do?"

Between mouthfuls of food he shared his plan to rescue Longwood. "I hope Papa will agree," he concluded.

"Have you decided not to marry that crude man's daughter?"

At the sound of a startled exclamation, they looked across the breakfast room. Neither of them had heard the door open nor noticed Miss Tomlinson enter the room.

Langley crossed the space between them, the heels of his boots clicking on the wooden floor. "You must be sharp-set. Please join us at the table."

A little colour rose in Miss Tomlinson's cheeks. "You reprimanded my father for calling the countess Missus." She trembled. "I am sure you will agree Lady Charlotte should not speak of him in a derogatory manner."

"I agree," his sister said before he could reply. "I am in the wrong. Please forgive me. Our parents are vexatious, are they not? However, your father was kind to give Margaret the parrot."

With a pang of remorse, Langley realised it took courage for one of Miss Tomlinson's disposition to correct them.

"Come," he said, gently, "please don't allow my sister's unfortunate choice of words to prevent you from eating your breakfast."

The young lady stepped toward the table. A ray of sunshine spread across the room, enhancing the rich colour of her hair, drawn into a knot high on the back of her head and allowed to form ringlets on either side of her face. Were it not for her excess weight, she would be attractive. In addition to a flawless skin, she possessed a fine pair of eyes and an exceptionally musical voice.

Chapter Four

15th March, 1815

"Good morning," Langley said to his father, who sat propped up in bed against a bank of pillows.

The earl replaced the coffee cup on his tray. "How can it be good? I have told you I have not a penny to call my own."

Testy! Papa was definitely out of humour. "Well, sir, even if you had a penny or more I am sure you would not want to venture into one of the new-fangled hot air balloons."

"Don't try to make me laugh or cozen me, Langley. You always tried to do so when guilty of childish misdemeanours."

Langley repressed an amused smile. His father had never chastised his children with a rod. Instead he gave them verbal lashings.

Papa stared at his unsteady hands. "Was ever a gentleman so plagued?"

Langley maintained a prudent silence.

The earl glared down into the empty coffee cup. "I look to you, Langley, to set all to rights."

"If you are referring to a match with Miss Tomlinson it will not do."

The earl transferred his glare to Langley. "Not do? Of course it will. You know your duty."

Langley's back tensed. Although Charlotte's darned sleeve came to mind, he loved Helen too much to sacrifice himself to Miss Tomlinson at the altar of matrimony. He took a deep breath in preparation for a cannonade from his father. "I shall not disgrace you and the family, yet nothing you say will persuade me to marry that man's daughter. I am convinced our temperaments don't suit." Langley admired the lady's interest in horticulture but knew he could never bring himself to share her enthusiasm for rhubarb. He checked a grin, visualising the scene if she launched into a lecture on the plant's medicinal properties in polite society. "Besides, her position would be uncomfortable. As my wife, although she would gain entry to the ton, she would be unwelcome. I shall not marry her."

For a moment, Langley believed Papa would throw the coffee pot at him. He prepared to duck.

"Will not marry her?" The earl gazed around the bedchamber from the commodious wardrobe to a looking glass appearing to seek advice from his reflection.

Langley steeled himself to speak frankly. "Your impoverished situation is not my fault. However, it is possible for you to bring yourself around if, to begin with, you sell those manors which are not entailed."

"I have already done so."

"You must sell the hunting lodge and half of the horses."

The earl picked up the coffee pot.

Once more, Langley prepared to duck. To his relief, Papa poured a cup of coffee to which he added brandy from his silver flask.

He hoped Papa would not be stubborn. "Longwood is filled with treasures. I suggest an auction. When I go to London I shall consult Mister Christie at his place of business in Pall Mall to find out how we should proceed. Afterward, I shall send word to you."

"The shame of it." The earl swigged some of his drink. "You should marry Tomlinson's daughter. Do you care nothing for your brothers and sisters?"

"Yes, sufficiently to fund a London Season for Charlotte, after which I shall rent a house in Brighton for her and Mamma to occupy in the summer, while you remain here to co-operate with Mister Christie. Please excuse me, for I must tell Mamma to prepare to go to London in April."

For all of his mother's languishing airs, Langley knew a practical core underlay them. He strode down the corridor to have a private conversation with her.

When he entered her bedchamber, he saw her sitting up in bed looking down at a jumble of letters, ladies' magazines and a newspaper or two spread out on her pretty rose-pink counterpane.

"You may go," his mother said to her dresser.

After Mamma adjusted her fine linen nightcap trimmed with lace, she looked at him with a hint of alarm in her large grey eyes. "Good morning, dearest boy, how nice of you to spare time for me." She patted the edge of the bed. "Will you not sit here?"

"No, it would discommode you."

He drew the bedroom chair to the side of the bed.

"Am I to congratulate you, Langley?"

He shook his head.

Mamma crumpled the letter in her hand. "I did not think you would agree to marry Miss Tomlinson."

She gazed around, a plaintive expression in her large blue eyes. "I spent the first night of my married life in this bedchamber. Will I be able to draw my last breath in it?"

"Yes, I think so, but hope it will not be for a long time."

"Your father said if you don't agree to marry Miss Tomlinson—"

He leaned forward. "Don't distress yourself, Mamma. All is not lost. The hunting lodge and most of the horses are to be sold. Also, many of the family treasures will be auctioned to pay Papa's debts. Thereafter, he must never gamble." He did not think it wise to mention the London House would probably be sold.

"Is there no alternative?"

Langley shook his head. "Well, there is some good news. Father has agreed for you and

Charlotte to go to London for the season after which you may spend the summer in Brighton."

"How good of him, I wondered how we would manage to present Charlotte to the Queen at her Drawing Room, but how will he meet the expense?"

He patted her hand. "If you are not extravagant, I have sufficient funds to meet your needs."

"Thank you." Mamma heaved a sigh. "When our circumstances become known, I fear Charlotte will not make a good match."

"There is time enough before anyone finds out. The auction will not take place for some months. Let us hope the news does not find its way into the broadsheets before Charlotte is betrothed." He stood. "Please excuse me, I must return to London today."

She clutched his hand for a moment, then smiled with obvious difficulty. "God keep you safe."

* * * *

16th March, 1815

His bags packed, Langley made his way to the blue parlour where he partook of nuncheon with his family and the Tomlinsons. He ate the last morsel of ham, then stood, prepared to leave.

In the hall, Papa shook his hand and wished him well. Mamma embraced him and pressed a piece of paper into his hand. "Put it in your pocket to keep it safe," she murmured.

Tears in their eyes, Charlotte and Margaret hugged him. To his annoyance, Mister Tomlinson not only remained, he also accompanied him to the drive.

"Where will you be putting up in Brussels?" the man asked.

Langley squared his shoulders. "Until I know where I am billeted, I might stay with my friend Major Tarrant and his wife." If he did, he must make it clear he would not make a proposal of marriage to Helen, not because he would succumb to his father's plan for him to marry an heiress, but because his financial circumstances forbade it.

He sighed; he doubted he would ever marry another lady. Unless he found some way to restore the family fortune, Helen would be lost to him forever.

Come to think of it, he might as well be honest. Eventually, news of the auction would spread. The reason for not asking Helen to marry him would become obvious. Not for the world would he wish to be considered a scoundrel who had aroused a lady's false expectations.

"Well, lad, I daresay we'll meet again before long."

Langley hoped they would not. "Good day to you, Mister Tomlinson. My regards to your daughter. I hope you will have a pleasant journey home."

"Not home, we're going farther afield, much farther."

* * * *

19th March, 1815

A footman opened the door of Major Tarrant's rented house in the Rue Royale. He raised his eyebrows. The voice, manner of speaking and somewhat flamboyant attire of the man standing at the threshold indicated the stranger should not call at the front door.

Fletcher stepped forward eyeing the unwanted visitor.

"Don't look down your nose at me," the man said before Fletcher could speak. "Inform Major Tarrant that Mister Tomlinson of Manchester brings news of Lord Langley."

"Fletcher," said a female voice from inside the hall, "admit Mister Tomlinson at once."

The butler stepped aside to allow the man to enter the house.

Mister Tomlinson looked at the tall young lady dressed in a jade green pelisse.

"Good day," she said. "My brother-in-law, Major Tarrant, will be delighted to have news of his lordship. Unfortunately, he is not at home, but my sister, Mrs Tarrant, will receive you. Follow me."

"Miss Whitley," Fletcher murmured in protest.

"Take these." Mister Tomlinson handed a supercilious footman his tall, felted beaver hat, yellow pigskin gloves and cane. He followed Miss Whitley up the stairs to a large drawing room in which a dainty, exquisitely gowned, black-haired beauty sat on a chaise longue, perusing a broadsheet.

"Georgianne, here is Mister Tomlinson, bearer of news about Langley."

"Good day, Mister Tomlinson, please be seated," said the lady, who appeared to be more than a head shorter than Miss Whitley.

He sat on the edge of a chair.

"Have you seen the viscount recently?" Miss Whitley asked.

Her cheeks flowered pink as the roses his daughter loved so much in the ornamental garden at their mansion on the outskirts of Manchester.

"I had the pleasure of seeing his lordship at Longwood Place, which I and my daughter visited at the earl's request."

A crease formed between Miss Whitley's eyebrows. "I see."

He leaned forward. "Maybe you're asking yourself why we were the earl's guests."

Mrs Tarrant's gaze flickered to her sister. "I confess I am curious. But how remiss of me, I have not offered you a glass of wine. Helen, dearest, summon Fletcher."

After Georgianne ordered wine, her butler returned within minutes and served Mister Tomlinson.

"Thank you, my good man," Mister Tomlinson began, "although a mug of ale is more to my taste."

His face expressionless and his back straight enough to satisfy any sergeant whose men were on parade, Chivers left the room.

Helen clasped her hands together. "You spoke of Lord Langley, Mister Tomlinson."

"Yes, I said you must be wondering why my girl and I stayed at Longwood Place. Well, I'll tell you. My daughter is to make a match with the viscount. It's not been announced but there's no need to keep it a secret. When my future son-in-law arrives, most probably in a few days, I daresay he'll break the good news to you." He finished his wine.

Mrs Tarrant stood. "Thank you for bringing the news. Please excuse us. My sister is going out."

Tomlinson heaved himself out of the chair. "Then I'll take my leave of you. I look forward to seeing you when I bring my daughter to call on you."

* * * *

"Dearest, it cannot be true. I don't believe Langley would marry that man's daughter,"

Georgianne said, palpably shocked but also sympathetic.

"Dreadful, odious, ill-bred man!" Helen exclaimed. She snatched up a porcelain vase filled with daffodils from one of the tall wooden stands on either side of the door, and hurled it into the fireplace.

"That vase did not belong to us. This is a rented house," Georgianne protested.

Helen put down the second vase. "That horrid man would not have dared to make a false assertion about Langley and his daughter," she snapped.

She marched out of the drawing room and hurried downstairs to the hall where Pringle, her elderly dresser, waited for her. Helen strode into the street without saying a word to the woman. Her breathing slowed to normal on her way toward the haberdashers where she intended to purchase rosettes for her dancing slippers. Several acquaintances impeded their progress. Helen greeted them cheerfully. Nothing would induce her to betray her broken heart to the world.

She decided to be the epitome of a well-bred young lady, careful neither to display her emotion in public nor laugh immoderately in polite society. She would speak, sit and walk elegantly with the utmost propriety. To avoid gossip, she would never dance more than twice with the same partner. Above all, she would not set out to attract any gentleman's notice. At all times she would behave with serene dignity. As for the nouveau riche of Mister and Miss Tomlinson's ilk, she would treat them with frigid courtesy.

Helen clenched her jaw. In future, if the viscount compared Maria Tomlinson to her, she hoped he would bitterly repent his choice of wife. She would not, as the saying went, 'wear her heart on her sleeve'. Inwardly, she wanted to swathe herself in deepest black for the loss of the man she adored. Outwardly, she would dress in the height of fashion and behave too prettily for either the most critical match-making mamma or the most severe dowager to find fault with her.

God willing, she would succeed in securing a well-born husband. When she married, she hoped Viscount Langley would suffer.

The Honourable Mister Lynton, younger son of Baron Westholt, approached her and bowed.

A pleasant young gentleman, fair-haired, with a round face and an honest expression in his blue eyes. She curtsied. "Good day, sir."

"Will you attend my mother's ball this evening?"

"Yes, I am looking forward to it." Helen gazed with deliberate demureness at the toes of her hand-made black leather half-boots.

"May I hope you will favour me with a dance—perhaps a waltz?" Mister Lynton asked.

She looked up at him for a fleeting moment. "You shock me, sir; I have not yet been presented at the Queen's Drawing Room or received tickets for Almacks. I am not permitted to waltz." She fluttered her eyelashes, a deliberate device which only yesterday would have been foreign to her nature.

"Your refusal wounds me."

Was he flirting with her? She was inexperienced in such matters. "No need to be, I have not refused to stand up with you for another dance."

Mister Lynton inclined his head. "I look forward to it. Good day to you." He crossed the road to the opposite side.

How many dances would there be, Helen wondered, after promising to dance with several well-dressed, well-heeled gentlemen. One in particular, Marcus, Captain Dalrymple, with hair as black as Viscount Langley's, dark eyes and a sun-bronzed skin, an officer in Langley's regiment, The Glory Boys, tore at her heart. How magnificent such courageous gentlemen looked even in their black service uniforms ablaze with gold braid, buttons and epaulettes. God protect all of them when they charged the enemy. Her breath caught in her throat. If Langley was wounded, how could she bear it?

Chapter Five

20th March, 1815

Every inch the fashionable lady, Helen entered her sister's breakfast parlour dressed in a black riding habit. One carefully modelled on the Glory Boy's dress uniform, it was embellished with two rows of gold buttons down the front of her jacket and gold braid on the sleeves.

"Have you already been riding so early or will you breakfast first?" Georgianne asked.

"I have just returned from my ride in the Allee Vert with Captain Dalrymple."

"Ah, an officer in my regiment!" Tarrant put down his coffee cup. "I hope a groom attended you." He opened his grey eyes wide in what seemed to be mock horror.

"Of course, I have no wish to ruin my reputation." Helen went to the side table. She piled a plate with buttered eggs, bacon, kidneys, and mushrooms sautéed in butter. "The fresh air has made me hungry." She took her place at the table spread with a crisply-laundered linen cloth. "Do you like my new riding habit, Georgianne?"

"Yes, but it is somewhat bold, dearest. It will draw attention to you."

Helen bent her head over her food. She wanted to be noticed—particularly by a hussar with dark eyes. Helen put her fork down. Strange that the mere memory of Langley should destroy her appetite.

"Coffee, dearest?"

"Yes, please, Georgianne." The strong beverage would revive her, but not compensate her for half the night passed in futile tears. Helen's jaw tensed. Even if she could not check her grief in private, she would present a brave face to the world. Her hand shook a little when she raised the coffee cup to her mouth.

"You look tired," her sister said.

"A headache during the night. I rode to clear my head."

"So, dearest, you did not have an assignation with the captain?"

"No, we met by chance." Her gaze flicked from her sister to Tarrant. "I intend to make a splendid match which will make both of you proud."

"I shall wait with interest. Have you chosen your fortunate bridegroom?" Cousin Tarrant asked, the hint of a smile appearing.

"No, nevertheless if he is a proper gentleman, he will ask you for my hand in marriage since my guardian is in England."

Helen blenched inwardly at the idea of marrying anyone other than Viscount Langley. Nonetheless, she could not face the alternatives. She was not cut out to be a maiden aunt living at her brother-in-law's expense, or even worse, a governess to a brood of over-indulged, unruly children—whose mamma did not want discipline to break their spirits—or a companion to some crotchety old lady.

"If I approve of your choice, I shall make a generous addition to your dowry." Immaculate in his black overalls, a black coat laced with gold, and a red sash around his slim waist, Tarrant stood. He raised his wife's hand to his lips. "I must hurry. Without doubt, General Makelyn will have new orders."

The door opened. "Major, Lord Langley has arrived," Fletcher said.

"Admit him," Georgianne said, a chill in her voice.

Although desperate to see him, Helen's first impulse was to flee. Her second was not to play the coward's part. Besides, even if she left the breakfast parlour, she would be sure to encounter the viscount on his way to it. In novels, the heroines were aflutter. Until now, she never believed she would ever emulate them. She speared a mushroom with her fork.

"Good day to you, Miss Whitley, I trust you are well," Langley said, after he greeted her sister and brother-in-law in his clear, deep tone.

His voice held the warmth Helen became accustomed to whenever he spoke to her in England. She transferred her attention from her fork to Langley, forcing the expression on her face to remain bland, in spite of her admiration at the sight of him, so handsome in his uniform. "Good day to you, my lord. I hope you did not encounter any problems during your journey from England."

With a slight crease between his eyebrows, the viscount regarded her for a moment. "I encountered nothing untoward, apart from a skittish horse when we disembarked." He looked at Cousin Tarrant. "By the way, I have brought the charger, which you asked for, from England."

"Thank you. How many horses did you bring for your own use? It is always advisable to have at least three remounts."

"Perhaps our army will not invade France," Georgianne said.

Tarrant rested his hand on his wife's shoulder as though he wanted to encourage her to be brave.

Georgianne's mouth quivered.

At the vision of Langley's horses being shot under him, or of him being killed or maimed, Helen pressed her lips into a firm line. No need to be maudlin. He was an experienced soldier, who miraculously survived almost unscathed for years in the Iberian Peninsula. She pushed her plate aside. "Please excuse me, Georgianne. I have an appointment with my modiste, the one who made my riding habit. She is a genius. You should order some gowns from her."

"I agree!" Langley exclaimed. "Your outfit is splendid, Miss Whitley. All the ladies will be jealous."

"Thank you for the compliment." Helen curtsied. "My congratulations on your betrothal to Miss Tomlinson. Good day to you, my lord."

Head held high she withdrew from the breakfast room before the viscount could say a word.

"Good God, I am not betrothed!" Langley exclaimed.

"According to Mister Tomlinson, his daughter is to marry you," Georgianne said.

Langley whistled low, understanding why Helen's eyes were so cold when she had looked at him.

"Georgianne," he began, for he addressed her in private as though he was her brother, "my father ordered me to offer for Miss Tomlinson. I refused."

She frowned. "Why did he think you would agree?"

"Georgie, you have not offered Langley a place at your table. Maybe the poor fellow is famished," Tarrant intervened.

"I am sorry. Langley, please be seated. Have you breakfasted?"

"Yes thank you, I had a bite to eat at headquarters but would not say no to some coffee."

Georgianne busied herself with the silver coffee pot. "I presume you will stay with us, Langley, while you are stationed in Brussels. I must have a room prepared for you."

"No, please don't, I am billeted elsewhere." It would be intolerable torture if he saw Helen every day.

"Nevertheless, I shall have a bedchamber readied for you. It will always be at your disposal."

"You are generous," Langley said, certain he would not avail himself of her hospitality.

"So," Tarrant began, when he and Langley were alone, "it seems you were coerced into one unfortunate betrothal with Miss Carstairs and you will be forced into another if Mister Tomlinson can bring it off."

"By God he will not!" Langley glared at his friend. He picked up his coffee cup. "I regret it is my misfortune to be unable to propose marriage to the lady of my choice."

Tarrant frowned. "I am sorry to hear it."

Langley finished his coffee. "Shall I see you at headquarters?"

"Yes, I was about to set off when you arrived. Shall we go together?"

He agreed, much relieved because although he could not marry Helen it would not affect his friendship with Tarrant.

* * * *

Pringle opened the door for Georgianne to enter Helen's bedchamber.

She took a moment to admire the room decorated with pale pink wallpaper sprigged with rosebuds, rose-pink velvet curtains and the palest pink muslin which hung in front of the window to protect the room from prying eyes. Except for the ball gown on the bed and Helen's sketch pad propped against the bedhead, everything was in perfect order.

Georgianne eyed her sister's back which was as straight as a hussar's at a review. "Dearest, Langley is not betrothed to Miss Tomlinson."

"Pooh, why should I care whether or not he is to marry the lady?" Helen asked. "If he changes his mind, I wish him the joy of having Mister Tomlinson for his father-in-law." She gestured to the white satin ball gown. "Do you like my design? I shall wear it to the Linton's ball this evening." She opened her jewel box. "Do you think grandmamma's gold and pearl parure will look well with it?" She fingered the arm clasps. "Mind you, when Mamma gave it to me, she said she would have given it to you if Cousin Tarrant had not given you magnificent pearls."

Georgianne winced, not fooled by Helen's nonchalance. "Dearest, stop, you cannot deceive me with such chatter. I am sure Langley cares deeply for you."

"No, he is not the same toward me as before. Something has changed." Helen took a step forward, her pretty mouth the only colour in her face other than her green eyes. "Don't look so worried, Georgianne. I intend to be admired this evening. I have a gold sash and artificial gold rosebuds to tuck into my hair. I also have kid slippers dyed gold which I intend to wear out this evening, for I already have partners for half of the dances, and am engaged to have the supper dance with Captain Dalrymple."

Georgianne's eyes narrowed. With only eleven months difference in their ages, she and Helen were not only sisters, they were best friends. A little heat stole into her cheeks. Of course, after she married Tarrant, there were personal matters it would not be proper to share with Helen. Apart from this, they always confided in each other. The gulf which now seemed to have widened between them dismayed her.

"Please sit down, Georgianne." Helen gestured to a chair set primly against the wall opposite her tent bed. "Don't fret about me. I shall enjoy everything Brussels has to offer— breakfasts, parties, soirees, picnics, balls, rides in the country, charming young men and—"

"Hush, Helen!" Georgianne exclaimed, aware of her sister's false cheerfulness.

* * * *

Langley's eyes narrowed while he observed Helen dancing with an officer in a scarlet uniform, her white satin and gold ensemble an effective contrast to it.

Tall and elegant, every strand of her pomaded hair gleamed in the candlelight, and her feet in dainty slippers executed each graceful step of the quadrille. She caught at his heart. If only he were free of obligations and could ask her to be his wife.

He should be pleased because, in spite of her many admirers, Helen did not seem to favour any one of them. After each dance she returned to her sister, her manner confident, but not bold. No unseemly laughter escaped her, and she could not be accused of bestowing flirtatious smiles on any gentleman. She conducted herself with such propriety that surely not even the most cantankerous dowager or avid gossip could find fault with her.

Apart from a moment when they looked at each other across the width of the ballroom, Helen ignored him. Although in the unhappy position of being unable to stand at the altar with her, he should be pleased because she seemed happy.

Langley caught his breath. Was she really enjoying herself? Previously, her charming smile was not forced as it now appeared to be.

He held back a sigh to avoid an ill-bred display of the least sign of emotion in public, and made an effort not to frown. He could have sworn, by all he held sacred, that Helen loved him. Had he been mistaken? In the past, could he have misread the significance of the warmth in her eyes whenever they were together? Well, this evening, she looked at him without affection. On the contrary, her eyes were cool as green glass scoured by waves advancing and retreating on the shore. Moreover, the expression on her beautiful oval face was enigmatic when she had merely nodded at him before looking up at Captain Dalrymple.

"Good day to you, my lord," said Mister Creevey, who was always in search of more titbits of gossip.

Langley inclined his head to the lively-minded Member of Parliament, who moved to Brussels to escape his debts at home, while clinging to the hope a change of air would improve his wife's health.

"Congratulations on your betrothal to Miss Tomlinson." Creevey's smile brought a voracious crocodile to Langley's mind.

"I am not betrothed," he said sharply, for he knew that in England the case for libel brought against the gentleman did not cure him of rumour mongering.

Creevey raised his eyebrows. "You must take action to refute the rumour, for a dozen or more people asked where your supposedly affianced bride is."

Did he imagine that Helen now looked with particular interest at the officer in the lifeguards about to dance with her? The damned fellows always appeared ready for parade and retired if even a smudge marred the perfection of their uniform or boots. Well, this particular one would soon learn war was a bloody business in which pristine uniforms were quickly sullied. Langley returned his attention to Creevey. "Perhaps you would be good enough to scotch the misapprehension," he said, although he did not entirely trust the gentleman to do so.

"You may rest assured that I shall." Creevey's eyes glowed with palpable curiosity. "Tell me, my lord, who do you think will command the cavalry?"

Langley shrugged. "Perhaps the Earl of Uxbridge."

Creevey tittered. "An appointment which could not please the Duke of Wellington."

"I daresay." Langley had no wish to speak of Uxbridge's scandalous affair with, and subsequent marriage to, the former wife of Wellington's younger brother, Thomas Wellesley. He nodded at Creevey before walking away from him. Time for him to leave, though in order to do so he must skirt the ballroom floor and pass by Helen, who with an unfurled gold-coloured fan in one slim-fingered hand, sat gazing up at several gentlemen.

Georgianne beckoned to him. A few steps took him to her side. Helen's soft laughter aroused his jealousy. He stood close to her, breathing in her scent, a mixture of flowers and citrus, a blend of sweetness and sharpness that suited her personality.

"Good evening, ma'am," he said to Georgianne. "Miss Whitley."

"My lord." Helen concealed the lower part of her face with her fan. Her beautiful eyes regarded him cautiously over its upper edge. One of her beaux spoke. She smiled at him.

Langley bowed. "I see you are a success—without question you will be the toast of the town."

"Unlikely, my lord."

"I have no doubt you will cut your teeth on as many unfortunate hearts as possible. Perhaps you would like to wear them like a garland around your neck, for young ladies are always fickle. Good evening." Ashamed of himself for his loss of self-discipline, he left the ballroom without a backward glance.

* * * *

"What," Helen asked herself, "have I done to deserve such sarcasm?" Yet she had discerned fire in Langley's eyes which could have scorched her most tender sensibilities. Pride would never allow her to reveal her susceptibilities in the face of his indifference. Yet, how dare he imply she was no more than a shallow flirt when he must know she would never flirt with another gentleman if he asked her to marry him.

She turned her attention to her next partner. Feigning great interest, she paid close attention to his description of his pack of hounds brought with him from England. "They are in the peak of condition, eager to scent the quarry." He looked down at her face. "By Jove, Miss Whitley, would you care to join a hunt?"

"I should like to, but doubt my sister would allow it," she said, unable to think of little she would enjoy less than staying on a side-saddle, while riding across rough country through water and over hedges, at the risk of falling and breaking her neck. "Yet", a small inner voice said, "I would risk anything for Langley." She could have cried. Suppose he broke his neck during a charge into battle, leaving her to mourn with no more words for her other than those which stung her this evening.

Chapter Six

21st March, 1815

Followed by a footman, Fletcher entered the yellow drawing room. "Letters and newspapers from England," he announced. "These are for you, Major." He handed a bundle to Tarrant, gave another to Georgiana and a third to Helen, while the footman put the remaining newspapers on a marble-topped table.

"Has The Lady's Magazine arrived?" Georgianne asked Fletcher.

"Ah," said Cousin Tarrant, "that hallowed magazine, An Entertaining Companion for the Fair Sex appropriated solely to their use and amusement."

Georgianne regarded him demurely. "'Pon my word sir, you are overly familiar with the publication. One would think you have read it. If so, I shall look forward to perusing The Gentleman's Magazine."

"If you please, but I doubt you will find much in it to interest you," her husband replied, with mock meekness while he broke the wax seal on a letter.

She maintained a dignified silence until her husband chuckled. "What amuses you, Major?"

"A letter from my mother. Your youngest sister is in disgrace. Bab persuaded my little sisters to dress like hussars and charge down

Broad Field on their ponies. After seeing them dressed in breeches, Miss Castleton, their governess, took to her bed for two days and threatened to resign."

"Spineless creature," Georgianne said, torn between annoyance and amusement.

Although Cousin Tarrant looked lovingly at his wife, he ignored her interruption. "My half-sisters, who love Miss Castleton dearly, wept when they were scolded. Bab remained unrepentant. She told my step-mamma that if she were not a female, she would join my regiment as a drummer boy."

"What a dreadful idea." Georgianne turned toward Helen. "Do you know the drummer boys are targeted when the line advances because they communicate the orders?"

"Yes, Father told me. But you and my cousin are speaking of Bab. Her behaviour is scandalous. She should be sent to a boarding school—a strict one where she will learn good conduct. Drummer boy, indeed!"

"You are too harsh, dearest," Georgianne said, although both of them knew their ten-year-old sister's wild behaviour must be curbed.

"Well," Helen said, "at least Bab is neither enacting funerals nor burying her dolls, as she did after Father's death."

Tarrant drummed the tips of his fingers on the arm of his chair. "Georgianne, perhaps you and Helen should return to England to take care of her."

Georgianne sprang out of her chair, her delicate needlework falling from her lap onto the carpet. "No, Tarrant, I could not bear to be separated from you."

"Georgie," her husband exclaimed, his voice a little unsteady. "Please think of the danger both of you might be in if Bonaparte attacks Brussels."

"Surely that is unlikely because our army will invade France before Boney can do so," Helen said.

"Georgie, what do you want me to do?" Tarrant asked.

"Perhaps, we should send for Bab. She is never so mischievous when she is with us, and she always obeys you."

Helen looked at Tarrant. "Georgianne, she behaves with Cousin Tarrant because he dotes on her, and indulges her."

"Georgie?" Tarrant asked.

"It would not be fair to expose Bab to danger" she replied slowly. She bent down to pick up her sewing, a tiny white gown, from the carpet woven from brightly coloured threads of gold, cobalt blue and scarlet.

"Although I would like to see the child, we are agreed," Tarrant said. "I shall write a placatory letter to my mother."

Georgianne smiled at him. "So shall I," she said, while her sister Helen crossed the room to leaf through the newspapers and periodicals.

"Ah, the Hertfordshire Gazette." Helen carried it to her chair opposite the sofa on which Georgianne and Tarrant sat.

"I wonder what Bab would think of this room." A wave of Cousin Tarrant's hand encompassed curtains the colour of old gold, the primrose satin and daffodil-yellow silk-striped wallpaper, and a profusion of gilded wood. "Georgie, do you remember Bab's derogatory comments on imitation Egyptian furniture with feet carved to look like a crocodile's?"

"Yes, and what is more, I agreed with them," Georgianne smoothed the tiny garment, which lay across the lap of her azure-blue gown.

"What are you making?" Helen asked. "I believed you prefer riding to sewing."

"Yes, I do." Georgianne's cheeks burned. She rolled up her handiwork and put it in her sewing bag.

A strangled sound escaped Helen. Her hands shook. The newspaper quivered.

"Dearest! What is the matter?" Georgianne asked.

Her sister frowned at Tarrant. "Did you know about this?"

"What?"

"How foolish of me, of course you don't know what I am referring to. There is a snippet hinting the treasures of Longwood Place are to be auctioned by Christies, and the earl will sell his London house, hunting lodge and most of his horses."

* * * *

Tarrant sat motionless for a long moment. So, his sister-in-law did love Langley. If she did not, why else would she be so distraught? He removed the newspaper from her tremulous hands. "Georgie, a glass of wine for your sister or, perhaps, some brandy."

While his wife busied herself with the decanter, Tarrant read the snippet. The author had taken care to word it so that an action for libel could not be brought. He sighed. The rumours that the earl could not meet his gambling debts were probably true. It was not unusual for a gentleman to be in debt to tradesmen to the tune of thousands of pounds. In the case of the reckless Prince Regent, tens of thousands, but it was a point of honour to meet losses at the gaming tables with promptitude.

Langley could not be held accountable for his father's folly. How could he help his friend? Well, thanks to the fortune inherited from his childless godfather, the nabob, he could afford to help Langley.

He cracked his knuckles. Of course, the earl must have attempted to arrange for Langley to marry Miss Tomlinson for her substantial dowry and future inheritance. Yet, although Langley refused the proposal, it seemed Mister Tomlinson remained determined to arrange the match. What a coil. He must return to headquarters where he would offer Langley financial assistance with the hope his friend would accept it.

* * * *

Outside headquarters, Tarrant dismounted and handed the reins to a hussar. The heels of his boots resounded on a short flight of broad stone steps. At the top, he acknowledged another hussar's salute. "Major Langley?"

"Upstairs, sir."

Tarrant hurried to the first floor where several officers took their ease in an ante-room while they awaited orders. He greeted them, then glanced at Langley, who stood with his back toward one of a pair of tall windows. With swift steps he crossed the parquet floor. "A word with you, if it is convenient." Tarrant indicated the door to a small room, in which private conversations often took place.

Langley raised his eyebrows. "Why so serious? Have you received bad news?"

"None other than my mother is in despair over Bab's naughtiness."

Langley's eyes gleamed with obvious amusement. "Bab is a mischievous kitten, albeit an endearing one."

"Yes, I confess I am fond of her although she is a red-haired imp of a child." He glanced at his friend. "Enough of her. Come." He crossed the spacious room, once part of a wealthy Dutch manufacturer's house, and opened a panelled door. After they entered,

Langley shut the door and Tarrant perched on the edge of a desk.

Langley frowned. "I take it you have something important to say."

"The Hertfordshire Gazette arrived." Tarrant cleared his throat, embarrassed by the necessity to mention the report.

His dark eyes wary, Langley sat behind the desk. "Is there anything in it of particular interest?"

Tarrant decided it would be best to come straight to the point. "Perhaps to you. It is claimed Mister Christie will auction Longwood's treasures."

"Only those which are not entailed," his friend said quickly. Perhaps too quickly.

"I would like to help."

"It is unnecessary."

Tarrant stood. "It is vulgar to speak of money, but we have been friends for—how long—more than twenty years? Nothing should stand between us. Due to my inheritance I can lend you whatever you need." Tarrant waved an admonitory finger to prevent Langley interrupting him. "If our situations were reversed, I know you would make the same offer. Don't be too proud to accept mine," he concluded, although in Langley's situation he would refuse.

Langley's eyes smouldered. "So far I am not reduced to a state of poverty in which I must accept crumbs. During our years in the Peninsular, I saved more than sufficient for my needs. I can also provide for my mother and sisters, so please don't say anything else."

"Very well." Tarrant visualised Helen. "Make sure you don't, as the saying goes, cut off your nose to spite your face."

"I shall not but thank you for your offer." He frowned. "Gambling is a curse. It is like a fever in many a man's blood. Have you heard Symonds lost everything? He blew his brains out because he could not meet his debts." His nostrils flared. "I have decided never to be in debt to anyone."

Tarrant knew Langley was too much the gentleman to criticise his father and that he would say no more on the subject.

A sharp rat-a-tat-tat sounded on the door. A fresh-faced young ensign entered the room. "General Makelyn's compliments. He has orders for both of you."

Tarrant returned the ensign's salute. "Thank you, Mister Garston."

After he and Langley exchanged a glance, they hurried into Makelyn's den where several maps were spread out on a large table.

"You took your time," the general grumbled, as he looked them up and down as though trying to fault their immaculate uniforms. He scowled. "I am not a shepherd who must send his collie to round up his sheep."

Makelyn is crusty today, Tarrant thought, avoiding the amused look in a young lieutenant's eyes. Well, the old man had more than enough to irritate him with the uncooperative King of the Netherlands—who objected to almost every suggestion made by the British—and his heir, the inexperienced Commander in Chief of the occupying forces and Dutch-Belgian army.

Thank God he was not one of the Prince William of Orange's staff officers. Twenty-three-year-old Slender Billy, nick-named because of his long neck, did not inspire confidence in either the army or those civilians who eagerly anticipated the Duke of Wellington's arrival. Nevertheless, he and Langley were well aware their Dutch counterparts had served the French. They also knew former French officials, who wanted the British to leave the Netherlands, influenced King William. Tarrant exchanged a rueful look with Langley. Any hussar sent to gather intelligence in areas of the Netherlands—where Roman Catholics favoured the French—would need the utmost tact and skill.

After several wasted hours with the General while the blood red sun sank toward the horizon, Tarrant rode home deep in thoughts of Helen and Langley. Before he wed Georgianne, he assumed love was not a necessity for marriage. Due to his harrowing experience in Spain, when French soldiers raped his betrothed, who subsequently died in childbirth, he had not wished to marry and father an heir. However, conscious of his duty, he knew he must tie the knot to please his family. At that time, like many gentlemen, he saw no reason why he should not have both a wife and a mistress.

Tarrant laughed at his former self. How could he have been so foolish? Since he fell in love with Georgie, he had never wished to stray from her bed. If only Langley and Helen could enjoy equal happiness.

During the next few days, army matters kept him too occupied to think about Helen. Then in the space of several hours, four gentlemen requested permission to court her.

"Deuced odd, I cannot account for Helen being so much sought after," he said later in the evening when he lay in bed, his wife's head snuggled against his chest.

"Why?" Georgie asked indignantly. "Helen is fair of face, a talented artist, a—"

"You need not praise your sister to me," Tarrant broke in. "I am puzzled because three of the gentlemen are known fortune-hunters. I shall let it be known that Helen does not have a fortune."

"I see." Georgianne traced a pattern on his nightshirt with the tip of her finger. "It is, as you put it, deuced odd."

"Georgie!"

"Don't worry; I shall not repeat such unladylike words in public." She propped herself up on her elbow, looking at him by dim firelight. "Who is the fourth gentleman?"

"Marcus Dalrymple, with whom she sometimes rides in the Allee Vert before breakfast."

"What did you say?"

"That I have no objection to him courting Helen, provided he applies to her guardian, Major Walton, for permission to marry her." Tarrant suppressed a yawn. It had been a long day during which he rode to Voord and back on General Makelyn's orders to gather information.

"Good. Dalrymple is the eldest son of a wealthy baronet who owns a large property in Essex. There can be no objection to him courting Helen if she likes him, only—"

"What?"

"Do you think she favours him because he looks a little like Langley?"

"Even if she does, don't worry. Go to sleep. If you stay awake fretting about Helen, you will lose the roses in your cheeks."

"Sleep? Are you sure you want to sleep?" Georgianne asked, her voice deepening.

Suddenly wide awake, he faced her, murmuring, "Heart of my heart."

* * * *

In the stillness of the quiet night, Helen sought oblivion in sleep but it eluded her. Even her toes were cold because the flannel-wrapped hot brick at her feet had long since cooled. Outside, the first spring flowers poked their heads above the ground, and even when the sun shone, the days were chilly. Helen shivered again in spite of the flames leaping in the grate and casting shadows on the walls.

She had no close friends, and since her father died several years ago, Mamma had grown dependent on the bottle, gradually becoming unfit to care for her daughters. Her mind turned to Georgianne. Since her sister's marriage, although they still loved each other, a rift had opened between them. Perhaps it would widen even more when she married.

She must tread a new path if she did not wish to remain the recipient of Cousin Tarrant's generosity. Oh, she appreciated it, but she wanted a home of her own. Her troubled mind strayed to Marcus Dalrymple, whom she liked more than any of her other beaux.

Chapter Seven

22nd March, 1815

Helen enjoyed her early morning canter when the Allee Vert was not thronged with those wishing to see or be seen, who were either riding thoroughbred horses or driving splendid vehicles. On her way home, she checked her mare by the bridge over the River Seine. When she dismounted, Collins, the groom, who followed her at a discreet distance, came forward to take Silk's reins. She peered around while Collins walked the horses.

No sign of dashing Dalrymple this morning. Doubtless, military duties prevented him from joining her.

The paving stones beneath her feet were slick with overnight rain. She slipped. For a horrifying moment, she realised she would fall if she lost her footing. In the next instant, strong hands steadied her.

"I beg your pardon, Miss Whitley. I feared you might take a tumble." A gentleman's voice resonated in her ear.

Helen recognised the voice. She could neither move nor speak. Her heart beat faster. To calm herself, she took deep breaths until she recovered her composure sufficiently to force herself to turn around. She stared at Langley's black cape open down the front and revealing gold buttons which shone by the light of the pale sun breaking through the pearl-grey clouds. Langley stood so close that she could smell his pomade. "Thank you, my lord." She took more deep breaths. Her legs a little unsteady, she made a small curtsey.

"There is no need for formality between friends."

Had he emphasised the word friends?

Langley scrutinised her. "Miss Whitley you are shivering. Are you cold?" He wrapped his cape around her.

When they were alone in England he had called her Helen. An awkward silence ensued, during which she admired him. The magnificence of his expertly-cut hussar service uniform, and his busby and boots with gold tassels almost stole her breath.

Langley frowned. "Your face is pale. Are you unwell? May I escort you home?"

Hooves clattered toward them. "There you are, Miss Whitley," Captain Dalrymple interjected, his cheerful face in sharp contrast to Major Langley's concerned one. "Sir," he continued, saluting from the saddle.

For a moment the officers eyed each other as though they would like to snarl. Then, the captain smiled at her before he spoke. "My apologies, Miss Whitley, duty detained me." He eyed Langley's cape. "It is cold this morning. I daresay the fresh air has given you an appetite for breakfast. May I escort you home, Miss Whitley?"

"Yes, thank you."

"Do I not have a prior claim?" Langley asked, while she returned his cape.

She looked uncertainly from one officer to the other, aware of her ghost of a smile. "No, my lord, you don't have any claim on me. Nonetheless, there is no reason why both of you should not accompany me."

Dalrymple nodded. "Thank you, it will be my pleasure."

Helen beckoned to Collins, who led her mare to her.

"I like your grey, Miss Whitley" Langley said. "Allow me to help you up." He laced his hands together to receive her foot.

Conscious of her flushed cheeks, Helen settled into the saddle, reins in her hand.

Dalrymple raised an eyebrow, "Shall I see you this evening at Lady Verulam's soiree?"

"Perhaps. I am not sure whether my sister accepted the invitation."

Dalrymple pressed his free hand over his heart. "I hope to see you there."

Helen liked the cheerful Captain, and she knew nothing about him which would displease even the most exacting young lady.

Suddenly, at risk of its life from Silk's hooves, a small terrier dashed across the narrow road in pursuit of an alley cat.

The mare shied. Regardless of danger, a plump matron wearing a fluttering white headdress pursued the yapping dog. "Bebe! Bebe!" she shrieked.

Silk reared. Helen lost control of the mare. Langley flung himself out of his saddle. A gig approached quickly from the opposite direction. It drew parallel to them, preventing Langley from coming to her assistance.

Langley dodged another vehicle with mere inches to spare. He grabbed the curb rein of Helen's horse, and then helped her to dismount. "My sweet girl!" He cradled her in his arms.

Tall for a woman, Helen dwarfed most men, but Langley stood almost a head taller. In his embrace, she could find no words to describe the sense of security his superior height gave her.

Langley kissed the top of her head. "Thank God you are not injured, but you must be shaken."

"Somewhat," she admitted, overwhelmed by the joy of being in his arms.

He held her a little tighter.

For a few moments, bubbles of happiness swirled within. They dispersed when she caught sight of Dalrymple's frown and widened eyes. Whether the danger she had faced or Langley holding her so close shocked him more, she did not know. "Please, forgive us for ignoring you, Captain." She freed herself from Langley's embrace. "The Major is a close friend of my family. My sister regards him as an honorary brother."

"Ah, he is fortunate." Dalrymple dismounted, looking with intense dislike at the

Belgian lady, who ran across the road, her little dog clasped in her arms.

Helen shook out her full skirt. Dalrymple picked up her hat and handed it to her. She fingered the plume. "Alas, it is ruined." She beckoned to Collins, who held her mare's reins and those of the Major and Captain's horses.

Langley frowned. "Are you sure you are fit to ride?"

"I must for fear of losing my courage."

Dalrymple's eyes shone. "Upon my word, I cannot tell you how much I admire you, Miss Whitley. Some young ladies would have hysterics or palpitations after such an experience."

She smiled in response. "You forget I am the daughter and sister of cavalry officers, although I fear they would have scolded me for not acquitting myself well."

"No such thing, you kept your seat." The captain helped her mount Silk once again.

"Will you come in to have breakfast?" Helen asked when the three of them reached Rue Royale.

"No, thank you," Dalrymple replied "You must rest after such a shock."

"No, no, I don't need to." She looked up at Langley. "My lord, I am sure Cousin Tarrant and my sister would be pleased to see you."

Langley shook his head, his dark eyes inscrutable. "Please forgive me for not accepting your invitation. I must hurry to headquarters. Without doubt, Makelyn will rebuke me for being so tardy."

A spring in her step, Helen almost danced up the stairs on her way to change from her riding habit into a morning gown. Delight flooded through her at the memory of his embrace and calling her his sweet girl.

The intoxicating scent of horse leather combined with his spicy toilet water seemed to linger. The tenderness in his voice echoed in her ears. Of course, after taking such a shocking liberty he should have proposed marriage. No matter, she was sure he would do so in the near future. Soon, she would be choosing her trousseau and bridal gown.

Pringle blinked when she entered the bedchamber. "You enjoyed your ride, Miss Whitley?"

"Oh, yes, I did." Helen tossed her damaged hat onto a chair.

"Which gown do you wish to wear?"

"My pea-green kerseymere," she replied, well-aware, green—her favourite shade—intensified the colour of her eyes.

"Very good, Miss."

Helen stripped off her riding gloves and handed them to Pringle, before going behind a screen, where she poured rose-fragranced water from a jug into a basin. "Langley loves me," she thought, while washing her hands and face. "I shall be his lifelong companion."

An ice-cold shiver ran down her spine. "Dear God, suppose neither the French Republicans nor the Royalists oust Napoleon." Langley might be killed if France invaded. "No," she told herself, "I shall not think of it. He will live to see our children." Lost in a dream of a happy future, she emerged from behind the screen imagining her unborn children with their father's dark eyes and hair. She sighed with satisfaction. Langley would be a tolerant husband and father. His sons would be equally honourable. His daughters, whom he would protect and indulge, would adore him.

"Do you want to take off your habit?" Pringle's voice jerked Helen out of her vision of the imaginary future.

"Yes, please."

With her usual efficiency, Pringle helped her to dress in warm kerseymere suited to the chilly weather.

Helen regarded herself in the mirror. She adjusted one of the pomaded ringlets bunched on either side of her oval face. "Vanity," she reminded herself, "is one of the seven deadly sins. But is it a sin to know I look my best? Surely not."

"Oh dear, what's happened Miss?" Pringle held up Helen's riding hat. "The plume is ruined, it will have to be replaced."

Helen frowned. Must the woman forever be interrupting her thoughts? "Yes, I shall buy a new one. If my sister has no plans for us this morning, you may accompany me to the haberdashers."

Without a backward glance at Pringle, she left her bedchamber. A spring in her step, she went downstairs to the breakfast parlour where Georgianne presided over the coffee pot.

"Good morning." Helen pressed a kiss on her sister's cheek.

Georgianne kissed her in return. "Delicious, Helen, you smell of fresh air."

Helen examined the silver dishes on the marble-topped buffet. Hungry, she helped herself to bacon, kidney, a poached egg, and bread and butter.

Georgianne eyed her plate. "You are hungry, Helen. Coffee?"

"Yes please."

"Did you ride with Captain Dalrymple?"

Helen laughed. "No, I rode alone in the Allee Vert."

Georgianne raised her eyebrows. "Alone!"

"Collins attended me." Helen hesitated. Better to describe what had happened during her ride, in case the groom blabbed to the other servants and word of her mishap reached Cousin Tarrant and Georgianne. However, she would neither mention Langley's embrace nor his kiss on the top of her head. Moreover, she would not tell Georgianne he called her his sweet girl. That was a private treasure; one to keep in her heart.

"Thank God you were not hurt!" Georgianna exclaimed, after Helen explained how she was nearly thrown from her horse.

"I have Langley to thank." Helen wanted to sing for joy at the sound of his name.

"I am grateful to him for rescuing you, dearest. He is so gallant and, poor Langley, the financial predicament caused by his father is regrettable. I understand why Mister Tomlinson proposed a match between his daughter and Langley."

No longer hungry, Helen pushed her plate away. "Langley loves you. Surely he means to marry you," her inner voice whispered in her ear.

"Unfortunately," Georgianne rattled on, "as the saying goes, although Langley rejected Tomlinson's offer, he needs to marry money."

"When Silk plunged, my hat fell to the ground." Helen deliberately changed the subject of the conversation. "The plume is damaged, so if you have no plans for us this morning, I shall go to the haberdashers to buy a new one."

"Why not purchase another hat?"

"I could, although my old one matches my riding habit. Will you come with me?"

"No thank you, I have too many letters to write."

Helen dabbed her mouth with a linen napkin. "Do you want me to buy anything for you?"

"Yes, please; two yards of the finest inch-wide Brussels lace."

Perplexed, Helen stared at Georgianne. "How you have changed. Before you married, you loathed sewing."

Georgianne flushed. "Now that I am no longer forced to sew in the schoolroom, I enjoy it."

Helen fingered one of her pearl earrings. Since her sister married, both of them had changed.

* * * *

Her purchases from the haberdashers carried by Pringle, Helen gazed into a milliner's shop at a charming high-crowned straw hat, trimmed with a broad lace frill on the inner edge of the brim. A commotion from behind drew her attention as she was on the verge of entering the shop to try it on. She turned around. Her eyes narrowed at the sight of a group of young Belgian soldiers surrounding an elderly gentleman dressed in clothes fashionable in the previous century.

"Please leave me alone," the old man said in English.

"Dance for us, old man! Let us see your coat skirts swirl." The soldier's companions laughed raucously.

The old man turned slowly. He looked from one mocking face to another.

The soldier drew his sword from its scabbard. "Dance," he repeated. "Perhaps the tip of my sword will encourage you."

"How dare they?" Helen stepped onto the road.

"Don't interfere, Miss," Pringle pleaded.

Helen hurried forward. Without hesitation she addressed the unmannerly men in French. "I am Major Tarrant's sister-in-law. You may be sure your commanding officer will hear of this outrage. What are your names?"

"Be careful, this isn't your business," Pringle cried out.

"Not my business! It most certainly is. I am a captain's daughter. Like the Duke of Wellington, he would have had these men flogged for their unmannerly conduct." She returned her attention to the soldiers. "Off with you!"

Two of the men went on their way down the street, whooping and turning frequently to jeer. The other four, including the one with the drawn sword, grinned mockingly. "Perhaps you will dance with the gentleman."

Helen scowled. "Certainly not! Neither of us will dance." With one hand, she reached into her huge sealskin muff, suspended to her waist from a cord looped around her neck. The soldier moved closer. His face beetroot red, he was sweating profusely. He reeked of alcohol. Helen withdrew a pocket pistol Cousin Tarrant had taught her to fire. Ever protective, he had requested her to always carry it.

"A pretty toy," the soldier sneered.

"It is loaded. If you dare to threaten me or refuse to let this gentleman proceed in peace, you will discover it is not a child's plaything."

Several members of the British Light Infantry rounded the corner of the quiet street and approached.

"Well?" she said to the Belgians.

Outnumbered four to ten, after several bungled attempts, the ringleader pushed his sword back into its scabbard before he made his way up the street with his companions.

Pringle fanned herself with the package of lace, in spite of the chilly March day. "Those rascals were tipsy. Who knows what might have happened if our soldiers hadn't arrived."

The old gentleman bowed to Helen. "I am forever in your debt." With one hand clutching his walking stick, he straightened.

"I am pleased to have been of help," Helen murmured.

A smile mitigated the gravity of his wrinkled face. With his free hand, he indicated his dull yellow brocade coat. "I am too old to wear new fashions." He laughed. "I shall not be intimidated by those ignorant young louts." Despite his brave words his hands trembled.

Before Helen could offer him further assistance, the British soldiers reached them. "Miss Whitley, is all in order?" a young lieutenant asked.

Helen gazed at him.

"Lieutenant Calverly at your service, Miss Whitley. We were introduced during a soiree." He bowed. "Do you remember me?"

"Of course I do."

"I am flattered." Calverly inclined his head. "Do you need assistance?"

"No thank you, nevertheless those soldiers should be punished."

"I agree." In a few well-chosen words, the old gentleman explained what had happened. "I am Mister Barnet," he added. "Don't hesitate to ask if I can ever be of service to you."

"Thank you, sir. We will follow those louts, try to apprehend them and ensure they are punished. Good day to you, Miss Whitley, Mister Barnet."

For a moment Helen stared after him. How old was he? Her own age, eighteen or a little older? She shivered, not from cold. All too soon, he might surrender his life for king and country.

"Would you have fired Miss Whitley?" The soft voice drew her attention.

Helen faced Mister Barnet. "If necessary, for although my sister is a better shot than I am, I could not have missed at such close range."

The gentleman chuckled. "Do you always carry a pistol?"

"Yes, when I am only accompanied by my dresser. My brother-in-law insists on it. What of you, sir? Will you allow us to escort you home after your dreadful ordeal?"

His eyes twinkled. "It is usually the gentleman who escorts the lady." He paused for a second. "My house is only two streets away so I will accept your offer."

"Miss…" Pringle protested.

Helen ignored her. "Were you frightened, sir?"

"No, I am old but not entirely defenceless. He raised his cane. This is a swordstick. I was once considered a master of the art of fencing."

She looked at him doubtfully. It must have been long ago.

They turned right onto a short street of large houses with scrubbed steps and well-polished door knockers. At the end of it, they entered another street with even larger houses.

Mister Barnet halted outside a four storey mansion. "I live here."

"Well, sir, I shall bid you goodbye for now."

"For now?"

"Yes. Tomorrow, if you permit, I shall call to make sure you have recovered from your unfortunate experience."

"You are kind. However, would it not be improper of you to call on an unmarried gentleman?"

It would be rude to imply she doubted one of his age would be a threat to her virtue, so she chose her answer carefully. "Not if my dresser accompanies me. Until tomorrow, sir."

"Good day, Miss Whitley."

She lingered until the door closed behind him. "Not a word of this to anyone, Pringle."

"I shan't say anything Miss, but the lieutenant might."

Helen frowned. She could not ensure Calverly would not mention the matter. Oh well, if he did, she would insist it was of no consequence.

Chapter Eight

23rd March, 1815

Langley sat at a table in headquarters, a sheet of writing paper before him. He picked up his quill and dipped the tip into the inkwell.

Dear Miss Whitley.

His hand hovered over the words. Should he write to Helen, or should he apologise in person for holding her in his arms and kissing the top of her head?

During his years in the army, he had faced fear in all of its many guises, yet he was terrified when her horse reared and the gig came between them. After he helped her to dismount, relief overwhelmed him. He had folded his arms around her wanting to keep her safe forever. Still, he should not have done so in public and in the presence of Captain Dalrymple.

Curse the young officer well-known for his pleasant manners and cheerful nature. Damn it! With his dark eyes and hair black and glossy as any of The Glory Boys' treasured horses, Marcus Dalrymple seemed to be one of Helen's most favoured beaux.

A bitter laugh escaped him. He must not be a proverbial 'dog in a manger'. Unable to marry Helen, he should not resent her other suitors.

Langley put the quill down. He crumpled the paper. Mere words could not express how much he admired Helen's steady nerve when faced with danger. She was not craven, so he should not take the coward's path by writing to her. Instead, he must speak to her in person. Perhaps he should accept Georgianne's invitation to dine tomorrow, and hope to have a private moment to apologise to Helen for his impropriety.

* * * *

24th March, 1815

On Sunday, Langley sipped from his glass of wine in Georgianne's salon furnished in salmon-pink and gold. He realised it would be impossible to speak in private to Helen. Langley did not begrudge Helen her popularity, but he wished he could oust two junior officers from her side. His fingers tightened around the stem of his glass. Eyes bright, she greeted him with a smile. Though he did not consider himself conceited, he sensed she reciprocated his love. His embrace probably led her to expect a marriage proposal would be forthcoming. "You are a scoundrel," he castigated himself. For her own good, he must disappoint Helen no matter how much he dreaded the day when she would marry another man.

Dalrymple entered the salon, as impressive as the other officers in his regiment who were gathered here. Indeed, the black and gold uniform contrasted well with the ladies'

Langley smarted in response to Dalrymple's polite reply. "It seems you are not aware Miss Whitley is a talented artist. She needs little practice. Her skill is far beyond that of many young ladies."

Helen blushed. "You flatter me, my lord."

Langley devised a plan. "It is no less than the truth,"

"If it is convenient, I shall call for you tomorrow at eleven of the clock," countered Dalrymple, who obviously feared he might be losing ground with Miss Whitley. He cleared his throat. "After our promenade, perhaps you would care to partake of refreshments at the pavilion."

"Yes, thank you, captain, I would," Helen replied.

* * * *

25th March, 1815

Langley arrived in Georgianne's salon when the clock struck the hour.

"Captain Dalrymple presents his apologies, Miss Whitley. General Makelyn's orders prevent him from escorting you to the park. I hope you will give me that privilege."

"I hope you had nothing to do with those orders," Helen said, the expression in her eyes mischievous.

"If I did?"

Her rosy lips curved into a smile. "Although I should reprove you, I shall not, for I am ignorant of the truth of the matter. Please be good enough to wait for a few moments while I put on my hat and pelisse."

"Of course."

Within a few minutes, Helen returned bundled up in a holly-green woollen pelisse lined with fur. "I am ready, Major."

"I thought you wished to draw."

"My dresser, who awaits us in the hall, has my sketch pad and pencils."

"Very well."

They proceeded to the front door and out into the Rue Royale.

Helen looked up at the pale blue sky decorated with puffs of white cloud. "In spite of the sunshine, it is a little cold."

"Which makes the world a more cheerful place."

"Yes, grey days don't enhance the spirit."

Side by side, they walked along the pavement, to the right were the railings enclosing rectangular Parc Royale. Inside the park, few people—other than nurses with their charges—were taking the air.

Helen slowed her pace, turned and beckoned to her dresser. "Are you cold, Pringle?" she asked, when the woman drew near.

"No, Miss."

"You need not deny that you are. Go to the pavilion. Have a hot drink to warm you. We will join you after our walk."

The dresser hesitated. Langley handed her a coin. She curtsied. "Thank you, my Lord." Nevertheless, when he took the portfolio from her, she looked from him to Helen with a question in her eyes.

"No need to worry," Langley said. "Your mistress will be safe with me. Come, Miss Whitley." He departed leaving Pringle with no option other than to obey.

He gazed into the distance at the fourth boundary of the park—part of the wall which enclosed Brussels—before he returned his attention to Helen. "Is there anything in particular you wish to sketch?" he asked, while they strolled beneath the bare branches of trees forming an intricate pattern reminiscent of black lace.

"There is a stone statue of a charming young girl dressed in a riding habit. It is this way." Helen turned around toward the east, where a seat faced the equestrienne captured forever in time.

Seated, Helen peeped sideways at him. He fancied she wanted to say something of a particular nature. While he considered how to raise the subject uppermost in his mind, she spoke, her hands idle on her lap instead of busy with a sketch. "My lord, we rarely have the opportunity to speak in private, so I hope you will not think me forward if I broach a subject I have long wished to speak of."

Good Lord! What did she intend to say?

Delicate colour tinged her cheeks before she spoke again. "I have never expressed adequate thanks to you for helping Cousin Tarrant rescue me from the Earl of Pennington. The old man was quite mad, you know."

"Yes, definitely queer in his attic, but there is no need to thank me." He frowned unintentionally, thinking of the old villain who had kidnapped Helen in an attempt to marry her and father a child.

"You look fierce. Are you angry with me for mentioning the subject?"

"No, I could never be angry with you."

"Judging by the expression on your face, you are enraged," Helen persisted, "but I had to thank you properly."

"I am not 'enraged' by you, it is the memory of Pennington's wickedness which infuriates me," he replied, more vehemently than necessary. Langley longed to take her in his arms to reassure her. Simultaneously, he knew he must not. Langley forced himself to smile although haunted by the moment when he discovered Pennington had abducted her. "I have already said you did not need to thank me."

"Thank you."

He cleared his throat. "I am glad I helped your brother-in-law save you from the old lecher's clutches. Rupes is my brother-in-arms, so you and Georgianne are my honorary sisters. I shall always be yours to command."

Helen bent her head, but not so quickly that he did not see tears before she blinked. He wished he had the right to kiss them away. Instead, he must make some sort of apology to her for raising false expectations. "Miss Whitley, since I last saw you in England, I regret the change in my circumstances. They oblige me to fulfil my obligations to my family. I hope you understand."

"All too well, my lord. I am sorry for your situation. No one could regret it more. I wish I could help you." She stood. The brim of her velvet hat concealed most of her face. "Well, I have thanked you and set my conscience at ease. Shall we proceed to the pavilion? The breeze is too chilly for me to remain here. I shall sketch the statue on another occasion." She squared her shoulders before hurrying away.

Both of them were suffering from unrequited love. He could do nothing to alleviate it. With no wish to examine the state of his heart, he quickened his pace to catch up with Helen.

To his surprise, Langley noticed Miss Tomlinson accompanied by the high-stickler Madame la Comptesse de Beaulieu in the distance. "Why," he asked himself, "would Miss Tomlinson be in her company?" He whistled low. Judging by the way the old lady's head inclined toward the manufacturer's daughter, she seemed familiar with the heiress.

* * * *

At the sound of fast footsteps crunching on the gravelled path, Helen looked back. By the time Langley reached her, she had gathered sufficient composure to speak calmly. "Good day to you, my lord."

"I must see you safely home."

Helen gazed at him wistfully, committing his face to her memory. If she spent more time with him, he would tear at her heartstrings. "There is no need for you to do so; my dresser is waiting for me. Please go."

His dark eyes sober, the viscount hesitated, seeming to debate with himself before he spoke. "Very well. Good day to you, Miss Whitley."

Grief-stricken, Helen turned away. She had been so sure that, in spite of financial difficulties, Langley would propose marriage to her. Well, whether he loved her or not, he would not be the first gentleman forced by circumstance to marry for money. She struggled to convince herself Langley was unworthy of her love.

Helen knew one thing, she must put the viscount out of her mind and never allow anyone to guess he had broken her heart. Helen straightened her back. There was much to be thankful for. Her popularity was assured. Captain Dalrymple and other gentlemen were paying court to her. Not by a word or deed would she reveal her bitter disappointment.

Helen reached the pavilion where Pringle sat. "Come," she said to the woman.

What could she do other than continue her daily activities? Where to go? Not to Georgianne, who knew her so well. No matter how hard she would try to conceal her misery, her sister would sense it and ask concerned questions.

Followed by Pringle, Helen left the park.

She walked slowly down the street. On the opposite side, a group of mannerly Belgian soldiers—unlike those who accosted poor Mister Barnet on the previous day—approached.

"Mister Barnet!" she exclaimed to herself. "I promised to visit him. I shall do so immediately." She nodded at acquaintances but did not pause to speak to any of them.

"Knock on the door," she ordered Pringle when they reached Mister Barnet's house.

The woman sniffed, an irritating habit employed when she disapproved of something. The door opened. A tall footman in dark green livery opened the door.

"Please tell Mister Barnet that Miss Whitley is here," Helen said in a crisp tone of voice.

"Step inside, Miss, the master told me you might call."

Helen entered a lofty hall with a domed skylight and a peach-veined, white marble floor.

The footman ushered her past walls covered with beautiful hand-painted paper to the staircase.

Helen removed her pelisse and gloves. She handed them to her dresser. "You may wait here."

Pringle opened her mouth, probably to protest it was her duty to chaperon.

"I said, wait here," Helen repeated every inch of her an authoritative officer's daughter.

Fine paintings, of exotic scenes she would have liked to examine, hung on the walls on either side of the broad staircase. At the top, the footman turned right. He led her too swiftly along a short corridor for her to pause to admire beautiful blue and white china on plinths. He opened one of a pair of double doors. "Miss Whitley, Sir."

Helen stepped into a small salon decorated in the Chinese style, and ornamented with gorgeous vases and bowls from the mysterious land of pagodas and silk.

"My dear young lady." Mister Barnet put down a journal. "You are welcome, most welcome." He stood. "Please sit by the fire. It is a little cold outside, is it not?"

"Oh, I am well wrapped up so I hardly felt the chill in the air."

He nodded at his footman. "Fetch coffee and biscuits, Thomas."

Alone with Mister Barnet, Helen watched him sit at the other side of the hearth. "My dear young lady, I hope you did not come here alone."

"No, sir, my dresser accompanied me. She is waiting for me downstairs."

"I hope you will not take offence when I ask if it is unwise for you to only be escorted by a female servant."

"Of course not, sir, I...I—" To her dismay, thoughts of Langley caused tears to fill her eyes and trickle down her cheeks. She dabbed them away with her gloved hand, furious with herself for revealing her unhappiness.

Mister Barnet scrutinised her face.

"I beg your pardon, sir."

"There is no need to do so. If you wish to confide in me I might be of assistance."

A long sigh escaped her. "No one can help me."

Her host's blue eyes gazed at her from a lined face. "In my experience, when a young lady sighs and is overset, the cause is a gentleman."

His percipience threw her into confusion. "You are...too acute, sir."

He chuckled. "Please forgive my amusement. I am old, an advantage because I have experienced and observed much."

He did not seem self-pitying but something undefinable in his tone told Helen he had suffered profound grief.

Thomas returned and put the contents of a tray on a low table in front of her.

"Miss Whitley, would you pour coffee?" Mister Barnet asked. "I regret I have neither wife nor daughter to do so."

"Yes, of course." She wondered if he were a childless widower. It would be impertinent to question him to satisfy her curiosity. She poured coffee from the heavy silver pot, without comment.

"You may go, Thomas." Mister Barnet held out his hand to take the cup from her. She noticed a gold ring on the third finger of his left hand. So, he had been married.

"Am I mistaken to assume, that like Romeo and Juliet, you and the gentleman who has caused you sorrow are a pair of 'star-crossed' lovers?"

"In a manner of speaking, however, he is not my family's enemy. Sadly, the stars are not in our favour."

Mister Barnet sipped some coffee. His silence invited more confidences. At the end of them, he smiled. "The gentleman is to be praised."

"Why?" The word escaped her as fast as a bullet from her pistol.

"If he is sincere, you should believe he loves you too much to marry you without the means to maintain you."

"I don't care about his circumstances."

"It is fortunate he does." Mister Barnet put his empty coffee cup on the table.

"You don't understand," she burst out.

"Yes, I do, only too well. Penury blights even the most ardent love."

Again tears threatened to spill over her cheeks. She wiped them away with a handkerchief. More tears oozed from the corners of her eyes.

"My dear, Miss Whitley, please allow me to say how much I admire you for your decision to hold your head high and participate in all society has to offer you. You are a beautiful, brave, intelligent young woman. I have no doubt you will find happiness one day with someone else."

"Thank you, sir. Please forgive me for taking advantage of your hospitality. I have to go. By now, my sister must be wondering where I am."

Mister Barnet stood. The stiff silk of his old-fashioned coat rustled. "Thank you once more for rescuing me from those louts."

"I am pleased to have helped you, sir. Indeed, I am sorry for burdening you with my woes. Please pardon me."

"There is nothing to forgive." He smiled. "I hope you will visit me again."

"I shall be happy to."

* * * *

With only the lingering fragrance of his guest's perfume to keep him company, Mister Barnet sank back onto his chair. He wiped his moist eyes. His dear wife would have known how to advise his guest. If his granddaughter had lived, her bravery might have equalled Miss Whitley's. He sincerely hoped the young lady would visit him again.

Mister Barnet frowned while he settled more comfortably. He must discover more about his visitor. Through a few discreet enquires, it would not be difficult to find out the name of her brother-in-law's best friend. He hoped the gentleman really was an honourable man, not an arrogant, insensitive officer who cast her aside for selfish reasons. After all, he could only judge by the young lady's interpretation of the matter.

Chapter Nine

26th March, 1815

Helen skirted a table covered with a miscellany of objects, any one of which might feature in a painting. They included a marble bust of Julius Caesar, a collection of peacock feathers, a damaged sabretache with gold and red embellishments, a mummified seahorse and a spray of dried lavender. She shut the door of a battered armoire in which she stored paintbrushes, her paint box and other items.

Helen walked across the spacious attic to the window at the front of the house, careful not to bang her head on the ceiling which sloped toward it. She peered through the glass. By the half-light before dawn, she could see cart horses pulling three wagons with iron-rimmed wooden wheels. When Helen opened the window, she heard the clip-clop of the horses and the clatter of wagon wheels. She gazed at the drivers, soldiers huddled into great coats. How could she capture the bustle of carts, mounted troops and foot soldiers, passing through the city on their way to towns on the border, in a sketch or watercolour? How could she depict the anxiety underlying brave smiles? She shivered, but not from the slight chill in the large room Georgianne and Tarrant allowed her to use.

If she had the skill to record preparations for war, could she depict individual fears, such as those of a mother or wife unable to conceal their anxiety?

Helen took a deep breath to clear her head. She stared past the street to Parc Royale at a well-endowed lady facing a tall gentleman. The ostrich plumes on her hat quivered. The man shook his head. He removed her hand from his shoulder. She reached out to him. He turned and hurried away.

The lady sank onto a seat and took out a handkerchief from her reticule. Helen's eyes widened. Maria Tomlinson! No sign of a maid or a footman. How improper!

The manufacturer's daughter wiped her eyes. Helen realized this might be her chance to try to capture the embodiment of a lady in distress. As she rushed to pick up her sketchbook, she experienced a twinge of guilt.

By the time she returned to the window, Miss Tomlinson was looking around, presumably to see if anyone had observed her. She stood, her legs seeming too weak to support her.

Sorry for the young lady, Helen's imagination began to sweep away her common sense. Thwarted love? The bearer of bad tidings? She turned to a new page in her sketch pad and placed it on the easel. To depict Miss Tomlinson with the unknown gentleman would be equivalent to eavesdropping. However, she wanted to portray a young woman's overwrought sensibilities. An imaginary picture of a slip of a girl, overcome by imminent separation from a handsome soldier, formed in her mind. The girl in tears—the soldier indifferent. No, not indifferent; his outward calm masked his fear that he might be killed and never return to the love of his life.

The minutes ticked away while she sketched. Her stomach rumbled. How long had she been up here? She put down her pencil. She had captured Maria Tomlinson's sorrow via the imaginary girl. Sharp as a shard of glass, a pain pierced her heart. Suppose she and Langley were parting forever. Would she ever smile again?

Yet he had made it plain they had no future together. Helen sank onto a chair. For sanity's sake she must remove him from her mind. It would be difficult, for they could not avoid frequently seeing each other.

She glanced at the window. The sun had long since risen in the sky from which the last traces of pale pink and gold faded from the horizon. Time to breakfast, but surely she should not be so hungry. In novels, young ladies crossed in love, lost their appetites and faded away. "Well," she thought, "I am healthy so I shall not languish like those weak-spirited heroines. Moreover, regardless of whatever Langley thinks of me, I am not a heartless flirt. Even if I cannot marry him, sooner or later, I shall wed, have my own home and—God willing—children." She left the attic room and went to the breakfast parlour, where her sister sat reading a letter.

"Are you unwell?" Helen asked Georgianne after they greeted each other.

Not only was her sister's face almost devoid of colour, her weight had decreased. Helen eyed her with concern. There were dark shadows under Georgianne's eyes. She must be fretting about Cousin Tarrant and wishing he had not purchased another commission after he heard Napoleon escaped. "You should eat more. Toast and weak coffee are insufficient."

Georgianne dabbed her mouth with her table napkin. "I cannot."

Helen helped herself to ham, eggs, and bread and butter.

"Coffee?" Georgianne asked.

Helen nodded.

"Dearest, you should take off your apron before leaving the attic." Georgianne gazed at her. "I must say I cannot understand why you want to leave your warm bed at such an early hour of the morning, either to practice your art or ride."

"Sometimes, as the saying goes, early birds catch worms." She chuckled. "I caught one this morning."

"Really?"

She hesitated. Perhaps it would be unkind to mention Miss Tomlinson's assignation. Yet Georgianne would not gossip. "I saw Mister Tomlinson's daughter, unchaperoned in the park with a gentleman. After he left, she wept."

"'Pon my word!" Georgianne frowned. "What an unfortunate lady. Before I married Tarrant, I always feared being the victim of an arranged marriage. When Mamma beat me with a riding crop for refusing to marry the Earl of Pennington—Oh! I have no words to describe my sentiments."

Helen sipped some coffee. "It is old history which I am sure you don't wish to recall any more than I wish to remember! I am sure you have not forgotten, the earl also tried to force me to marry him after you rejected him. Yet what does it have to do with Miss Tomlinson? Why should you pity her?"

Georgianne's bosom rose and fell faster than usual. Once more she dabbed her mouth with a table napkin. "If Mister Tomlinson is still set on her marriage to Langley, I pity her if she does not wish to marry him."

"Why should she not want to?" Helen burst out. "He is agreeable and handsome, besides being well-born."

"Perhaps you are right. She might be in love with the man you saw her with in the park. Someone her father disapproves of. After all, it does not take half a brain to understand the manufacturer is ambitious. If he is trying to force her into a marriage against her wishes, she is to be pitied."

Fletcher entered the breakfast parlour. "Lieutenant Calverly has called to speak to Miss Whitley."

"You may admit him," Georgianne said.

Helen stood to remove her apron. Before she could do so the fresh-faced lieutenant, wearing the silver-laced black service uniform of the 7th Light Dragoons, and a scarlet sash around his slender waist, entered the breakfast parlour. He bowed while looking at Helen with palpable amusement.

To her annoyance, her cheeks grew hot.

"My sister is an artist," Georgianne explained, while Helen wrestled with her apron strings.

"Allow me."

Somewhat ill at ease when the lieutenant could not avoid touching her back, Helen fidgeted while he teased open the knot.

Before she could thank him, he turned and bowed to Georgianne.

"Please forgive me for waiting on you so early in the morning, ma'am. My excuse is duty which sends me to Nivelles, so I have called to set Miss Whitley's mind at rest before I leave."

Helen handed the grubby apron to Fletcher, who looked down his nose at it before leaving the room.

"Do sit at the table before you explain." Georgianne's hand hovered above the coffee pot. "Will you partake of coffee? Something to eat?"

"Thank you, ma'am."

Georgianne waved her free hand in the direction of the buffet. "Please help yourself."

The lieutenant piled his plate with steak, kidneys, sausage and eggs. He looked at it appreciatively. "I shall enjoy my breakfast. The food in my billet is not as good as this, and you cannot imagine what our rations taste like when the army is on the move."

Georgianne gave him a cup of coffee.

"Thank you, ma'am." He smiled. "I beg you not to look so dismayed, soldiers must do their duty."

"Quite," Helen commented, aware of her sister's distress at the indirect mention of war. "You said you have some good news."

"Yes." He laid down his fork. "Those impertinent Belgian soldiers have been disciplined."

Helen smiled. "I am pleased. Poor Mister Barnet; being made fun of and ordered to dance at an age when he should be respected. A disgraceful matter."

"Who is Mister Barnet?" Georgianne asked.

Helen wished she had told her sister about the incident. "An old gentleman insulted by the soldiers."

"Who your sister rescued," Calverly explained.

Georgianne raised her eyebrows but made no comment.

The lieutenant broke a brief silence. "You paint, Miss Whitley?"

"Yes." She did not like discussing her endeavours.

"Of course, it is fashionable for ladies to dabble in watercolours. The more eerie the

115

subject, the more enthusiastic they are," Calverly said.

Georgianne laughed. "My sister does more than dabble, and she does not paint ruined gothic abbeys and churches which send chills down the back and cause nightmares. She painted the oil painting of my husband above the mantelpiece. I like it so much that I brought it with us from England."

The lieutenant looked at it for a long moment. "Upon my word, I hardly know what to say. It is clear Miss Whitley is exceptionally talented."

"Thank you, sir," Helen replied, somewhat amused by his astonishment.

Calverly put down his knife and fork. "Miss Whitley, I would be honoured, if you would show me more of your paintings."

"Oh, they are not worth viewing," Helen declared. "Oil paintings take a long time to dry, so I only work in pencil and watercolours in Brussels."

The lieutenant ate the last morsel of sausage. "Thank you for your hospitality, Mrs Tarrant." He stood, bowed and took his leave.

"A nice young man. God bless him," Georgianne said softly when they were alone.

"What are you going to do this morning? You still look unwell. Should you rest?"

"No, I could not sleep knowing Tarrant might need something. Come."

Helen accompanied Georgianne to her comfortable parlour, where Cousin Tarrant's mahogany medicine case with silver mounts and a close-fitting lid stood on a low table.

Georgianne sat down. She opened the case to check the contents of several small boxes. "Rhubarb pills," she murmured. "Of course, though Tarrant has an excellent digestion, he might need them." I must order some. He needs more plaisters and James Powders for fever. Ah, here is his tongue scraper. Where is his bleeding cup?" She pressed her hands to her mouth, her pupils dilated.

Helen knelt by Georgianne's chair. She drew her sister's small hands into her own. "I shall purchase a new one for him today. Perhaps I could also buy a few things for you to give Langley. After all, he regards you as a sister, so he would probably appreciate them. Some rhubarb pills and James Powders perhaps; no maybe not—some laudanum and-and bandages."

"Dearest, your hands are trembling."

"I am cold."

"If you say so, although your hands are warm." Georgianne smiled. "It is kind of you to suggest providing Langley with some necessities."

Aware of unspoken words on the subject of the viscount, Helen forced herself to return her sister's smile. "I shall purchase them today from the English Apothecary."

Georgianne replaced the hinged lid of Tarrant's round case. She stood. Poker-straight she fainted.

Women's troubles? Horrified, Helen could not act for a second or two. She recovered her senses and tugged the bell rope.

Distraught, she fetched a cushion, knelt by Georgianne, and inserted it beneath her sister's head. "I knew you were feeling poorly." She patted Georgianne's cheeks hoping to revive her.

When Dawson, Georgianne's dresser, entered the parlour she regarded her mistress thoughtfully.

"Fetch some sal volatile, some cool cloths and—" Helen commenced.

Georgianne's eyes fluttered open.

"Lie still," Helen said, relieved because Georgianne had regained consciousness, but still greatly alarmed. "I shall send for the doctor."

The dresser returned with a tiny, silver-chased vial of the pungent salts which she passed to Helen.

She removed the stopper. "Sniff this." She held the vial beneath Georgianne's nose.

Georgianne obeyed. Tears poured down her cheeks. She pushed Helen's hand away. "Enough, dearest!" She sat up, rejecting the cool, damp cloths Helen wanted to apply to her forehead. Some colour returned to her face. With Helen's help she stood. "No need to send for a doctor, Helen. There is nothing untoward."

"Please, I must send for one."

Georgianne sank onto the sofa. The palms of her hands rested on her stomach. A smile hovered around her mouth.

"Tell me what is happening. Why you don't want me to summon a doctor? If you feel shy with a strange physician, perhaps we can send to London for our own doctor."

"Truly, it would be ridiculous, dearest! There is no need for you to be so worried."

"A glass of brandy to bring the colour back into your cheeks?"

"No, thank you."

"No matter what you say, I insist you sip some cherry brandy. It will restore you." Helen crossed the carpet to a table on which small bottles and crystal glasses stood. She poured a generous measure of the ruby drink and gave it to her sister. "Please explain why you are pale and heavy-eyed. I think it is due to more than a monthly female affliction."

Georgianne sighed. "I see you will give me no peace until I confide in you; so I will if you promise not to tell Tarrant."

The door had opened in time for her brother-by-law to overhear.

"Secrets?" he asked. "Perhaps you have lost a fortune at cards."

Georgianne laughed. "Of course I have not been so reckless."

"Then?"

Helen took the empty glass from Georgianne.

Tarrant narrowed his eyes. "Never tell me you have become a secret drinker."

"No, no," Georgianne replied, "The wines and spirits are for your refreshment when you take your ease here. I…er…felt a little faint so Helen suggested a sip or two of brandy. Please don't worry, I am quite well now."

Helen looked anxiously at Dawson. Servants always gossiped below stairs which meant their chatter spread from person to person. Doubtless, Dawson would spread the news that her mistress fainted, and then Tarrant's valet would probably tell him Georgianne lost consciousness.

Tarrant sat next to Georgianne. He rubbed her hands in his large, well-shaped ones. "Heart of my heart, be honest, is all well with you?"

"Yes, all of us are subject to occasional ills. I promise there is no need for concern."

"If you say so."

"I do."

"Very well, I know you never lie to me." Tarrant raised her sister's hand to his lips and pressed a kiss onto it. "I came to tell you I shall be away for two nights on Makelyn's orders."

"Be careful. No rough riding," Georgianne said.

Tarrant stood. "You fret too much." He bent to kiss the top of her head. "Lavender. Heaven. When I am away from you, I always remember your perfume."

Georgianne laughed. "I hope you remember more than that."

"Of course I do." He straightened. "Helen, take care of your sister."

"I shall; so will Dawson."

Georgianne glanced at her dresser. "You may go."

Tarrant turned back to Georgianne. "Adieu, my dear love."

Georgianne smiled up at him. "Hush! Choose your words carefully or you will make Helen blush."

Tarrant lingered for another moment. He reached the door then turned back to give Georgianne another kiss on the cheek before he departed.

Georgianne buried her face in her hands. "Heaven above, what is written in our stars?" Georgianne buried her face in her hands. "I am afraid for Tarrant! Suppose—"

"Don't think the worst. Instead, believe you will have long, happy lives together." She sat opposite her sister. "What is your secret?"

Georgianne smoothed her gown over her stomach. "Promise to keep it."

"I cannot swear not to tell Cousin Tarrant until you tell me what you are hiding from him."

Georgianne toyed with a gold tassel which ornamented a plump cushion. "Very well." A smile illuminated her beautiful face. "God willing, you will be an aunt."

Helen's eyes rounded. "You are with child."

"Yes."

Helen hurried to embrace her. "Congratulations. This is wonderful news," she said before fear clutched her. So many women died in or after childbirth. So did their babes.

Yet, last year Georgianne had reassured their little sister that their mother and aunt survived many births and their children survived. She squinted at Georgianne. "Why don't you want Cousin Tarrant to know?"

"Before he met me, a lady he knew died in childbirth. When he married me, he did not want to have a child for fear I would also die."

Helen hesitated. "Unless there are grave concerns for your well-being, I promise I will not tell him you are increasing." She spoke as though her words were dragged out of her.

She saw the glint of tears in Georgianne's eyes. How fortunate her sister and brother-in-law were to love each other unselfishly. She believed he would do anything in his power for Georgianne which would not compromise his honour.

Well, sitting here, indulging in sentimental thoughts and maudlin fears, served no purpose. "This morning I shall purchase James Powders. I will also buy anything else you require." She forced herself to smile. "If you are well enough to chaperone me, we shall attend the Greville's ball. If not, you must put your well-being and your baby's before me."

"Don't fuss, dearest. I cannot remain at home until the baby introduces itself to us. Besides, I am only indisposed in the early mornings. Dawson assures me the nausea will end soon. In the meantime, she suggests I drink a cold ginger infusion to mitigate the vomiting.

Enough of that. I am looking forward to this evening. What are you going to wear?"

Helen ignored the question. "You fainted. Are you sure you would not prefer to stay at home?"

"Yes."

Helen frowned. Could marriage and motherhood ever be worthwhile? Yet, what were the alternatives for a lady? Those who loved, like Georgianne and Cousin Tarrant, reaped the rewards. But marriage without love? Such whims! In her milieu, love was not a requirement for marriage—although the goal of many men and women was to wed and have a happy home. For now, even if Langley considered her a cruel flirt, she would enjoy the company of Dalrymple and other gentlemen.

Chapter Ten

26th March, 1815

Gowned in gleaming white silk, Helen stood next to Georgianne halfway up the stairs. Above them on the landing stood Sir Hugh and Lady Greville greeting their guests as they were announced.

Helen looked sideways at her sister. "Are you sure you don't want to dance this evening?"

"Yes, but please don't fuss. I am well."

From the ballroom came the sound of a minuet, the first dance executed by individual couples at some balls. Did her sister, who excelled in its intricate steps, not want to participate this evening because of her condition, or because Cousin Tarrant could not accompany them? Helen could not dismiss the subject from her mind. "Why have you decided not to dance?" she whispered in Georgianne's ear.

"I am not sure if it is wise. I must think of the baby," her sister whispered back.

"I see." Helen looked around. She gestured discreetly with her fan. "Georgianne, look! Miss Tomlinson is making her curtsy to our host and hostess."

Her sister raised her eyebrows. "Lud! I am surprised to see her here. Despite hearing her name mentioned by gossips, I did not know she moved in the first circles. Who is the lady with her?"

"Madame la Comptesse de Beaulieu," Helen replied. "When I saw them in Parc Royale, I wondered why such a high stickler accompanied Miss Tomlinson."

"How do you know she is a 'high stickler'?"

"Madame, our grandmother's friend, often visits her. Last year, when I stayed with our grandparents, Madame never mentioned Miss Tomlinson."

Georgianne watched the young lady. "It is said the heiress is well spoken and has pretty manners."

They reached the top of the stairs. Sir Hugh inclined his head to them while his wife spoke to Georgianne. "Mrs Tarrant, it is good to see you. How charming you look. Your gown is almost the exact colour of your eyes."

The colour in Georgianne's cheeks bloomed. "Thank you for the compliment."

"I trust you and your husband are well."

"How kind of you to ask. We are in good health. I regret the Major is unable to accompany us this evening. Duty has called him to the border."

"Ah! How unfortunate; I hoped to speak to him. Our son, our only son, is in Major Tarrant's regiment. He is the reason for our being in Brussels." She cleared her throat. "Forgive me. This is not the moment to speak of such matters." Her ladyship inclined her head. "Miss Whitley."

Helen made her curtsy, her sympathy with the anxious mother—even as she tried to commit the fear in her ladyship's eyes to memory, in order to capture it in a sketch.

* * * *

With Georgianne at her side, Helen entered the ballroom which was festooned with evergreen garlands and swags brightened with colourful berries. Lit by numerous chandeliers, their crystal pendants glittering, the decorations were beautiful.

"It is hot," Helen said in response to both the fragrant beeswax candles, and the large company of officers in dress uniforms laced with gold or silver, alongside fashionably dressed gentlemen and modish ladies.

"Yes, it is." Georgianne unfurled her ostrich feather fan and looked at the doors which were open to admit cool night air and led onto the long balcony.

Helen gestured to a row of chairs on the opposite side of the ballroom for the use of chaperones and their charges. "Do sit down, Georgianne." She gazed anxiously at her sister. "Are you sure you don't want to go home?"

"Quite sure dearest; I shall enjoy meeting my friends."

She and her sister edged their way around the crowd at the side of the ballroom.

Madame la Comptesse tapped Helen on her arm. "Miss Whitley," she said in a voice loud enough to be heard above the hub-bub of conversation and music, "'Ow do you go on. 'Ow is your grandmother?"

Helen curtsied. "I am very well, thank you, Madame. Grandmother is in good health. By the way, have you met my sister, Mrs Tarrant?"

"No I 'ave not 'ad ze pleasure."

"Please allow me to introduce her? Madame, Mrs Tarrant." Georgianne curtsied. "Mrs Tarrant, la Comptesse de Beaulieu."

"You are a beauty, Mrs Tarrant. 'Ave you met my granddaughter, Mademoiselle Tomlinson?"

Astonished, Helen stared at the elderly lady. Her granddaughter!

"No, Madame, although I have met Mister Tomlinson."

The Comptesse pressed her hand to her flat bosom. "'Ave you indeed?" She sounded displeased. More than likely because she considered her late daughter made a mésalliance.

An awkward silence ensued before Madame spoke again. "Miss Whitley, I think both you and Maria 'ave eighteen years. I daresay you 'ave much in common so you may become friends. Mrs Tarrant, we shall call on you tomorrow."

"Indeed," thought Helen, "for all Madame knows, we might not have any mutual interests—other than Langley, who I am sure is important to both of us."

She eyed Maria, resplendent in a white silk gown, ornamented with tiny, pale pink artificial roses on her puff sleeves and at the hem; a ball gown so well cut that it flattered her large figure. As an artist, she admired Miss Tomlinson's wealth of glossy brown hair. Yet her large hazel eyes seemed haunted. Did the gentlemen she saw her with this morning in Parc Royale, cause it?

Georgianne curtsied to the Comptesse. "Please excuse us, Madame."

Helen made her curtsy to the French lady before following her sister to the row of upholstered chairs. Yet due to the number of people who greeted them, and the necessity of conversing, a half hour or more passed before Georgianne sank onto a seat. "Sit down, dearest, before your beaux solicit your hand."

"Half of the dances are already spoken for, including the supper dance which I granted to Captain Dalrymple."

"I like him," Georgianne remarked.

The minuet ended to the sound of polite applause. "Look" Georgianne gestured toward the ballroom floor, "Mister Colchester is leading Lady—oh, I did not hear her name. What is it?"

"Lady Cecilia," Helen replied.

"Ah, yes, what a pretty girl she is. Her brother serves with the Cherry Pickers."

Helen suppressed a vulgar chuckle remembering an Ensign in the 11th Light

Dragoons, who bitterly resented his regiment's nickname. It was the result of an attack by the French while some of the regiment raided a cherry orchard at San Martin de Trebejo in Spain.

From the corner of her eye, Helen noticed Captain Dalrymple pace along the line of chaperones seated next to their charges. She hoped he would never ask her to perform the complicated steps of the minuet. "Of course," she mused, "at most balls the minuet is no longer the first dance because it takes so long to complete."

Helen held her breath. She had never performed the minuet at so large a function. The prospect of being the only couple on the ballroom floor alarmed her. "Two passes left then two passes right," she murmured to herself, mentally reviewing the steps.

"Mrs Tarrant."

At the sound of the Langley's familiar voice, Helen looked up. Although he bowed to Georgianne, he looked at Helen with an amused expression in his eyes. "No need to be nervous, Miss Whitley, you dance delightfully. I am sure you would excel at the minuet."

"Oh no, I am not sufficiently proficient," she answered, treasuring his compliment.

"You are too modest."

Helen looked down at her lap. To say 'I am,' would seem boastful. To say 'I am not,' would appear bold. She peeped up at Langley, who frowned as he observed Georgianne.

"Mrs Tarrant, please forgive me for saying you are flushed. It is too warm. Is the heat overpowering you? Would you care for a glass of wine? Shall I fetch one?"

Georgianne pressed a dainty handkerchief to her forehead. "How kind you are, but wine will not cool me. Perhaps some lemonade."

"Of course. May I also fetch one for you, Miss Whitley?"

"Yes, please."

Before long, he returned and gave them two full glasses.

If only Langley would ask her to dance, she would even throw caution to the wind by accepting his invitation to waltz—although she had not received permission to stand up for the dance from a patroness at Almacks.

A gentleman's voice caught her attention. "Good evening, Miss Whitley."

"Captain Dalrymple."

"If Mrs Tarrant permits, would you care to stroll on the balcony?"

Aware of Langley watching like a dog fox prepared to pounce to protect his prey, Helen's cheeks warmed.

The captain bowed to Georgianne; the expression on his face serious. "It is very hot here, so may I have your permission?"

Georgianne raised an eyebrow. "Dearest?"

"Some fresh air would be welcome."

"Very well,"

Dalrymple made way for Helen through the crowd and led her outside.

They were not the only couple to escape the ballroom, and stroll up and down past potted orange trees and other plants well lit by lanterns.

The captain held out his arm. Helen placed the tips of her fingers upon it. She walked by his side to the end of the balcony where a bench stood between two tall trees. Not until she sat did she realise the foliage hid them from view. "Most improper, Captain."

"Not at all, what harm can there be in a lady having a private conversation with a gentleman who respects her?"

Enough light penetrated the branches for her to see the serious expression on his face.

"Miss Whitley, you have many admirers, so please don't think I am impertinent for asking if you would welcome a proposal of marriage from any of them."

Well, he certainly came to the point in swift military fashion. What should she say? She liked him very much so he deserved honesty.

Helen chose her words with care before she spoke. "I hoped a gentleman would ask me to be his wife, but he did not and will not."

"Do you expect him to do so in future?" Dalrymple asked, the expression in his eyes intent.

She shook her head.

"If he had, would you have accepted him?"

Helen nodded.

"Thank you for your honesty." Dalrymple peeled off her elbow length glove. He enfolded her hand in his warm one and raised it to his lips. Head bent, lantern light gleamed on his dark hair. His kiss on her knuckle sent a strange shiver through her.

He replaced her hand on her lap. "Forgive me for taking the liberty which expressed my admiration. I hope it is not unwelcome."

She pulled on her glove. "No, but it surprised me."

He chuckled. "According to Major Tarrant, surprise is an excellent tactic, although, of course, he was not speaking of matters of the heart. So, please allow me to ask you if I may request your guardian to grant permission for me to pay my addresses to you."

Indeed, he had taken her by surprise.

"I hope you are not shocked by my boldness. Your brother-in-law has no objection to my paying court to you."

She bent her head. What should she say? She wanted to marry, to have her own home and forget Langley. "Would your parents approve of me?"

"Yes, they married for love and wish me to do so."

"Your parents might not like me."

"Why, are you ill-natured?" he teased.

"I hope not."

"Miss Whitley, I am not asking you to decide now what your answer will be, merely for your consent to write to your guardian. While we wait for his reply, we can become better acquainted. When we are, you might dislike me."

"Oh, no, I cannot imagine that!"

Dalrymple smiled as he looked deeply into her eyes. "That is all I need to know for now. I shall escort you back to your sister."

* * * *

27th March, 1815

On the following evening, as she was about to change before they dined, Helen received a request to join Cousin Tarrant.

When she entered the study, lined with shelves containing handsomely bound books, he gazed at her from his chair behind the large mahogany desk without uttering even a single courteous word.

Apprehensive, Helen looked into his eyes, which were grey as the sky on a cold winter's day. "Why did you summon me?"

"To warn you not to be careless with your reputation. I refer to your regrettable tete-a-tete with Captain Dalrymple on the balcony."

What right did he have to complain of her dalliance? She wanted to remind him that prior to his asking Georgianne to marry him, he had entered her bedroom while she slept at an inn. Helen glared at him, discomfited because he considered it necessary to upbraid her. Anger combined with embarrassment warred within her. She held back irate words.

"Cousin Helen, I don't expect you to seclude yourself with one of your beaux and allow him to kiss your hand."

Some wretched old cat of a woman must have observed them and spread gossip. "Georgianne gave me permission to walk on the balcony with the captain."

"You have condemned yourself with the word 'walk'. Your sister did not expect you to flirt with him while seated on a secluded bench." Cousin Tarrant's cold expression softened a little. "Dalrymple wishes to marry you. If you refuse his proposal now, gossip will attach itself to your hitherto good name." He cleared his throat. "Helen, I wish your mother or another older lady could explain the way of the world. I am sorry because you cannot rely on anyone for advice other than Georgianne and myself. I must depend on your good sense. Confound it!" He broke off for a moment. "Sorry for swearing." He drummed the tips of his fingers on the mahogany desk spread with maps and correspondence. "Oh, sit down, Helen."

Afraid he would send her back to England, she sank straight-backed onto the chair opposite him.

"Helen, please believe I have your welfare at heart. One day, I sincerely hope you will be happily married."

She smiled at him, relieved by his kind words. "Thank you."

"From now on, I hope your good sense will prevail." Tarrant stood. "I shall say no more." He crossed the room to hold the door open for her to leave. "Duty at headquarters prevents me from attending the concert with you and Georgianne after we dine. I hope you will enjoy it."

* * * *

29th March, 1815

After it became known she was not an heiress, a few of Helen's gallant beaux did not desert her, and Dalrymple sought her out at a rout, rode with her in the early mornings, and accompanied her and Georgianne to the theatre. She welcomed his presence but behaved prudently, careful not to risk a stain on her reputation by any further incautious conduct.

Other gentlemen began to seek her out, their admiration obvious. Yet, if she were honest, Helen realised she cared little for those who ignored her after they discovered she only had a small dowry. After all, she only craved Langley's attention. Unfortunately, she must come to terms with both the change in his attitude toward her, and his change of circumstance.

Soon she must decide. If her guardian approved of Dalrymple, would she or would she not accept his proposal?

* * * *

31st March, 1815

Pringle, neatly dressed in grey, her white apron spotless, entered the bedchamber carrying a tray. "Good morning, Miss. I hope you slept well."

"Yes, thank you." Helen covered her mouth with her hand to hide a yawn.

"Your hot chocolate, Miss."

Helen sat up, and then plumped up her pillows and arranged them behind her.

Pringle placed a tray on Helen's lap, then crossed the room to draw open the heavy silk curtains at the window. "A lovely day. The sun's shining. Shall I lay out your riding habit?"

"What time is it?"

"Nearly ten o'clock."

Helen hoped Dalrymple had not sought her this morning in the Allee Vert. "No, I don't have time to ride before breakfast. In future, no matter how late I return, please wake me at half past eight; I don't want to forgo my daily ride. If I need to, I shall rest in the afternoons. She looked down at the tray and picked up a letter. "Who sent this?"

Helen broke the red wax seal and unfolded the smooth, expensive paper. "Oh! It is from Mister Barnet. He invites me to drink coffee with him this morning."

Pringle sniffed.

"No need to disapprove." Helen sipped some chocolate before adding, "He is a good-hearted old man."

"If you say so, Miss."

"I do. Please don't frown." She shook her head reprovingly. "Sometimes I think you and the other servants are more conscious of my position in society than I am."

The dresser's cheeks reddened. "Well, Miss, I know what is fitting. Mister Barnet will not add to your consequence."

"Is that so?"

Pringle nodded vehemently. "Yes, we take such pride in you."

Helen laughed. "To hear you talk, someone would think I am a duchess instead of an army officer's daughter." Of course, her father, the youngest son of a baron, was well-born nonetheless. Although respected for his courage and courtesy, he had not ranked high in society. If Cousin Tarrant were not well-born, and extremely wealthy due to an inheritance from his godfather, a nabob, her position amongst the ton would be negligible.

After finishing her drink, Helen got out of bed to attend to her morning ablutions, and retired behind a screen. "The sun is deceptive at this time of the year, Pringle. I shall wear my cream kerseymere gown, my jade-green pelisse, the matching hat and dark green leather gloves.

Refreshed after washing with water scented with essence of roses, Helen cleaned her teeth with coral powder, before she allowed her dresser to help her into a cotton chemise with a square neckline and short sleeves trimmed with lace. With resignation, Helen eyed the buckram stays with cup-shaped supports for her breasts. At a ball, she had overheard a dowager comment on her good figure and elegant deportment. Perhaps the rigid garment helped to achieve it along with her determination to make a proverbial mark on society. She sighed. Stays were not designed for comfort. Constrained by them, how did any ladies manage to eat sufficiently to keep them alive? Well, she did not intend to starve. "Pringle," she said, somewhat irritably, "don't pull the laces too tight for me not to be able to eat enough to satisfy my appetite."

The stays fastened, Helen put on her pink silk stockings and knee-length cotton drawers. Next, she allowed Pringle to help her with a cambric petticoat with a deep border of Moravian work. She fastened the buttons at the front of the bodice while Pringle tied the tapes at the back.

Helen glanced at the clock on the mantelpiece. Time to partake of a late breakfast.

She sat at the dressing table looking at her reflection in the mirror. Impatient, she waited for Pringle's clever fingers to arrange her hair in a knot high on her head and tease short, pomaded tendrils into place across her forehead and at the sides of her face.

"My pearl earrings," she said, even more impatient to complete her toilette.

Pringle found the earrings in the jewel case. Helen slipped them into her ears. Aware that she looked her best, she hoped that if Langley joined them at breakfast he would admire her. Even if she must accept they could never be married she also hoped they could be friends and always at ease with one another.

* * * *

After breakfast, Georgianne asked Helen to go shopping with her, so it was not until they partook of a late nuncheon that Helen settled in Mister Barnet's parlour.

"Are you comfortable, Miss Whitley?" the old gentleman asked. "Are you warm enough? Although it is nearly spring, there is still a chill in the air. A good fire is the answer."

"I assure you I am both comfortable and cosy, sir."

As Helen stared into the heart of the burning wood, she remembered lying on the rug in front of the nursery fire with Georgianne beside her, watching fiery caverns, and castles and dragons which formed in its depths. Well, her childhood days were over.

A footman placed refreshments on the low table in front of her. At her host's request, she poured coffee.

"I forget what young ladies like. Would you prefer cherry brandy or tea to coffee?" Mister Barnet asked. "Should I send for biscuits?"

Helen cut a slice of feather-light cake for him. "No thank you, this young lady is perfectly content."

"Good. How are you, Miss Whitley? I hope you are a little happier than when I last saw you."

"Yes, thank you, I am." Her voice lacked conviction.

"Something is troubling you?"

"A little. I am in disgrace." The entire sorry tale tumbled from her.

Mister Barnet put his empty cup and plate on the table. "Perhaps you were incautious. Nevertheless, I like what you have told me about Captain Dalrymple. With regard to gossip, people in your milieu will forget your misdemeanour when they have something new to chat about. You are wise beyond your years to hold your head high, and dress exquisitely to carve a place for yourself amongst the ton."

Appreciative of his encouragement, Helen looked across the space between the table and his chair. His face, slightly tinged with grey, was somewhat thin, with two deep lines extending from each side of his nose to either side of his mouth. Yet Mister Barnet's visage expressed good humour, and his sky-blue eyes revealed exceptional kindness. At one moment they were soft, at the next, sharp as a sword-edge. Life must have dealt him equal shares of happiness and distress. Dressed in dove-grey velvet, the coat with silver lace, silver buttons, and a long pearl-coloured waistcoat embroidered in silver thread, his garments were fashionable in a bygone era. He would be an excellent subject for a sketch or even an oil painting.

A little embarrassed because she had confided in him so recklessly, Helen finished her refreshments.

She put her cup and plate on the table spread with a linen cloth of the finest quality. Indeed, everything in this withdrawing room spoke of Mister Barnet's good taste and great wealth. Even the Prince Regent might envy the gentleman's exquisite collection of blue and white vases, other Chinese porcelain, and a magnificent black-lacquered screen, embellished with exotic scenes painted in shades of brown, cream and red.

Mister Barnet stood. "I have a gift for you.

"For me?"

The elderly gentleman crossed the room. He unlocked a cabinet which matched the screen, opened the doors and took a dark blue leather box from one of the many small drawers. He put it on her lap. "Yes, a present, Miss Whitley, to thank you for rescuing me from those ruffians."

"There is no need to give me anything."

"I disagree, for it would give me great pleasure if you will accept this small token of my appreciation." His eyes shone like an enthusiastic young man's.

It would be rude to refuse. Helen opened the box lined with indigo-blue watered silk. She gasped with pleasure at the sight of a delicate suite of brilliants set in silver. Any young lady would be delighted to adorn herself with the tiara—into which ostrich feathers could be fitted—necklace, brooch, ring and arm clasps. Speechless with delight, she admired the delicate floral design reminiscent of spring.

"Do you like it?"

"Yes, but it is too much, I cannot—"

"No, it is not." The light left his eyes. "You must accept it." He pressed his right hand to the left of his chest. "At my age, I might have died if those ne'er-do-wells had forced me to dance. My gift is valueless compared to your gift of my life."

Were his eyes moist? "You are persuasive, sir, but—"

"I commissioned the jewellery for someone I loved who never had an opportunity to wear it. The pieces should not be wasted in a box. If you accept my token of gratitude, it will give me great pleasure."

However well-meant, Helen knew she should not accept the present. She sought a way to refuse it without causing hurt or offence. "There is something which would give me even more pleasure, Mister Barnet."

"What?"

"I want to sketch you, sir."

"Ah, like so many other clever young ladies, you claim you are an artist. Is it not the fashion to draw mossy stones, deserted places inhabited by ravens, or tumbledown abbeys surrounded by neglected graves?"

"Such gothic subjects are of little interest to me."

"When I return to England, I hope you will visit me so I can show you the works of art I have been collecting for many years."

"If my sister and her husband permit me, I shall be pleased to accept your invitation." She closed the lid of the hinged box. "Will you allow me to sketch you instead of accepting this?"

"No, you may paint me only if you keep the trinkets."

Helen hesitated. She caught her lower lip between her teeth. After all, brilliants and silver could not be costly, could they?

"Thank you for your gift. With your permission, I shall sketch you later in the week."

* * * *

The door closed behind Miss Whitley. Contented Mister Barnet removed his wig and scratched his head. He admired her. She had entered his life like a welcome broom which swept away cobwebs.

Mister Barnet replaced the wig. The knowledge that Miss Whitley would wear the dainty pieces, lovingly designed for his late granddaughter, pleased him. He sank back against his padded chair. Would her sketch of him be like one drawn by a child in the nursery?

Every young lady with pretensions to an education considered herself an artist.

* * * *

Helen looked up at the sun low in a sky streaked with pale gold and powder-pink. It took little to imagine God's almighty hand had painted it.

Dusk approached so Helen walked a little faster, conscious she had stayed for longer than she had intended with Mister Barnet. She glanced at Pringle, who followed behind her carrying a parcel containing the jewellery box. From the opposite direction, she heard horses' hooves. Seconds later, she saw Langley at the head of a contingent of mounted troopers, their horses' coats glossy black and satin-smooth. Langley drew rein, dismounted and spoke to a lieutenant. The trooper's horses clattered away while Langley led his horse over to her. "Miss Whitley, you should not be out alone at this hour of the day."

Overcome by his kind concern, she could not speak.

He frowned. "I hope you are in good health."

She recovered her voice. "Yes thank you. As you see, I am not alone. My woman is with me."

Langley glanced at Pringle, who still walked behind her. "She could not protect you from a dastardly attack."

"I refuse to allow fear to prevent me from going out. Besides, I have a pocket pistol in my muff."

"Indeed!"

"Yes, Cousin Tarrant gave it to me."

"I shall not ask if you know how to use it, for I am sure Rupes has taught you. Now may I escort you home?"

"Yes, thank you."

His smile revealed evenly-spaced white teeth, unlike so many gentlemen's discoloured ones, which she considered repulsive. Why had she fallen in love with Langley? How could she define what set him apart from her other beaux? Oh, he was brave, gallant and handsome, yet so were many other officers in His Majesty's army. Besides, she was in his debt, although he had been too modest to allow her to express her appreciation for rescuing her from the Earl of Pennington. She admired all his qualities, his common sense, his—

"Miss Whitley, you seem to be wool-gathering," Langley's deep voice sounded somewhat amused.

"Do I?" she asked, embarrassed. "I mean, how discourteous of me. I beg your pardon," she gabbled.

The Major cleared his throat. "Perhaps I should not broach certain subjects, nevertheless for your peace of mind I shall."

A head taller than most ladies, she appreciated his superior height when he looked down at her. It imparted a sense of delightful femininity.

"I don't know how the rumour you are an heiress took root. Now it is scotched, your friends will value you only for your many admirable qualities." Her heart seemed to flutter girlishly. "The gossip I heard is of no significance. I could never imagine you behaving with gross impropriety."

As the distance to Georgianne and Cousin Tarrant's house lessened, tears formed in her eyes. "Thank you for your reassurance, Major. You shall always be one of my dearest friends." She stared down at the pavement, wishing she could say much more.

"And you, Miss Whitley, shall be one of mine. Whatever befalls you in the future, you may always approach me for help."

"Lud, how serious we have become. Please let me know if I can ever mend your quill, sew on a button, or perform any greater service."

"Oh, my quill often needs to be mended and my man constantly reprimands me for losing my buttons," he explained with laughter in his voice, "so I shall remember your kind offers. Now, as Romeo said to his Juliet, 'Parting is such sweet sorrow.'" He smiled and the harsh lines on his face softened. "Fortunately or unfortunately, we are not a pair of star struck lovers. Our friendship shall endure."

Was his voice huskier than usual? Did he want to say much more that was not permissible?

The Major mounted his horse and rode away. The empty sleeves of his gold-embellished black pelisse, worn over one shoulder, streamed behind him in a sudden blast of cold wind; a wind which chilled her entire being and almost swept away all her erstwhile hopes.

Helen shivered as she entered the house. She hurried up the two wide flights of stairs to her bedchamber, where a bouquet of narcissi lay on her dressing table. On the card, Captain Dalrymple had written, "No flowers can compare to your matchless beauty, which I hope to have the pleasure of seeing this evening at the soiree." 'Pon her word, the gentleman knew how to compose a pretty phrase. She buried her nose in the fragrant blooms and relished their scent. She would pin a spray in her hair. Its delicate colour would complement her new cream, silk, evening gown.

Pringle spoke a few quiet words to someone who knocked on the door, then turned around to face her. "Major Tarrant and Mrs Tarrant request your immediate presence in the drawing room."

Helen picked up Mister Barnet's gift to show it to Georgianne.

Chapter Eleven

1st April, 1815

In the drawing room the curtains were pulled across the windows, effectively shutting out the dark. The candles cast a warm glow. A cheerful fire burned in the grate. Regrettably, the expression on Cousin Tarrant's face did not match the cosy atmosphere.

"Ah, Helen, please be seated," he said, a distinct chill in his voice. "Your sister has been uneasy. She wondered where you were this afternoon."

"Oh, I am sorry; Georgianne was resting when I went out, so I left word with her dresser." She sat on a chair opposite the chaise longue on which her sister took her ease.

Georgianne frowned. "Dawson did not give me your message."

"Where were you?" Cousin Tarrant asked.

Why did they seem so suspicious? Did they think she had committed another indiscretion?

"A glass of ratafia?" Cousin Tarrant poured a drink for himself from the decanter on a low table by his chair near the fire.

"Yes please."

He handed her a glass almost full to the brim.

"I visited Mister Barnet," she answered, annoyed because he spoke to her as though she was a mere schoolroom miss.

"Mister Barnet?" Cousin Tarrant frowned and sipped his drink while waiting for her reply.

"The old gentleman Helen rescued," Georgianne explained.

"Why should you visit a person your family is not acquainted with?"

Although Cousin Tarrant put the question in even tones, she sensed his displeasure. Confound Dawson! If the woman had given her message to Georgianne, Cousin Tarrant would not be questioning her. "I called to enquire whether or not he had recovered from the shock."

Her cousin raised his eyebrows. "A letter of enquiry would have sufficed."

Helen decided to be honest. She found it difficult to keep secrets. Besides, she wanted to show Georgianne the silver suite set with brilliants. "Perhaps I should have written to him, but I am concerned for Mister Barnet, who is very kind. He even insisted on giving me a token of his gratitude."

"What did he give you?" Cousin Tarrant asked.

She quailed inwardly. He seemed unreasonably disgruntled. "Some jewellery made for someone he did not have the opportunity to give it to. I suspect she died." She shrugged. "Anyway, Mister Barnet really wanted me to accept his gift. It would have been ungracious to refuse."

"May we see it, dearest?"

"Of course, I am going to wear the suite this evening. I think it will look well with my new satin gown, the one with silver net. My present is pretty, but silver and brilliants are not valuable, so Cousin Tarrant need not be so cross with me."

"Who said I am?" he asked.

"You seem annoyed," She gave the box to Georgianne. "Look inside."

Tarrant crossed the floor to look down over Georgianne's shoulder.

Her sister held up the necklace.

"Brilliants!" Cousin Tarrant exclaimed. The word almost sounded like a swear word. "Not brilliants, they are diamonds worth a fortune. You must return them."

"D…diamonds," Helen faltered, knowing it was almost, if not quite out of the question to keep them.

Georgianne stared at the jewellery in amazement. "Tarrant, are you sure they are diamonds?"

Helen sank onto the nearest chair. "I never thought."

Cousin Tarrant glared at her. "That is the problem. You did not think. You helped this Mister Barnet, called at his house, and did not return here until almost dark, after which you accepted this token of his gratitude. You must return it and never visit him again."

Of course, if she had realised the stones were diamonds, she would not have accepted the gift. However, having done so, she could not be cruel enough to give them back. Moreover, she really liked Mister Barnet. "No, Cousin Tarrant, I cannot return them."

Her cousin's shoulders stiffened beneath the fine cloth of his uniform.

"I beg your pardon?" His glare intensified with each word.

"I shall continue to call on the gentleman."

"We have not met him in polite society, so it seems he is not a gentleman," Georgianne said, as though she explained matters to a defiant child.

In return, Helen wanted to stamp her feet like an angry child in the nursery. "His manners are better than some so-called gentlemen born, whom I have met."

Her cousin strode backward and forward across the carpet before he halted in front of her. "No more arguments, Helen. You shall return the diamonds and may not visit him again."

Her temper rose. "I appreciate your generosity. Please remember that although you are the master in this house, you are neither one of my parents nor my guardian. You don't have the right to dictate to me. I am not a junior officer from whom you expect instant obedience."

Tarrant stepped toward her. He halted no more than a foot away. "Look at me."

Somewhat reluctantly, she gazed up at him, noting the dark shadows under his eyes. No matter how demanding his duties were, he always found time for Georgianne. Grudgingly, she admitted he was good-natured and generous. She pressed her lips into a mutinous line. She would not obey his order.

If only Papa were alive, her life would be so different. Tears rolled down her cheeks.

"Helen, you are crying!" Cousin Tarrant sounded horrified. "Please understand I became responsible for you when I married your sister. It is my duty to look after you."

She wiped her face with the back of her hands. "Mister Barnet means no harm." She sniffed. "You don't need to protect me from him. I am going to sketch him. I shall ask him to come here so you may assure yourselves he is perfectly respectable. As for the diamonds, only he and the three of us know how I came by them."

"Poor dear, Papa," she thought. A few more tears spilled out of her eyes.

Cousin Tarrant withdrew a handkerchief from his pocket. "Dry your face with this." He faced his wife. "Georgie," he appealed.

Georgianne swung her feet onto the floor. She patted the seat of the chaise longue. "Sit beside me, dearest. When Mister Barnet visits us, you shall return the diamonds without offending him," Georgianne said gently.

Helen sank down next to her sister. "No, it would insult him. I shall keep them, not because of their value, but because they were given out of the goodness of an old gentleman's heart. I shall wear them tomorrow to the Omerod's soiree." No matter how understanding Tarrant and Georgianne were, on this occasion, she would not allow them to impose their will upon her. She retrieved the box from her sister. "Please excuse me. It is time to change my gown before we dine."

* * * *

After the door closed behind Helen, careless of his deceptively casual hairstyle, Tarrant ran a hand through his hair. "The sooner your sister is married, the better. Let us hope her guardian consents to Dalrymple's courtship and she marries him."

"I am not sure she will. I think her heart is with Langley."

Tarrant poured another glass of excellent French wine. It was unpatriotic to buy it, but if he did not, someone else would.

"A green girl's fancy." He sat down, dismissing his wife's words.

"Maybe, but you married a green girl, and you are not a mere fancy."

She moved restlessly on her chair.

"What is wrong? Are you unwell?" he asked, always perceptive where she was concerned.

Georgianne's dimples deepened. She shook her head, the little ringlets on either side of her face dancing and gleaming in the candlelight.

"Should I send your sister back to England?"

His wife looked at him with some alarm expressed in her eyes. "The state of the country," she murmured. "Would it be safe for her to travel?"

"Yes, unless you wish her to stay."

"I do. Where would she live in England? Even if she went to our grandparents, they are too old to take her to London to be presented at the Queen's Drawing Room. We cannot be sure Mamma will stay away from the bottle, so Helen cannot live with her."

"My parents?"

"Your Papa is nice, but he does not want another female in his household."

"So, Helen stays here with us?"

"Yes, and I shall visit Mister Barnet with her to find out what sort of a person he is." A mischievous smile formed around his wife's pretty lips. "I shall thank him for the brilliants and say we cannot allow my sister to accept the token of his esteem."

Almost speechless, Tarrant stared at his wife, as beautiful as an empty-headed, exquisitely fashioned china ornament, but also exceptionally kind and intelligent. As he well knew, a core of steel—which he could always depend on—ran through her. Yet, surely on this occasion he would not be cast as the villain. He accepted the inevitable.

"If you wish to, heart of my heart, call on Mister Barnet."

"Thank you." Georgianne sat on his lap and kissed his cheek. "No one could have a more amiable, more agreeable husband. I am the luckiest wife imaginable."

What could he do other than kiss his wife?

* * * *

2nd April, 1815

Helen's refusal had turned to reason. With great reluctance, she had allowed Georgianne to persuade her to return the diamonds. On the day after she incurred Cousin Tarrant's wrath, she accompanied Georgianne to Mr Barnet's house.

The footman rapped the dragon shaped knocker on the front door.

Helen followed her sister up the broad, shallow steps.

Thomas opened the door. "Good day, Miss Whitley, I shall inform Mister Barnet you and another lady have called."

"My sister, Mrs Tarrant," Helen said, while Georgianne withdrew her card from her reticule and gave it to Thomas, who stood aside to allow them to enter.

Georgianne stared at the Chinese wallpaper, hand painted on a cream background. "How beautiful." She eyed the design, a tree with branches which sprouted green leaves, fanciful pink and blue flowers, and strawberry shaped orange fruit. "I think the Prince Regent would envy this." With a discreet wave of her hand, she indicated an ornately ornamented porcelain flower pot on a red-lacquer stand.

Mister Barnet's butler came forward to take the card. He opened a door. "Mrs Tarrant, Miss Whitley, please wait in the reception room while I see if Mister Barnet is at home."

To Helen's amusement, her sister's eyes opened even wider when she looked at a china pagoda that stood at least three feet higher than herself. "Extraordinary! What bright colours! I wonder if the Prince Regent has anything to compare favourably with it."

"This house is full of treasures. Look at the mantelpiece."

Her sister turned. A gasp escaped her. "How lovely!"

"Yes, it is." Since she first saw it, Helen delighted in the ivory replica of a Chinese boat, carved with intricate latticework, and admired the boatmen, the flagpoles, and the roofed area on the top deck, beneath which painted greenery emerged from a tiny terracotta pot.

"The door opened. This way, ladies," the butler said. He led them upstairs to the drawing room where Mister Barnet sat turning a jade cup around in his hands.

He put it down on a black, gold lacquered, wooden table at the side of his chair, stood and bowed.

"Mrs Tarrant, Miss Whitley, you are welcome. Please be seated. A glass of canary wine for both of you?"

"Thank you." Georgianne looked around, obviously amazed by the beautiful Chinoiserie.

Helen waited for Georgianne to sit before she seated herself on the chair opposite Mister Barnet's.

The footman, supervised by the butler, served the wine with thin biscuits dotted with caraway seeds, then left the room in response to a gesture from Mister Barnet.

Georgianne cleared her throat before she spoke. "My sister told my husband and myself that she wishes to paint a portrait of you. Perhaps you would allow her to do so in her...er...attic at our house where she...um...daubs."

Mister Barnet shook his head. "I regret I don't have time for her to do so due to my imminent return to England with my treasures. If Napoleon attacks, I don't want to be in a war torn country. Besides, I have no more business here."

Helen exchanged a glance with Georgianne. Although they were curious about his business, it would be rude to question him.

He inclined his head to Georgianne. "If you and Major Tarrant permit, Miss Whitley may come here to sketch me on any morning of the week."

Georgianne seemed indecisive. Helen caught her breath while she waited. Her sister had accepted Mister Barnet's hospitality so it would be ungracious to refuse.

Georgianne inclined her head. "Very well."

"Shall we agree on Wednesday morning?"

"Yes." Helen nodded her head, eager to sketch him, for, in his old-fashioned clothes and wig, he represented a bygone age. "I shall breakfast early and arrive at ten o'clock."

"I look forward to seeing you," Mister Barnet replied.

"There is another matter," Georgianne spoke again. "Please take this back. It is far too valuable for my sister to accept."

"Nonsense! She probably saved my life, which is more valuable than anything I could give her."

Georgianne looked around the room for a few seconds, seeming to search for inspiration. "Nevertheless—" she began.

"Nevertheless," the old gentleman repeated, "I wish you and your husband to allow Miss Whitley to accept the suite."

Before Georgianne could protest, Mister Barnet shook his head. "Please say nothing, Mrs Tarrant, unless you wish to distress an old man who is thinking of the young lady who departed this world before he could give her the jewellery. Knowing Miss Whitley wears it, will give me great pleasure."

It seemed Georgianne could think of nothing to say in response to their host's words.

Helen stood. "I look forward to sketching you, but for now I don't wish to tire you so it is time for us to take our leave."

Before Georgianne rallied and could forbid her to accept the diamonds, Helen retrieved the box from her sister.

Mister Barnet bowed. "Miss Whitley, I hope you will forgive me if my house is in a state of upheaval when you come to sketch me. My treasures are to be packed in crates."

"I hope none of them will be damaged during transport."

"I have already brought many of them here intact from China while padded in straw. There is no reason why they should not travel well by barge, ship and wagon."

He grasped his cane, stood with visible effort, and then walked slowly across the room with the ladies.

With her sister at her side, Helen returned to the carriage. When they were settled, Georgianne shook her head, obviously bemused. "'Pon my word, the man must be a nabob. I daresay he either served the East India Company or traded independently in Canton."

Helen knew Georgianne read the broadsheets from beginning to end so she was remarkably well informed.

Georgianne shook her head. "How he persuaded me to allow you to keep the diamonds I cannot imagine. Now, no matter what Tarrant might say, it would be impossible to insist on returning them."

* * * *

That night, Georgianne lay in bed with her head on her husband's shoulder. "I tell you, Tarrant, I am sure if I had said 'open sesame' the walls would have swung open to reveal a treasure cave. To Mister Barnet, the value of the diamonds must be almost insignificant. Please don't be cross with me. He spoke so movingly about someone they were intended for—someone who is no longer of this world—that I could not insist on returning them."

"When am I ever cross with you?" he asked, his eyes soft by firelight.

"Every day," she teased.

"Ow," she exclaimed when he pinched her bottom, but not hard enough to hurt. "Brute!"

"Not a brute, a slave to your charms."

Georgianne giggled and snuggled a little closer.

"I hope Major Walton will approve of Dalrymple."

She sighed. "So do I, but only if Helen wants to marry the captain." She spoke in a small voice. "I love you so much and am so content that I want Helen to be equally happy." Georgianne stroked her stomach, thinking of the new life within. She hoped if she gave birth to a son, he would be like his father in every way.

Tarrant stroked her cheek. "Heart of my heart," he murmured.

She lay in silence while sleep evaded her and considered her sister.

"Georgie?"

"Yes."

I think we should hold a ball for Helen. After all, she has already entered society. A ball would be her formal introduction to it."

"How considerate of you. It is an excellent idea." Full of enthusiasm, she sat up, trying to see his beloved face in the darkness. "It must be exceptional. The decorations, the refreshments, the music, everything, and we must invite the cream of society." She lay down, yawned and her eyelids closed. "I love you, Tarrant."

"And I you."

Chapter Twelve

3rd April, 1815

Conscious of her diamond suite sparkling with rainbow hues, Helen made her way through the throng with Cousin Tarrant and her sister, toward the salon where the soiree was being held. However, many people greeted them which considerably slowed their progress. Due to the rumour that Wellington would soon be on his way to Brussels to join the Army of Occupation, Cousin Tarrant was forced to field many questions, which delayed them even more.

Near the door to the spacious salon, they were greeted by Madame la Comptesse de Beaulieu and Miss Tomlinson.

"A zouzand apologies, Madame Tarrant, I did not keep my promise to call on you with my granddaughter. Please excuse me. Maria has been unwell."

To have lost so much weight, Miss Tomlinson must have been very ill. What would Langley think of Miss Tomlinson when he next saw her?' Annoyed with herself, she caught her lower lip between her teeth. Langley, always Langley. She wished for a magic medicine to remove him from her mind.

"Magnificent diamonds, Miss Whitley," the Comptesse commented "Ze setting is so simple zat zey are suitable for a young lady."

Helen curtsied. "I am glad you approve, Madame." With an artist's eyes she noted the pearls nestling in Miss Tomlinson's hair, in her ears, and at her throat. The young woman looked attractive in an ivory-coloured silk gown. The deceptively simple design relied on an expert cut to minimise the lady's shapely, but still generous figure.

"Come, Maria, we must not be late for your performance on the harp."

Colour flooded Miss Tomlinson's cheeks. "Please, Grandmere, I don't wish to—"

Madame rapped the unfortunate young lady on the arm with her ebony fan. "Don't make yourself ridiculous, child, it is arranged for you to delight us."

"Unfortunate," thought Helen, "why do I also think of her thus?" The image of Miss Tomlinson weeping in Parc Royale returned.

At that moment, Captain Dalrymple greeted her and then whispered. "The harp! Another amateur fumbling her way through the music!"

"Miss Tomlinson might be an excellent musician. Let us hope you will enjoy her performance," she whispered back.

They followed Cousin Tarrant and Georgianne into the salon, in which gold brocade curtains were drawn to exclude the night air that some still believed injured their health.

Georgianne looked back. "Good evening, Captain Dalrymple."

The press of other guests was too great for him to bow, and so he inclined his head politely. Her sister beckoned to her. "Come, Helen."

With the captain on one side and her sister on the other, Helen settled on a chair in the centre of a row, from where she had a good view of a temporary stage concealed by more gold-coloured curtains.

The buzz of conversation ceased when Lord Ormerod appeared. "Welcome to my house." He beamed at his audience. "I look forward to the entertainment my dear wife has arranged for our pleasure. Pray, silence for Major Lord Langley and my daughter who will perform the minuet."

His lordship stepped aside. The curtains drew apart to reveal Langley, smart in his dress uniform, and Miss Ormerod, a young lady considered one of the best amateur dancers in Brussels. An unseen orchestra played. Langley's passes were perfect. Miss Ormerod did not falter. Although Helen did not want to perform the minuet in public, her jealousy of the young lady's opportunity to dance a solo with Langley consumed her.

"Will you entertain us?" Dalrymple whispered in Helen's ear.

She shook her head, aware that one of her short, pomaded ringlets brushed his face.

"Why not?"

"I don't possess sufficient talents."

Dalrymple's eyes glinted. "Nonsense, you dance beautifully. I would be happy to take the stage with you."

"Shush," Helen scolded. Her fingers itched to sketch Langley and Miss Ormerod, who wore a gown in fashion before the French Revolution. From her dainty shoes with large silver rosettes, to the top of her white-powdered wig, adorned with flowers and feathers, Miss Ormerod looked exquisite.

Helen's stomach tightened. Had Lady Ormerod asked Langley to dance with her daughter? If Langley had offered be her partner was it of particular significance? Miss Ormerod's dowry would probably be as large if not equal to Miss Tomlinson's. Did Langley intend to marry Miss Ormerod? She must stop tormenting herself with such speculations.

The minuet ended. Langley bowed. Miss Ormerod curtsied. Enthusiastic applause sounded while they left the impromptu stage.

The Ormerod's eldest son, a copper-haired gentleman wearing brown velvet and cream, came onto the stage. "Alas," be began, "I have few accomplishments so I shall recite the bard of bard's famous words.

"Let me not to the marriage of true minds
Admit impediments. Love is not love
Which when alteration finds,
Or bends with the remover to remove."

Helen caught her breath. Shakespeare's poignant words could have been written for her. She looked down at the silver net draped over her white silk gown. A spider's web seemed to trap her. A hand clasped hers. Startled, she looked around to see if anyone had noticed. She doubted they had, for young Ormerod's melodic voice still entranced the audience. The hand squeezed hers. She looked up at Dalrymple.

"Could not have expressed my sentiments any better, Miss Whitley." He released her hand.

Two footmen carried a harp onto the stage. A third placed a chair for Miss Tomlinson who walked slowly to take her place.

"Must we listen to an amateur playing?" Dalrymple complained.

"Don't be cruel. When Miss Tomlinson plucks the strings, I daresay we shall be delighted by her accomplishment. If so, she may entertain her future husband and his guests."

"I can think of better ways to entertain her husband," Dalrymple muttered.

"Shush!" Helen exclaimed, aware of the colour spreading over her cheeks. Without doubt, as the vulgar saying went, the captain was 'hot for her'. Helen sighed. She hoped for a happy marriage but did not know if she would welcome his attentions in the marriage bed, whatever they might be.

The first notes of a half-remembered Bach sonata rippled like a gently flowing stream, sweeping Helen into another world. At the end, she burst into spontaneous applause while Miss Tomlinson curtsied, then, with maidenly modesty, hurried off the stage followed by the sound of thunderous appreciation.

"I take my words back," Dalrymple said. "You see a chastened man at your side."

Helen moved her foot awkwardly and caught her toe in the hem of her gown. As she extricated it, the net ripped. Embarrassed, she made her way along the row of seated guests on her way to the ladies' withdrawing room to repair the damage.

She held her skirt a little higher than usual to prevent the torn net dragging on the floor. With careful footsteps she ascended the stairs. On the landing, she heard sobs. Someone needed comfort. Entering a small boudoir, she found Miss Tomlinson seated on the edge of a chaise longue, her shoulders heaving, and her hands covering her face.

Helen coughed to announce herself before she spoke. "Forgive my intrusion; I could not ignore your tears."

Heedless of her expensive gown, Miss Tomlinson wiped her hands on the skirt. She sniffed. Helen withdrew a handkerchief from her reticule. "Take this."

Miss Tomlinson accepted the white linen square, edged with broad lace. She mopped her face and blew her nose. "You will not tell my grandmother you found me in tears, will you?"

"Why should I?"

"Everyone gossips in this hateful town. I want to go home to England; back north where I belong."

Helen remembered the nights when she and Georgianne were children who could not sleep for fear of the Corsican monster. "Are you frightened of Napoleon?"

"A little, but Boney is not why I want to go home."

Helen hesitated. Should she or should she not mention she had seen Miss Tomlinson in the Parc Royale speaking to a man who had left her in obvious distress? She decided to refrain for fear of causing embarrassment. "Why do you wish to return to England?"

"I miss my father and...and.... Oh, I cannot tell anyone!"

Helen changed her mind. "I am not a gossip. Anything you tell me will be in confidence. Do you want to leave Brussels because of the man I saw you with in Parc Royale?"

Miss Tomlinson nodded, her magnificent hazel eyes open wide.

"Have you confided in your grandmother? Have you told her you are unhappy?"

The lady shook her head so hard that a silk rose pinned in her hair fell onto her lap. "It would be useless. She would be disgusted if I told her the truth."

"Disgusted?" Helen repeated.

"Grandmere has made her low opinion of me quite clear." Miss Tomlinson wiped her eyes on the handkerchief. "On the morning you saw me in Parc Royale, I paid her dresser not to tell her, I would slip out of the house on my own. After the wretched woman took my money, she told Grandmere, who questioned me when I came home." Miss Tomlinson straightened her back. "Of course, she demanded to know where

I had gone. I did not tell her. Since then I have not been allowed to leave the house my father rented for us unless Grandmere accompanies me. To make matters worse, the diet she imposed on me has become stricter than ever. All she cares about is arranging my nuptials to a member of the ton. The bait, of course, is my dowry."

"I see."

"My father wants me to marry a nobleman who has a great estate. Grandmere despises him. She constantly refers to my mamma's mésalliance, although Father is a dear man— even if he is stubborn."

Miss Tomlinson needed a knight errant who would snatch her up on his white charger and bear her away from the dragon of a grandmother.

"In the eyes of Mamma's world, she should not have married Papa but she did not care. Always too full of her own self-consequence, Grandmere never took proper care of Mamma." Now that Miss Tomlinson's flood gates were open, words flowed from her mouth. "I swear if Grandmere says another unpleasant word about Father, I shall scream. Father loved my mamma. I am sure they were happy. Moreover, he is the best of fathers."

"I see," Helen repeated. "Now, do you want to explain what the man whom you met has to do with all this?"

"I don't know what you will think of me if I confide in you."

Helen patted Miss Tomlinson's hand. "What does my opinion matter? Besides, I might be able to help you."

Miss Tomlinson half-turned to face her. "The gentleman, you referred to, is a scoundrel whose name is Mister Midhurst. I met him when I was sixteen, soon after I left school in Bath. I went for a walk with my companion, Miss Brent, to choose holly with the most berries to adorn the house for Christmas. My companion broke her ankle when she slipped on an icy patch. By chance, Mister Midhurst was on his way to the house with a report for Father about a mill for sale. When Mister Midhurst heard my companion cry out, he rode toward us.

"He helped Miss Brent onto his horse and took her to the house. Confined indoors after Christmas while Father was away for two months, Miss Brent did not know Mister Midhurst visited me." Cheeks scarlet, she eyed Helen. "I found him agreeable, so much so that I believed I loved him and often wrote to him. He is threatening to publish my letters if I don't pay him one thousand pounds. That would ruin my reputation, because, although it is not true, they imply I lost my virtue." She choked back a sob. "In short, the wretch is blackmailing me. If I give him the money, he says he will return the correspondence." She gripped Helen's hand. "I don't have the money. Oh, I can't bear it. Father will be so disappointed. As for Grandmere, I can't stomach the thought of what she will say." She burst into tears.

Helen regarded her blotched face with sincere sympathy. "Shush! Even if you gave him the money, you cannot be sure he will return the letters."

Eyes wider than ever, Miss Tomlinson stopped crying. "Do you really think he won't?"

Helen nodded. "Yes. Have you heard the tale of the goose which laid the golden egg?"

"Yes."

"I am afraid you are the goose Mister Midhurst expects to provide gold coins instead of an egg. I shall help you. When your grandmother calls on Georgianne, I will offer to show you my studio. You will accept. Before your grandmother can speak, follow me out of the drawing room."

Her face pale, Miss Tomlinson looked queasy. "How can you help me?"

"Major, Lord Langley is a good friend to my family. I shall ask him to find out where Mister Midhurst is putting up so that he can retrieve your letters."

Miss Tomlinson shook her head. "Oh, no, please don't. What would he think of me? Besides, he is the gentleman Father wants me to marry." Some colour returned to her cheeks. "Although he assured Lord Langley's father I would agree to the marriage, I refused!"

"Why?" Helen asked, her curiosity aroused by the vehemence in Miss Tomlinson's voice. She patted the distraught lady's hand. "I am sure Langley will sympathise with a young girl who became a scoundrel's victim. He is a gentleman who would never betray a confidence. I shall speak to him this evening."

A maid entered the room. Helen indicated her torn net. "Please pin this up for me," she instructed the woman, while Miss Tomlinson washed her face.

Helen returned to the salon in time to watch Miss Carruthers dance the saraband, but her mind was still occupied with Miss Tomlinson's predicament. Oh well, she trusted Langley. More than likely, he could help the unfortunate girl.

"May I escort you?" Captain Dalrymple asked.

"Where to?"

"The supper room."

Helen stood. "Yes, you may."

After a brief word with Georgianne and Cousin Tarrant, she followed Dalrymple to the adjoining salon. She looked around at the paintings of Egypt, wooden replicas of sphinx and pyramids on stands while the captain guided her to a table.

"Wait here for me," he said, after she sat down, "I shall serve you."

The captain made his way to a large table, where dishes and platters of cold food were spread on a linen cloth decorated with swags of greenery, and blue and white delft vases filled with daffodils.

Where was Langley? Gentlemen were never at hand when they were required. Ah, there he was, speaking to a lady gowned in primrose yellow who nodded in response to something he said.

Helen beckoned to a footman. "Please tell Major, Lord Langley, I wish to speak with him in the library after the other guests have returned to the soiree?"

The footman stared at her with obvious surprise at the impropriety of her request.

She ignored it. "Where is the library?"

"It is the last room on the right at the end of this corridor."

"Thank you. Now deliver my message." How could she ensure his silence? "Not a word of this to anyone. It is a matter of life and death. If murder is committed, you would be held responsible."

The footman's eyes widened. "I'll say nothing about it Miss. Gawd save me if I break my word."

She sat down again, moments before Dalrymple returned. He put the contents of a tray, on which were two glasses of white wine, two gold-rimmed plates laden with lobster patties and tiny curd tarts, and two smaller plates heaped with little cakes and sweet pastries on the table. About to sit, he remained on his feet when Cousin Tarrant and Georgianne joined them with General Makelyn and his wife, Lady Anne. If the arrival of his commanding officer discomposed Dalrymple, good manners prevented him from revealing it. He left to fetch more refreshments and wine.

Chapter Thirteen

3rd April, 1815

Helen glanced along the corridor to make sure she was unobserved before she entered the room illuminated by the faint radiance of a dying fire. Would Langley come soon?

Careful not to bump into anything, Helen made her way to the fireplace. She reached up to the white marble mantelpiece. Her hand brushed against a piece of china; she steadied it to prevent it falling to the floor. She stood back peering through the dim light. Ah, a candlestick complete with a beeswax candle. Helen picked it up and stooped to touch the wick to a glowing ember in the hearth. Within moments she lit more candles in a candelabrum.

With tongs, Helen replenished the fire with coal from a conveniently placed iron-banded wooden bucket. She applied a poker to encourage the fire to blaze. How long would it be before Georgianne sent someone in search of her?

The door opened. "Langley," she said, appreciative of his handsome appearance.

He walked across the large room until he faced her. "What?" he asked in a level tone, "is so urgent that you must summon me to a clandestine meeting which, if it became known, would ruin your reputation?"

Although Langley's words reproached her, his dark eyes, glinting by candlelight, did not. She stared up into their depths, her heart full of deep feeling it would be unmaidenly to express. "Yes my conduct is shocking, but I must consult you on a matter to be handled with discretion."

A smile played around his well-shaped mouth. Theatrically, he pressed a hand to his forehead. "Never tell me you played cards and cannot meet your debts. Or are you going to confess you stole those magnificent diamonds you are wearing? No, I think not. I daresay you borrowed them from Georgianne." His eyes, which were full of suppressed merriment, widened. "Perhaps you wish me to caution a beau who is too ardent, but that is Rupes' task not mine."

"What a poor opinion you have of me." Amused by his play-acting, she smiled.

"To the contrary." The mirth fled from his eyes, "I am sure your admirers pay you so many compliments that you need none from me."

"Yours would mean more to me than any others," she replied in a small voice.

The viscount's breath rasped in his throat before he spoke. "Miss Whitley, I fear you are a hardened flirt. I shall not add to your vanity."

She pressed her lips into a firm line, for fear she should call him a fool for not believing she would treasure even a single word of admiration from him.

Langley scrutinised her face. "If you would be so good, please, tell me why you asked me to meet you here."

"An acquaintance of ours is being blackmailed."

Langley whistled low. "Who is the victim?"

"Miss Tomlinson."

The expression on his face hardened.

"No, my lord, please don't poker up, and please don't refuse to help her unless you wish to lose my good opinion of you."

Langley sighed. "Heaven forbid I should forfeit it."

"There is no need to be sarcastic."

"You misjudge me." Langley reached out to catch hold of her but did not. He shook his head as though admonishing himself. "I hope your request will not foster either Miss Tomlinson's or her father's wish for me to enter the parson's noose."

"You are not in danger; she does not want to marry you. She loves another man."

Langley looked steadily at her, the expression on his face inscrutable. "I once said—it seems somewhat foolishly—I am your servant. No, don't smile at me thus, my girl, you have not got the better of me."

She glanced down at the toes of his black evening slippers.

"There is no need to pretend to be demure after you tempted this poor fool to have an assignation with you, only to find out you want me to help a lady, who, in spite of my father's acute displeasure, I have refused to wed."

She resisted the temptation to ask why he had said no to the proposal which would have solved his father's financial problems. "In my opinion, my lord, you are an officer and a gentleman, so honour binds you to help Miss Tomlinson."

"I am an officer, though when I look at you I am not sure my instincts are those of a gentleman."

Puzzled she stared at him. "What do you mean?"

Langley shook his head as though bemused. "Please ignore my words before I say something I will regret, and also do something disgraceful."

"You could never act disreputably."

He looked away from her at the regiments of books which lined the shelves. "Thank you for your good opinion of me. Please tell me how I can serve you and Miss Tomlinson."

"I knew you would help us." Impulsively, she reached up to put her gloved hands on his shoulders. His hands clasped her waist; he bent his head. Oh, how she hoped he would kiss her. If Langley did, he would be obliged to ask for her hand in marriage without delay. Of course, she would accept, despite Mister Barnet's words of caution.

Langley released her, removed her hand from the epaulette on his left shoulder and stepped back. "If you tell me why Miss

Tomlinson is being blackmailed and who the blackmailer is, I shall try to help her."

"Thank you." She related the facts in a flat voice.

"If I find the scoundrel I will deal with him."

Completely at ease with Langley, Helen hugged him. "I knew it; I knew you would help." She stood on tiptoe with the intention of kissing his cheek. At the same moment, he turned his head. Langley's dark eyes smouldered.

He squared his shoulders. "How green your eyes are. A man could lose himself in their depths as easily as he could in the sea."

She could scarcely breathe. The softness of his lips surprised her when he kissed her forehead. She wanted to ask him to kiss her on the mouth but could not bring herself to voice words she believed would shock him.

"No!" Langley disengaged himself. "Miss Whitley, I hope to return the letters to Miss Tomlinson, and to have the pleasure of thrashing Mister Midhurst." He raised his eyebrows. "However, please understand there can be nothing other than friendship between us."

"I shall treasure that, my lord." She restrained her incipient tears over her dreams which would never become real. He bowed, turned and left the library.

* * * *

Langley walked swiftly along the corridor. Miss Whitley's innocence meant she did not understand the effect her embrace would have on any gentleman. How he had summoned the iron will not to kiss her passionately he did not know. Yes, he did. He loved Helen too much to take advantage of her. The sooner she accepted a proposal from Dalrymple or some other pleasant young gentleman, the better it would be.

Damnation! Miss Whitley netted a reluctant catch when she asked him to help Miss Tomlinson. With Wellington's arrival expected in the near future, Makelyn would most probably issue more and more orders, so he did not want to feel obliged to find the time to help the heiress. Curse the foolish young lady for having been indiscreet. He shook his head. No, he should not be unkind. Suppose one of his sisters were caught in such a coil. He would be grateful to anyone who came to her rescue.

Langley scowled. He would deal with the blackmailer while he bivouacked well away from Miss Tomlinson. God forbid anyone, particularly her ebullient father or her formidable grandmother, misinterpreting it if he ever did more than greet her briefly out of politeness.

* * * *

Helen lingered in the library. She must accept Langley would never marry her. Yet she revelled in the remnants of warmth she imagined emanated from his body and thawed her frozen heart. His intoxicating choice of sandalwood toilet water, mingled with a cavalryman's odour of leather and horses, still hovered in the air. The fool, the dear fool! She would be delighted to marry the viscount in spite of his change of circumstances. If only she had more to remember than his lips against her forehead. If only he had kissed her on the mouth.

Shame overcame her. What did Langley think of her disgraceful conduct? Would he know why strange but sweet sensations stirred deep within her when she hugged him? Oh, why think of it? She could never speak of it to him.

Dalrymple entered the library. "Miss Whitley, there you are. When Major and Mrs Tarrant wondered where you were, I offered to search for you." Candlelight flickered over him, adding ruddy colour to his face as he drew closer. He frowned. "Are you quite well? Pardon me for saying you don't seem yourself."

"My head aches a little," she replied, truthfully, for it began to hurt after Langley strode out of the library.

She gazed at her beau. Her mind flitted away from Langley. Dalrymple was perceptive. Did he love her, truly love her? He must. Why else would he want to marry her despite her small dowry?

"Shall I fetch your sister? Do you want to go home to lie down in a darkened bedchamber?"

"No thank you; my headache is not severe."

"Shall we join my sister and the Major?" Dalrymple asked, too much the young gentleman to take advantage of the impropriety of their being unchaperoned.

Would she prefer Dalrymple to be more impetuous? He treated her with utmost respect, unlike some of the rakes Georgianne warned her of; libertines, who would not hesitate to ravish a young woman for their own enjoyment. She wondered what ravishment entailed. When she had asked her sister, Georgianne blushed before she responded. "There is no need for you to know."

The captain stood aside for her to leave the library.

* * * *

4th April 1815

At breakfast the following day, her head filled with the memory of her assignation with Langley on the previous evening, Helen ate the last morsel of toast spread with butter and apricot conserve. Instead of thinking of him, she would consider the sketches she intended to make of Mister Barnet this morning.

Georgianne entered the room. How dainty her beautiful sister looked. Helen admired her sister's charming cap edged with delicate lace, and her white muslin gown sprigged with china-blue posies.

"Good morning, dearest."

"Good morning. Are you well?"

"Yes, thank you. Ginger helps with the nausea that afflicts me every day upon awakening."

"Is there anything I can do for you?"

"No, thank you." Georgianne helped herself to some toast and coddled eggs, before she sat at the table. She looked at her plate with obvious satisfaction. "How hungry I am! But dearest, we came home late last night, so I am surprised to see you have almost finished your breakfast."

"Have you forgotten I arranged to draw Mr Barnet today? Shall I go in the carriage or take a footman with me to carry my folder, paint box and other materials?"

"Your paint box?"

"Yes. I shall make a chart of the colours of his clothes and his complexion."

Georgianne poured a cup of coffee.

"The carriage or a footman?" Helen persisted.

Georgianne looked out of the window. "There might be April showers. Go in the carriage with Pringle."

* * * *

Thomas opened the black-painted door. "Mister Barnet is expecting you, Miss Whitley." He took her equipment from Pringle.

The first fat drops of rain fell. Grateful for Georgianne's permission to use the carriage, she gave orders for it to return to take her home at three of the clock.

Why did Thomas look so glum?" She looked around the hall at packing boxes. Perhaps Thomas feared Mister Barnet would dispense with his service when he returned to England.

"This way, Miss." The footman shrugged as if his coat were too tight. Observant as ever, Helen admired the effect of the gold braid on his livery.

She followed him up the stairs to the spacious landing, now bare of oriental rugs, where Thomas halted. "I hope you will not be offended, Miss, by my informing you that Mister Barnet is unwell."

"I am sorry. Should I return on another day?"

"No, Miss, he is looking forward to your visit. If may be so bold, please don't tire him."

Helen nodded, appreciative of the servant's concern. She looked back at Pringle. "You may wait downstairs."

The dresser sniffed loudly and then retraced her footsteps.

Helen ignored the almost silent protest. One would think the woman would be pleased to sit in idleness. She followed Thomas into a parlour.

A beautiful cream-coloured quilt patterned with scallops was draped over his lap, Mister Barnet smiled. "Welcome, Miss Whitley. I am delighted to see you." He waved his hand—an invitation to look around the small room. "I apologise for receiving you here instead of in the drawing room, where my butler is supervising the servants who are packing my treasures."

"No need to say sorry. This room is charming." Helen admired the miniature paintings clustered together on one wall, an ornate mirror on another, and exquisite snuffboxes on several tables. "How do you go on, sir?

"Well enough, well enough." Mister Barnet glanced at some small bottles of medicines, a glass and a jug of water, on the table beside his chair.

Helen set up her easel, placed her sketch pad on it, and then arranged her pencils and paint box on a table next to it. While she did so, she noted the dark circles under her host's eyes and the hectic colour in his cheeks. If she were not mistaken, his complexion was even greyer than when last she saw him.

"Do you require anything else?" Mister Barnet inquired.

"Only some water."

He poured some into one of the glasses on the table beside his chair. "Will this be adequate?"

"Yes, thank you." Helen put it next to her wooden paint box. She opened the lid, removed the upper tray to reveal the lower one, and admired the myriad of colours, each in separate china compartments.

"Something to drink, to eat?" Mister Barnet suggested.

"Please don't tempt me. You have been good enough to allow me to sketch your likeness; I don't want to further intrude upon your time."

The old gentleman chuckled. "Miss Whitley, I enjoy your company. You could never be an imposition. We shall partake of refreshments while we talk, before you wield your pencils and brushes."

The door opened.

Mister Barnet looked at her with a childish gleam in his eyes. "I gave instructions for refreshments to be served as soon as you arrived."

"Thank you, I shall enjoy them." She sat in front of a low table. "Shall I pour coffee, sir?"

"Yes, please." The gleam in his eyes deepened. "You may lace it with cream— though my doctor would disapprove. He expects me to survive on slops. At my age!" He shrugged.

"Perhaps you should follow his instructions," Helen suggested, although she handed him a cup of coffee with cream floating on its surface. "A biscuit, cake, or a bon-bon?"

"No thank you, my child, I have little appetite."

Helen tried to decide whether she objected to his addressing her as a child. No, she did not, although she might resent it from anyone else.

"Please serve yourself, Miss Whitley."

Helen selected a small cake covered in marzipan.

Mister Barnet sipped his coffee. "Does all go well with you?"

"Yes, thank you," she replied, although Maria Tomlinson's predicament came to mind.

Shrewd eyes scrutinised her face. Her cheeks became hot.

"Something troubles you."

"Yes." Once again the temptation to confide in him proved irresistible. "I cannot reveal my acquaintance's name. To be brief, when she was still in the schoolroom she wrote some indiscreet letters. The man she imagined she loved is blackmailing her."

"I see. Does she need my help?"

Her eyes widened. How could he be of assistance? "With my friend's permission," she continued, "I related her sorry tale to Viscount Langley. Hussars are accustomed to gathering information. Langley, with a few of his most trusted men, will search for the scoundrel."

"Miss Whitley, I deplore crime. I would be pleased to help bring the fellow to justice. If you furnish me with his name, one of the people I know might be able to discover his whereabouts."

She pondered this strange offer, while the delicious flavour of the cake she nibbled, which tasted of chocolate and brandy, distracted her. Well, so long as she did not mention the victim's name, there would be no harm in revealing the blackmailer's.

She finished her coffee, stood, picked up a pencil and quickly drew Mister Midhurst from memory.

"You seem distrait," Mister Barnet said.

"A little." She gave him a page torn from her sketchbook. "I have drawn a likeness of the blackmailer. His name is Mister Midhurst."

"Upon my word, you are talented, Miss Whitley. Please forgive my previous comment about clever young ladies who paint mossy stones and other gothic subjects. It seems your skill exceeds some of those who believe they are talented artists."

Flattered, she curtsied playfully. "Thank you, sir." She returned to her easel. For the next hour, she concentrated on drawing the elderly gentleman, adding, adding a range of colours to each sketch.

The clock struck three. "So late, by now my carriage will have returned." She packed up her equipment.

Mister Barnet pulled the bell rope. "Has Miss Whitley's carriage arrived?" he asked when Thomas answered the summons.

"Yes, sir."

"Good, you may carry her paraphernalia to the carriage."

"Thank you for your kindness, Mister Barnet." Helen wished propriety allowed her to kiss his cheek. "When I have finished the watercolour, I shall present it for your opinion. You must be honest. I will not be cast down if you don't like it, for I constantly try to improve."

He winced. "I shall send you a message if I receive news of Midhurst. Good day to you, child." He pressed a hand over the left side of his chest.

Something in his tone forbade her from either asking if he were quite well, or if he needed to dose himself with medicine.

Chapter Fourteen

5th April 1815

The morning brought heavy rain and gusts of wind, so instead of enjoying an early morning ride, Helen went to the attic before breakfast.

After several hours of intense concentration near the window which provided natural light, she stepped back to consider her partially completed watercolour. Would she ever be completely satisfied with anything she painted?

Helen looked forward to painting the old gentleman in oils when she returned to England, where she would have time for the paint to dry. With the moistened tip of her brush, she mixed a little sepia into the mid-grey on her palette, to achieve the right tone to edge Mister Barnet's coat. Good, it defined the collar and cuffs.

Helen smiled; she had finished the portrait in time to have nuncheon with Georgianne, who had not put in an appearance at the breakfast table. Oh well, last night they came home only a few hours before dawn. Georgianne's condition justified her sleeping late if she wanted to.

Helen rinsed her brushes, then poured the dirty water into a bucket. She took the key to the attic out of her pocket. To avoid the temptation to return to the watercolour, she hurried out and locked the door as usual, to prevent the servants entering her private domain.

In her small dressing room, Helen washed her hands with purified soap. She dried them with a soft linen towel, then massaged her hands with almond milk to keep them white and soft.

A quick glance in the mirror showed tidy hair. She took off the apron which protected her white muslin gown. Since the day on which Lieutenant Calverly untied her apron strings, she never made the mistake of wearing one stained with paint when she came downstairs.

Georgianne smiled when she entered the small parlour where they dined en famille. "Good day, dearest, I hope you did not ride this morning. The weather is miserable. I don't want you to become chilled because it might cause an inflammation of the lungs."

Helen sat opposite her sister. "Good day, there is no need to worry about my health. How are you? I hope you are not too fatigued?"

Her finger to her lips, Georgianne looked sideways at the footman, warning her not mention her condition.

"Would you care for some broth, dearest? The weather is so bitter that if Tarrant joins us, he might appreciate something hot instead of ham sandwiches. I also instructed Cook to make apricot tarts which Tarrant is partial to. To be sure, he and his men are busier than ever gathering news inspecting the borders. Who knows whether or not they will be in danger?" She gained control of her sensibilities before addressing the footman. "Peter, you may serve Miss Whitley before you leave the room."

The odour of the steaming broth, ladled into her soup plate from a silver tureen, made Helen's mouth water. "It will be delicious," she thought, in anticipation of succulent cubes of carrot, turnips and sticky texture of barley.

"What did you do this morning, dearest?"

"I worked on my watercolour of Mister Barnet." While she dipped her spoon into the broth, she fretted about his dull complexion and the hectic colour in his cheeks.

Georgianne raised her eyebrows. "Why do you look so sad?"

"He seems ill."

"It is obvious he can afford to be well-looked after, so don't worry."

"I know, but I am concerned." A deep sigh escaped Helen. "Our acquaintance is short, but I have grown fond of him."

Georgianne frowned. "Fond! I admit I like the gentleman, but don't forget Mister Barnet is not a member of our milieu. You must be careful of your good name."

"Nevertheless, he is everything a grandfather should be. It is easy to confide in him."

Georgianne's knife, poised to cut a bread roll in half, clattered onto her plate. "I beg your pardon! What have you confided in him?"

"Nothing worth mentioning." Maria Tomlinson relied on her not to mention her name in connection with blackmail. If she hinted at the subject to Georgianne, her sister would want to know the victim's name. She tasted the broth. "This is excellent. I must compliment your cook."

"Well," Georgianne began, "you will have more than Mister Barnet to concern yourself with. Tarrant proposes holding a ball for you in mid-May. He thinks you should make your formal curtsy to society. Of course, when we return to England, after—" she broke off then continued, "you shall be presented at the Queen's Drawing Room."

"How generous of him." Helen wanted to tell Georgianne not to agonise over Cousin Tarrant. Yet, although he survived gruelling years fighting against Napoleon, her cousin would soon be in danger, once again. Her throat tightened at the thought of Langley, Captain Dalrymple and her cousin.

Georgianne smiled at her. "So much to arrange."

"Are you sure it will not overtire you at such a time?"

"Quite sure. We must order the invitation cards. By the time the ball is held, I am sure the Duke will have arrived in Brussels. I hope he will attend."

"It would be an honour," Helen murmured.

Georgianne dabbed her mouth with her table napkin. "The ballroom must be transformed, but neither with a mass of greenery nor with ribbons and bouquets." She frowned. "Chinese lanterns and temple bells are all too common." She clapped her hands. "India! A Moghul court! Unfortunately, we cannot procure a live elephant. Besides, even if we could borrow one from a menagerie, it would be inappropriate in a ballroom. Oh, dearest, the servants could wear splendid turbans decorated with aigrettes and...oh, I don't know. Helen, what do you suggest?"

"Papa only served in India for two years before he returned to England when the Duke of Wellington did. However, his memory of the land remained vivid. He was very impressed by Gwalior Fort. Perched hundreds of feet above the surrounding plains, Papa said it measured almost two miles in length." Her words came slowly. "Do you remember his description of one of the Hindu gods, a blue-skinned boy with a peacock feather in his hair?" Her artist's imagination captured a picture in her mind's eye. "Papa told me that his devotees believe he plays a flute so sweetly, that all who hear his music are entranced. What did our papa say he is called?"

"Yes, I remember Papa mentioning him, Helen. What was his name? Did it begin with 'Kli'?" Georgianne shook her head. "No, I remember thinking it begins with 'Chr' as Christ does."

"Krishna!" Helen exclaimed, memories flooding her mind. "I remember Papa describing a black marble statue of Krishna clad in yellow silk. He also spoke of white marble temples on dusty plains; of people dressed in bright colours. I shall transform the ballroom with scenes of Hindu India."

"In six weeks?"

"There are sure to be artists who can be employed to help me and, maybe some of the hussars under Cousin Tarrant's command can paint the background for my designs."

"Perhaps we could serve some Indian food," Georgianne mused. "Maybe my chef has some receipts."

"If not, there are sure to be army men who served in India, who can make suggestions."

"I daresay. And there is an Indian restaurant in London. Perhaps the owner could lend us a cook. That would be splendid."

"What would?" asked Cousin Tarrant.

Georgianne raised her eyebrows. "Must you enter a room so stealthily, sir?"

"Stealth, Georgie, is a hussar's friend. He never knows what he might hear to his advantage." He crossed the room to kiss her.

Georgianne held up her hand in protest. "Desist, Major, you will shock my sister." She patted his cheek. "How cold you are. I am glad you have joined us. The weather is so bleak that I ordered Scotch broth to warm you."

"Thank you."

Georgianne beckoned to Peter, who had followed Cousin Tarrant into the room. "The broth in the tureen is cold. Fetch more from the kitchen and make sure it is hot."

Cousin Tarrant sat opposite Georgianne. "Please tell me what you ladies are plotting."

"Helen will transform the ballroom for her ball. Imagine an Indian paradise painted around the beautiful blue boy, a Hindu god our father once described. It is sure to be spoken of as the most splendid event of the year."

"Painted!" Tarrant sounded alarmed. "Helen, you can't strip the paper from the walls to paint them. The house does not belong to me."

"I shall paint my designs on heavy cloth which will hang from poles on the walls in the ballroom."

"I see."

"Perhaps The Glory Boys' band could play for our guests," Georgianne suggested.

"Maybe. I shall speak to Makelyn."

"Good. Can you imagine the strains of a waltz?"

"No, though I am sure the two of you can." Tarrant sounded amused. He cleared his throat while helping himself to a sandwich. "Where is the broth? I must hurry. Georgie, I shall be away for a week or more."

"Why? Where are you going?"

"To gather information and inspect troops quartered at various places along the border."

"Be careful—" Georgianne broke off when Peter served Tarrant.

"This is very tasty," Tarrant remarked. "Did I hear a mention of an Indian restaurant when I arrived?"

"Yes, it is. I would like to serve some Indian food when we dine before the ball, and during supper."

"I shall leave everything in your capable hands." About to bite into the sandwich, he paused. "The blue boy sounds fascinating, but please remember this is a Christian country. You must not shock either the Glory Boy's chaplain—who will most probably attend—or any of the other guests."

Helen nodded, imagining a sweep of hyacinth blue sky above plains made verdant by the heavy rains Papa had described.

"Helen?" Cousin Tarrant spoke in a sharp tone.

"Yes."

"I repeat that I don't want any of the guests to be affronted."

"Trust me, Cousin, if you don't approve of my designs, they can be painted over."

"Good." He finished his broth and refused Georgianne's offer of an apricot tart. "I must leave."

Her sister peeped up into his eyes.

"Don't look at me thus!" he murmured. "There is no need for apprehension. I have the lucky heather you gave me in my sabretache."

Georgianne's smile did not warm her eyes.

"Take care of each other, ladies. I shall return as soon I can." He kissed her sister's cheek.

Half way to the door, he turned around and returned to the table. Smiling like a mischievous schoolboy, he helped himself to two apricot tarts. "Greedy, I know, yet I can no more resist them than I can resist you, Georgie."

Conscious of her sister's blush, Helen studied the crumbs on her plate. Did Langley like apricot tarts?

* * * *

Helen hoped Mister Barnet would be pleased with the watercolour. In the afternoon, while she waited for admittance to his house, she tried to decide whether she had captured the soft texture of velvet and the sheen of silk. Once again, she wondered if she would ever be satisfied with anything she painted.

The door opened; her footman handed the watercolour to Thomas and she stepped indoors, followed by Pringle.

Thomas put the wrapped painting on a table in the hall, now denuded of its treasures. Presumably, they had been packed prior to Mister Barnet's departure.

Helen handed Thomas her furled parasol before she stripped off her sage green gloves, the colour of which matched her pelisse. She gave them to Thomas, who put them beside the watercolour, but not before he glanced at Greaves, the butler, who stood opposite the front door.

The butler nodded to the gentleman, who stood with his back to them. "Soup, steamed fish, a little chicken, no rich sauces and, most definitely, no brandy or other strong liquor. I shall return tomorrow to see how Mister Barnet is. In the meantime, please send for me if you have further cause for concern."

"I shall, Doctor Longspring," Greaves replied.

"Mister Barnet's relatives must be informed of his state of health."

The butler shook his head. "He has no relatives."

Doctor Longspring frowned. "A pity. I daresay Mister Barnet's attorney is in charge of his affairs."

His face impassive, Greaves looked at Doctor Longspring. "Yes, Doctor, he has given me instructions."

"See that you carry them out. I must go. I have other patients to attend."

Shocked by the severity of Mister Barnet's illness, Helen frowned.

The butler's glance flickered over the carefully wrapped watercolour. "Thomas, if that is for Mister Barnet, you may take it to him." He turned his attention back to Helen. "Miss Whitley, I regret Mister Barnet is confined to bed, therefore, unable to receive you today."

Helen looked around the bare hall and up the equally bare stairs. "Nonsense, Mister Barnet is always delighted to see me. Thomas, show me to his room, immediately."

Greaves thrust his chest out. Rich colour flooded his cheeks, but unless he manhandled her, he could not prevent her from making her way up the stairs to the landing. "I protest," he said, rigid with disapproval.

198

"Miss, I don't think you should visit him." Pringle sniffed.

"Nonsense!" Helen exclaimed, surprised by the depth of her affection urging her to see the old gentleman. However, she would observe the proprieties, such as they were, by allowing the woman to accompany her. "Come with me. This time you need not wait downstairs."

"This way, Miss," said Thomas from the top of the half-landing.

Judging by the warm expression in the footman's eyes, he approved of her determination to see Mister Barnet.

Thomas led them up another flight of stairs and opened the door to a small parlour. "Please wait here, Miss Whitley, while I inform Mister Barnet you are here."

"Thank you."

A door further along the wide corridor opened.

"You have been most helpful, sir," said a familiar voice.

Langley! For her sister's sake, she regretted Cousin Tarrant's orders which sent him to the borders. For her own, she was glad Langley remained safe in Brussels.

Langley strode toward her. "Miss Whitley, I did not expect to see you here."

Like a guilty schoolgirl, she fidgeted with the satin bow securing her bonnet beneath her chin. "Nor did I anticipate seeing you." She cursed the heat rushing into her cheeks. "Why are you here, my lord? I did not know you are acquainted with Mister Barnet."

"He sent for me."

Helen pressed her gloved hands to her hot cheeks. Why did Mister Barnet send for him? To betray her confidence? Surely not. Her face cooled but she could not speak.

"You seem alarmed, Miss Whitley. There is no need to be."

Had he sensed her inner turmoil? "How fortunate."

"I presume you have come to call on him."

She wanted to warn him to keep out of danger, but, tongue-tied, could only nod in answer to his question.

Langley inclined his head. "It will be my pleasure to escort you when you are ready to leave."

Before she could say another word, he strode to the stairs.

"If you'll be good enough to wait here, Miss Whitley, I'll inform my master you're waiting to see him." Thomas said.

"Thank you." She looked at her gift for Mister Barnet. She did not want Thomas to give it to him. "Pringle, take the watercolour from Thomas."

Pringle obeyed while sniffing even more loudly than usual.

"Blow your nose," Helen ordered her, irritated by the conventions designed to fetter young ladies with a chaperone. "Thomas, why did the doctor attend Mister Barnet?"

"When he stood after breakfast, he staggered. If I had not caught hold of him, he would have fallen. Mister Greaves persuaded the master to return to bed and allow him to summon the doctor."

Alarmed, Helen scrutinised the footman's impassive face. The old gentleman's condition must be serious.

Chapter Fifteen

5th April, 1815

When Thomas ushered Helen into the bedroom, Mister Barnet smiled at Helen from his chair, every hair of his snow-white wig in place. "Good day, Miss Whitley, thank you for visiting me." A wry expression on his face, he indicated his opalescent grey silk dressing gown, embroidered with gold oriental lettering. "I apologise for my appearance. My doctor forbade me to dress for the day. He ordered me to remain in bed, but I prefer to sit by the window to enjoy the view of my garden. The primroses and bluebells are in full bloom and the birds are busy building their nests."

"Good day, sir." Helen glanced at the large, neatly made bed with a primrose yellow quilt folded back at one corner to reveal linen sheets, a plump bolster and pillows.

Concerned for his health, she scrutinised him. "Perhaps I should not have disturbed you."

"Yes, you should. Thomas, fetch a chair for Miss Whitley. We shall admire the view together."

While she waited for the chair, she looked around. Although patches on the pale blue and primrose-yellow striped wallpaper marked spots where paintings once hung, everything in the bedchamber was comfortable.

Pringle, who had followed her, sniffed several times, presumably to express her disapproval of their presence in a gentleman's bedroom.

Impatient with propriety, Helen's breath caught in her throat. Did she need a watchdog? No, she did not. "Pringle, I have changed my mind, you may wait for me downstairs." She frowned at the woman. "Please stop sniffing."

Helen moved aside to allow Thomas to fetch a small wing chair, upholstered in velvet the same colour as the bedspread.

She placed the folder across Mister Barnet's knees before she sank onto the chair. "Please look inside. I hope it will please you."

After the old gentleman opened it, he whistled low. His head bent over the painting, Helen could not see his face. Did he like it? She could hardly breathe while she waited for him to speak. At long last, he smiled at her. He held his portrait up to examine it more closely. "I congratulate you, Miss Whitley. Were you not born a lady, your paintings could be exhibited by the Royal Academy in one of the galleries at Somerset House, and your talent would earn you a living."

"Thank you, sir."

Mister Barnet studied the watercolour for a minute or more before he beckoned to Thomas. "Take this downstairs. Make sure it is packed carefully. And, Thomas, fetch coffee and cake."

"I shall bring it immediately, sir."

Alone with her, Mister Barnet smiled again. "I don't know how to thank you for my portrait. It is beyond me to understand how you captured the glint of silver and the texture of velvet with your paintbrush."

Helen shrugged. "I try to show what I see." She considered the designs for the supper and ballroom. "And sometimes I picture what I have not seen."

"Do you have a subject in mind?"

She nodded. "Yes, my brother-in-law and sister plan to hold a ball for me. Mrs Tarrant wants the decorations to be superior to those of every other ball held this season. I suggested the ballroom should be transformed with vistas of India, temples and palaces, elephants and tigers."

"An ambitious scheme." Mister Barnet chuckled. "How will you accomplish it?"

"Not without a lot of help from artists I shall employ."

Before Mister Barnet could reply, Thomas arrived with a tray of coffee which he put on a table. The elderly gentleman dismissed him with a wave of his hand.

Helen poured coffee for Mister Barnet and handed him the cup. After she ate a small cake and drank some coffee, she stood. "I must go, sir," she told him, for fear she would exhaust him. "I shall call on you soon to see how you are. When will you leave for England?"

"As soon as the doctor permits." His wrinkles deepened as he spoke. "Although I hope to see you beforehand, I shall understand if you are too busy to call."

She pitied the frail, lonely invalid. "I shall visit you several times before you go home."

"Thank you again for the watercolour. I shall treasure it."

"Au revoir, Mister Barnet. I look forward to seeing you again. I hope you will soon be in the best of health."

* * * *

As soon as Helen stepped into the street with Pringle close behind her, Langley stepped forward. Surprised because he had waited for so long, she gazed at him, appreciative of his delightful smile which softened the somewhat harsh contours of his face. She curtsied. Conscious of her dresser's acute hearing, Helen searched for something innocuous to say. After several seconds passed, she spoke, flustered by his mere presence. "It is good of you to have waited for me."

"My pleasure, Miss Whitley. May I escort you home?"

Helen hesitated. It would be improper to return in the carriage without a chaperone. Yet she did not want to be seated inside with Pringle listening to every word she exchanged with Langley. She opened her cream-coloured parasol which was shaped like a giant toadstool edged with broad lace dyed to match the fabric. "Langley, the sun is shining. If you wish, you may walk home with me while my servant returns in the carriage."

He inclined his head. "With pleasure, Miss Whitley."

"Thank you." Vexed, she glared at Pringle. "If my dresser continues to sniff disapprovingly, I shall be tempted either to scream or—well never mind about that—it would not be ladylike," she muttered, too low for her dresser to overhear. "Oh," she continued when Langley laughed, "It is all very well for you to be amused, my lord, but you are not hemmed in by an attendant."

His gypsy-dark eyes seemed to continue to laugh at her. "Please accept my sympathy, ma'am."

"Be good enough not to tease me by calling me ma'am."

"I beg your pardon." he responded, as meek as a lamb, although the laughter in his sloe-dark eyes appeared to increase.

She frowned at him in spite of her amusement. "Wretch, I don't believe you are sorry."

"A truce, Miss Whitley. I apologise for annoying you." Hand over his heart, he inclined his head. "What may I do to make amends?"

As ever, she found him irresistible. "By telling me why you visited Mister Barnet."

"He sent for me."

"May I ask why?"

"Yes, you may ask, but I am not obliged to offer you an explanation."

"Please don't provoke me instead of answering my question," she replied, with mock haughtiness.

His face expressionless, Langley spoke again. "Why did you visit him? Should I assume you unburdened your heart to the gentleman?" The teasing note returned to his voice.

"No, of course not," she answered too quickly.

What did Mister Barnet tell the viscount? That she loved Langley? Surely the ailing gentleman had not betrayed her confidences. She wished the ground would open, and then close over her head to rescue her from embarrassment. "Why did you visit him?" she asked, afraid of the answer.

Langley's eyes widened a little. His eyes searched her face in response to which her body seemed to explode into countless shards of delight. Before she had time to consider the extraordinary sensation, he spoke. "I called on him at his request. He told me Midhurst lodges in Antwerp. I shall ask Major Makelyn to send a small detachment of Glory Boys there to gather necessary information for the army. If he agrees, I will order my men to search Midhurst's rooms and take possession of any papers they find."

"How good you are! Miss Tomlinson will always be in your debt. I shall tell her the letters might be retrieved."

Langley cleared his throat. "Let us hope they are in his rooms. We must avoid scandal.

Unfortunately, Midhurst cannot be prosecuted, for it would ruin the lady's reputation."

"He deserves the worst possible punishment," Helen commented when they turned the corner into Rue Royale.

"Upon my word, Miss Whitley, I would not care to have you for an enemy. You are as fierce as one of Napoleon's famous Old Guard, any one of whom is capable of making me shake in my shoes."

She looked down at his gleaming black boots. "A gazetted hero frightened of one of the ogre's toy soldiers. Impossible!" Yet again the possibility of him sustaining a fatal wound or being seriously hurt terrified her. She forced herself not to reveal her fear by as much as a blink of her eyes.

"Thank you, Miss Whitley. Ah, here we are outside Rupe's house. I shall see you safe indoors after which I must return to headquarters. Although everything is quiet at the moment, by now Makelyn will probably be asking where I am."

From the hall, she looked back at Langley who stood on the doorstep. "Are you sure you don't wish to come in to partake of a glass of wine?"

He shook his head. "No, thank you, I regret time does not allow it. Good day to you, Miss Whitley." He turned around, his pelisse swirling, and marched in military style up the street toward his headquarters.

The butler stepped forward. "Mrs Tarrant instructed me to ask you to join her when you returned, Miss."

"Where is she?"

"In her parlour."

Was all well with her sister? Helen undid the wide satin ribbons tied in a coquettish bow beneath her right ear. She removed her hat and tossed it onto the head of the marble bust of a Roman emperor placed on a rosewood table. Her fingers made clumsy by her concern for her pregnant sister, she struggled to unfasten her three-quarter length, sage-green woollen pelisse. Finally, she slipped her arms out of the sleeves, and handed it to a footman.

Later, she would exchange her forest-green kid half-boots for slippers. Now, regardless of dirty marks made by her footsteps on either the shining wooden floors or costly carpets, she rushed to join Georgianne, who was taking her ease on a chaise longue.

A swift glance revealed she did not need to be alarmed, so she came to an abrupt halt. "Don't be foolish," she chastised herself. "I daresay a healthy baby is born every minute and its mother suffers no ill effect, so there is no need for me to fuss like a watchful mother duck."

Georgianne put down a letter. "The mail arrived. It contains a letter, in your guardian's handwriting, addressed to Tarrant."

The moment when she must make a decision which might affect the rest of her life drew near. Helen reminded herself she wanted to marry; to be free of Cousin Tarrant's charity. She did not want to be the poor relation. Although Tarrant would add to her modest dowry, there were few beaux of the captain's calibre who called on her.

"Dearest?"

Georgianne's voice cut into her confusion. "Yes?" she forced herself to reply while thoughts rushed through her mind.

"Your hands are trembling. There is no need to be agitated. If Captain Dalrymple asks you to marry him, you only have to say yes or no. Neither Tarrant nor I wish you to agree unless you are certain beyond all possible doubt, that you want to be his wife."

"Thank you. I do like him." She enjoyed their early morning rides, his admiration of her artistic skills, his delightful gifts of flowers and books, and his consideration at balls, soirees and routs, where he catered to her every need.

She forced herself to smile at Georgianne before changing the subject. "Mister Barnet is delighted with my portrait of him."

"So he should be. It is a good likeness."

"Thank you for the compliment." She sighed. "I am sorry for him. Not only has the doctor confined him to bed, it seems he has no friends or relatives in Brussels to visit him."

"I am sorry. Is his condition serious?"

Helen shrugged. "I hope not. Mister Barnet is confident he can return to England in the near future."

A knock on the door preceded the butler, who handed Helen a large parcel and a sealed letter.

"Thank you, Chivers." Helen broke the red wax wafer. She read the letter. "Mister Barnet is generous. He has sent illustrated books of India. I must write to thank him."

Later, she leafed through the volumes and marvelled at the vistas of the sub-continent, and drawings of its inhabitants dressed in clothes unfamiliar to her.

* * * *

Seated at a table in the ballroom before it was time to change into an evening gown, Helen added details to her sketches. At intervals between the tall windows would stand large, one dimensional painted wooden elephants or tigers. A wooden representation of the blue boy—as she thought of Krishna—with his bluish-black complexion, and black curls decorated with a peacock feather, would be on a plinth between the centre windows. Oh, she could imagine the splendid decorations.

Helen stood to stretch her back. Excitement possessed her at the prospect of the ball. With nimble feet, she danced the waltz with an imaginary partner. She forgot the apron which covered her muslin gown, and imagined a silk skirt and petticoat swirling at her ankles.

The door opened. Peter stared at her in astonishment. The footman must consider her mad. Embarrassed, she waved a dismissive hand at him. "You may go."

Peter's mouth twitched. Obviously hard-put to restrain his amusement, he withdrew.

So much to do. The strains of imaginary music died away.

Helen stepped through the double doors onto the landing. Voices sounded from the entrance hall. She peeped over the banister at one side of the broad, red-carpeted stairs, at the top of which the guests at her ball would be received by Cousin Tarrant and her sister. She smiled with pleasurable anticipation of the occasion.

Who had called so close to the hour at which they would dine? Ah! Captain Dalrymple. She watched him remove his busby ornamented with a small scarlet bag, scarlet feather and gold braid. Uniform improved the appearance of any man. Yet, she decided, the captain would be as handsome in civilian clothes as he was dressed as an officer.

Curious, she wondered what her suitor gave to Chivers. A message for Cousin Tarrant?

After Dalrymple left the house, she hurried to her bedchamber where Pringle had laid out fresh undergarments, together with a white silk gown with a satin ribbon around the high-waistline. About to disrobe, Helen raised her eyebrows at the sound of a knock.

Pringle opened the door. She spoke a few words then turned around, and held out a bouquet of spring flowers and greenery. "With Captain Dalrymple's compliments, Miss."

"Thank you, Pringle."

Helen sniffed the fragrance of narcissi and hyacinths which filled the room. "How beautiful."

Her dresser handed her a sealed missive.

Helen broke the sealing wax wafer, and opened the sheet of paper.

Flowers for the most elegant flower of all, a matchless lily. I look forward to seeing you this evening at the soiree,

Your servant,

Dalrymple

Helen giggled, for she had never compared herself to a flower. She smiled, touched by her beau's compliment. In silence, she prepared to dine.

When would Cousin Tarrant return? Had her guardian given permission for Captain Dalrymple to do her the honour of asking her to be his wife? If so, what reason did she have to decline his proposal? She knew of two ladies, of some thirty years of age, who were now 'on the shelf'. Did they regret refusing offers of marriage from pleasant, respectable gentlemen?

An ivory fan dangled from a cord around her wrist, as she made her way to the parlour, in time to join her sister before Chivers announced, "Dinner is served."

"You are unusually quiet," Georgianne said when they were seated at the table.

"Oh, my mind is busy with plans for the ball."

"Dearest, I don't think it is why you are so quiet."

Helen sighed. Georgianne knew her too well. Her thoughts drifted to the soiree. Whom would she meet there besides the captain? Langley?

Chapter Sixteen
5th April, 1815

The company retired to the supper room during the interval between recitations of poetry, performances on the harp, flute and pianoforte, and renditions of favourite songs.

Miss Tomlinson sidled up to Helen and her escort, Captain Dalrymple. "I must speak to you," she whispered, her mouth close to Helen's ear. Shall we sit at the table in the corner?" She grasped Helen's arm. "Grandmere will scold me for slipping away from her but I don't care."

Helen feared her arm would be bruised. "Maria, please let go of me." Sure that—due to the sound of many voices—her beau, Captain Dalrymple, could not have overheard Maria's whisper, she turned her head toward him. "Please, would you escort us to the table near those Roman marble busts decorated with gilt wreaths of laurel leaves?

"A pleasure; I am always at your service." His self-depreciating smile made him appear younger than his years. "I would be embarrassed if someone put a laurel wreath on my head after a battle." His cheeks reddened. "Oh, I beg you not to misunderstand me. I did not mean to imply I could be a hero. I shall say no more for fear of seeming vain."

Helen smiled at him with genuine admiration. "Every soldier who fought in the

Peninsular is a hero who deserves to be honoured."

He gazed into her eyes, a warm expression in his own. "You are kind."

Helen sat at the round table opposite Maria while Dalrymple fetched refreshments. "What is urgent enough to risk your grandmother's displeasure?"

Maria clasped her hands to her breast. "Father has arrived in Brussels. If Mister Midhurst publishes those foolish letters I wrote to him, Father will be outraged." Her cheeks flamed scarlet. "He...he might believe I allowed Mister Midhurst to rob me of my virtue. As for Grandmere, I cannot bear to imagine what she would say."

"We must hope Langley retrieves the letters and ensures Mister Midhurst receives the thrashing he deserves."

Maria's shoulders shook. "And if he does not? If Father finds out, what shall I do?"

"Calm yourself; you will attract unwelcome attention." Helen glanced around and saw the Comptesse approaching like an unwelcome brisk breeze. "Shush, your grandmother and my sister are coming toward us."

"Ah, zere you are, Maria," the Comptesse said, her displeasure revealed by the hard glint in her dark eyes.

"I am sorry, Grandmere, I lost sight of you in the crush, so Miss Whitley suggested I join her while she waited for her sister," Maria gabbled.

The Comptesse frowned. "Come, we shall join Monsieur le Baron de Montpellier."

Maria stood. "It would be improper for me to leave you, Miss Whitley," the Comptesse continued. "Young ladies should always be chaperoned."

"I am; my sister is only a few feet away engaged in conversation with Miss Omerod." In an effort to mollify the old lady, she added. "Now there is a lady who is mistress of the minuet, and dear Maria is an accomplished harpist."

Madame's eyes softened. "Yes, my granddaughter plays well enough." She sighed. "Oh, you should have seen my queen, poor, poor, Marie Antoinette, perform ze minuet; she was incomparable. Ah, zere you are Mrs Tarrant. Only a moment ago I remarked zat young ladies must be chaperoned at all times."

"Just so," Georgianne murmured politely. "Madame, will you join us?"

Before the lady could reply, Captain Dalrymple arrived, carrying a tray loaded with glasses of white wine, tiny sandwiches, little patties and other delicacies.

Madame glared at the food instead of replying to Georgianne. "Maria, I hope zat if I 'ad not found you in zis crush of people, you would not have been tempted to abandon your reducing diet."

A brief, awkward silence ensued during which Helen sympathised with Maria, who stared mournfully at the delicious selections.

"No, Grandmere."

"I am glad to hear it. Come, child, it is rude to keep the Baron waiting. Good evening Mrs Tarrant, Miss Whitley, Captain Dalrymple."

The captain watched Madame retreat. "If Napoleon's troops were of her calibre, we might have been defeated in the Peninsular."

Georgianne sat at the small table, "Oh, you forget the Comptesse is a Royalist. She would have fought on our side."

Dalrymple's boyish laugh rang out. "True, ma'am."

Helen craned her neck in an attempt to see Langley's tall figure in the throng. She wanted to inform him of Mister Tomlinson's arrival in Brussels and Maria's fear that Mister Midhurst would publish those letters.

* * * *

5th April, 1815

Yearning for a taste of the succulent fish, Maria looked at her serving of salad leaves dressed with lemon juice. She sighed, well aware of Grandmere's impotent fury when her son-in-law joined them at luncheon in the commodious house he had rented for their stay in Brussels.

"Well, Countess." He poked his portion of trout—dressed in a cream sauce—with his fork; for he preferred plain food. "What of Viscount

Langley? Has he shown a marked interest in Maria?"

Grandmere's lips thinned.

"Comptesse, Father, not countess," Maria murmured.

As usual, her grandmother did not speak to him unless she was forced to. Grandmere shook her head.

Maria sighed before she spoke to her parent. "It would be best for you to accept that Viscount Langley does not wish to marry me."

"The fool! I can afford to set Longwood Place to rights. What reason does he have to reject a beautiful, well-educated prospective bride?"

Although she loved him dearly, she was not blind to his imperfections, but it seemed he did not notice hers. Maria sighed, well-aware that she did need to reduce her weight, and with reluctance, admitted she should be grateful to Grandmere.

If Mister Midhurst published her letters, it would break Father's heart. Whatever the cost, it must never happen. No longer hungry, she stared down at her plate.

Maria decided to write to Viscount Langley asking him to meet her in Parc Royale. She hoped he would keep the appointment. However, The Duke of Wellington had arrived in the early hours of the morning, so General Makelyn might not be able to spare the viscount. Maria shrugged. What did she care for army matters provided they did not prevent

Lord Langley from refusing to meet her? If it was unpatriotic, so be it, for she could only think of her own predicament.

Mister Tomlinson thumped the table with his fist. "Maria, you've become a little too skinny. No wonder, if you are kept on short commons. There's not enough on your plate to keep a minnow alive. Have you lost your appetite?" He beckoned to the footman. "Serve my daughter with some trout."

Her grandmother shrugged with long-practiced daintiness.

"Grandmere fears no gentleman will court me if I don't adhere to a reducing diet," Maria explained.

Mister Tomlinson scowled. "She is wrong. Your fortune guarantees they will."

Maria bowed her head. She wanted to be married for more than that.

With a tiny portion of trout on his fork, Mister Tomlinson looked balefully at Grandmere. "Your grandmother is mistaken. Most noblemen are in debt due to the insanity of the gaming tables. They wager on foolishness, such as which raindrop will reach the bottom of the window first. At the races, they place an outrageous sum on a horse they think is certain to win, or they bet on—" he broke off for a second. "No, it is unfit for your ears."

If only Grandmere would say something. Instead, straight-backed, shoulders squared, she took a sip of wine while regarding her son-in-law contemptuously.

"Surely you don't want me to marry a gentleman who would gamble away my fortune?"

"Can't say I do, but there's ways to make sure your fortune's safe and see you mistress of a fine estate."

"You could buy me one instead."

"How would that establish you in the ton?" He scowled. "No, no, I want the best for you, my girl."

Unknown to him, the man she now loved was not that scoundrel, Midhurst, but the son of another manufacturer. A man who would never blackmail her or treat her badly. Although his family's fortune from iron works and foundries was substantial, Maria knew her stubborn parent would not consider him a suitable son-in-law. Yet, more than anything else in the world she wanted to marry her beau, who shared her exceptional interest in gardening and music. But, if she summoned the courage to explain that she had given her heart to a worthy man, who cared nothing for the ton, what would her father say? Undoubtedly he would be furious. But why was he so determined for her to marry an aristocrat? Was it because he did not want her to be looked down on by the beau monde as her mother had been after she married—as the saying went—beneath her?

Mister Tomlinson pushed his plate aside. "Considering how much I pay your chef, madam, I would have expected him to provide better than this."

Grandmere looked at him with a distinct hint of implacable frost. She stood. "I can eat no more." Her tone made it clear her son-in-law's presence at the table had caused her sudden loss of appetite. "Come, Maria, we shall call on Monsieur le Baron de Loches."

Glad to escape from the clearly drawn battle lines, Maria dabbed her mouth with her napkin and then stood.

Mister Tomlinson frowned. "I don't want to see you wed to some damned Belgian, or even worse, a French royalist."

"No danger of that." She kissed the top of his head. "I love you."

His eyes softened. "Enough sentimentality, my girl."

His brusque words did not deceive her. Whether she were overweight or not, she knew he would always love her.

Maria gazed at the curd tarts topped with whipped cream and slivered almonds. Could she hide one from her grandmother in the folds of her gown? Her mouth watered. One day, she would faint from hunger if Grandmere did not increase her diet of boiled or raw vegetables, and salt meat—which was believed to encourage weight loss through perspiration.

Grandmere paused in the doorway. "Hurry up, Maria." She deigned to offer Father the smallest possible courtesy by nodding her head.

She followed her grandmother, abandoning all idea of eating a tart in the privacy of her bedchamber.

* * * *

9th April, 1815

When the news of Wellington's arrival spread through Brussels, the British were optimistic. Whatever Napoleon's plans were, Old Hooky—the soldiers' nick-name for the Duke due to his prominent Roman nose—would defeat them, and the veterans of the Peninsular were jubilant.

Within days of the great man's arrival, Langley and Helen's cousin commented on Wellington's need for more experienced veterans. As the great man had said, on more than one occasion, no one could have more regret over the lack of those seasoned officers who had served in the Peninsular, and were now either deployed in America, or had sold out of the army.

Helen supposed Langley and Cousin Tarrant would be too busy to attend balls, the theatre and other enjoyable events, but they were not. Wellington expected his officers to acquit themselves well in society.

Captain Dalrymple managed to escape the demands on his time to join Helen while she rode in the Allee Vert early on the morning of the 9th of April.

"Good day, Miss Whitley. I have something particular to say to you." He dismounted. "Would you stroll with me for a while?"

"Yes, Captain." Apprehensive, she allowed him to help her out of the saddle.

Helen walked by his side, appreciating the fresh, early morning air and the greenery on either side of a broad path. Mindful of the proprieties, she did not allow him to guide her out of her groom's sight.

At first, he seemed somewhat hesitant to speak, but after several minutes, he began. "Miss Whitley, I am kept so busy by Major Makelyn, perhaps this is not the best time to broach the subject of another possible engagement." He ran a finger between his neck and his stiffly starched shirt collar, as though it suddenly had become too tight. "I hardly dare ask if Major Tarrant received the letter which your guardian referred to when he wrote to me."

Helen stared down at the path riddled with tree roots. "Not yet; he is away from home."

"Miss Whitley, if the major had read it, I daresay he would have told you that provided my parents have no objection to our marriage, he gives us his blessings."

Helen peeped up at him, glad that unlike so many gentlemen, he was taller than she, yet still unsure whether or not she would accept his proposal.

The captain's smile seemed to light up his face. "I have mentioned you several times in my correspondence with my parents, so I believe

Papa will write to assure your guardian that he approves."

With the tip of her toe, Helen traced a pattern on the ground between two exposed roots which resembled hands reaching out to grab her.

"I have not forgotten you told me you have a tendresse for another gentleman," the captain continued, his voice gentle. "By now, if he reciprocated, I think you would be betrothed to him. So please be frank. Tell me if you could ever care for me?"

"It would be improper for me to say more than that I like you." She looked down again. Never had she imagined she would employ the proprieties like some milk and water miss.

The captain's boyish laughter rang out before he spoke. "Despite my best efforts, I could not compose an ode to you which fully expressed my admiration. To be honest, I have few talents, but I am full of praise for yours."

She permitted Dalrymple to tuck her hand into the crook of his arm. At ease with her ardent beau, she allowed him to lead her forward.

"You are a talented artist." He looked at her with honest pleasure. "If you become my wife, I shall encourage you to continue painting. If you wish, maybe your finest work could be displayed anonymously by the Royal Academy."

She glowed at the suggestion of some of her paintings being viewed amongst those displayed from floor to ceiling at the exhibition.

The captain smiled. "I shall make enquiries when the business with Napoleon is finished."

Her eyes widened as she remembered Mister Barnet's opinion. If he and Dalrymple considered her talented, maybe, just maybe, she was. Helen warmed even more to her suitor.

"How good of you, sir."

Dalrymple patted her gloved hand. "Nothing is too good for you, Miss Whitley."

She did not deserve such a commendable beau? Her hand trembled due to the dangers the captain and so many other fine young men, including Langley and Tarrant, faced with insouciance. Intrepid officers, who took their duties seriously, rode magnificently on and off the battlefield, were efficient, and as Wellington demanded, accomplished in society.

Helen turned her head to look at him full in the face. He swung round to stand before her, his head inclined. A flutter in her chest! Would he kiss her? They were only inches apart. Her groom cleared his throat loudly.

"Time to go home to have breakfast," Helen remarked with reluctance. "The morning air has given me a sharp appetite. I expect it has whetted yours."

"You could say so," Dalrymple replied, as if he were thinking of something other than breakfast.

* * * *

Langley turned Miss Tomlinson's letter around. Why did she want him to meet her in Parc Royale so early in the morning, at a time when he would prefer to ride in the Allee Vert where he might encounter Helen? Well, even if it meant he would not have time to breakfast, he must be quick before finding out if he had new orders.

Accompanied by a trooper, who would look after his horse while he rendezvoused with the lady, he rode to the wrought iron gates. After he dismounted—trained to observe every detail— he scanned his surroundings while he strode along the path. Near the pavilion, he did not know if he imagined a movement by an oak tree, where sunlight kissed bluebells at its base. An errant breeze wafted their fragrant perfume, one very different to smoke-laden air on battlefields. The sight of Miss Tomlinson, seated on a bench near the pavilion, diverted his sudden thought of war. She appeared to have seen him. Langley whistled low. She must have dieted to reduce her weight.

Beneath the grey sky which threatened an April shower, Langley walked toward the manufacturer's daughter. His sixth sense, sharpened on missions to gather information about the French during his years in the Iberian Peninsula, gave him the impression he, the spy, was being spied upon. Alert, he looked around, but saw no one.

He reached the table by which Miss Tomlinson stood. In spite of his annoyance at her request for this meeting, he noticed how well her cornflower blue pelisse, and pearl-grey hat, trimmed with artificial forget-me-nots, suited her. Perhaps most gentlemen did not observe ladies' ensembles in such detail. However, no brother growing up with a bevy of sisters and female cousins could be oblivious to the fair sex's turnouts. Langley chided himself for being remiss. He bowed. "Good day to you, Miss Tomlinson."

She curtsied and spoke simultaneously. "Good day, Major. You must think it is scandalous of me to have asked you to join me here, nonetheless, my letters must be retrieved before my father finds out about them." She covered her face with her hands and sobbed.

"My dear Miss Tomlinson, I have every sympathy for your predicament and am pledged to do all I can to help you," he said in spite of his embarrassment at her tears in a public place.

"Oh, you are so kind." She removed her hands from her face. Her beautiful eyes glistened with tears. "I don't know who else to turn to."

"There, there," he said, as soothingly as he had spoken to his sisters when they were still in the nursery and full of childish woes. He patted her on the back. "Please stop crying. Tears will accomplish nothing."

She wrapped her arms around him.

"Miss Tomlinson!" He tried to disengage himself but she clung to him as though she had tentacles.

"What is the meaning of this?" demanded an outraged voice.

Chapter Seventeen
7th April, 1815

Miss Tomlinson swung around as though a swarm of bees had stung her. "Father!" She tottered.

Forced to support her, Langley tried to decide whether he or Miss Tomlinson were more shocked upon being discovered in the lady's embrace.

"Yes, you may say 'Father'." Mister Tomlinson's harsh tone made the words sound like a curse. "I'm not a so-called fine gentleman who lies in bed until the morning is half-gone. I saw you sneak out of your grandmother's house, so I followed you. I'm shocked. I trusted that French woman to take care of you. She failed me, but you, should know better. His chin thrust forward, he glared at her. "I should disown you."

Disentangled from Miss Tomlinson's clutches, Langley squared his shoulders.

The young lady sat and sobbed into her handkerchief. The manufacturer glared at him, his face as red as a cockerel's wattle.

Langley's mind filled with the hideous memory of that manipulative heiress, Amelia Carstairs. Words could not describe his relief when she had realised they did not suit each other, and she had released him from their betrothal. He forced himself not to scowl at the furious man standing before him, the effect of his impeccable blue coat, cream waistcoat and biscuit coloured pantaloons, spoiled by a pin, thrust into his cravat, with a diamond head so large it was vulgar.

The hard glint in Tomlinson's eyes softened. "Well, well, my lord, I can't say I approve of such doings in a public place. And you, Maria, whatever your grandmother may think, you've been gently brought up. You should know better."

All his senses alert, Langley regarded the top of Miss Tomlinson's hat. Her sobs grew louder, as the manufacturer continued. "There, there, my girl, it's all I have dreamt of. What more could you ask for, than for you to be married to a peer of the realm, and become mistress of a country estate and a grand house in London?" He scrutinised the viscount. "My lord, I felt sure you had enough sense to make a match of it with my daughter. Now she's to be mistress of Longwood Place, I'll be generous."

Good lord, the man's desire for his daughter to have a great estate has obsessed him. Langley resisted the temptation to give him a set down. "You are mistaken, sir."

Mister Tomlinson's eyes narrowed. His daughter stood, her handkerchief, as sullied as trodden snow, fell to the ground.

Head held high, her eyes reddened by tears, she glared at her father. "You are determined for me to have a place in the ton. Neither you nor Grandmere ask what I want. Well, I'll tell you.

I've no desire to wed either the viscount or any other snobbish member of the ton assumed to be a gentleman; one who would accept my fortune and look down on me because I am a manufacturer's daughter."

Much chastened by the young lady's words, and with the hope that she did not regard him as 'a so called gentleman', Langley waited with interest to hear what she would say next.

"What is more, both of you, I don't want to attend ball after ball, or soiree after soiree, where Grandmere expects me to play the harp and—"

"You ungrateful chit!" Mister Tomlinson's cheeks suffused with an unhealthy looking flush. "Haven't I surrounded you in luxury and given you the best education money can buy?"

Maria sank onto a chair. "Money, money, money! Do you never think of anything other than what it can purchase, which includes—if you have your way—a husband for me? All your wealth can't buy the happiness which you and Mamma knew."

Langley noticed a man, whom he presumed was the owner of the pavilion, unlock its door and then look at them curiously. Embarrassed by the attention the furious parent and his indignant daughter had attracted, Langley touched his busby with the tips of his fingers. "Miss Tomlinson, if you should require my assistance in future, I remain at your service. Good day." Tempted to tell her never to ask for another assignation, he resisted. It would be ungentlemanly to let her father know they met at her request. He nodded at the manufacturer. "Mister Tomlinson."

Langley failed to prevent the incensed manufacturer from grabbing hold of the sleeve of his pelisse. "Not so fast, my lord. I demand an explanation of why I saw my gently-reared daughter in your arms."

A man clattered open the shutters of the pavilion.

"Release me," Langley commanded, acutely conscious of a small, interested audience, which had begun to gather near the pavilion. "If you want to know why your daughter needed to be comforted by an embrace that I did not instigate, I suggest you ask her."

His expression impassive, he noted the horror in the lady's large eyes. He did not need her to remind him of how much she feared her father would discover her indiscretion. Even more, he knew she feared the blackmailer would publish her foolish letters. Langley castigated himself. He should not have spoken in anger. Had he learned nothing from years during which he spied during the campaign in the Iberian Peninsula, when a careless action or word could have cost him his life?

Tomlinson stamped his expensively shod foot, stirring up dust, which would probably precede another verbal storm. "Why should Maria need to be comforted when she has everything to make her happy?" He let go of the pelisse.

Langley smoothed the sable fur that edged the short garment. "Mister Tomlinson, I suggest you sit with your daughter at a table, order coffee or hot chocolate, and have a private conversation."

This time, Miss Tomlinson clutched his sleeve. "Please don't leave, my lord."

Judging by the alarm in her hazel eyes, she might as well have asked him not to abandon her in the proverbial lion's den. He lowered his head slightly to speak too quietly for her father to overhear. "Under most circumstances, it is best to tell the truth."

"What's that, my lord, what did you say to my girl?"

Langley struggled not to reveal his dislike of Maria Tomlinson's parent. He did not understand his attempt to force her into an unwelcome alliance. Damn it all. Arranged marriages were not as fashionable as they had been when his parents were young. Today, most ladies and gentlemen anticipated a happy marriage. Some even believed they should marry for love. Yet, he should not condemn Tomlinson. His own father had tried to make him wed without the least regard for his wishes.

"Will you not be seated, Miss Tomlinson?" he asked, aware that she shivered, and not only because the sun had retreated behind a bank of grey clouds.

Miss Tomlinson seated herself.

"Well, my lord?" the manufacturer sat opposite his daughter. "I'm still waiting for you to tell me what you said to my girl."

"Messieurs, Madame. May I have your order?" a boy asked.

The Tomlinsons ignored him so Langley ordered a pot of coffee.

"Father." The unfortunate girl did not look at her angry parent. "I am unhappy. Please take me back to England."

He shook his head. "I don't understand you, Maria. You have more than most young ladies ever dream of. Whether you like it or not, I've the right to demand an explanation. You can't be too careful of your reputation. If you ruin your good name, no decent man—let alone a peer of the realm—will wed you. If the gossips spread the word that you and Viscount Langley embraced in the park, I'll insist the pair of you make a match."

Langley sat between the Tomlinsons. The boy returned to ask if they wished to order croissants. "Yes," Langley replied to be rid of the youngster. He scrutinised the manufacturer. "Mister Tomlinson, please believe me when I say I have not ruined your daughter's reputation. No one will gossip about us, but if they did, I would do my best to ensure your daughter's name remained unsullied." There, he had given Miss Tomlinson an opportunity to confess to her father.

"Father, you have always been the kindest parent imaginable. Can't you understand I am miserable living with grandmere?"

"Yes, for she's a disagreeable woman." Like a piece of crumpled paper, Mr Tomlinson's face creased in a multitude of fine lines, making him appear older than his fifty or more years. "All I've ever wanted is the best for you. Moreover, I'm sure your mother would have wanted you to marry a born gentleman."

"Why do you want me to? You are not a member of the ton. But Mamma married you although she knew her equals would condemn her for doing so."

"It is why I want you to make a splendid match. I want you to have the position which would have been your ma's had she not married me."

"But—"

"No more, Maria," Mister Tomlinson interrupted. He glared. "My lord, I'll see what your commanding officer has to say when I tell him you refuse to marry my girl."

Langley tensed. "Don't attempt to blackmail me."

At the word blackmail, even the plume on Miss Tomlinson's hat quivered.

They remained silent while the boy placed their order on the table.

"Coffee, Father?"

Mr Tomlinson nodded, his face still an unnatural shade of red.

Langley pitied the young woman, whose hands trembled too much for her to pour the drink. Yet, how dare the ill-mannered man threaten him? "Mister Tomlinson, you may say whatever you wish to my commanding officer, General Makelyn. I think you will find out that he is too preoccupied to have time to consider my conduct toward your daughter." His sense of humour almost caused him to chuckle, as he imagined the haughty reception Tomlinson would receive from Makelyn, whose demeanour varied from affability to being extremely high in the instep.

The manufacturer's eyes narrowed. "Makelyn, eh, I'll see what he has to say. For now, all I can think is that your father must regret the day your mother gave birth to so disobedient a son."

Langley ignored the insult. "You must excuse me, Miss Tomlinson, Mister Tomlinson. Duty beckons." While he marched away, he castigated himself for having agreed to rendezvous with Miss Tomlinson.

* * * *

Maria spilled some coffee onto the table before her hands stilled enough for her to fill a cup for her father, who glowered as he watched Langley march out of sight.

Father was much angrier with her than he had ever been before. If only she dared to confide in him. Tears welled up in her eyes.

Nauseous at the prospect of his outraged reaction if she mentioned those foolish letters, she quailed. His suspicious mind would refuse to accept she was only guilty of folly. He would suspect she allowed Midhurst to take liberties with her person. To father, black was black, and white was white. To him, grey did not exist. Without doubt, he would not believe she was not guilty of impropriety. He would never pardon her. His interpretation of Christianity was an unforgiving one.

Her head ached. What a wretched situation. She should be able to confide in the father who loved her more than anyone or anything else in the world. Thank God for Miss Whitley and Lord Langley's tolerance. They neither ranted nor raved, as Father would if he knew about the sorry business with Mister Midhurst. The sun emerged from behind the bank of clouds and cast a ray of brilliant light over the wooden table. No matter how shocking, she could only do one thing regardless of the consequences.

Father looked at her over the rim of his coffee cup. "Maria, I don't have the words to explain how disappointed I am."

"I know, but you don't need to repeat yourself." Sorry for him because she could neither fulfil his ambition nor accept his rigid beliefs, she reached out to clasp his hand.

He scowled and tugged his hand away. "I know what's fitting for you, my girl. It is improper for you to be in any gentleman's arms in public, or private, before you're married.

Until I wed your mother, I respected her too much to take advantage of her innocence by so much as a kiss. It's wrong of the viscount to take advantage of you."

"There is nothing I can say," Maria thought, "for he will deliberately misunderstand me unless I tell him the odious Mister Midhurst is blackmailing me. If only Father had remarried, he would not be a lonely, well-meaning man, who showers me with love, and places the burden of his expectations upon me." Maria shut her eyes. She would welcome a kind step-mother; one she could turn to for advice.

"Look at me, Maria."

Apprehensive, she glanced across the small table for a few moments.

"If you ever shame me again with wanton conduct, I'll disinherit you and disown you."

Now, she knew she could never tell him about Mister Midhurst. Maria sighed.

"I mean it." He shook his clenched fist at her. "I would cast you out of my house with only the clothes on your back."

Maria gasped. Would he really do so? Could he be so hard-hearted? She covered her face with her hands. Suppose he meant it. How would he react if those letters were published? With extreme care, she put down her cup. From somewhere deep within, she summoned previously unsuspected strength. "I love you, so I would never deliberately do anything to make you ashamed of me. You misjudged what you witnessed. For once and for all, please understand, the viscount and I are not romantically attached. I flung myself into his arms because I am miserable."

She knew what she must do in order to be happy. So be it if Father cut her off without a penny.

Chapter Eighteen
20th April, 1815

Helen broke the wax seal on a letter from England written in an unfamiliar hand. Before she could read it, two of the gentlemen who had danced with her on the previous evening, arrived to pay their respects.

Seated with Georgianne in the spacious salon, Helen forced herself to ignore the letter while she conversed with Lord Omerod's younger son and Captain, Lord Avery, both of them well-turned out in rifleman's green. They bowed after the fifteen minutes customary for morning calls.

"Must forgive me, ladies, if I am too engaged to call on you in the near future," Lord Avery said.

Helen shuddered, unable to imagine these fresh-faced young men, who were untried on the battlefield, marching with great enthusiasm to confront the Corsican monster's army. "You are forgiven. I look forward to dancing with both of you again when time permits." She forced herself to speak cheerfully in spite of her dry mouth. Not for a moment did she believe war might be averted.

After they left the salon, Chivers entered. He held out a silver salver to Helen on which there were a number of cards and a letter. Most of the officers she danced with at the ball were too busy to pay morning calls so, in accordance with protocol, they sent their cards. Not to do so would have been considered a breach of courtesy. Helen fingered them. Society's unwritten rules seemed trivial while the Duke made preparations for confrontation with his opponent on the battlefield.

She laid the cards aside and opened the letter.

"Who is it from?" Georgianne asked.

"A moment, if you please, while I decipher the signature."

She scanned the closely written lines. Hesitant, she looked up. "It is from Captain Dalrymple's mother. How nice she is. Mrs Dalrymple writes that because her son wants to marry me, she is sure she will love me. She also assures me that she looks forward to welcoming me into her family. Oh, it seems she takes it for granted that I will wed the captain."

Somewhat flustered, Helen looked at Georgianne, who put down her sewing, a tiny white muslin gown. She turned her attention back to the letter. "Mrs Dalrymple has also written to her son." She sighed. "At the moment, he is not in Brussels." After a moment's hesitation, she added, "When he returns, do you think he will propose?"

"Yes, dearest."

"He is not my only suitor," Helen murmured. She still wished Langley would court her. Somehow or other she could not imagine marrying anyone else, yet she needed to be a wife instead of an unmarried girl dependent on relatives.

Georgianne smoothed the little garment over her knee.

Helen's habitual calm deserted her. She stood, heedless of the letter which fell to the floor. Agitated, she stalked around the room. "What should I do?"

"There can be no objection to Captain Dalrymple who, it seems, loves you."

"Yes, I think he does." Helen flung herself down onto the chaise longue so hard the gilt legs creaked.

Georgianne threaded a needle. "Did Mrs Dalrymple mention her husband in the letter?"

Helen picked up the letter and perused it. "Yes, she writes that he is looking forward to meeting me. She also explains my marriage settlement is generous. Oh dear, what has Captain Dalrymple told them? They really do assume we shall marry."

"Is there any reason why you should not?"

"Yes. I don't love him."

"Believe me," Georgianne said, her eyes soft, "it is possible to learn to love a husband after marriage."

"Even if one loves someone else?"

Georgianne cut the thread with scissors. "I am sure widows learn to love again. If they can, so can you."

The word 'widows' seemed to hang in the still air. Georgianne must be afraid Cousin Tarrant would not survive. Helen decided it would be tactless to acknowledge her sister's fear. She stood. "Thank you for your good advice."

"Where are you going, dearest?"

"I don't think any more visitors will call this morning, so I shall see how the work for the ball is progressing. Everything needs to be ready in good time."

* * * *

Accompanied by Pringle, Helen descended the stairs to the basement where artists were busy painting the backdrop, wooden shapes of elephants, tigers, peacocks and Krishna, the blue boy.

She paused to watch the artists add jewel bright colour to the elephant's painted howdahs and smiled. The effect in the ballroom would be impressive.

Careless of her pretty sprigged muslin gown, Helen ignored Pringle's remonstrance as she picked up a paint pot and brush, approached one of the elephants and began to edge with gold the tear-shaped decoration which extended from the forehead to the top of the trunk. Soothed by the work, she allowed Pringle to help her into an apron. The paint glinted in the light of many candles. Only a few more brush strokes before this elephant would be finished. She stepped back to view it. Magnificent. She hoped the guests at the ball would be swept into the mysterious world of India.

A footman stepped into the cellar. "Nuncheon is served," he announced.

Helen passed the brush to one of the artists. "Please clean this." She turned to allow Pringle to untie the apron strings. Conscious of hunger, she hurried to the small dining room to sit opposite Georgianne.

A footman entered the room and spoke to Chivers. "I beg your pardon, Madam," the butler began, "Miss Tomlinson begs for a word with Miss Whitley."

"You may ask her to join us," Georgianne replied.

Chivers inclined his head. "Please forgive my presumption, madam, but I think I should tell you that the young lady is agitated."

When Maria joined them, a casual admirer might have praised her beautifully cut, pale yellow pelisse, worn over a crisp white cambric gown, and her straw hat ornamented with artificial primroses. However, all too aware of the wild expression in Maria's reddened eyes, Helen knew she was distraught.

"Mrs Tarrant, Miss Whitley, I apologise for my intrusion. It is good of you to receive me. Indeed, I am sorry to disturb you but I must speak to Miss Whitley."

"You are welcome, Miss Tomlinson," Georgianne gestured toward the table. "Please be seated. Some wine? A sandwich, or bread and cheese and some of Cook's excellent pickled vegetables?"

Maria sat next to Helen at the circular table. "A glass of wine, if it is not too much trouble."

"Are you well?" Georgianne asked. "Your cheeks are flushed. I hope you are not feverish."

Her guest fidgeted on the chair. "Yes, yes, quite well, thank you."

Helen picked up the plate of ham sandwiches. She held it out toward the young woman. "Some food might bring the colour back into your cheeks. Do have one."

"Thank you." Maria's eyes glistened with unshed tears.

Helen looked at her with sympathy. "Something has upset you,"

Maria nodded.

"There is nothing you cannot say to either of us. We are not gossips." Helen sighed, weary of the burden of the young woman's secrets.

Words tumbled from Maria. Helen stiffened when she described embracing Langley.

"All I want," the overwrought manufacturer's daughter ended, "is to return to England. Even if Mister Midhurst publishes those wretched letters, there is someone who will understand I am only guilty of naivety."

Georgianne nodded. "Good."

"Thank you, Mrs Tarrant."

A small crease appeared between Georgianne's eyebrows. "I hope Langley will retrieve them. If he does not, I advise you not to be foolish."

Maria looked down at her sandwich. "I assure you I shall be neither unwise nor imprudent."

The bright colour in Maria's cheeks subsided. She seemed less agitated.

Maria stood. "Mrs Tarrant, thank you for listening to my sorry tale. Miss Whitley, thank you for all your help." She bobbed a curtsey to Georgianne. "I must go."

"Well!" Georgianne exclaimed, after Maria left the dining room, "who could have guessed she would be embroiled in such a horrid tangle, one into which she has dragged you?"

Helen shook her head. "I could neither ignore her, when I found her in tears in the ladies withdrawing room, nor refuse to help her after she confided in me."

Georgianne chuckled. "Poor Langley, for the second time, he has been discovered with a young lady in his arms, by an outraged relative who expects him to propose marriage."

"You are heartless," Helen teased, and then every trace of amusement left her. Langley's father, the profligate earl, and Mister Tomlinson, the brash manufacturer, would be delighted if Maria married Langley.

* * * *

Helen reclined on a chaise longue in her small parlour, decorated in shades of pearl-grey paint and lilac wallpaper enhanced with small, gold-embossed lilies. She gazed at the wall on

247

which hung some of her sketches, which included one of Captain Dalrymple and another of Langley. Two handsome men, the former with the bloom of youth revealed on his rounded cheeks, the other a lean, battle-hardened officer ten years her senior.

Eyes closed, she visualised Langley, who exuded…what? Ladies were drawn to him, obviously appreciative of a gentleman who stood a head taller than most men, spoke confidently, and walked with natural grace. Helen ruffled the lilac-coloured velvet which covered the chaise longue. She longed for the right to run her fingers through Langley's blue-black hair.

Helen scrutinised her sketch of Langley. Had she flattered him? No, she had captured his sculpted cheekbones, square jawline and well-formed mouth. What would his kisses be like? Why did she burn to find out? Why did he disturb her dreams and much of her days?

Did Langley want to marry her? She believed he did. Sometimes, when off guard, he watched her like a famished man. She took deep breaths. If only his pride did not stand between them. She frowned. In spite of Mister Barnet's explanation, if Langley loved her, surely nothing should prevent him from making her his wife. If only she could marry him, she would be prepared to suffer any vicissitudes. Yet perhaps her belief that he loved her was an illusion.

Once again, she closed her eyes for fear she would cry. Tears would not help. Her attention turned to her sketch of Captain Dalrymple, a gentleman with hair as black as Langley's, a face in which the cheekbones were not so sharply carved, and slightly fuller lips with dimples on either side of them. She could not imagine being kissed by the young captain. Yet she really did like him, appreciated his consideration, gentle nature and kindness. When he proposed marriage to her, what would she answer?

Chapter Nineteen
25th April, 1815

Thunderous knocks sounded on the front door. Startled from sleep, Helen sat up. What was so urgent? Was Cousin Tarrant safe? She swung her legs over the side of the bed, and then made her way to the window to loop back the curtain.

Yesterday evening's harvest moon had yielded to the sun, but was still low on the horizon framed by dawn's delicate colours. She turned. While her eyes adjusted to the change of light, she squinted at the clock on the mantelpiece. Six o'clock. Dear God in heaven, if bad news about Cousin Tarrant had arrived, what effect would it have on Georgianne and her unborn child? She hurried across the bedchamber to snatch up her dressing gown from the end of the bed. The sleeves would not fit over her nightclothes. Fingers made clumsy by anxiety, she untied the ribbons which fastened her night jacket and slipped off the garment. Impatient, she pulled on her silk dressing gown, twitched the lavish lace trimming into place and adjusted her frilled nightcap.

Regardless of the impropriety of appearing downstairs in her night clothes, she hurried to the hall where her sister—also attired in her nightgown and dressing gown—Chivers and several tall, strong footmen had gathered. A series of more insistent knocks sounded.

Chivers, who seemed unconscious that his knitted nightcap shaped like a jelly bag detracted from his usual dignity, nodded at a footman, who opened the door.

Mister Tomlinson erupted into the hall like molten lava sweeping everything before it. Hatless, hair disordered, face red as fire, he glared at them. "Where is she? Where is my girl?"

Georgianne squared her shoulders. "Your daughter? I have no knowledge of her whereabouts."

Mister Tomlinson continued to glare at Georgianne. "Since she visited this house, neither her grandmother nor I have seen Maria."

Although he stood no more than five feet six inches tall, the high heels of the burly manufacturer's fashionable black leather shoes made him seem taller. He towered above Georgianne, who stepped back. "I repeat, we don't know where your daughter is."

Mister Tomlinson raised his fist.

Georgianne gasped, her hands cupping her stomach.

"How dare you threaten my sister" Helen shouted.

"Simon, Colin, seize him," Chivers ordered two of the footmen.

"No need for that." The distraught father lowered his fist, a shocked expression on his face. "Hit your sister, Miss Whitley?" He scrutinised Georgianne, whose face had turned deadly pale. "No, lass, for as long as I've lived, I've never struck a female. What's more, I'd never strike a pregnant one."

The ill-bred man's blunt description of her sister's condition horrified Helen. Polite society delicately referred to pregnancy as 'increasing' or by the biblical term, 'with child'.

Her sister swayed. Surely Georgianne's sensibilities were not so fine that, in response to Mister Tomlinson's crude announcement, she would faint for the second time in her life.

Georgianne fingered the button at the throat of her nightgown. "H...how did you..." she began.

"Know you're expecting a baby?" Georgianne nodded. "My dear wife, may God rest her soul in peace, cupped her belly as you did when she expected Maria." He pulled free from the footmen. "A chair for Mrs Tarrant," he said to Chivers.

The butler and footmen seemed to be fixed to the spot by the unexpected news.

A smile appeared on Chivers' face. "An heir for the Tarrant family," he breathed.

"A chair, at once," Helen ordered.

"Some brandy for your mistress," Mister Tomlinson added

Georgianne shook her head. "No, I am quite well, thank you." She glanced at the manufacturer. Follow me, we shall talk in private. There is something you should know."

"Never tell me my Maria is with Lord Langley." The harsh lines of Mister Tomlinson's face relaxed.

"I doubt it." Georgianne led him and Helen into an ante-room situated on one side of the hall.

As composed as she would be if she wore a morning gown, Georgianne sat and gestured to Mister Tomlinson to do so.

Chivers instructed a footman to open the shutters and draw the curtain aside to admit daylight, while Simon fetched a candle from the hall which he used to light the kindling in the grate.

"You may go," Georgianne instructed her servants.

The door closed. "There is something you should know, Mister Tomlinson." Georgianne began. "Although my sister and Lord Langley were bound to secrecy by your daughter, I am not. To be frank, his lordship has done his utmost to rescue Miss Tomlinson from a Mister Midhurst, who is blackmailing her."

Mister Tomlinson's mouth gaped, while little by little Georgianne revealed the whole, sorry tale.

"Blackmail! By God, if that snake's harmed a hair on her head, I'll kill him."

Georgianne frowned. "Mister Tomlinson, you should be mortified."

"Why?" he asked.

"Your daughter feared you would not believe she was innocent of anything other than writing some ill-judged letters to Mister Midhurst." Georgianne paused to take a deep breath, as though she doubted she could make Mister Tomlinson comprehend. "Oh, what can I say to convince you that if you love your daughter, she should have been able to divulge anything to you, confident you would safeguard her?"

Mister Tomlinson sank onto a chair, pulled a handkerchief out of his pocket and mopped perspiration from his forehead. "Mrs Tarrant, I admit that if Maria had told me, I'd have been angry with her for writing indiscreet letters, but I'd not have doubted her virtue. Indeed, I would have protected her. If you tell me where my girl is, I'll deal with Midhurst."

"We don't know where she is." Helen separated each word as if she spoke to a person slow to understand even the simplest explanation.

"You befriended her, Miss Whitley. Surely you know where she might have gone?"

What could she say to make him believe neither she nor Georgianne were privy to the girl's whereabouts? Helen opened her mouth to answer. Mister Tomlinson forestalled her by slapping his knee. "Of course, my Maria said she does not like Brussels and asked me to take her home. Although I refused, she must have returned to England." His face creased. "Dear Lord, let her be safe."

Before either of them could respond, the door opened. Cousin Tarrant and Langley stepped into the room, the folds of their scarlet-lined cloaks swirling elegantly around their ankles.

At the sight of Georgianne and Helen, sitting opposite Mister Tomlinson and garbed in their night attire, their eyes widened.

Langley's gaze scorched Helen. Her cheeks so hot that she did not need to look in the mirror to know they were scarlet, Helen smoothed the ribbons of her nightcap.

"What is the meaning of this?" Cousin Tarrant demanded.

Mister Tomlinson, seemingly unaware of Cousin Tarrant's outrage, stepped forward to seize his hand. He pumped it up and down. "Congratulations, Major."

Tarrant pulled his gloved hand free from Mister Tomlinson. "For what?"

"Your wife's pregnancy."

The muscles around Cousin Tarrant's mouth twitched. His grey eyes were ice-cold. "Georgie! Is it true? Are you increasing?"

Georgianne nodded.

"Why didn't you tell me?" Without the slightest warning, Cousin Tarrant fainted.

Georgianne rushed across the room to kneel by her husband.

Mister Tomlinson's uproarious laugh rang out. "Stap me, I've never before seen a man drop unconscious to the ground when told he would be a father."

Helen looked at him with intense dislike. She tugged the bell rope. "Simon," she commenced when the footman answered the summons, "ask Pringle to bring my sal volatile as fast as she can."

Langley chuckled. "Who would have imagined my friend would be felled by such news?"

Georgianne's anxious expression reproached him.

"Please accept my apology for laughing," Langley said hastily, "and please accept my felicitations." He stepped toward Mister Tomlinson. "I suggest you take your leave."

"The letters? Have you got Maria's letters to Mister Midhurst?"

Langley raised an eyebrow. "Miss Whitley, if you broke Miss Tomlinson's confidence, an explanation is due."

"When Maria confided in Georgianne, she did not swear her to secrecy, so my sister told her father she is being blackmailed."

"Ah," Langley breathed. "One would have supposed the lady could have told her father the truth. It would have saved me a lot of trouble. To answer his question, besides Miss Tomlinson's letters, I have those of other unfortunates whom he blackmailed." He brushed his gloved hands together as though he removed dirt.

"I know you are almost penniless, how much do you want for them?" Mister Tomlinson asked.

Langley's hand shot out to throttle the man. At the last moment, he lowered it. "Mr Tomlinson! How dare you? Get out."

"Nay, lad, I didn't mean to insult you. I only intended to recompense you for the trouble you've been to on Maria's account."

"Out!" Langley exclaimed, his face a mask of fury.

Tomlinson stood. "Good day, Mrs Tarrant, Miss Whitley." He ignored Langley.

Pringle hurried into the ante-room and gave a tiny flask to Georgianne, who sat with her inert husband's head on her lap.

Georgianne removed the stopper. She wafted the flask beneath Cousin Tarrant's nostrils. Within seconds, he opened his eyes.

Langley held out his arm. "Come, Miss Whitley, I am sure my friend and his wife have much to say to each other."

She wanted to protest, to say she wanted to help Georgianne and Cousin Tarrant.

"Come," Langley repeated, this time in an authoritative tone of voice.

With uncharacteristic meekness, Helen allowed him to guide her to the salon where she sat. Still frightened because Cousin Tarrant fainted without the least warning, she did not pause to consider her words. "I neither understand why my sister refused to tell Cousin Tarrant she is with child, nor why he fainted."

"It is a long story which someone else should tell you." Langley smiled down at her. "A glass of wine, I think, or perhaps brandy to calm you." He opened a panel, papered to make it seem part of the wall, and selected a bottle from one of the concealed shelves. "Ah, cherry brandy for you, Miss Whitley. No, no, don't protest, I promise it will restore you."

She frowned. "Thank you, but I don't need it." Her eyes widened. "I want to know why Cousin Tarrant fainted."

"Yes, I know, there is no need for repetition." Langley closed her hand around the barley-twist stem of a glass.

The touch of his strong hand, with its long, slender fingers and well-shaped nails, sent quivers through her as she looked down; quivers almost as strong as those she experienced at the first sight of Langley when she considered him more handsome than the much admired Lord Byron. Now, when he removed his hand, she wanted to clutch it and ask him if he loved her.

"Drink up like a good little girl."

Her hand shook. Although brandy spilled onto the expensive Brussels lace, which edged her sleeve, she paid no attention to the stain. "Don't insult me! I am not a small child."

* * * *

Langley eyed Helen from the tips of her slippers to the button at the throat of her nightgown. Although her nightclothes revealed far less of her than any of her fashionable gowns worn at balls, against his will, he imagined their marriage bed, in which he divested her of them and introduced her to the pleasures of the flesh. "I am well aware that you are not a small child. May I suggest you finish your brandy then attend to your déshabillé.

They stared into each other's eyes until Langley shook his head and looked away.

"I must go, Miss Whitley."

"Please stay for a moment, my lord. I want to know why Cousin Tarrant fainted," she repeated.

"Yes, but it is not for me to tell you."

For the second time that day loud knocks sounded.

"Have we not had enough to endure today without a visitor?" Helen asked.

"If I am not mistaken, either Mister Tomlinson has returned, or Miss Tomlinson is about to seek your help."

Her eyes widened. "I hope not, for I think her father would be prepared to commit murder if he discovered Maria in this house."

He laughed. "Good day, to you, Miss Whitley."

Before he could reach the door, Chivers, now attired in a black coat and pantaloons, white shirt and black waistcoat, opened it. "Miss Tomlinson apologises for calling upon Miss Whitley at such an early hour. She asks if she will receive her." His expression blank, Chivers added, "Miss Tomlinson's baggage is in the hall and so is her dresser. Should I have a bedchamber prepared while Mrs Tarrant is preoccupied with the Major?"

"Yes. Conduct Miss Tomlinson to my parlour, then have her luggage removed to a bedchamber."

Langley turned around. "Miss Whitley, please give my regards to Mrs Tarrant. Good day to you."

Chapter Twenty
25th April, 1815

Without a backward glance at the imposing mansion, Langley took the reins from the groom. The viscount mounted, settled on the saddle of his well-schooled black gelding, and then patted the powerful animal's glossy neck.

A wagon pulled by Percherons approached from the opposite direction. When it drew level, the burly driver muttered an imprecation. Presumably another French sympathiser who resented the British army of occupation. In the face of such hostility, now that Rupes knew about Georgianne's condition, maybe he would send her back to England with Helen.

Struth, never had he found Helen more desirable than when he saw her in her night attire. He did not know why. Feminine fashion with high waistlines and low necklines revealed more of Helen's figure than her nightgown and dressing gown. A bolt of desire shot through him at the thought of Helen's wealth of thick brown hair, which followed the line of her spine in a sinuous plait reminiscent of the snake that tempted Eve. He longed to remove her night cap, loosen her hair and run his fingers through it. Yet he desired far more than physical contact with her.

Langley wanted Helen's daily companionship. He wanted to ride with her and sit before a fire on long winter evenings where they could read aloud to each other. He wanted to converse, flirt, and with pride, introduce her to friends and neighbours. Curse his situation which prevented him from asking her to be his wife. His bitter laugh rang out in the quiet street. What accounted for an experienced soldier of his age losing his heart to a lady so much younger? Even if Papa had not squandered his fortune, he would still consider her an unsuitable wife for a viscount.

He clicked his teeth as he rode toward headquarters. Should he have answered Helen's questions? Did she know Rupes had been betrothed to Dolores, a modest Spanish lady, who was raped by French soldiers? Nine months later, when Tarrant seized an opportunity to visit her, he listened to Dolores' anguished screams until death silenced her after she delivered a stillborn baby.

Despite Tarrant's happy marriage to Georgianne, and although he had only spoken once about the ordeal, Langley did not doubt gentle Dolores' agony still haunted Tarrant. No, it was not for him to explain to Helen, an innocent young lady, why Tarrant had collapsed when he found out Georgianne was with child. Uncomfortable with his thoughts, he spurred his horse forward.

* * * *

"I should have been the first to know," Tarrant said. His back turned to Georgianne, he stared out of the window of the small anteroom. "It is beyond tolerance for Tomlinson to have informed me you are with child."

Georgianne's slippers made almost no sound on the carpet as she hurried to him. She wrapped her arms around his waist and pressed her head against his back. What should she say to her furious husband? She understood both his humiliation—because he had fainted—and his outrage at Tomlinson's unintentional blunder.

Their marriage had not been consummated for a long time due to Tarrant's fear that, like Dolores, she might lose her life during childbirth. Only when he realised her mother, his late mother, and his step-mother had delivered healthy children, had he shared Georgianne's bed. Now, with the news of her pregnancy, his horror of childbirth had returned.

"Let go of me." Tarrant turned around. The expression in his eyes hard, he stared down at her. "Why didn't you tell me?"

Although he had never before spoken to her in such a harsh tone or looked at her with such coldness, she would not allow him to intimidate her. "I did not tell you for two reasons. The first is because Dolores' death scarred you. The second is because a confrontation with Napoleon is inevitable, and I did not want your judgement to be impaired."

Tarrant's jaw tightened. "You consider me a coward." He accused her, through tight, almost bloodless lips.

"You know that is not true." Vexed by his wilful misinterpretation of her words, Georgianne almost lost her temper. "I know you are a courageous officer." She took a deep breath to calm herself. "We all have fears we think we have buried, but they re-emerge when something brings them back to mind. Then we realise our worst apprehensions are foolish because nothing may come of them."

Her husband stared at some point past her head. "So?"

"You are too busy to be burdened with worry about me. I am in the best of health and no longer retch every morning." She was glad his duties had kept him away from her too often for him to have become aware of that. "There is no reason why you should not meet your son or daughter in November." A tremor ran through her, for no reason other than the danger of childbirth for even the healthiest women.

He transferred his gaze to her. "Don't humour me. I am not a child."

Tears filled her eyes. Even if he did not mean it, why could he not congratulate her; tell her he looked forward to their baby's arrival? "I am not 'humouring' you by saying I am well. Even if you don't want our child, I hope to have a son with your kind heart who looks like you."

On the rare occasions when he realised she would cry, Tarrant was always shocked and comforted her. Today, absorbed by his reaction to her condition, he continued to glare down at her.

He should be pleased. An unexpected rush of love, mingled with pity, seized her. She reached up to cradle his cheeks with her hands. "God has given us the gift of a child. Can you not be happy? Imagine the joy of being parents, of meeting our baby?"

He shook his head. "I can only envisage the pain of losing you."

Her patience seemed futile. "Don't you know I am terrified of losing you, either in a skirmish or on the battlefield? Do I burden you with my fears? No, I don't. How can you be so selfish? Do you think I want to die, want our child to die? You should congratulate me and take pride in the knowledge that we will have a child to love as much as we love each other."

"Georgie, I—"

"No, if you have nothing to say which I want to hear, please be silent." She turned around to leave the room.

Tarrant moved swiftly to block her way. "I am sorry. Please forgive me."

To her astonishment, he knelt. His arms around her, he pressed his forehead against her stomach. "Hello, little one, I am your father." He looked up, his eyes moist. "There," he said, his voice shaky, "I have introduced myself to our daughter."

"Daughter?"

"I hope so. I would like to have a little girl who is as like you as a proverbial pea in a pod, with all of your admirable qualities." He stood and enfolded her in his arms. "I shall not lie. Although I am still frightened, I am glad we will have a child." He kissed the top of her head. "Perhaps I should send you and Helen to England, where you, your precious cargo and your sister, will be safe."

"How dare you, sir, our baby is not cargo." She smiled up at him. "As for going to England, you would have to tie me up and drag me aboard ship because I will never consent to be separated from you."

"Heart of my heart, I admit I would be sorry to be parted from you." His grey eyes soft, he gazed into hers for a moment before he kissed her.

* * * *

Helen entered her small parlour in which Maria sat straight-backed, her gloved hands clutching the arm of the chair. After a single glance at her guest, she rang the hand bell.

The door between the parlour and her bedchamber opened. Pringle bobbed a curtsey. "You rang, Miss?"

Helen nodded at her dresser while addressing Maria. "I think you need a restorative. Would you prefer coffee or tea, or perhaps a glass of wine or cherry brandy?"

"Thank you, some coffee would be welcome." Maria's eyes seemed larger than usual in her pale face.

"I think you would be more comfortable if you take off your hat and pelisse. Pringle, please assist Miss Tomlinson."

Maria remained seated. "No, I don't want to be an inconvenience."

Helen restrained a sigh. If Maria did not want to be one, why had she come here? "Allow me." She removed her guest's hat and put it on the small table beside Maria's chair. "Take off your gloves." She spoke as patiently as she would to a stricken child.

Maria gave them to Pringle, who put the pair next to the hat. "Now, Miss," Pringle said, "please stand so I can help you take off your pelisse."

As though Maria feared her legs would not support her, she gripped both arms of the chair to push herself up. Pringle eased her out of her mustard-yellow, sarcenet pelisse. She folded it neatly, put it over her arm and sniffed loudly.

Irritated, Helen frowned.   Although servants were expected to be humble, they found ways to express their disapproval.

"Pringle, you may take Miss Tomlinson's hat, gloves and pelisse to her bedchamber. Also, arrange for coffee to be served immediately."

The dresser sniffed again before she left the parlour.

Helen glared at the closed door. Did the woman's nose never become sore? Later she would order her to stop the habit.

"Miss Whitley," Maria began in a soft tone of voice, "I cannot imagine what you must think of me."

Helen sympathised with Maria, and her father's total lack of consideration for his daughter's wishes.

"Miss Whitley, you are my only friend, so I could not think of where else I could claim sanctuary."

Sanctuary? Should she explain she was dependant on Cousin Tarrant, and she did not know if he would object to Maria's arrival with the expectation of being accommodated?

"Miss Whitley, I hope you don't despise me because I could not tolerate my situation."

"No I do not. I think you are brave, but don't you have some regrets?"

Maria stood, this time without the assistance of the arms of the chair. She paced backward and forward. "Yes, of course I do. I love Father, although his mind is so fixed on what he desires for me that he is incapable of accepting the idea that it would make me miserable." She stood still and faced Helen. "I have tried to make him understand. He cannot. So I dare not name the gentleman I love, who asked me to marry him. I have accepted his offer. In two or three days, I shall meet him at the pavilion in the Parc Royale. We shall elope.

In the meantime, I don't want Father to know where I am."

At the mention of her husband-to-be, the glow in Maria's eyes and the tender smile curving her mouth softened her face in a manner Helen could not put into words. She hoped to capture Maria's expression in a painting.

"Father would say Philippe—"

"The man you love is a Roman Catholic? A Frenchman?"

"No, his family are Huguenots who fled France and settled in England a century or more ago. Father would say Philippe wants to marry me for my fortune. It is not true. He owns a small but beautiful estate, and his business prospers." Some colour returned to her cheeks. "I never knew my mother, and know little about her other than Grandmere never forgave her for making a mésalliance. Father still mourns her loss, so it is too painful for him to speak of her. Yet I know one thing, Mamma married for love in spite of grandmere's fierce opposition. I believe Mamma would have sympathised with me and been happy for me."

Helen swallowed. Maria's love for Philippe shone in her eyes and the tender expression on her face.   Unbidden, unwelcome jealousy bubbled up from within because fortune had smiled on Maria.

"Miss Whitley…"

"No need for such formality." Helen forced herself to smile. "We agreed to address each other by our Christian names."

"You are very kind and—" she broke off when Pringle entered the parlour, followed by a maid carrying a tray.

Helen decided to ask Tarrant if Maria could stay with them until Philippe arrived in Brussels, but then changed her mind. The servants would be sure to gossip. News of Maria's presence in Cousin Tarrant's house might reach either Mister Tomlinson or his mother-in-law.

Helen dismissed Pringle and the other servants and poured coffee for Maria from the silver coffee pot.

"We must decide what to do. I think it would be unwise for you to stay here for more than a night, because your father might find out where you are."

Maria's hand trembled. Coffee spilled onto her gown. "Oh, no, Grandmere will be furious with me. She often chastises me for my clumsiness. "'Pon my word, I doubt the stain can be removed." Her forehead creased. "Let me think. Maybe, it should be sponged with the finest laundry soap, dissolved with spirit of wine and potash, then spread on grass and sprinkled with alum water. After three or four days it should be washed again with soap and fuller's earth, or maybe—"

"Why fret over the stain or your grandmother's temper and unkindness now that you are on the verge of marriage?" Helen interrupted. She was surprised by Maria's knowledge of how to launder clothes, something with which she had never concerned herself. She frowned.

Maria clapped her hands. "How foolish of me, within the week I shall be wed and free from Grandmere's criticisms." She stood and shook out her skirt. "Mind you, Miss...I mean, Helen, I should thank her for one thing. I wonder what Philippe will think of my improved appearance."

"I am sure he will admire you," Helen murmured. "Your figure has improved; you have beautiful hair, which I think waves without resort to artifice." She smiled. "I am sure many ladies envy your large eyes and long eyelashes and your perfect complexion."

"Thank you. At home my skin was not so fair. Although Father did not consider gardening a proper occupation for a lady, I enjoyed sowing seeds and tending plants. However, I took Grandmere's advice to wash my face with milk before applying cucumber pomade" Her eyes widened. "That does not matter now, for by birth, I am not a lady, so I am sure Philippe does not care if my complexion is a little darkened by the sun. And I am sure he will allow me to garden and have a glass house, for he is interested in horticulture."

Again jealousy, combined with pity, warred within Helen. According to Maria's description of Philippe, it seemed she would be happy with him. As for Mister Tomlinson, he was convinced his opinions were always right. Although he provided a luxurious cage for his daughter, Maria's wish to break the lock did not surprise Helen. She stilled her mind, which envisioned a painting of a beautiful young woman surrounded by luxury, with a key in her hand, staring at a prison door. "Maria, please sit down, while we decide what to do.

"I shall pen a note to Mister Barnet, an elderly friend of mine. With your permission, I will explain your circumstances and ask him to put you up until Monsieur Philippe arrives. If he sends his carriage for you, none of Cousin Tarrant's servants will know where you have gone."

Maria finished her coffee. "Do you think your friend will agree to your request?"

Helen nodded. "Yes, he is very kind-hearted."

"How can I thank you for your help?"

"There is no need," Helen replied, ashamed of her jealousy. On Sunday, at the English Church, acceptance of whatever situation the Almighty placed His servants in had been the subject of the vicar's sermon. Her envy made it almost impossible to speak. She found it intolerable to submit to the end of her dream of marrying Langley.

A knock on the door heralded Pringle's return.

The woman bobbed a curtsey. "Lord Langley is waiting for you and Miss Tomlinson in the salon."

If only he had not arrived at the moment when her conscience strangled her.

Maria glanced down at her skirt. "I must change my gown."

"Yes, of course, Pringle can show you the way to your bedchamber. In the meantime, I shall wait with Lord Langley for you to join us." The rare opportunity to be alone with him delighted her.

Chapter Twenty-One

25th April, 1815

Helen entered the salon where Langley stood in front of the fireplace, a glass of ruby-red wine in his hand.

"My lord, I did not expect to see you so soon."

Langley bowed. "I should not be here. My excuse is, before I carry out my orders to go to Courtrai with a troop of Glory Boys, I want to be rid of the sorry business of Miss Tomlinson's letters to Mister Midhurst."

"Take care," she said with more depth of emotion than she intended.

"I shall. Don't be concerned for me. Enjoy all that society in Brussels has to offer a young lady."

She would think of him while he was away.

"May I see Miss Tomlinson? I have little time to spare."

Alarm fluttered in her throat. "It seems your mission is urgent." The daughter, sister, and sister-in-law of military men, she knew better than to question him about it.

"I would neither describe it as a mission nor as urgent, however General Makelyn is not a patient man. He expects his aide de camps to carry out his orders without even the slightest delay."

"Yes, of course," she murmured, "but I think it will take her some time to change her gown."

"Then I must bid you good day. I shall leave her letters to Midhurst with you." He held out a small package tied with string.

"She will be so grateful. Please tell me how you obtained them?"

"Part of The Glory Boys duty is to gather information. After my sergeant found out where the blackmailer lived, we broke into his lodgings. Midhurst must have been certain no one would discover his whereabouts, as the letters were not well-hidden. My sergeant smashed the lock on a trunk and there they were."

Helen laughed.

"What is funny?"

"I can imagine the look on abominable Midhurst's face when he realises someone has stolen the letters. Are you sure you cannot wait to give them to Miss Tomlinson yourself?" She held out the package but he did not take it back.

"Before I go, please tell me why she came here."

"She plans to elope."

Langley raised his eyebrows. "What! Good Lord, how improper. I should inform her father."

"No." She prepared to launch into an explanation of Maria's reason before she realised Langley seemed amused.

"Miss Whitley, the young lady continues to amaze me, but I confess I am grateful not to be obliged to have any further dealings with her."

"I daresay you are, but Miss Tomlinson still needs my help. She does not want her father to know she is here while waiting for her betrothed to arrive in Brussels. Yet, if she remains in this house the servants are sure to gossip, so in all probability, Mister Tomlinson will return once again to pound on the front door."

"I hope you will not ask me to house her elsewhere. The idea terrifies me. If her father found out, I fear he would either hold a gun to my head, or suffer a fatal seizure."

Helen stamped her foot. Alas, her slipper did not make a satisfactory sound on the carpet. "Please be serious, my lord. Such an idea never entered my mind. Mister Barnet's health has improved, so I shall ask him to put her up for a few days. What do you think of my plan?"

Langley stepped toward her. "I think anyone who has you for a friend is fortunate." His hands closed around her upper arms. "Despite everything which lies between us, I hope we shall always be friends."

Taken by surprise, tears filled her eyes. The proximity of battle made her bold. "Can we be no more than friends?"

His dark eyes searched hers. Slowly, very slowly, he shook his head. "No, circumstances forbid it." His hands slid down her arms to her wrists. He held them, oh so gently. "I shall wish you well if you marry Captain Dalrymple or some other worthy young man."

"How can you say so when I am sure you lo—"

Before she could complete the word, Langley pressed one finger against her mouth.

"Hush. There are some things we should never say to each other."

Why not be truthful for once? Captain Dalrymple would never cause her such pain. If she said she returned his affection, the captain would be delighted. Perhaps she did love Dalrymple in a different way to the one in which she loved Langley. Could it be possible to hold two gentlemen in equal regard? Should she fear the violence of her love for Langley and welcome the calm lagoon of Captain Dalrymple's?

Helen looked deep into Langley's eyes. Pride came to her rescue. "When you marry, I shall wish you well."

The door opened. Miss Tomlinson glanced at them. "I beg your pardon for disturbing you."

"No need," Helen answered hastily, "there is something in my eye which the Major is trying to remove."

Langley released her wrists and took the package. He turned around and held it out. "This is for you, Miss Tomlinson."

Maria hurried to him, nearly tripped over the edge of the carpet, steadied herself and seized the letters. "How can I ever thank you?"

Langley smiled. "By not writing any more incautious letters."

"Never," she promised.

Helen looked past Maria to Langley, who bowed. "I must take my leave of you both. Miss Whitley, Miss Tomlinson, good day to you."

* * * *

Helen knelt by the fireplace and struck a flint to ignite the kindling. A tiny flame flickered and spread. She added some small logs, then sat back on her heels watching them catch fire.

Maria untied the string around the package. One by one she fed the fire with her 'incautious' letters.

Helen used the poker to disperse the ash of Maria's dreams which had turned into nightmares. If only her own dreams would turn to ash and arise like a phoenix to become reality.

She stood looking at the rosy-cheeked bride-to-be whose eyes glowed. "So, Maria, you are free to marry your Philippe without fear of Mister Midhurst. I can imagine how relieved you must be." She hesitated. Maria seemed so certain she and her betrothed would be happy. Nevertheless, perhaps she should put the question which troubled her to the young woman. "Are you sure you are not about to make a mistake? How can you be certain the man you intend to marry will be a good husband?"

Maria plopped down onto a chair which creaked beneath her weight. "At school, his sister, Suzanne, and I were the best of friends. Father allowed me to visit her during the vacations so I have been acquainted with Philippe since the age of ten."

Helen sank onto a sofa. "Surely his family will be shocked by an elopement."

Maria shook her head. "His parents are dead. Suzanne is married. I think she will understand why we eloped."

What would it be like to run away with Langley in the whirlwind of his family's opposition? "Maria, I shall write a letter to my friend, Mister Barnet, to ask him to permit you to stay with him for a few days." She walked toward the door. "You must be tired. I suggest you rest until it is time to change before we dine, after which I hope Mister Barnet will send his carriage to convey you to his house."

* * * *

Helen sealed her letter to Mister Barnet, confident he would help. She pulled the bell rope to summon her dresser. She suspected Pringle gossiped about her to the other servants. On this occasion, she must caution the woman.

"Ah, Pringle," she said when the dresser entered the parlour.

"Yes, Miss."

Helen held out the letter. "Deliver this to Mister Barnet in person, immediately."

The woman sniffed. Slowly she put out her hand to take the letter.

"There is no need to mention this to anyone."

For once, Pringle did not sniff again. However, her light blue eyes gleamed with obvious curiosity. "I'm sure I don't know why I should speak of it, Miss."

"Good. And Pringle…"

"Yes, Miss."

"Summer is nearly here, so it is time to consider my wardrobe. There are a number of items I shall not wear again which I will give to you. For example, the muslin gown sprigged with lilac, the lilac pelisse, and the hat made to match."

Like most dressers, Pringle regarded cast-off clothes as one of her perquisites, which she could keep or sell.

"Thank you, Miss Whitley. You may be sure I shall not mention your letter to anyone."

"I am pleased to hear it. You may go," Helen spoke without the slightest sense of guilt for bribery. Sometimes she wished for Georgianne's permission to dismiss Pringle. Yet, it would be unfair to dispense with her dresser's service for no better reason than her sniffing when she disapproved of something, and her gossiping, a tendency common to most servants.

She gazed out the window. A troop of Glory Boys rode past the house, their horses curried until they gleamed like the finest satin. By now, Langley would be on his way to the border with France. Hot colour flooded her cheeks. After she had made it quite clear to Langley that she wanted to marry him, he had rejected her. Did he despise her forwardness? No, she would not think of him. It was too painful. She would go to the cellar to see whether some of the wooden figures were ready for her to add the last details.

Helen fetched a paint-spattered smock from her dressing room. With an image in mind of the blue boy, flute in hand, and a peacock feather in his thick, black, curly hair, she descended the narrow flight of stairs. "Splendid," she said to the three artists, "the elephants look so lifelike and Krishna is beautiful. Perhaps his eyes should be a little larger. In the book a friend lent me, they are described as shaped like lotus buds." She stepped closer to examine the blue boy's figure. "I think his lips should be redder."

In her imagination, Langley's gypsy-like eyes laughed and hovered at the back of her mind, yet somehow or other the blue boy almost eclipsed them, although she could not account for her fascination with him.

Helen began to paint the peacock feather. To grace Krishna's hair, she felt it must be perfect. She hummed until, within the hour, Pringle entered the cellar and held out a sealed letter.

"For you, Miss."

"Thank you. Please wait for a moment."

Helen laid aside her paint brush and stepped back. A perfect peacock feather. The colours glowed against the sheen of Krishna's painted black hair. She cleaned her hands and then read the letter. Mister Barnet had not failed her. He would be pleased to accommodate her friend and her friend's maid until alternative arrangements could be made for them. Helen smiled, for she had not considered it wise to tell him Maria planned to elope. His carriage would call for the lady this evening at nine of the clock. She went to her sister's parlour to tell her Maria would be leaving.

* * * *

"May I come in?" Helen asked Georgianne, who appeared comfortable on her chaise longue.

"Of course." Georgianne put a book on her lap.

"What are you reading?"

"I am re-reading Pride and Prejudice by an unknown lady. I wonder who the author is. For all we know, we may have met her and never guessed the sly creature wrote such an entertaining novel."

"Sly?"

"Yes, for I cannot imagine the characters are fabrications. Surely they are founded on people the lady is well-acquainted with. What do you think, dearest?"

Helen gazed at the realistic watercolours she had painted of her parents and sisters which hung on the walls. Yet some of her other portraits were born of her imagination. What had Shakespeare written in The Merchant of Venice? Ah, yes. "Tell me where is fancy bred? Or in the heart or in the head? How begot, how nourished." A question she could not answer. She only knew something within drove her to express both reality and imagination.

"Dearest?"

"I beg your pardon, Georgianne. Perhaps the lady's observations in her novel are merely based on the pride and prejudice she observes in society."

Georgianne clapped her hands. "How clever you are. Now, do sit down instead of towering above me."

"I beg your pardon." Helen sat by the window, in the clear daylight which intensified the colour of the aquamarine wallpaper echoed in the curtains and upholstery.

"I must say," Georgianne continued, "the characters seem to be alive. As for Mister Darcy, I had no patience with him until his true nature was revealed." She laughed. The expression on her face sobered. "I have found my own Mister Darcy, although my dear husband is nothing like him. I hope you will find yours and be as happy as I am, in spite of the threat which Bonaparte poses." She sighed. "If only one knew what the odious little man intends."

"Little in stature, but from all one hears, not in ambition," Helen replied. Ashamed—for she envied her sister—Helen relegated the thought to the back of her mind. "Why think of him now? Georgianne, I realised Cousin Tarrant might not wish for Maria to stay in his house, so I have arranged for Mister Barnet to accommodate her until her betrothed joins her."

Round-eyed, Georgianne regarded her for a moment. "Although I sympathise with Miss Tomlinson's situation, I am pleased to be rid of her. I would not care for the scandal of her elopement to be attached to my name." Her eyes grew even rounder. "Besides, it might damage your reputation; for your friendship with a manufacturer's daughter, no matter how wealthy her father is, has caused unfavourable comments."

Helen mulled over the gossip about herself and Captain Dalrymple which had angered Cousin Tarrant. Now there was criticism of her unsought for involvement in Maria's affairs. Perhaps she should draw a series of sketches called The Heiress' Progress. No, it would be too cruel. "I fear you and Cousin Tarrant find me a trial."

"Dearest, you could never be a burden, but Tarrant is aware that he must account for you to your guardian, so he never wants a whisper of scandal to attach itself to you."

"Cousin Tarrant is kind," Helen murmured with genuine appreciation. "I don't understand why you didn't tell him you are increasing. Why did he faint when Mister Tomlinson told him?"

"There are questions you should not ask because married people are entitled to privacy." Georgianne picked up Pride and Prejudice and snapped it shut.

"I beg your pardon." Helen could not help feeling resentful, for in the past she and Georgianne had not kept secrets from each other.

Her sister shifted position. "Where is Captain Dalrymple? He has not called on you for some time. Have you rejected him?"

"No, he wrote to me yesterday to explain he is very busy."

"He is a charming gentleman. I look forward to seeing him again."

Did her sister expect her to marry him? Should she ask her for advice? No, she did not want to be urged into a life she might regret. Helen stood. "I shall leave the two of you to rest."

"The two of us?"

"Yes, you and my niece or nephew." She looked forward to the baby's appearance in the world. Would he or she be dark-haired and blue-eyed like her sister, or have Tarrant's fair hair and grey eyes? If she married the captain, what would her children look like? Did she want to risk her life in childbirth? Fear coiled its way around her heart. Years ago, Helen witnessed a favourite mare birth a foal and guessed that the birth of a human was similar.

Of course, Mamma would have whipped her if she knew her gently-reared daughter had witnessed the scene. Moreover, she suspected that even her tolerant father would have been angry. Afraid for her sister, Helen wished she had remained ignorant.

Chapter Twenty-Two
20th April, 1815

In the garb of an English gentleman of moderate means, Langley rode out of Brussels on the orders of General Makelyn. A wig, a subtle application of powder and paint—the art of which he learnt from an actor—and pads in his cheeks to make them seem plumper, reduced his chance of being recognised.

Before long he passed ploughed fields and lush meadows, neat farmers' houses, barns, stables and plump cattle and flat landscape so different from Spain and Portugal where he and Rupes spent so many years spying in both town and country. He shook his head. Instead of thinking about the past, he must concentrate on his instructions to discover the whereabouts of one of Napoleon's pernicious spies, a merciless man who killed with no more compunction than a farmer's wife wringing a chicken's neck. He dismissed the ugly images.

Unbidden, Helen crept into his mind. Confound it! If only the last battle against Napoleon was won, he would be free to— what? In spite of money, which would be raised when the valuable contents of Longwood House were auctioned by Christies to pay his father's debts, he feared the sum would not be sufficient for him to marry Helen. He suppressed a groan.

It took every scrap of control he could muster not to admit to her that he loved her.

Helen would never know what it cost him to reject her overture when her soft, luminous eyes searched his, before she asked if they could be no more than friends. He could only guess how embarrassed she was when he denied his fervent desire to ask for her hand in marriage, and draw her into his arms to kiss her until they were breathless with desire. Her stricken expression when he told her he would stand her friend at her wedding to Captain Dalrymple, or some other gentleman, tore at his heartstrings, for she held them in her long-fingered artist's hands.

* * * *

Seated at her escritoire in the small parlour adjacent to her bedroom, Helen perused a note from an anxious Maria.

"There is no news of Monsieur Lamont who should have arrived two days ago. You can imagine," Maria wrote, "I am in great anxiety about my betrothed. Although Mister Barnet has been all that is kind, I would appreciate it if you would call on me as soon as possible, for he advises me to confide in my father and ask for his permission to marry Philippe. Mister Barnet is in poor health therefore I don't want to argue with him, but his advice is unacceptable.

If my husband-to-be does not arrive within the next three or four days, I don't know what to do, because I am reluctant to impose any longer on my host whom the doctor attends twice a day."

Helen stared across the road at the Parc Royale. She reproached herself for her neglect of Mister Barnet. In future, she would be more attentive.

After nuncheon Helen set out for the old gentleman's house, with Pringle in attendance. Halfway there, sunshine submitted to dull grey clouds. Drizzle fell, further dampening her low spirits, which she found almost impossible to conceal since Langley's visit. By the time Thomas opened the door of Mister Barnet's house, her clothes were damp.

Helen shivered and took off her pelisse. "I hope Mister Barnet's health has improved,"

"I'm sorry to say it hasn't," Thomas replied.

Greaves came forward from the other side of the large hall. "You may go, Thomas."

Helen turned her attention to the lugubrious man. "Please inform your master I am here."

"Doctor Longspring gave orders for Mister Barnet not to be disturbed," said Greaves, who could not be much younger than his employer.

Helen looked straight into the butler's eyes which were as cold as those of a dead fish. "Ask your master if he wishes to see me."

"Miss Whitley, perhaps you did not understand. Mister Barnet is in bed so it would be improper for you to visit him."

"Nonsense! On previous occasions, I have visited him in his bedchamber. I am certain your employer would be glad to see me." She stressed the words 'your employer' to remind Greaves that not even an upper servant had the right to make decisions for his master. "Please inform Miss Tomlinson I wish to see her."

At the mention of Maria's name, Greaves looked down his nose as if he smelt something offensive. "I don't think Miss Tomlinson will receive you."

"I am sure she will."

Greaves opened a door to the small room in which she had waited with Georgianne to see Mister Barnet. A quick glance informed her the ivory Chinese boat, they so much admired, was no longer on the mantelpiece. Doubtless it had been packed for transport to England. She remained in the centre of the hall. "Greaves, I am sure it will not take long for you to inform Miss Tomlinson I wish to see her."

Greaves turned around and left the room. What caused him to be so put out and unhelpful?

Pringle coughed. After a severe reprimand concerning her habit of sniffing, the woman had replaced it with equally annoying coughs.

She ignored the dresser while she looked around. The beautiful hand-painted Chinese wallpaper still graced the wall, but the ornately ornamented porcelain flower pot on a red-lacquer stand, which Georgianne had remarked the Prince Regent would envy, no longer stood in its place.

She frowned. Apart from such large treasures there were many small objet d'art which could be pilfered. It would be easy to slip a jade figurine or a small, valuable piece of porcelain into a pocket. Did Greaves discourage her visits because he feared she might suspect him of theft? She had only met a few of Mister Barnet's servants. Did he have a secretary? Did he have a steward? Were the items packed for transportation to England itemised?

A door opened. Maria, her eyes reddened by tears, erupted into the hall. "I knew you would come." Maria crossed the floor so fast that she reminded Helen of a galloping filly. She came to a halt in front of her and seized her hand. "Do come to the parlour."

"Wait here," Helen ordered Pringle. She followed Maria to the hall where Greaves stood. Maria called over her shoulder. "Please bring refreshments, Greaves. What would you prefer, Miss Whitley, tea, coffee or ratafia?"

"Coffee."

"Odious man," Maria said when Greaves went through the door leading to the kitchen. "He dare not disobey me for Mister Barnet has told him to make sure I am comfortable, but Greaves makes it obvious he resents my presence." She gestured to a chair. "Please sit yourself down."

Helen held her sprigged muslin skirts taut to prevent them creasing as she sat, back straight, feet placed demurely side by side on a small footstool. "How is Mister Barnet?"

"In spite of his cheerfulness, I am very worried. His face is ashen and his lips have a bluish tint. The doctor has ordered him to stay in bed."

"Do you know the cause of his illness?"

"I am told his heart is weak."

Thomas arrived carrying a silver tray which he put on a low table beneath the sash window that overlooked the garden.

Maria stood. "Shall I pour coffee?"

"Yes, please."

Maria busied herself with the silver pot and delicate porcelain. She handed a cup to Thomas to give to Helen. "Some seed cake? A biscuit?"

"No thank you."

Maria gave Helen a cup of coffee. "You may go, Thomas."

Alone with the young woman, Helen sipped a little of the aromatic drink. "Are you comfortable here? By the way, does Mister Barnet have many servants? Does he, for example, employ a steward and secretary?"

"There are several footmen and maids besides the cook and the kitchen girls. His steward fell down the stairs. His ankle is sprained and he is badly bruised. The secretary has gone to Bruges on Mister Barnet's business." Her eyes glistened. She dabbed them with an embroidered handkerchief. "What do the servants matter when I am beside myself with fears for Philippe? There is no word of him. I fear his ship sank, thieves attacked him, or he encountered some other misfortune." She hurried and went to the window. "Oh," she cried out, "the first tulips of the year are in flower. I wish father never brought me to Brussels. I could be at home in England enjoying our garden." She covered her face with her hands. Her shoulders shook. "Forgive me for my outburst, Miss Whitley. You have only known happiness. How can you understand my despair?"

Only known happiness! Surely Maria must have heard Papa died of gangrene and both of her brothers died in battle in Spain? Of course, she could not know the family secret of Mamma's addiction to the bottle. However, perhaps Maria could understand she did not want to continue her life at Cousin Tarrant's expense, and that she loved a gentleman who would not propose marriage. Helen pressed her teeth together for fear of her sensibilities becoming as uncontrolled as Maria's. "My father always said bad tidings travel faster than good news. Don't despair. There are many less dramatic reasons than yours for Phillips arrival being delayed."

Maria turned around. "I don't know what to do." Tears filled her eyes. "I can't expect Mister Barnet to house me for more than another two or three days. If Philippe has not come to Brussels by then, where shall I go?"

"If he does not arrive, I think you have only two choices. The first is to return to your father, who must be distraught about your whereabouts. If you have the funds, the second is to return to England to make inquiries about your betrothed." Helen put her cup down. "Maria, please compose yourself before we visit Mister Barnet."

"I shall try to." Maria walked slowly out of the room.

In the hall, Helen looked at Pringle, who sat on a settle, lemon-faced—to indicate her disapproval of the visit to Mr Barnet, whom she regarded unworthy of a young lady's attention. On stage, Helen thought, Pringle would give an excellent role of a martyr. She nodded her head at Thomas, the footman on duty. "Please take my dresser to the servant's hall and see she has something to drink."

Maria beckoned. "Come, Miss Whitley." She led her up the stairs to the third floor, along the corridor and knocked on a bedroom door, which opened almost immediately.

Helen caught her breath surprised by the sight of a nun, who wore a grey tunic, emblazoned with a red cross on the chest, a black gown with full skirts, and a spotless white wimple and veil.

"May we see Mister Barnet?" Helen asked.

Not a ripple of emotion disturbed the nun's tranquil face. "I regret—"

"I know that voice. Miss Whitley, how good of you to visit a sick old man. Sister Imelda, be good enough to admit my guest."

"Monsieur Barnet, you know Doctor Longspring said you should not have any visitors."

"Confound him—beg your pardon Sister—what harm can passing the time with a charming young lady cause."

"Don't agitate yourself, Monsieur Barnet," Sister Imelda then turned her attention to them. "Only one visitor at a time."

"I shall visit him later," Maria said.

The Sister opened the door a little wider to allow Helen to enter.

"Please leave us," Mister Barnet said to the nun. "I wish to speak to my guest in private. If you don't allow me to do so, I shall be agitated."

Sister Imelda fingered the rosary suspended from her belt. "Very well, Monsieur." She spoke without a hint of displeasure. "My child, please help him to make his peace with the cher Dieu. Don't be surprised," she continued, in a lower tone, "if my patient nods off to sleep in the middle of a conversation, and don't be taken aback if you cannot make sense of his words. Sometimes, he relives the past in a disjointed manner."

Helen remembered the last days of her father's life. Now and then he had believed he was still a happy child in his parents' house. Helen gazed past the nun into the dimly lit room with a crucifix on the wall opposite Mister Barnet's bed. She did not remember seeing it before. Did Sister Imelda hang it there?

"I shall return within the quarter hour." The Sister closed the door behind her.

"Ah, you are looking at the crucifix which the good nun hung on the wall. It does no harm so don't be dismayed. She belongs to an Order dedicated to nursing the sick and wounded."

Helen shivered. Unless a miracle occurred in the near future, the nuns' services would be needed to tend countless soldiers.

"Please come closer, Miss Whitley."

Helen stepped quickly across the spotless floorboards to his bedside.

"Ah, pretty and well-turned out as ever. Now, please draw back the curtain and open the shutters. I can't abide this gloom. Anyone would think I'm almost in the grave."

"I don't think you are." Somewhat embarrassed by his remark, she hurried to let light into the room.

"Sister Imelda seems to think I am." Mister Barnet chuckled. "If I gave her the least excuse, I think she would send for a priest to administer the last rites."

Brought up in the Anglican faith and taught to despise the Roman Catholic Church, Helen shifted from one foot to another, unsure of what to say. The last rites were as foreign to her as Bengali, which her father learned to speak—in his own words, 'tolerably well'—during his time in India. "Don't allow the Sister to bully you, Mister Barnet."

"No fear of that, I've never allowed anyone to do so."

His eyes closed. Had he drifted off to sleep? She hoped he was merely tired, not drugged to ward off discomfort. Should she leave? No, she would sit in the small wing chair by the window and look out at the garden in which he took so much pleasure.

She watched a tree sparrow flying backward and forward with grubs in its beak, presumably to feed its nestlings. Her shoulders drooped. If only she possessed a nest to share with—

Mister Barnet stirred. "Emily, there you are. Give your grandfather a kiss."

His granddaughter! He had said she died, and also that he had no living relative. Saddened, Helen turned to look at him. Of course, Sister Imelda had warned her the old gentleman sometimes retreated into the past. What should she say or do?

"No? Now that you are a young lady, do you think you are too old to give me a kiss?" Eyes half open, Mister Barnet tapped his cheek. "I remember the days when you sat on my lap, shook your pretty brown curls and pouted your little cherry-red lips. Somehow you always persuaded me to give you whatever you wanted. Sweetheart, do you know you have been the joy of my life since your father died?"

She should humour him. "Y…yes grandfather and I know how much you love me."

The sick man's eyes fully opened. "Ah, Miss Whitley, there you are. For a moment I thought you were Emily."

Helen dabbed her eyes with her handkerchief. "Yes, I know. May I fetch you anything?"

"No, thank you. I am grateful for your visit."

She patted the back of his gnarled hand. "It is a pleasure. You only have to send for me whenever you wish to see me."

Mister Barnet's eyes closed again so she resumed her seat on the chair by the window.

"Everything for you," he muttered, presumably back in the past with his beloved Emily.

The door opened. Sister Imelda seemed to glide into the bedroom on noiseless wheels. Vivid blue eyes, set in an alabaster-white face, regarded her. "You appear distressed, my child."

Helen shook her head while she tried to analyse her reaction to the old gentleman's poor health. "I wish I could help Mister Barnet."

"You can pray for son âme immortelle."

"Oh, his immortal soul, yes, I shall." Helen looked down embarrassed by such talk. She glanced at Mister Barnet. He slept, his breaths shallow. "Good day to you. I shall visit him again."

* * * *

When Helen left the bedchamber, Maria came out of a room a little further down the corridor. "I left the door open so I would hear you take leave of Mister Barnet's bedroom. How is he?"

"He is tired but peaceful."

"I'm glad, and I'm sure you understand why I hesitate to impose upon his hospitality for much longer. Come to my bedroom while I put on my cloak. I shall go to Parc Royale to see if Phillipe's arrived." She wrinkled her forehead. "I must take precautions to make sure I'm not recognised." A nervous laugh escaped Maria. "I dare say you think it's over-dramatic to suppose Father might have employed people to search the streets to find me."

Helen followed Maria into a large bedroom, and stared at an old-fashioned tester bed with brightly embroidered curtains tied back to each carved post.

A plump, rosy-cheeked dresser turned away from her task of dusting the mantelpiece, put the cloth down and curtsied.

"Susie, my black cloak, bonnet and gloves," Maria ordered.

The young dresser helped her mistress envelop herself in the cloak. Maria put on her bonnet, pulled the black net veil over her face, and tied the ribbons beneath her chin. Susie drew the hood over Maria's head and pulled the edge over her mistress's forehead.

Maria looked in the mirror. "I don't think Father would recognise me."

"No, I don't think so," Helen agreed.

As Helen followed Maria onto the landing and down the stairs, she looked down at the butler, who was crossing the hall. "Greaves, send for my dresser." To assert her position as Mister Barnet's welcome guest, she did not say please, although, unlike some members of the ton, she usually accorded the servants that courtesy.

A few minutes later, with Pringle and Susie in attendance, Helen walked with Maria at a steady pace to Parc Royale. When they entered it, Maria hurried toward the pavilion outside, where well-dressed patrons relaxed at tables eating and drinking in spite of the cloudy sky that threatened more rain.

Maria halted. A long drawn out breath escaped her. "Philippe is not here," she murmured, her tone of voice desolate.

"Yes, he is, cherie," came a voice from behind them.

"Philippe!" Maria tottered. An unusually tall, well-proportioned gentleman, with hair the colour of newly minted sovereigns, reached out to steady her before drawing her into his arms.

He pushed back Maria's hood and raised her veil. "Why did you hide your lovely face?"

Maria blushed as pink as a peony in full bloom. "Because of my father! I am staying at a friend's house. I don't want him to find me." She gazed lovingly at Philippe. " How did you recognise me?"

He laughed. "You spoke my name, but even if you had not, I would have recognised your voice."

"You can't imagine how anxious I have been while waiting for you to arrive. I imagined you might have been thrown from your horse and lost your memory, or attacked by thieves and mortally injured. Or, I even thought you decided you don't want to marry me." She stood as close to Phillipe as possible without touching him, and stared up at his face, her eyes tender with emotion.

"Of course I do. The chaos in Ostend—a miserable place, a filthy unhealthy town with endless sand hills along the shore—delayed me." The expression of disgust on his face was comical. "When the military were disembarking, the Duke of Wellington's orders for the troops to land and their boats to return to England without delay, led to frantic horses being lowered into the sea and paraphernalia thrown overboard." He emphasised the shocking scene with a wave of his hands. "Oh, it is impossible to describe the chaos during which my horse bolted. My groom could not find the wretched animal. Fortunately, my portmanteau was safe. Anyway, to be brief, I travelled here in comfort by canal. So here I am, entirely at your disposal.

"Sweetheart, my sister looks forward to receiving you." He held her hand. "Are you sure Mister Tomlinson will not change his mind?"

"Father is too stubborn. I love both of you, but am glad you want me to be your wife."

"My beauty, it is for me to be grateful for your trust in me. We shall leave Belgium after we are wed."

Helen coughed to attract their attention. "Miss Tomlinson, I must go."

Maria turned to face her. "How discourteous of me not to have presented Monsieur Lamonte to you." she said and made the introductions.

The gentleman bowed, Helen inclined her head. "Good day, to both of you."

Followed by Pringle, Helen walked toward Rue Royale. Her footsteps slowed. She remembered her late father's good humour and tenderness. Confronted with the same dilemma as Maria, she could not imagine having married without Father's consent. Yet, an inner voice whispered, would I not give up everyone and everything for the opportunity to marry Langley? Yes, I think I might whatever the consequences.

She halted, causing other pedestrians to have to step around her. Honesty compelled her to admit she envied Maria. She castigated herself for being guilty of envy, one of the seven deadly sins. She brushed away a tear.

"Miss Whitley, are you unwell?" Pringle asked.

Helen shook her head. With great effort, she abandoned the painful memory of her father, thoughts of Maria, and her own covetousness.

Chapter Twenty-Three

23rd to 28th April, 1815

To find an excuse to question Doctor Longspring about Mister Barnet, Helen pretended to be ill.

After he examined her, he addressed Georgianne. "Well, ma'am, it is possible Miss Langley is feverish due to an unknown condition, which might worsen during the next few days. At the moment, I find little amiss with her." He gazed at Helen, the expression in his eyes sharp. "Your sister's cheeks are merely a little flushed, and her pulse is only a bit rapid. We must hope its rate will decrease."

His comment did not surprise Helen. Until now, she prided herself on her absolute honesty. Doubtless guilt brought colour to her face and increased the beat of her pulse. The experienced doctor could not know she lied about her condition even if, for some reason, he harboured suspicion. She looked at her sister who would never imagine she fibbed. Dear Georgianne had fussed over her since she stayed in bed. Her self-reproach swelled when her affectionate sister bathed her forehead with a cool cloth perfumed with lavender before she sent orders to the cook to make barley water and gruel. Gruel! No matter how tasty it would be, Helen's appetite demanded something more substantial.

Doctor Longspring released her wrist and patted her hand. Helen looked up at his round, plump face. If she were ill, his confident manner would reassure her.

He turned his attention back to Georgianne. "Mrs Tarrant, your sister is not my only young patient to neglect her health while swept up by the gaiety of balls and suchlike. I prescribe bed rest for five or six days"

For so long? How on earth would she maintain her pretence? She wondered while she listened to the doctor.

"Afterward we shall see how Miss Whitley goes on. In the meantime, if her temperature rises please don't hesitate to send for me."

Georgianne nodded. "Thank you for your good advice, Doctor. I know I can depend on you."

Doctor Longspring glanced at her rounded stomach. "You, ma'am, must take good care of your own health. Do summon me if you suffer even the slightest indisposition." He smiled, amusement revealed in his light blue eyes. "Major Tarrant has already consulted me on your behalf. I assured him he has no cause for his excessive concern."

"So I have told him, but the major is too solicitous on my behalf," Georgianne explained, somewhat breathlessly.

"Just so, ma'am," he looked at Helen. "Miss Whitley, although ladies have stronger constitutions than it is generally believed, if you are chilled while you walk in the rain, it will do you no good. Now, I must bid you good day. I have patients who need my urgent attention."

"A moment more of your time, Doctor Longspring," Helen requested, in spite of her shame because she deprived those in genuine need of him. "When I visited Mister Barnet, both his butler and nurse told me that in accordance with your orders no visitors are allowed to see him."

Doctor Longspring raised his shaggy eyebrows, as though surprised by the visit of a young lady of good birth to a tradesman. "My instructions have been misinterpreted. Mister Barnet's heart is weak, so I gave orders for him to be kept calm. However, it is not for his butler and the good Sister to decide whether or not he should see someone."

Helen frowned. "I have his former guest, Miss Tomlinson, to thank for admittance to his bedchamber."

Doctor Longspring frowned. "If you call on my patient again, please remember he soon becomes exhausted, so you should not stay for long. In the meantime, I shall speak to the butler and Sister Imelda—who is an excellent nurse even if she is sometimes too protective of her patients."

"Thank you," Helen replied, still annoyed with Greaves and sorry for Mister Barnet.

"Dearest," Georgianne began, after the doctor left the bedchamber, "I am sure there is no need for you to worry about Mister Barnet."

"I am anxious about him. As I have told you, he is frail and at the mercy of his servants."

Georgianne applied a cool cloth to Helen's brow. "There now, don't fret. It will make you even more feverish. Sit up. I'll plump up your pillows. Would you like some barley water?"

"Yes please." Helen despised herself for her charade, "There is no need to fuss. I am much better." The idea of being confined to bed for nearly a week irked her, but unless she confessed her deception to Georgianne, she must endure it.

* * * *

After Helen did not ride on two consecutive early mornings in the Allee Vert, Captain Dalrymple called at the house. Told she was unwell, he bombarded her with pretty nosegays and letters, in which he expressed his hope she would soon recover. He also sent gifts of handkerchiefs edged with broad borders of exquisite lace, and a bottle of Hungary Water. They were well-chosen gifts which did not exceed the bounds of propriety. On the morning of the fourth day, a note accompanied a copy of *An Account of the Kingdom of Nepaul* by Major Kirkpatrick.

With pleasure, Helen read the note. "Look, Georgianne." She turned the pages and admired the maps and pictures. "It was so kind of Captain Dalrymple. He hopes it will help me to plan the Indian theme we have chosen for my ball. Of course, he is sworn to secrecy because I want to surprise the guests." She chuckled. "Polite society feeds on chatter and rumour while every hostess attempts to provide more lavish and spectacular entertainments than any other. When questioned, I merely say I am sure the decorations will not disappoint."

"It is good of Dalrymple to be so attentive. Tarrant and I like him."

"So do I." Helen said, conscious of her sister's unspoken words 'we hope you will marry him,' that almost hovered in the air.

Georgianne kissed her forehead. "Well, dearest, I shall leave you to rest until nuncheon. You must not overtire yourself."

Helen restrained herself from protesting that there was no question of becoming fatigued. She kept silent, fearful of her sister's reaction if she admitted her fraud. She passed the time by first reading the book and then finished Cook's tasty barley gruel to which a little white wine had been added. Sweetened with sugar, flavoured with mace and enhanced with raisins and currants, she savoured every mouthful. Unfortunately, her stomach rumbled after she finished it. Helen considered bribing Pringle to fetch a ham sandwich. Her mouth watered when she imagined succulent ham between slices of bread spread with butter fresh from the country. No, no matter how hungry she became she would not stoop so low. A second parcel, containing a copy of Oliver Goldsmith's Vicar of Wakefield and another note from her suitor, distracted her. With a sigh, she put the book and note on her quilt.

Surrounded by luxury, she considered Captain Dalrymple. If she married him, she believed he would wrap her in kindness for the rest of her life. She sighed. "Love", some of the ton have stated, "is not a prerequisite for marriage." Many of its members considered the mere notion of romantic love unrefined. Nevertheless, she found no vulgarity in the masterpiece Pride and Prejudice, which she had read three times with increasing appreciation and enjoyment. Yet perhaps those who disapproved of romance were wise. One's heart would not be broken if one's husband took a mistress, an all too common occurrence. What more did she want than a husband such as Dalrymple? "Langley," an inner voice whispered, and continued. "How foolish to hanker after a gentleman who ruthlessly rejected your overture."

* * * *

On the afternoon of the sixth day, glad to exchange her nightgown for a well-cut white muslin gown, Helen joined Georgianne in the drawing room. No sooner had she sat on a chair from which she could look out of the window toward Parc Royale, than Cousin Tarrant arrived. He strode across the carpet to Georgianne and raised her hand to his lips.

Eyes wide, Georgianne clutched his arm with her free hand. "Why have you come home so early? What has happened?"

Cousin Tarrant removed Georgianne's hand from his sleeve. "Nothing to alarm you. I only came to tell you I shall be away for a week."

"Why? Where are you going?"

He smiled down at his wife. "Makelyn ordered me to gather information around the border. No need to sigh; I shall return before you have time to realise I am away."

"I shall miss you every moment until you come back safely." The passion in Georgianne's voice startled Helen. "Why, Tarrant," her sister asked, "do I always suspect there is something you have not told me? That your duties are not as straightforward as you claim? I am your wife. You should have no secrets from me."

Cousin Tarrant sat next to Georgianne on the sofa.

"You know better than to question me about my orders."

Her sister stood. "No, I don't." She glared down at him. "Neither Helen nor I would ever repeat anything you confided in us."

The major stood. "One never knows who might overhear and gossip, or whether, in an unguarded moment, you might say something in all innocence. Something which might be misinterpreted and put my life and the lives of others at risk."

Georgianne's hands fluttered above his gold epaulettes. "You speak as though you are more than a dedicated officer." She closed her eyes. "If I did not know you better, I would think you are a spy, and maybe Langley is also one, for the two of you are constant companions."

For a moment, the major remained silent, his grey eyes hardened, and his features seemed to alter, to become sharper.

Helen stared at him in horror. Could her sister's hunch be true? She caught her breath. As usual her artist's eyes were aware of something most people did not seem to observe.

Cousin Tarrant stood. His face an inscrutable mask, although his grey eyes were tender when he spoke to Georgianne. "You know part of 'The Glory Boys' duty is to gather information. Now, if you please, no more nonsensical speculation. I have heard ladies who are increasing, are prone to whimsies."

"I am sorry," Georgianne whispered.

The major slipped an arm around his wife's waist. "There is nothing to apologise for. Now, I must get ready to leave."

"I shall come with you to make sure you have everything you need," Georgianne murmured.

The door closed behind them. Helen took a deep breath. Her heart beat fast. Perspiration beaded her forehead. She looked at the delicate china ornaments on the mantelpiece, the broadsheets and magazines on a table and Georgianne's rosewood sewing box. Everything seemed so ordinary, so commonplace. Yet something even more terrifying than the imminent threat of armed combat, in which Cousin Tarrant and Langley would participate, crept into the drawing room. Helen shuddered. She found it almost impossible to visualise the gracious house being vandalised if Napoleon's army invaded Brussels.

"Captain Dalrymple," a footman announced.

Chapter Twenty-Four
28th April 28, 1815

Captain Dalrymple bowed, a tussie-mussie of delicate spring flowers in his hand. He straightened his back, walked toward Helen and halted three-feet—or a little more—away from her.

Helen curtsied, conscious of the footman, who could hear every word they spoke. " Good day, sir." His smile warmed her heart as he gazed at her with a glint in his dark eyes. She smiled back at him with admiration for his exceptional good looks. "Please be seated."

"Before I do so, please accept this." He bowed and then handed her the flowers.

She inhaled the fragrance of the multi-coloured blossoms. "Freesias, narcissi, some of my favourites. They smell delicious. And yellow rosebuds, how charming."

"Not as charming as you." Her suitor spoke too low for the footman to overhear.

"You flatter me, Captain."

"No, Miss Whitley, a mere mortal's words could never do you justice."

"You are too kind, sir."

"I could never be too kind to you." With an economic movement common to so many military officers, he sat opposite her.

Conscious of her blushes and his ardent expression, Helen gazed out of the window.

Nervousness made it impossible to continue looking at him. "A glass of wine?"

"Yes, please."

"Thomas, a glass of Canary wine for the captain," she ordered the footman.

She smiled at her suitor with genuine gratitude. "Thank you for your gifts. Kirkpatrick's book about Nepaul is fascinating. It has given me many more ideas for the décor for my ball. And thank you for your other gifts. I fear you are spoiling me."

"It is my pleasure. I would enjoy doing so for the rest of our lives."

Oh dear, the captain might be on the brink of a marriage proposal. It seemed the moment to decide whether to accept or reject her beau had arrived. "I am sure I would not deserve such devotion."

"I think you will always be worthy of it."

Surely he would not ask her to marry him while at risk of being interrupted by Thomas when he brought the wine.

She buried her face in the soft petals of the tussie-mussie. The perfume almost overcame her senses and, somehow or other, added to her indecision.

"What are you thinking of, Miss Whitley?"

By now her cheeks must be rosy. "Nothing in particular."

"I hope you have recovered."

"Recovered?"

"From your indisposition. Upon my word, I burned with anxiety."

All confusion, she peered at him over the top of the flowers. He seemed as calm as the sea on a tranquil day. But one never knows what undercurrents lay in its depths. "You did not need to concern yourself, sir."

What would her devoted admirer think of her if she confessed her deception? Would he despise her? She decided to confess. If he were not dismayed by her dishonesty, it would prove he loved her. "I was not ill." She faltered for a moment. "I confess, I needed an excuse to question Doctor Longspring about Mister Barnet, one of his patients."

The captain whistled low. "Mister Barnet, the nabob?"

"You know him?"

"I know of him. He is the only son of Sir Roderick and Lady Barnet, my parents' deceased neighbours."

"I am not surprised to hear he is of good birth. His conduct is that of a gentleman born. Please tell me if he has any living relatives?"

The captain shook his head. "None that I know of."

"How sad."

"Indeed," the captain began. He broke off when the double doors opened to admit Thomas, who served the wine.

A wave of her hand dismissed the footman.

Dalrymple leant forward. "So, Miss Whitley, do you wish to tell me more about your charade?"

He did not seem put out by her confession.

She found the courage to explain her motives.

"Thank you for confiding in me. I admire your concern for the gentleman." He put his glass on the small table by his chair.

Her cheeks warmed. "I feared you would think ill of me."

The captain knelt on one knee in front of her chair. "To the contrary, I honour you for your compassion."

Surely the moment to decide her future had arrived. Still indecisive, she looked up at the ceiling.

"Miss Whitley, we have your guardian's consent, and my parents' and Major and Mrs Tarrant's approval, so, will you agree to be my wife?" he asked, his words somewhat rushed.

She gazed down at him. Flames burned in the depths of his dark, fathomless eyes. She took a deep breath. Langley had made it clear he would not marry her. Here was a prospective husband whom she believed would do his best to make her happy. Although Georgianne and Cousin Tarrant had not been in love when they married, they doted on each other. Helen respected the captain. She could learn to love him, could she not? Only a fool would reject a proposal of marriage from such a man. Her cheeks cooled. "Yes, Captain Dalrymple, I shall be your wife."

Every trace of anxiety left his face. His eyes blazed. Never had she seen such joy on a gentleman's face.

He took a small green and gold box out of his pocket and opened the lid to display the contents.

She regarded the gold ring set with a large, square cut emerald surrounded by small diamonds.

"Green to match your eyes. Please hold out your left hand." He slid the symbol of their betrothal over her third finger.

"Thank you, it is beautiful. I shall always treasure it." In return, she believed Dalrymple would treasure her. After the pain of Langley's rejection, the captain's love acted like balm, which brought unexpected peace.

Dalrymple drew her to her feet. "How can I ever thank you for agreeing to marry me? I know you don't love me, but I hope you will in the future. If not, I have enough love for both of us."

How did he know she did not love him? Oh yes, while secluded on the balcony at the ball—after which Cousin Tarrant upbraided her—she had been honest when she told her captain she expected a proposal of marriage from another gentleman which she would be pleased to accept.

Dalrymple encircled her with his arms and kissed the top of her head. Always conscious of being taller than most ladies, she relished his superior height. Her nose was level with his black collar edged with gold braid as dazzling as her future. For a moment, she wanted to escape his possessive embrace. Common sense

"Thank you, but perhaps I am mistaken. For now, I don't think we should broach the matter."

* * * *

Helen erupted into her bedchamber and tugged the bell pull to summon Pringle.

Impatient to see Mister Barnet, she flung opened the closet and assessed her wardrobe. Her long-sleeved, light grey walking dress trimmed with swansdown, and the dark grey pelisse edged with white braid, would do. She shook her head. No, they were too funereal for a newly betrothed lady. She chose a cream-coloured, long sleeved gown and her emerald-green merino pelisse.

Pringle entered the bedchamber and raised her eyebrows. "I should be laying out your clothes, Miss. Your hands are trembling. What is wrong? Allow me to help you."

A little later, high-crowned hat upon her head, Helen pulled on her gloves.

For once, the dresser took one look at her face and did not speak.

"Pringle, fetch your hat and cloak. I shall visit Mister Barnet."

Pringle coughed to indicate her disapproval.

Helen glared at her but made no comment. Instead, she hurried downstairs to join her betrothed, who stood the second he saw her. He took her hands in his and spread them wide apart. "How beautiful you are. You should always wear green to complement your eyes. It is why I chose an emerald ring."

Beautiful? No, Georgianne was the family beauty. She was merely fashionable in clothes she designed. Yet Dalrymple's admiration warmed her heart.

"I chose grey, then decided the colour is too dull for a bride-to-be." She spoke somewhat breathlessly to distract herself.

His endearing, boyish laughter rang out. "I adore you too much to ever think you look dull."

"Even when I grow old and wrinkled?" she teased.

"I shall be so accustomed to your face that I will not see the wrinkles, but I am sure you will notice the havoc time has wrought upon me."

What had she done to deserve this charming, sincere gentleman? For the first time, she began to look forward not merely to being mistress of her own establishment, but to becoming Captain Dalrymple's wife.

"Ah, judging by your expression, you like me a little."

"More than that, sir." Yes, she liked him very much indeed. If she could rid her mind of Langley, surely it would not be difficult to love him.

* * * *

Helen waited with Pringle in the reception room after being admitted to the house by

Mister Barnet's impassive butler. It had been emptied of everything other than a sofa, with a long narrow seat and two matching chairs. Now devoid of ornamentation, it seemed the soul of the house had departed.

The door opened. A tall, slim man joined her. She found no fault with his black cloth suit, white shirt with stiffly starched collar not too high for him to turn his head, and a simply tied muslin cravat. He bowed. "Miss Whitley, please allow me to introduce myself. George Hempstead, Mister Barnet's secretary."

Helen inclined her head. "Mister Hempstead."

"I am pleased to see you. As I wrote, Mister Barnet is extremely restless. He has repeatedly asked for you."

So far, she approved of Hempstead—whom she judged to be more or less thirty years-old—a gentleman of medium height, with an oval face and a head of russet-brown hair. She looked into his hazel eyes. "I cannot help comparing the house, as it is now, to my first visit. I hope there is an inventory of all its treasures."

"Yes, there is."

The expression in his eyes hardened as he spoke, but that might have been because he considered her question impertinent. Yet, could Hempstead and Greaves have robbed their employer? "Ah," Helen began, "I can only hope none of the servants are dishonest."

Hempstead frowned. "So do I."

"I shall not take up more of your time."

The secretary held the door open. Helen looked at her dresser. What did she make of her conversation with Mister Hempstead? "You may wait here, Pringle." At the bottom of the stairs, she hesitated with one foot on the first one. "Mister Hempstead, I hoped Mister Barnet's health would improve after my last visit during which he seemed exhausted and a little confused." Should she mention that, not for the first time, the nabob mistook her for Emily? Why not? "Sometimes he confused me with his late granddaughter."

"Ah. Her parents died when she was three years old. Afterward, Mister Barnet cared for her. When she died, it appeared—I hope this does not seem too fanciful—Mister Barnet's heart and soul had left him."

"No, Mister Hempstead, it does not strike me as too whimsical." She understood completely. The deaths of her brothers and father had destroyed her mother. Day-by-day Mamma drank more and more wine and spirits in an attempt to obliterate her grief, until only the carapace of the woman she had once been, remained.

"Although Mister Barnet continued to trade and to fulfil his obligations to those he employs in England and elsewhere, after Miss Barnet's death he became reclusive. Since her funeral, Miss Whitley, he has been indifferent to everyone."

But not, Helen thought, to me. "I should visit him immediately.'

Mister Hempstead followed her. "Please forgive me if I have said too much."

"You have not."

Side by side they walked along the corridor on the second floor. Mister Hempstead knocked on the bedroom door. It opened to reveal Sister Imelda's concerned face.

"Ah, it does my eyes good to see you, Miss Whitley. My patient needs you."

With mingled dread and pity Helen crossed the threshold.

Chapter Twenty-Five

28th April, 1815

Helen stood next to Mister Barnet's bed, her back toward Sister Imelda, who sat opposite it, her rosary in her right hand.

"How happy you look, Miss Whitley." As he spoke his voice wavered.

She looked down into his eyes as guileless as a small child's. "Not because you are confined to your bedchamber pretending to be a little unwell, sir." A chuckle rewarded her for the sally. She tugged off her glove and held out her hand. "My happiness is due to this."

"Ah, a handsome ring, set with an emerald to match your eyes."

"Thank you, Mister Barnet. That is what my future husband said."

"Who is the fortunate gentleman, Viscount Langley, Captain Dalrymple, or maybe someone whom you have not mentioned to me?"

At the viscount's name, pain lanced through her. "Captain Dalrymple," she replied, her voice choked with emotion.

"I must congratulate you." His eyes gleamed.

Helen studied his linen sheets, primrose yellow quilt and the crucifix above the bed while she decided how to phrase her question.

"Must? Don't you think I should have accepted the captain's proposal?"

Mister Barnet's chuckle wheezed from him. "It is not for me to say." His eyes closed and he drifted off to sleep.

She looked at Sister Imelda who murmured something. Helen distinguished the words, 'at the hour of our death'. She wanted nothing to do with Popery. The fragment of the soft spoken prayer both fascinated and scared her.

"Congratulations on your betrothal, Miss Whitley."

"Thank you," Helen answered, her voice strained. She wondered what a woman who had chosen marriage to the Lord could know of earthly matters.

"I wish both of you every happiness. May the Good Lord bless both of you."

"Thank you, Sister."

Helen looked down at the infirm nabob. His chest did not stir the covers. She groped for the pulse in his wrist. To her relief, it beat steadily.

A smile appeared on the nursing Sister's face—a white oval framed by her wimple. "No need to be alarmed, Miss Whitley. You already know that my patient slips in and out of sleep. It is only to be expected. Do you wish to sit by him?"

Helen nodded. Sadness for the old gentleman, who had been so vital when she first met him, overwhelmed her.

Sister Imelda placed a chair by the bed. In spite of the nun's Roman Catholic faith, Helen found strange comfort in her calm presence.

She sat. Toward the end of life, did old age inevitably mean being cared for like an infant? The thought dismayed her until she answered her own question. No, both of her paternal grandparents enjoyed good health to the end of their lives.

His eyes flickered open. "Miss Langley." She leaned forward to hear his quiet voice. "It is good of you to sit here with such patience. I hope I shall live long enough to know you are married."

She chose not to voice a platitude. "If Cousin Tarrant and my sister approve, to please you, I shall wed soon."

"Good. You know, I am not without influence. I can help you to obtain a special licence from an ecclesiastical court at Doctor's Common's in London." His voice gathered strength. "I shall send a letter to our ambassador requesting his aid. Perhaps you could marry at the embassy, on the morning of your ball, in the presence of your sister, brother-in-law and a few friends."

Astonished, Helen opened her eyes wide. How much influence did Mister Barnet wield?

"Miss Whitley, when the guests at your ball are received, you may be introduced as Mrs Dalrymple."

Doubtless her betrothed would agree to Mister Barnet's plan, even if Georgianne and

Cousin Tarrant objected to such haste on the morning of the ball when there would be so much to do. She did not regret her decision. It would be best to tie the matrimonial knot so she could put aside every memory of Langley—and what might have been—behind her. "An excellent suggestion, sir, for I neither wish to postpone my wedding for long, nor invite many people to it. Nevertheless, I must consult my sister and her husband." Could the old gentleman retain his hold on life until the fourteenth of June? She brushed the back of her hand across her eyes. "If they approve, I shall marry in mid-June." While she spoke, she vowed she would be a good wife.

"Good, I won't detain you any longer provided you promise to visit me again."

She stood, not immune to his understated request. "Every day, if it is possible. If I cannot visit you, I shall send a footman to ask how you are."

"Thank you."

Helen waited until he slept before she stood. "Sister Imelda," she whispered, "is he in much pain?"

"No child, the laudanum keeps him comfortable and helps him to sleep."

"Good, I cannot bear to think of him suffering."

"May God bless you for your compassionate heart."

"Thank you. Good day, Sister. I shall visit your patient tomorrow."

"God willing."

Helen walked slowly with Pringle at her side, her mind disturbed by thoughts of death, Mister Barnet's, the possibility of Georgianne's in childbirth, Tarrant, Dalrymple's and Langley's during the inevitable war.

The dresser neither sniffed, coughed, nor spoke until they were close to Rue Royale. "I am sorry Mister Barnet is not expected to live for much longer."

Surprised, Helen looked at her attendant. "Thank you." She was tempted to question the woman about her changed attitude toward the elderly gentleman.

"Well, Miss, I am a Christian so I shall pray for the old gentleman."

Her surprise must have communicated itself to Pringle. Helen suppressed a smile. Presumably Pringle now knew Mister Barnet came from an upper class family. Servants were often more snobbish than those they served. If Pringle knew the nabob was well-born, it would explain her changed outlook. "Very commendable, Pringle. I shall also pray for him."

The dresser's black gown swirled at the hem as she increased her pace to keep up. "If I may be so bold, please accept my congratulations on your betrothal."

How did the woman know she had agreed to marry Dalrymple? Oh, she had probably noticed the emerald and diamond ring.

"Please forgive me for asking if you are to wed Captain Dalrymple?"

"You may ask, but until I have broken the news to my sister, please don't tell anyone."

"You may depend on me not to, Miss. Please forgive me for saying if you don't want them to know, be careful not to let them see your ring."

"Thank you for your good advice. I shall follow it."

With sympathy, Helen observed the thin woman, who must be thirty years-old or more. Servants were expected to devote themselves to their employers at the cost of marriage. Those in service usually lost their positions if they wed. How dreadful to be denied matrimony and children. Most servants took great interest in every detail of their employer's lives and gossiped about them.

"Pringle, I don't think I have ever expressed my genuine appreciation for your excellent service. What would I do without you to keep my clothes in order, attend to my toilette and chaperone me?"

Her dresser's cheeks reddened. "Thank you, Miss, you cannot imagine how gratified I am by your words."

She really should be less curt with all the servants, other than Greaves, for Mister Barnet's secretary seemed to agree the man might be guilty of theft.

Pringle walked a little straighter until they entered the house and Helen hurried to Georgianne's boudoir.

Nestled on the day bed, a pile of pretty silk-covered cushions at her back, when Georgianne sat up quickly, the satin coverlet fell onto the pastel coloured Aubusson carpet.

If only she could be so dainty. Impossible! She was happiest in her paint spattered apron.

Helen held out her hand.

Georgianne stared at the ring. "Dearest! Who? When?"

"Captain Dalrymple. I accepted his proposal a few hours ago," she explained, torn between the urge to smile or cry over her decision.

"I am pleased. So will Tarrant be. We like the captain very much." Her eyes rounded. "Dearest, why didn't you tell me immediately?" Georgianne asked, her eyes quizzical. "Why don't you look as radiant as you should?"

Helen's vision blurred with unshed tears which she blinked away. "I have, this moment, returned from a visit to Mister Barnet. Although he is so ill, he is always pleased to see me." Aware of a tremor in her voice, she swallowed before she spoke again. "I fear he has not long to live."

Georgianne stood and put her arms around Helen. "I am sorry, dearest. The only certainty in life, is that we come into this world, and must leave it. What happens in between cannot be predicted. Don't let the old man's sickness impinge upon your happiness."

Again, fear for those she loved crept through her. "Gentleman, not old man, Georgianne. His late parents, Sir Roderick and Lady Barnet, lived near the Dalrymples."

"I see."

Helen withdrew from her sister's arms. "I have grown fond of Mister Barnet so I shall try to visit him every day."

"Will your captain approve?"

If her judgement was right, Dalrymple would be a less authoritarian husband than Cousin Tarrant, who, although he adored his wife, was very much the master of his house. Curious, Helen realised how much she needed to learn about Dalrymple. Did he intend to remain in the army until old age forced him to resign?

"Helen…" Georgianne prompted.

"I am sure my captain will have no objections. Moments after I agreed to marry him, I received a note which asked me to call on Mister Barnet without delay. Dalrymple did not object, although—" She broke off, too self-conscious to admit the captain had been about to kiss her for the first time. To distract Georgianne, she explained why she wanted to marry at the embassy on the morning of the ball. "And," she concluded, "Mister Barnet is confident that a marriage licence can be obtained from England so Dalrymple and I may be married quietly on the morning of the fourteenth of June. If Dalrymple consents, do agree, Georgianne. We could help you and Cousin Tarrant to receive your guests, and be introduced as husband and wife. Oh, please don't look so dismayed."

Her sister sank back onto the daybed and swung her legs up. "Tarrant might disapprove of the suggestion."

Helen doubted it. Indeed, she suspected Cousin Tarrant would be pleased to see her leave his house so he and Georgianne could devote whatever time he could snatch from the army, to each other.

"Dearest, I cannot imagine what Captain Dalrymple will think of your plan."

Amused, Helen restrained a smile. She did not doubt her ardent suitor would approve. He wanted to marry her as soon as possible. "I think it will please him." Butterflies seemed to flutter in her stomach at the idea of being married so soon. She must not reveal it, for the slightest hint of indecision would alarm Georgianne.

"Why do you want to accept the old gentleman's suggestion?"

"Because I like him so much, and because he prays to live long enough to know I am married."

"Very well, when Tarrant returns, I shall ask him to agree, and to approach our ambassador on your behalf."

Helen bent to kiss her sister's cheek. "I hope your husband knows he is married to an angel."

Her sister's eyes glinted with mischief. "I doubt one would please him." She giggled. "Remember it when you are married."

* * * *

7th May, 1815

Georgianne and Helen faced each other on either side of the massive oak desk in the centre of the library.

Helen smiled. Dalrymple was delighted by the prospect of their marriage on the fourteenth of June. She sharpened her crow's quill and looked down at each list, one for the ball, the other for her wedding. So much to do and so little time to accomplish it. The menu had been chosen for the dinner which would precede it. The owner of the Indian restaurant in London had signed an agreement to provide exotic spices, and to send two cooks to prepare some of the food for the supper halfway through the ball.

Georgianne frowned. "There is the question of the wine to be served at dinner and throughout supper. My butler is invaluable. He has advised me to purchase stocks of light French or Rhenish wine to serve with each course, and hock or Barsac to be served between each one." She frowned. "Fletcher also pointed

333

out that although the gentlemen will not be encouraged to linger over it, the finest port wine must be served after the ladies retire."

Helen continued to make notes while her sister spoke.

Georgianne peered across the table. "You script is beautiful. I am ashamed to admit I always blotted my copybook when we were in the schoolroom, but our governess praised your copperplate. No matter how hard I tried, mine became squiggles instead of elegant loops." She frowned. "How foolish I am to mention my handwriting when I should be discussing wine. For the ball, champagne is the only possible choice, isn't it?"

Helen quailed. The wine would be expensive, not to mention all the other expenditure.

Her sister tapped her fingernails on the desk. "If only I knew when my husband will return. Of course, I trust Fletcher's advice; even so, I need to consult Tarrant about the wine. He has been away for longer than I anticipated. How I dislike being separated from him."

"With Wellington in command of the entire army, and Uxbridge in charge of the cavalry, it is not surprising Cousin Tarrant is fully engaged. When Major Makelyn found time to call with his wife to congratulate me on my betrothal, he looked exhausted. At heart, he is considerate. He even apologised for sending Dalrymple on a mission to gather information at such a time."

"How good of him," Georgianne gesticulated with her quill. She gazed with dismay at the blob of ink which fell onto her apple blossom pink gown. "How vexatious, this is the first time I have worn this morning gown." She put the quill down. "I shall depend on you to finish writing our lists."

"What else is there to discuss?"

"Dearest, how can you ask such a question when there is so much to decide? We must order your wedding gown and sufficient clothes for a year, so Dalrymple will not be put to the expense of buying any. I shall enjoy helping you."

For a moment, Helen caught her lower lip between her teeth. "Dalrymple is attentive and generous. He writes to me every day and sends gifts. I want to buy him a present, something he will treasure. I can't decide whether to purchase a medicine chest and fill it with necessities— because he mentioned his old one is in a sorry state—or a snuff box."

"I think a snuff box would be more appropriate. If you wish, you may give him a medicine chest filled with necessities after you are married."

"Very well," Helen agreed, still unable to imagine the reality of being a wife.

Next time she saw Dalrymple, would he claim their first kiss? She caught her breath and swallowed a sob. The kiss she always imagined receiving from Langley.

Chapter Twenty-Six

10th May, 1815

The clock struck two. Helen spared a moment to look outside through the window at the moon, which hid behind a veil of silver-rimmed clouds. She yawned and turned toward her bed on the end of which lay a prim, high-necked linen nightgown, cambric sleeping jacket and a lace edged nightcap.

Helen sank onto the edge of the feather mattress. Sleepy-eyed, she bent to untie the satin ribbons of her slippers, the soles of which were almost worn out from dancing at several balls.

Pringle, her cheeks flushed—probably because she had been dozing in the dressing room—joined her. Doubtless the dresser also looked forward to settling into bed. However, no matter how late at night Helen retired, she needed Pringle to untie the strings of her stays.

Almost ready for bed, Helen nodded at her. "Thank you. You may go," she said, when freed of the stays. There is no need for you to fasten my buttons and tie my ribbons."

"Thank you, Miss." Pringle gathered the discarded clothes and slippers.

Helen wriggled her aching toes. She buttoned her nightgown at the throat, fastened her sleeping jacket and pulled her nightcap over her head. Exhausted by a busy day, which included a visit to Mister Barnet and ended with hours of vigorous dancing, Helen snuffed out the candles.

Helen stretched and relaxed on the feather mattress then turned onto her right side and closed her eyes. Thoughts crowded her mind. Dear Dalrymple, always solicitous, made every effort to ride with her in the mornings and attend her at balls and dinners, breakfasts and soirees.

She turned over but could not still her mind. In spite of Cousin Tarrant's kindness since he returned to Brussels, she still suspected he might look forward to her departure from his house. "Are you certain?" he had asked, when she told him of her decision to marry Dalrymple.

She had known why he put the question but, her face expressionless, she had blocked Langley from her mind.

"Yes, I am," she had replied, with no regret for her decision.

"I congratulate you for accepting the hand of such an upstanding gentleman and wish you every happiness." He had smiled at Georgianne before he summoned his butler. "Ah, Fletcher, a bottle of champagne is in order to toast the bride-to-be." Before they sipped from their glasses, her cousin saluted her in military style. "Will you permit me to have the honour of saying 'I do' when the clergyman asks 'Who giveth this woman to this man' at your wedding?"

Filled with gratitude for his many kindnesses, she had said, "I shall be honoured."

Helen never slept on her left side, so she turned over again. The palm of her right hand tucked under her cheek, her mind turned to Mister Barnet who slept for most of every day. Only a fragile thread bound him to life. She had known him for such a short while but knew she would grieve deeply for him when he departed this world, which, last Sunday, the vicar at the English church described as a cesspit of vanity.

A contented sigh escaped her. Mister Barnet's pleasure, when she told him she had taken his advice to marry at the British Embassy on the same day as the ball, made the inconvenience worthwhile.

Of course, there would be few guests at the wedding, but in the meantime, congratulations continued to swamp her. She giggled. Several young gentlemen had sworn their hearts were broken. One even threatened to shoot himself. 'Not fatally, I hope,' she had responded, for she knew he would not.

Helen turned onto her back. She hoped Dalrymple would be pleased with the snuff box she ordered as a memento of their betrothal. Somehow or other, she and Dalrymple never had a moment alone so she still did not know how she would react to his first kiss. Sometimes, when he looked at her, his eyes smouldered, and unfamiliar but pleasurable sensations gripped her.

What would her future hold with Dalrymple? He had told her, "I am country bred and have a love of the land—which is not to say that I am not well-educated. I attended Eton and Oxford before I joined the army."

She yawned repeatedly. Enough of such matters, she must sleep. Once more, she planned the design of her wedding gown. No frills and flounces for her. It must be elegant. Her eyes closed. An inner voice whispered she should be planning a wedding gown to wear when she married Langley. She punched her pillow. No, no, no, she would not think of him.

* * * *

15th May, 1815

The carriage drew to a halt. A footman opened the door and lowered the step. Her feet on the ground, Helen approached a shop which sold snuffboxes and received orders for them to be made for customers. Monsieur Lucay, the elderly proprietor, came out to greet her. He bowed low and ushered Helen inside, but paid no attention to Pringle who accompanied her.

Monsieur beckoned to an assistant. "Jean-Paul, chair for Miss Whitley." A smile hovered around his mouth, Monsieur Lucay rubbed his smooth hands together. "Jean-Paul, fetch Mademoiselle's snuffbox."

Helen sat and looked down at the magnificent display beneath the glass counter. There were so many small treasures; some shaped like shells and hexagons, others were fanciful designs of animals and birds, fruit and flowers, boats and even sedan chairs. Each one was made of gold or silver, jasper or onyx, and many others materials such as ivory, malachite, papier-mâché and tortoiseshell.

Her artist's eyes revelled in the etched or engraved patterns on the lids, some of which were embellished with precious gemstones. She particularly admired one with a fine cameo.

Helen examined an outstandingly pretty box, with an enamelled lid that depicted a bluebell wood, each tiny flower perfectly executed. Neither she nor Georgianne took snuff so she resisted the temptation to buy it.

She frowned at the sight of a silver snuffbox edged with tiny diamonds which framed a mother of pearl moon and stars. Where had she seen the charming object? If she partook of snuff, she would have bought it.

Jean-Paul returned and handed her order to Monsieur Lucay.

"Regard, your treasure, mademoiselle." With a theatrical flourish Monsieur placed a circular snuffbox on a square of black velvet.

At the sight of the enamelled figure of a 'glory boy', Helen caught her breath. Every detail of the dress uniform was correct with even a hint of red silk which lined the jacket and pelisse.

"Allow me, mademoiselle." With a practiced flick of his left thumb, Monsieur Lucay opened the lid to reveal a ruby heart pierced by a golden arrow. Monsieur closed the lid. "Regard." He pressed a tiny catch to reveal a false bottom in which Helen intended to hide a minute self-portrait executed in watercolours.

"Mademoiselle is satisfied?"

"Yes, Monsieur. May I examine another snuffbox, the silver one decorated with the moon and stars?" She assumed nonchalance when he handed it to her. "Perhaps I am foolish to think I saw this somewhere else."

"You might have. I purchase snuffboxes from those who wish to sell them."

"I see." She could have seen it in any one of a score or more hands.

Jean-Paul put the gift for Dalrymple in a red leather box and handed it to her.

Helen stood. "Good day to you, Lucay."

Jean Paul hurried to open the door.

With Pringle a pace or two behind, Helen left the shop.

Perhaps she should purchase some snuff and snuff jars for Dalrymple. No, gentlemen were very particular. At least Papa had chosen his after much consideration, and Cousin Tarrant, whenever he could spare the time, blended his snuff.

Her next purchase would be some exquisite lace for the sleeves of her wedding gown. On her way to the coach, a display of antiquities, behind two bow windows on either side of a panelled door, brought her to a halt. Amongst Grecian urns, Egyptian jewellery, gothic rings, and ancient coins, stood an ivory boat, the one which she last saw in Mister Barnet's house. She peered through the whirls of glass at it.

Could she be mistaken? No, there was the artificial greenery in a miniature terracotta pot. So, one of the nabob's servants had stolen it. Furious, she pressed a hand to her throat. Should she ask how the proprietor obtained it? Helen shook her head. No, but she must take some action. Perhaps the best thing would be to inform Hempstead. The secretary would be the best person to make enquiries. She would speak to him tomorrow.

On the other hand, maybe she should ask Dalrymple for advice. For a second or two she considered Langley, who had retrieved Maria's letters from the blackmailer. Efficient Langley, six years older than her betrothed, and therefore more experienced, would be the gentleman to deal with this. Helen castigated herself. What reason did she have to think Dalrymple might not be capable of dealing with the matter?

She made her way to Madame Dumont's small shop where shelf after shelf of exquisite pillow lace lined the walls.

"For a special gown?" Madame asked, after Helen explained she wished to purchase lace sufficient for a pair of long sleeves.

"Yes, my wedding gown."

"Congratulations, Mademoiselle."

"Thank you."

Madame's eyebrows arched. "Have you decided on the fabric for your gown? If you have, it will help me to decide which lace to show you."

"I have chosen lily-white silk."

"Ah, the contrast between that and Brussels' famous lace will be magnificent. Your jewellery, Mademoiselle?"

Of course, she would wear some from the suite Mister Barnet gave her. "Diamonds set in silver."

Madame clapped her hands. "Magnificent." She indicated chairs set around a table. " Please sit down." She gestured to a high-backed wooden chair on one side of the door. "Your attendant may sit there."

"Thank you." Georgianne appreciated her consideration toward a servant. It would be a pleasure to purchase the lace from Madame Dumont.

Madame fetched two parcels of lace wrapped in paper. She spread the first across the table. "Point Duchesse," she breathed. "See the pomegranates, a symbol of fruitfulness intertwined with vines and leaves."

At the mention of fruitfulness, Helen blushed.

Madame rolled the lace up and handed it to an assistant. "Or perhaps you prefer Point Anglaise." She removed it from the paper, flicked the length open and laid it out on the table.

Helen gazed at the spider's web of fine threads linking roses and leaves to each other. If she decided to have puffed sleeves edged with scallops, there was also enough for a bodice, which, for modesty's sake, would be lined with cambric and silk.

Madame displayed more and more lace, but Helen selected the Point Anglaise because its pattern of roses reminded her of the blooms in summer which filled the gardens of her childhood home with sweet perfume.

"An excellent choice," Madame Dupont complimented her, all smiles.

"I think so," Helen murmured, thinking of the sketches she had made. She beckoned to her dresser, who walked across the well-polished floorboards to her side.

"Yes, Miss."

"Please carry the parcel."

Helen sighed. While she made her choice, the question of what to do about the theft of Mister Barnet's ivory replica of a Chinese boat remained at the back of her mind. Her eyes opened wide. The silver snuffbox edged with tiny diamonds which framed a mother of pearl moon and stars! Of course, she first saw it amongst a collection in a glass display case in Mister Barnet's drawing room. Anger boiled in her. How dare Greaves, or—to give him the benefit of the doubt—some other person steal from the nabob? The sooner she acted on Mister Barnet's behalf, the better. Perhaps the thefts should be drawn to the attention of the British Ambassador.

In the street, Helen took several deep breaths. She hoped Dalrymple would find time to call on her. If he did, she would give him the snuffbox and tell him someone had robbed Mister Barnet.

Chapter Twenty-Seven

10th May, 1815

For four days, Helen wrestled with the problem of whether or not to inform Hempstead about the thefts from Mister Barnet's house. The matter weighed heavily on her mind.

"Is something troubling you?" Georgianne asked.

"I am a little tired."

Cousin Tarrant had looked up over the edge of the most recent copy of The Times to be delivered to him from England. He shook his head in mock reproof. "Early morning rides, hours spent painting, visits to Mister Barnet, dancing until almost dawn and I don't know what else must be exhausting. I fear you becoming a mere shadow of your former self before I hand you over to the Captain on your wedding day. The roses will fade from your cheeks and he will cry off."

"Tarrant, stop teasing my sister," his wife scolded indignantly.

* * * *

"How is Mister Barnet?" Helen asked Greaves.

"I am told he is the same as ever since he took to his bed."

346

Should she have a word with the secretary? Yet suppose, only suppose, Hempstead was involved in the thefts.

Helen sat with Mister Barnet who retreated into the past, speaking of his childhood among the gentle folds of the Cotswolds, his kind nurse, and his first pony, a dapple grey called Merry. After a half hour, or a little less, he closed his eyes. Certain he slept, Helen took the opportunity to leave.

* * * *

On the ground floor, Greaves sent for Pringle, who as usual waited for her in the servant's hall.

Thomas responded to a knock on the door. To Helen's astonishment, Maria burst into the entrance hall.

"Miss Whitley!" she shrieked and embraced her.

Helen emerged from Maria's arms, her nostrils filled with the bride's strong perfume.

"Oh, my dearest Miss Whitley, I intended to visit Mister Barnet to thank him for his hospitality, but shall return later. Come with me. You shall ride home in my carriage."

Pringle came into the hall and pursed her mouth at the sight of Maria.

Well she might, thought Helen, dazzled by the bride's bright pink gown worn beneath an apple green pelisse and an Angoulême bonnet adorned with green feathers and artificial rosebuds.

Helen allowed Maria to lead her out to a carriage drawn by a pair of matched sorrels. "In with you, Miss Whitley," Maria said. "Your woman—what-is-her-name?—may walk, so we may have a comfortable coze in private."

Maria shepherded her into the carriage. "Rue Royale," she ordered the coachman. "How kind Mister Barnet is. I'll never forget his generosity."

"His health does not improve."

"I'm sorry." Maria seized her hand. "You can't imagine how agreeable it is to be a married lady."

With a tinge of envy, Helen laughed. Maria had defied her father, her dragon of a grandmother, and convention, to marry the man she loved. "I am happy for you, but I assumed you and your husband were in England. Why have you returned to Brussels?"

Maria clasped her hands together at her breast. "Oh, it is extraordinary. Only imagine Grandmere spoke to Father on my behalf?"

"I cannot envisage it."

"Well she did. Grandmere told my father that until the day she dies, she will regret the rift with my mamma. She told him to consider whether he would ever be sorry for the gulf between us."

"Really."

Maria nodded so vehemently that the feathers on her bonnet bobbed up and down.

"Yes, she did. Of course, she reiterated she never approved of their marriage. However, she believed mine would do well enough for a granddaughter whose aristocratic French blood is diluted by a commoner's."

"Good gracious!"

"Much struck by her opinion, but indignant by her words diluted blood, Father invited us to visit him. My angel, Monsieur Lamont, is so tactful and deferential that my father soon treated him as a son. Father has not quite forgiven me our elopement, but he declares that if he had known my affections were engaged, he would not have tried to force me into marriage with Viscount Langley." She shrugged. "Of course, that is nonsense, but Monsieur Lamont persuaded me to allow Father to colour the truth to avoid an argument."

"I am pleased to hear all is well with you."

"Yes, it is." Maria nodded so emphatically that the feathers embarked on another vigorous dance. "What of you, Miss Whitley? Are you still surrounded by beaux at every ball?"

"If I say yes, you will think I am conceited."

"So, you are."

"I have a single beau," Helen murmured, in an attempt to be modest

"Never tell me," Maria cried out, "you are betrothed to the viscount."

"I beg your pardon!"

"I'm not blind. Whenever the two of you are in the same room, the viscount doesn't blink when he watches you. He is spellbound." She cleared her throat. "There's no need to colour up. I suspected you love his lordship. Please accept my congratulations. I'm so happy for you."

Helen clenched her fists so tightly that her gloves might split at the seams. "You are mistaken. I am betrothed, but not to Viscount Langley."

"Oh, please forgive me. I apologise for my assumption." Maria twisted the end of one of the bright-pink ribbons which anchored her bonnet beneath her chin. "To whom are you betrothed?"

"To Captain Dalrymple."

"Ah, the officer whose looks resemble those of Lord Langley."

Her throat, too choked for her to speak, Helen nodded, well-aware of the similarity between Langley and Dalrymple's appearance.

Maria patted her hand. "Are you certain you wish to wed him? I speak as a happy bride, who can imagine nothing worse than the choice of the wrong husband."

Helen jerked her hand away. "I am sure," she said, although her previous uncertainties returned. She peered sideways at Maria, across whose face a shadow seemed to have fallen while the carriage drew to a halt. "I am sure," she repeated.

"Then I'm pleased for you," Maria replied, her tone of voice gentle.

"Will you come in to partake of refreshment?"

"No, I think not. Since my marriage, I'm no longer a part of your world." No, don't protest. Of course, I shall always be grateful for the help you and Viscount Langley gave me. If I can ever reciprocate, never hesitate to ask."

Helen scrutinised the young matron. "Thank you, Madame Lamonte." She stepped out of the carriage. "Good day to you."

With slow footsteps, Helen went up the steps. A footman answered her knock on the door.

"Is Mrs Tarrant at home?" she inquired.

"Yes, Miss, she is in her parlour."

A cheerful rat-a-tat sounded on the front door.

Helen turned around to see who had arrived. She forced herself to smile, her sensibilities still overwrought by Maria's assumption that she would marry the viscount. "Dalrymple, here you are, I hoped to see you soon" she said with forced cheerfulness.

The captain stepped inside. "My apologies for not calling on you for several days."

"Don't look so worried, I promised not to reproach you when duty commands."

Dalrymple's eyes glowed. "What have I done to deserve an angel like you?"

At the memory of Georgianne's amusement when she said she doubted Tarrant wanted an angel for a wife, Helen choked back a chuckle.

"Don't deceive yourself, sir. You have yet to discover my faults."

Dalrymple smiled while he tucked his black busby under his arm. "I doubt you have any, but I hope you will tolerate mine."

She seized the opportunity to be alone with him and give him the snuffbox. "Please come with me."

"To the ends of the earth and beyond if you insist."

A giggle escaped her. She led him up the stairs to a small drawing room, where the family gathered before they dined on the rare evenings when they did not entertain guests.

Helen stripped off her cream pigskin gloves, removed her hat, and tossed them onto a chair upholstered in hyacinth-blue and white-striped heavy silk which matched the curtains. "Please be seated."

Instead, he stood. His intense scrutiny made her toes curl

Unaccountably nervous, she withdrew the small red box from her reticule. A little shy, she offered it to him. Would he like it? "I had something made for you."

Dalrymple pulled off his gauntlets, removed his busby from under his arm and put them next to her hat and gloves.

* * * *

Dalrymple's hands quivered when he opened the box. Although he had referred to

Helen as an angel, he wanted to worship her in an earthly manner. The words of the marriage service drifted into his mind. With my body I thee worship. At his image of Helen naked in their bed, her nightcap removed and her thick hair loosened, red-hot lava seemed to flow through his veins.

Helen drew closer to him. He wanted to pull her into his arms, kiss her forehead, her eyes, her mouth, her neck...no, he should not think of such liberties. She was his future wife, not a mistress.

"Dalrymple, I hope you will like it."

What could be inside the box? She took the trouble to commission a gift to mark their betrothal so, whether he liked it or not, he must show his appreciation. He tipped the snuff box into his hand. Speechless, he stared at it.

"If it is not to your taste perhaps you would prefer something else."

He shook his head while he traced the design with his forefinger. "It is exquisite. I shall treasure it for as long as I live."

She took another step toward him. "I am so pleased you like it. I insisted on the exact shade of red for the Glory Boy's uniform."

Their bodies almost touched. He breathed in her cologne, an intoxicating blend of what? Roses and lilac combined with something sharp—a fragrance he would always associate with her.

His past dalliances faded from his mind. He believed Helen reciprocated his love. By now, the gentleman she once wanted to marry could be no more than a distant dream. Otherwise, she would not have taken so much trouble over his gift. Besides, why else would she have agreed to marry him? He did not have a title, and his means were modest.

Dalrymple put the snuffbox on a nearby table. He encircled her with his arms. Although Helen gasped, she did not attempt to escape him. He gazed into the brilliant green eyes of the only lady he had ever wanted to marry. Helen trembled. He did not want to frighten her so first he kissed the smooth silk of her forehead. She sighed. He kissed her satin soft cheeks, then the place where a pulse beat fast in her neck. Although she still trembled, he tightened one arm around her. With his free hand, he cupped the back of her head. Helen was his, all his to love and make love to. They belonged to each other.

Dalrymple paused to look at her face. Since she agreed to marry him, he had longed for this moment. With pent up passion, he kissed her mouth, which remained closed. So, was this her first kiss? In spite of her many admirers, it seemed she had kept them all at a distance and reserved her favours for the gentleman she would marry.

With the tip of his tongue he first traced the outline of her lips. Helen breathed fast. Delighted because she did not shrink from him, he knew he would lose control of his desire if he did not release her. With reluctance he freed her.

Helen's eyes opened. Her breathing slowed. Her full breasts no longer heaved. He clenched his fists to prevent himself cupping them while she returned from wherever he had transported her.

"I never knew," she whispered, her eyes soft.

"What?" he breathed

"That my first kiss would be so wonderful," she whispered, her cheeks poppy-red.

His heart pounded. He had won a prize beyond compare. Helen would not be a reluctant, missish bride.

This time he sat on the sofa when Helen asked him to be seated. He patted the space next to him. Without a moment's hesitation, she sat beside him. What should he say to his intelligent wife-to-be, now that he had mastered his urgent desire to possess her without delay? He cleared his throat before he spoke. "I am glad we are to be married soon."

"So am I." Her half smile hinted at shyness. She looked down at the hyacinth-blue and jade-green carpet. "But there is so much to do before our wedding day."

"Yes, I know, for I remember the preparations for my sister's marriage. I shall never forget the endless discussions about the bridal gown, and her trousseau, sufficient to last her for a year."

"Ah, you understand. I have chosen fabrics my modiste will have made up in accordance with my sketches."

"Oh, you design your own clothes. That is why you are always so elegant. I am fortunate to be betrothed to so talented a lady." A vision of Helen in an exquisite nightgown on their wedding night, popped into his mind. He took a deep breath and did not resist the temptation to slide his arm around her waist. If only he could feel yielding flesh instead of rigid stays.

Although Helen did not seek to escape from his possessive hold, to his surprise, she did not respond to his compliment. Instead she frowned, the expression in her eyes grave. "I have matters other than my bridal clothes to consider; in particular, one which concerns Mister Barnet. He is too ill for me to tell him someone is stealing his treasures." Helen's eyes smouldered. "Mister Barnet is gentle and generous. I cannot bear to think of him being robbed."

Dalrymple frowned. If someone was stealing from the nabob, the culprit must be caught. He removed his arm from around Helen's waist, stood and walked up and down the room. After a minute or two, he came to a halt before her. "I agree that if you are right, it is shameful to fleece an old gentleman. It is even more so in Mister Barnet's case, for he has no relative to depend on. I am glad you confided in me, but before any action can be taken, what proof of burglary do you have?"

"When I collected your snuff box, I saw one which seemed familiar. Later, I remembered seeing it at Mister Barnet's house. I also saw an ivory replica of a Chinese boat in a shop window. Both items are distinctive. I think both unique items were stolen."

"I shall visit each shop and question the proprietors. It will go ill with them if they don't furnish me with descriptions of the culprits. The next step is to inform our Ambassador—whose duty is to protect His Majesty's subjects. You may be sure the thief shall be brought to justice with the least possible delay." He frowned. "Do you suspect anyone?"

Relieved by his intention to take immediate action, Helen spoke. "Well, it might be Greaves, the butler, but his rudeness on one occasion when I called on Mister Barnet, does not mean he is guilty. It could even be Hempstead." She frowned not wishing to make unjust accusations. "Oh, I don't know who the culprit is. Any one of the servants could be to blame."

Dalrymple bowed. "Forgive me for leaving now. I want to act before Makelyn sends me on another mission. When there is something to report, I shall inform you." He tucked the snuffbox into a pocket, before retrieving his busby and gauntlets. "Good day, my love."

Dalrymple could have kissed her before he left. Bemused by his abrupt farewell but impressed by his decisiveness Helen pressed her hand to her mouth. Well, her first kiss was everything she had hoped it would be. In response, another extraordinary but not distasteful excitement stirred within her.

Chapter Twenty-Eight

14th June, 1815

In her dressing room, Helen caught sight of her own and her sister's reflection in the full length mirror.

"You have no regrets, dearest?"

The question, which Helen knew referred to her decision to marry Dalrymple, seemed to hover in the air. Helen shook her head. Langley would never tie the knot with her. Well, as a gamester would say, she had cast the dice. Dice! She cursed Langley's father for being an inveterate gambler. If he were not, she could have—Helen checked her thoughts. She would not give Dalrymple cause to regret the marriage.

She looked down at her white silk drawers, with rows of tucks at the hems edged with Brussels lace. She choked back a giggle, relieved to find something to divert her mind. Old ladies still considered the garment immodest, but after it became known Princess Charlotte wore drawers, they became popular. She blushed. What would her bridegroom think of them?

Her admiration for Dalrymple grew when he proved himself decisive and efficient. Only days after she confided in him, Dalrymple established Hempstead's guilt and arrested the secretary. Like a knight in times past, sent on a quest by a lady, her captain had fulfilled it as competently as Langley had dealt with Maria's blackmailer. No, she did not want to think of the viscount on her wedding day.

Pringle tightened the laces.

Helen sighed. She did not need to go on a reducing diet, but sometimes she wished she were not a giantess among smaller ladies. She shook her head. Dalrymple admired her, so what did her height matter? At least—she consoled herself—she did not need to complement the fashionable high waistline with a false bosom to enhance her figure.

What would Dalrymple think when he first saw her in the fine linen nightgown, lavishly trimmed with ribbon and lace, which she had chosen to wear on the first night in their bed? Would he say, "You are beautiful?"

Deep in contemplation, Helen slipped her cambric petticoat over her linen shift and stays. She stood still while Pringle fastened the tapes around her waist and did up the tiny buttons at the back of the bodice.

She glanced at her sister. Sometimes, Cousin Tarrant dismissed Georgianne's dresser and helped his wife prepare for bed. Aware of her blushes, she wondered if Dalrymple would allow Pringle to disrobe her, but if not— she could not complete the thought.

"Now, Miss," said Pringle, her tone of voice respectful. She picked up the silk wedding gown. With a deft movement, she drew it over Helen's head.

"You have never looked more beautiful," Georgianne breathed.

Her feet in dainty white slippers, Mister Barnet's gift of the diamond parure in place, Helen peeped into the mirror at the gleaming white silk and exquisite Pointe Anglaise lace.

"Dearest, you are beautiful."

"No, you are the family beauty." Helen gazed at Georgianne's pink silk gown. "You resemble a rose in full bloom."

Her sister laughed and patted her stomach. "How poetic, but you are unkind to remind me of the reason for 'the full bloom'."

"You misunderstand me. I refer to your pink cheeks and your elegant gown."

"In that case, thank you for the compliment."

Georgianne handed her a posy of white roses and sprigs of rosemary. "Rosemary, so you will never forget me."

"As if I could!" She reached out to embrace her sister.

Georgianne warded her off with her hands. "You will crush your gown and that is Dalrymple's privilege. Now, hurry if you still want to visit Mister Barnet so he can see you in your wedding finery."

"I insist on it."

"You are so stubborn, Helen, I cannot understand why you wish to— Oh, I shall say no more on the subject. We have already argued enough."

Helen sighed again. Her sister and Tarrant would never understand her affection for the nabob.

"Your cloak, dearest."

Her wedding gown concealed by the ankle length garment, Helen made her way with her sister to the carriage.

"Your visit must be brief, if we are to return in time for Tarrant to escort us to the Embassy," Georgianne warned her.

* * * *

"Ah," breathed Mister Barnet, "Captain Dalrymple is fortunate to have a beautiful, good-natured bride." He smiled. "Oh, I am delighted you are wearing the jewellery made for Emily."

Helen leaned forward to pat his hand.

"My child, don't pity me. I believe I shall soon be reunited with those I love." He turned his head on the pillow. "Mrs Tarrant, it is good of you to accompany Miss Whitley. Do you know your sister rescued me from a rabble of hooligans who are a disgrace to their uniforms?"

"Yes, indeed," Georgianne replied.

"She is dear to me." Mister Barnet beckoned to Sister Imelda, who seemed to keep constant vigil in her patient's bedroom. "Please give my letter to Miss Whitley.

The nun opened a drawer. She removed a missive sealed with red wax and held it out to Mister Barnet.

"No, it is for Miss Whitley." Mister Barnet clasped Helen's hand for a moment. "It is my farewell letter, but don't open it until I am dead."

Helen drew her breath in with an audible gasp.

"My dear child, there is no cause to be sorry for me. I am ready to meet my Maker, who I hope will not judge me harshly." He covered his mouth with his hand to conceal a yawn.

"Indeed, I am sure He will not." Her eyes filled with tears. She decided to let him sleep for now. She would visit him again in a few days.

Mister Barnet sat up. His eyes opened wide. "Emily!" he cried out, and, even as he voiced the name, fell back onto his pillow.

Sister Imelda rushed forward to check his pulse. The nun put his hand down. She made the sign of the cross on his forehead then closed his eyes.

"Is he…?" Helen faltered.

"Yes, he has gone—in his own words—'to meet His Maker'."

Georgianne put an arm around Helen's waist. "I am very sorry."

Sister Imelda fingered her rosary. "Don't cry, child. Mister Barnet would not wish it. To be sure, it is more than kind of you to have visited him on today of all days. He looked forward to seeing you in your wedding gown."

Helen squeezed her eyes shut. "It has been a pleasure to know him, Sister."

"You have a loving heart, child. May God bless you and keep you all the days of your life. I hope your marriage will be happy and fruitful."

"You are very kind." Helen allowed Georgianne to guide her out of the bedroom.

Thomas handed Helen her cloak. "Congratulations, Miss."

She thanked him, conscious of the many servants who busied themselves in the hall in order to see her wedding gown. Even crusty old Greaves smiled. Should she tell them their employer had died? No, if she did she would lose her composure and weep.

Wrapped in the cloak, she stepped out to the carriage with Georgianne.

Still numb with shock at the suddenness of Mister Barnet's death, Helen clutched the stems of her flowers and remembered the letter. She laid the fragrant posy on the seat beside her. With tremulous fingers, she broke the seal and unfolded the paper. Her eyes misted with tears. She read Mister Barnet's words twice in order to understand them. They thanked her for taking pity on a lonely old man, and explained he had left her a memento, which he hoped would please her.

She picked up the posy. Rosemary, for remembrance. How apt. She would never forget Mister Barnet. "Farewell, my friend," she murmured.

* * * *

"Dearest, I am sorry the nabob has died just before your wedding," Georgianne commiserated, when they reached home.

"I knew he did not have long to live," Helen replied, despite the lump in her throat.

"I know, but it does not make it any easier. I suggest you go to your bedroom to compose yourself, while I tell Tarrant that Mister Barnet is no more." She looked at her butler.

"Major Tarrant is in the library, Madam," Fletcher informed her.

About to follow Georgianne up the stairs, Helen caught her foot in a fold of her cloak. She put a hand on the wall to steady herself while Fletcher answered a knock on the door.

"My lord." The butler's voice conveyed surprise.

"Good day, Fletcher."

Helen recognised Langley's all too familiar voice. Why had he come?

She heard his footsteps approach. "Miss Whitley, a moment of your time, if you please."

Helen did not please. Her foot freed, she turned. "I regret—"

Langley frowned, "Say no more. I have not come here to be fobbed off with a platitude."

At the sight of the angles of his handsome face, unlike Dalrymple's with more rounded cheeks, she tried to ignore bubbles of excitement which exploded in her like those of the finest champagne. "To say the least, your visit is ill-timed," she replied, careful not to reveal the sudden but unwanted thrill in response to his presence.

"I disagree. It is well timed." Langley grasped her arm, but not hard enough to hurt.

Unless she wrenched her arm from his, her only choice was to allow him to propel her into the ante room.

"My lord?" She sank onto a small, hard-backed chair, aware of the closed door.

"Why are you bundled up in a cloak? Are you cold? Your voice is icy enough to freeze the life from any gentleman."

His words brought Mister Barnet to mind. He had always asked her if she was too cold or too hot. Tears filled her eyes. She blinked them away.

Langley stepped back. "Don't cry. Surely you are not frightened of me. Don't you know I would never hurt you?"

Someone on God's earth should shed tears for the dear old gentleman's passing. She swallowed to gain control. "No, I don't fear you. I am not quite myself because Mister Barnet has breathed his last," she managed to say in an even tone. She took a handkerchief out her pocket to wipe her eyes. "I should not mourn. Until the end of his life, he bore his illness with courage and dignity. I am glad he no longer suffers."

"You will miss him."

"Yes, I shall."

Langley drew nearer. He stood too close to her. "Well, I am here on a different matter. One which I hope will please you."

Puzzled, she waited for him to continue.

"Helen, I am not conceited but I am sure of one thing, your marriage to Captain Dalrymple would be a travesty."

Helen stood. "I beg your pardon?" Only inches away from him, his dark eyes commanded all her attention. The scent of leather, blended with horses and spicy pomade, almost intoxicated her. "A travesty?" She managed the question in a level tone. "It is less than an hour from the wedding ceremony, my lord." She stepped away from him with the intention of leaving the room.

Langley caught hold of her hand. His eyes blazed. "My situation has changed."

"How? What has it to do with me?"

"Forgive me. You must think I am mad because I am as inarticulate as a tongue-tied schoolboy."

"I would not describe you as inarticulate." She resented his touch which sought to claim her.

"My apologies. I must explain."

She sank back onto the chair to force him to release her.

"I have won the Government Lottery. When some officers discussed whether or not to share their resources to buy a ticket for the next lottery, and share the proceeds if they won, I remembered my mother gave me a ticket."

She stared up at him. "I am delighted, but what has it to do with me?"

"Oh, my love, she gave me the winning ticket. I can marry you and save Longwood Place."

The fool! She would have married him— even slept on the ground wrapped in his cloak. Did he value money more than her? "You call me 'my love' but I think you have always cared more for that pile of stone than me."

"You must know that is not true."

"No, I don't."

Helen's inner voice whispered. I know, that although he loved me, his pride did not allow him to marry me if he could not support me in comfort. Now it is too late for us to marry. Not only gentlemen pride themselves on their honour. Does Langley really believe I will reject Dalrymple?

He stood before her. "Helen? Have you nothing to say to me?"

"What should I say? Should I be flattered because a viscount wants to marry an insignificant army officer's daughter?"

"Sarcasm does not become you. I shall be flattered if you agree to marry me."

If only…no, she would not allow herself to travel down the road of regret. She had chosen to marry another upstanding officer and gentleman.

"Helen, you don't understand how desperate my circumstances were. Both of us have been brought up to understand duty. I owed it to my family."

"What have your relatives to do with your earlier rejection of me, when I summoned the courage to sacrifice my pride to ask you to be my husband?" Although her heart beat faster, she remained loyal to Dalrymple.

"It has everything to do with it. My sister wore a darned dress. Papa gambled everything on the turn of a fatal card. Unless I paid for it, Charlotte could not have the London Season she deserved. Although I had accumulated the funds to do so, I knew it would take almost every penny." He slammed his left fist onto the palm of his right hand. "Moreover, I also had an obligation to Mamma, my younger sisters and brothers. I was not selfish enough to have married you at the cost of their plight. However, I loved you too much to agree to marry Miss Tomlinson."

Helen stood. "I cannot reject Captain Dalrymple."

"Is there nothing I can say to change your mind?"

In turmoil, she shook her head.

Langley's eyes raged. "My God, I have always admired your calm. Now, I wonder if you are thus because you lack sensibility."

Langley could not know what it cost her to appear unruffled. Snakelike, her breath hissed between her teeth before she spoke. "How dare you? Do you think I could shame my family by jilting Dalrymple? If I acted so disgracefully, they would be justified if they disowned me. And if society rejected me, I would deserve it."

Before Langley could reply, Georgianne entered the room.

Her tiny sister drew herself up to her full height. She looked at Langley, her manner accusatory when she stepped forward. "Langley, thank you for calling on my sister to offer your congratulations." She looked away from him. "Leave your cloak here, dearest. Tarrant is waiting to escort us to the Embassy." Georgianne returned her attention to Langley. "We shall see you there. I also look forward to receiving you at our ball."

At the threshold, Helen could not resist the temptation to look back.

The viscount bowed.

Georgianne pinched her arm. Helen obeyed the unspoken instruction to leave.

Langley's impassioned plea for her to marry him clamoured in her mind. Had she made the right decision? Of course she had. She must not succumb to a hysterical outburst.

"Dearest, you are too pale, but it is understandable. Every bride is nervous on her wedding day."

It would be hours before she and Dalrymple were alone; time to become calm enough to recover from the shock of Langley's outrageous proposition.

After the ceremony, she would return here to supervise the last minute arrangements for the ball. No wedding trip for her. Moreover, due to the uncertain future, Dalrymple neither wished to set up house in Antwerp, Bruges or Brussels, nor for her to live in a hotel when Wellington invaded France on—rumour claimed—the 25th of June. For the time being, they would live with Cousin Tarrant and her sister. Indeed, she would spend her first night of marriage in this house.

Arm in arm with Georgianne, she made her way to the library.

Resplendent in dress uniform, Cousin Tarrant saluted her.

Georgianne gestured toward her. "I am sure you will agree Helen is the most beautiful bride you have ever seen?"

He laughed. "If I had a magic mirror and asked it, if your sister is the fairest bride of all, it would reply, 'She is fair; but fairer still was your wife on your wedding day'."

Georgianne blushed. "Dearest, it is time to leave."

Tarrant held up his hand. "A moment, if you please. My sympathy, Helen," he began.

She held her breath. Did the butler tell him Langley was closeted with her? Could he have guessed his friend asked her to marry him instead of Dalrymple?

"I am sorry to hear Mister Barnet is dead," Cousin Tarrant continued. "I know how much you liked him."

"Yes, I did. We became friends."

"Don't allow anything to spoil your day." He looked sharply at her. "Captain Dalrymple is an exemplary gentleman. I have no doubts about your future happiness."

"Thank you."

"God bless you, Miss," her dresser said, when Helen approached the front door.

"Thank you, Pringle," Helen murmured. She stepped from the cool interior of the house out into the sunshine.

* * * *

Langley cursed fate. He had tried to make Helen understand that before now, marriage to her would have been selfish. His nostrils flared. In spite of his disappointment, he respected her refusal to reject Dalrymple.

Distraught, he wanted to gallop away from Brussels, away from the bride and groom. Impossible! People knew of the strong bond forged between himself and Rupes since they went to Eton, after which they shared the same campaigns. In all probability, if he did not smile and congratulate Helen after her wedding, and attend the ball, speculation would be rife.

He cursed himself for being an arrogant fool. He should not have intervened on Helen's wedding day. But not for a moment had he imagined she would reject him now that he could provide for her and his family. Of course, if she had accepted his proposal, scandal—which would have shocked his mother—would have ensued. His jaw tensed. If it would help, he would swear, get drunk or—what?

The high collar of his uniform seemed to strangle him. He choked back the tide of thwarted love. Helen, he groaned inwardly, knowing she would always be embedded in his heart. Mothers were right to tell sons and daughters that love was too painful to be a necessity for marriage. Well, one day he would marry and have an heir, but never again would he risk his heart.

Damnation, why could he not have won the lottery before Helen accepted Dalrymple's proposal? He would always regret his father's folly.

His mouth formed a grim line. Well, she chose Dalrymple. Maybe she loved him. The possibility lacerated his heart.

* * * *

At the British Embassy, Helen entered the large parlour prepared for the wedding. Her fingers clutched Cousin Tarrant's arm. For the first time in many years, she missed her mother. Not the one who drank to try and forget her grief, but the tender parent she used to be, before she lost her sons and husband.

Oblivious to the few guests, she walked down a short aisle toward the drumhead altar, behind which the Glory Boy's chaplain stood. Only Dalrymple, who waited as straight as a lance in the uniform of The Glory Boys, commanded her attention. For a moment, she faltered. He turned. His eyes widened at the sight of her. A joyous smile brightened his handsome face. Her grief over Mister Barnet's death, and her turmoil caused by Langley, dispersed along with her momentary panic.

She stood beside her bridegroom, who clasped her hand in his strong one. Yes, she could rely on this officer for all the days of her life. Every vestige of strain flowed away. Her mind cleared. The clergyman spoke. "I am required to ask anyone present who knows a reason why these persons may not lawfully marry, to declare it now."

Did she imagine Langley staring at her back with the hope that she would refuse to marry Dalrymple? Conscious of his presence, she straightened her spine.

Later, she could not remember making her responses, but when the service ended she became aware that a thorn in her wedding posy had pierced flesh as tender as her bruised heart.

Georgianne came forward to embrace her before Cousin Tarrant congratulated her. He moved aside to make way for Sir Charles, the ambassador. "A long life and happiness to both of you." He kissed her cheek, and then made way for Langley.

"Congratulations." His lordship spoke in a clipped tone of voice. "Mrs Dalrymple, please give me a favour which, like a knight of old, I may carry into battle."

Her hand tightened on her bridegroom's arm.

Dalrymple laughed. "Will you not give the Major one?"

She forced herself to uncurl her fingers. From the posy, she plucked a golden-hearted rose, its stem entangled with a sprig of rosemary.

Langley bowed. "Thank you, rosemary for remembrance."

Her gaze lingered on him as he made his way out of the parlour.

Chapter Twenty-Nine
14th June, 1815

"A triumph, dearest. I cannot count the number of guests who congratulated me on the decorations and supper. I swear there is not a morsel left of the dishes prepared by the Indian cooks." Georgianne sank onto a chair in the ball room.

"Yes, so I have been told," Helen responded. "I have been besieged by compliments from gentlemen who served with the army in India." She smiled at her bridegroom who stood next to her.

His eyes concentrated on her face. "I am proud of you. I can't count the number of ladies who asked me if I would allow you to design the décor for their balls."

Georgianne fluttered her ivory fan. "What did you reply?"

"I said that Mrs Dalrymple does not need my permission."

Aware most husbands believed they had the right to control every aspect of their wives' lives, Helen his generosity warmed her heart. "Thank you," she whispered. She transferred her gaze to the wooden figure of the blue boy, the main feature in the ballroom thronged with gentlemen, either wearing colourful uniforms or well-tailored civilian clothes, and bejewelled ladies in elegant gowns.

The crowd near the door parted and the Duke of Wellington entered. In accordance with its instruction, the orchestra played Handel's See The Conquering Hero Comes.

Georgianne stood. "How provoking of the Field Marshall to arrive after Tarrant and I decided he would not attend, and after we had received all our guests," she murmured. "Look at him. 'Pon my word, while troops mass, one would think His Grace has nothing better to occupy himself with than balls and routs and I know not what else."

Dalrymple looked gravely at his sister-in-law. "If he seemed alarmed and did not assume a high-spirited façade, ma'am, French spies would soon report to Napoleon that our field marshal is rattled."

"How astute you are," Georgianne commented. "But where is Tarrant? Ah, there he is greeting His Grace."

Followed by Helen and her new brother-in-law, Georgianne crossed the floor to receive her illustrious guest, whom she had known since childhood.

"No need for formality," Wellington remarked, when Georgianne executed a graceful curtsey.

Her eyes laughed up at him. "I regret I don't have a wreath of combined myrtle and roses to crown you."

His Grace laughed while Dalrymple bowed and Helen curtsied.

"My felicitations," the great man boomed.

Gratified by his attention, Helen smiled. "Thank you."

"Amazing." The Duke looked around the ballroom. "I like the Hindu God, and the elephants. Quite takes me back to my days in India. Congratulations, Mrs Tarrant, you have outshone every other hostess."

"Thank you for your kind words." Before Georgianne could say more, the Duchess of Richmond joined them.

Wellington bowed and greeted her. "Splendid, is it not?" He waved a hand at the painted hangings on the walls.

The sparkle left the duchess' eyes. "Compared to this ball—which will be remembered for many years—I fear mine will fade into insignificance."

"Of course not." Wellington turned his attention to Helen. "Dalrymple, don't allow your bridegroom to neglect his duty. Tomorrow, ensure he attends Makelyn's review in the Allee Vert in good time." He nodded at Cousin Tarrant, who stood beside Georgianne. "Glad you and Langley are here. By God, Peninsular veterans know their duty unlike many of the new fellows."

"Mrs Tarrant, I look forward to seeing you at my ball," the Duchess began. "Bring the bride and bridegroom with you." She patted Helen's arm. "I wish you and your captain everything good. Now, Captain, dance with your bride."

Helen glanced up at her husband's happy face. His smile warmed her heart. She tingled remembering their only kiss. Helen put the tips of her fingers on his arm.

Dalrymple smiled when they took their place in the centre of the ballroom floor. "Our first waltz as husband and wife." He held her a little closer than the prescribed distance between partners.

"The first of many," Helen replied, relieved by the Duke's assurance that the Duchess did not need to cancel her ball since Napoleon posed no immediate threat. However, at the thought of the inevitable invasion of France, her hand trembled in Dalrymple's.

"Are you tired?" her bridegroom asked.

It was not the right moment to mention war. "Only a little."

He guided her toward the door. "Perhaps it is time to escape. I am sorry there is no carriage to carry you off on a wedding trip." His eyes shone. "We must make the best of our situation." To the strains of the music, he guided her out into the hall.

As if on well-oiled wheels, Fletcher stepped forward. "Captain, please follow me."

Pringle came to Helen's side to accompany her upstairs.

She pressed a hand over her heart which beat faster than usual. Her footsteps slowed. She lost sight of her bridegroom before reaching the landing and turned toward the left.

"No, to the right, madam," Pringle directed.

Helen hesitated before she followed the woman, who opened a door at the end of the corridor. "Your new apartment, madam. Mrs Tarrant considered your old one unsuitable for a married lady and gentleman. She prepared this as a surprise for you and the captain."

Apprehensive, Helen lingered at the threshold. One of the reasons she married was to become mistress of her own household, and here she was, still obliged to her sister and Cousin Tarrant. Every muscle tensed. She could not force herself to step over the threshold. For the first time in her life she would be alone with a gentleman in her bedroom.

"Come," Pringle urged.

Helen entered the bedroom. The scent of beeswax candles sweetened the air. Vases filled with fragrant red roses adorned the mantelpiece. A bower for a bride.

Pringle pointed to the right of the room. "The Captain's dressing room is through that door, and yours is through the opposite one. Please follow me, madam. Mrs Tarrant wants you to be comfortable. Your parlour is next to your dressing room."

"Oh." Helen battled nervousness. She wanted nothing more than to get into bed on her own and go to sleep.

Pringle closed the bedroom door. "There's a bowl and a pitcher of water behind the screen if you wish to wash your hands and face, but first allow me to help you take off your wedding gown."

Like a puppet, Helen stood still while Pringle disrobed her, but her mind would not be silent and submissive. A wave of grief for Mister Barnet swept through her. He approved of her decision to marry Captain Dalrymple, but neither of them could have forecast Langley would win the lottery and be in a position to marry her.

"You're nearly ready, madam," Pringle announced, the fine linen nightgown lavishly trimmed with ribbon and lace in her hands. Pringle drew it over Helen's head and fastened the mother of pearl button at the throat. "Please sit down at your dressing table."

Pringle removed the pins from her hair, then brushed and plaited it. What would happen when Dalrymple joined her? What would they do? What would they say?

"You are shivering, madam. A glass of wine to warm you before you go to bed?"

Helen opened her eyes wider. To bed? Now? "No, thank you, Pringle. I have drunk enough this evening." The spectre of her mother in her cups, ever present, she always drank sparingly.

The dresser opened the door to the bedroom. Helen shook her head. "I must wash my hands and face." She retreated behind the screen, sponged her face and soaped her hands, careful neither to splash water onto her nightgown nor wet the long sleeves. Glad to be alone, she took her time rinsing her hands. She squared her shoulders, chastising herself for being a fool. Dalrymple's kiss had thrilled her and she anticipated more kisses from her captain, the personification of gentleness. Her fears were foolish.

She dried her hands and entered the bedroom.

Pringle bustled in after her, and laid a dressing gown at the end of the bed. She turned back the sheet and quilt. "Why not get into bed while you wait for the captain, madam?"

Helen's sense of humour bubbled up. The woman sounded like a nursemaid coaxing a reluctant child. How inappropriate for her to be so amused at such a crucial time in her life. She should thank her dresser for her discreet suggestion.

A knock on her bridegroom's dressing room door. Her heart seemed to beat an irregular tattoo. Pringle said something. Dalrymple's deep voice answered.

Alone with the man to whom she would be answerable for as long he lived, Helen clenched her fists. Except for murder, a man could treat his wife as he wished. Ridiculous to imagine Dalrymple would turn from a tender giant into an ogre. Never before could she have imagined being so missish.

* * * *

"Dalrymple," Helen whispered.
"Please call me Marcus."
"Very well."

"Thank you." He smiled at her. "I love your musical voice. Now, please humour me by sitting opposite me."

He would never tell her how hard he had found it to make this decision.

With fluid grace, his wife walked toward the empty chair. Heat surged through him. He wanted to draw her down onto his lap but resisted the temptation. However, the touch of her delectable curves might change his mind. Thinking of them, he swallowed hard. "Perhaps I am selfish to have married you on the brink of invasion."

"Selfish?" she repeated, while she perched on the edge of the chair.

"Yes," he replied, determined to control his passion. "I love you so much, I was frightened to wait."

Helen's eyes rounded. "You! Frightened?"

"Yes, I feared you might marry someone else. So many gentlemen, with far more to offer than I, admire you. I feared you would break my heart by accepting one of them. I took no more interest in the prospective wives, whom my mother introduced me to, than they did in me." He smiled. "As I became better acquainted with you, I sensed your kind heart, appreciated your talent, and fell in love with you. I wanted you to be my wife more than anything else in the world. Tonight, I know I am the luckiest man alive."

Her green eyes soft by candlelight, Helen looked deep into his. "I hope you will never regret marrying me."

"How could I? But I suspect I shall regret the waste of this night."

His bride frowned. "I don't understand?"

"I know the precise relationship between husband and wife is not explained to most young ladies. However, I am sure you know they share a bed, and as a result, have children." In response to his urge to make love to Helen, he looked at the wall behind her. "In the Peninsular, too many married men were killed leaving widows and orphans to mourn them. None of us know what the future holds. I don't wish to father a child who might not have an opportunity to know me."

"I-I don't know what to say."

"Say nothing." He stood and held out his hand. "Come."

Helen slipped her hand into his and allowed him to guide her across the room.

* * * *

Before they got into bed, Dalrymple drew Helen into his arms. "One kiss," her bridegroom murmured. His face swooped closer to her. He cupped the back of her head with one hand and kissed her, even more passionately than he had the first time.

Why had she feared him? She knew he would never deliberately hurt her.

Dalrymple released her mouth. "My love, you are worn out by your grief over poor Mister Barnet's death, the wedding, the preparations for the ball and the ball itself. Get into bed and sleep as peacefully as a princess." His rueful smile enhanced his charm. "My queen, queen of my heart, come to bed, and please allow me to hold you in my arms."

Wonderful to look up at a man taller than herself, instead of looking down on one. Wrapped in his love, she felt feminine and protected.

* * * *

Helen turned over and opened her eyes. Slowly she returned to full consciousness. What had awakened her? The sound of a door closing? Comfortable and warm, she turned her head to look at Dalrymple. Where was he? Her mouth curved in a smile. Last night she fell asleep with her head nestled on his chest, her apprehension calmed by his strong arms. Half asleep, she closed her eyes and stretched.

A door opened. She must have dozed. Dalrymple, in his uniform that flattered his fine figure, walked quietly to the bedside. He bent and pressed a kiss on her forehead. Helen opened her eyes and smiled at him. She reached up and drew his head down to kiss him on the cheek. "Good morning, husband."

He returned her smile. "Good morning, my sweet siren. You have years ahead in which to tempt me."

"But I am not a siren," she protested, still sleepy.

"I am not sure. Your voice is part of your allure." Dalrymple sat on the edge of the bed. "Will you invite me into your parlour to breakfast with me before I attend the review?"

"Of course."

Helen sat up, completely at ease with her bridegroom. Whatever passed between them in the future, she would never fear him. "You are so nice, Dalrymple."

"Thank you for the crumbs from your table, but please call me Marcus." His eyes glinted. "One day, I hope to prove I am more than nice."

"How?"

His eyes burned like a forest fire. "It is my secret."

A knock on the door heralded Pringle's arrival. Granted permission to enter the bedchamber, the dresser announced breakfast awaited them.

There was, Helen decided as she poured coffee for Dalrymple, distinct pleasure in attending to a husband's needs while he ate a hearty meal.

"Thank you," he said, when she handed him the cup. "I shall return as soon as I may. What will you do in the meantime?"

"Supervise the servants who are clearing the ballroom, after I ride in the Allee Vert and watch the review."

"With your groom in attendance."

"Of course."

"Good. I want you to be protected at all times and would prefer you not to ride alone. Brussels is full of soldiers, some of whom are undisciplined."

"Yes, I know; some rascals insulted poor Mister Barnet." At the memory of him, tears filled her eyes.

"Don't cry, Helen. If your eyes are red, Major Tarrant will think I have mistreated you." He pretended to tremble. "I fear he would horsewhip me."

She laughed. "You are so funny." She buttered a roll. "After the review, will there be manoeuvres?"

His mouth full, he nodded.

"Why must they be practised so often? By now, surely the cavalry knows its drill."

"Yes, but it is difficult for the men and horses to reform after a charge. The more we practise, the better it is."

"Of course, I should have remembered that."

Dalrymple finished his coffee. "Don't tire yourself out today. I intend to dance with you again and again at the Duchess of Richmond's ball."

Oh, she was fortunate to be married to such a considerate gentleman.

Chapter Thirty

15th June, 1815

Helen wanted to watch the review while mounted on Silk, but when Georgianne insisted on attending it in her landau, she accompanied her.

At a distance, Helen found it difficult to identify individuals among motionless rows of soldiers astride their sleek black horses. However, she recognised Makelyn, the foremost figure, who was inspecting the regiment.

A rush of pride swelled within her as she eyed the spectacle—rows of mounted hussars; the scarlet plumes on their flat-topped busbies fluttering in the breeze.

She caught her lower lip between her teeth. What did fate plan for these magnificent men? She glanced at Georgianne, whose eyes glittered with unshed tears, and guessed a similar thought had crossed her sister's mind.

"Dear God," Helen prayed, "please spare my husband's and Cousin Tarrant's lives." After a moment's hesitation, she also prayed for Langley because—she told herself—he was a friend of the family.

Georgianne's eyes widened. "Do you remember that after our brothers and Papa died, I said I would never marry a soldier, for fear of him being wounded or killed?"

Helen nodded; the enormity of the possibility was too great for her to speak.

Her sister's shoulders heaved. " Now here I am, consumed by fear for Tarrant." She pressed a hand over her rounded stomach. "Oh, I am sorry. That is no way to speak to a bride."

Helen's mouth trembled. She pressed her lips into a thin line. The review ended. A battery of six pounder horse artillery moved forward. Too moved by her sister's words to speak, Helen focussed her attention on the squadrons which formed up, and in response to drumbeats and trumpets, began manoeuvres.

A horseman galloped to the side of the carriage.

Dalrymple bowed from the saddle. "Good morning, Mrs Tarrant." He smiled, the delightful dimples on either side of his mouth deepening. "Mrs Dalrymple. I regret only having time for a quick word before I return to my brigade. Makelyn's given me more orders than I can count on the fingers of one hand, so I am sorry I will not see you again until we dine before the Duchess of Richmond's ball. I have instructed my man, Jarvis, to lay out my dress uniform." He bent from the saddle to remove her glove and press a kiss on the back of her hand.

In response to the sombre expression in her bridegroom's eyes, Helen found it difficult to breathe. "Is there any cause for alarm," she asked, forcing herself to speak in a level tone.

"Brussels is a hive of activity. Have any regiments been ordered to stand at arms?"

"No, they have not. Don't be alarmed. At the moment, there is nothing to worry you."

Dalrymple spoke fast, perhaps too fast, for she knew Napoleon commanded the French army.

He squeezed her hand, but not hard enough for it to hurt. "If Wellington had given the order to prepare to be on the move, The Glory Boys would not be practising manoeuvres." He released her hand. "No reason to worry. The closest French vedettes are forty miles away on the other side of the River Sambre. Our army and the Prussians are guarding the border."

"What a goose I am," Helen retorted. "For four months, and particularly during the last few days, so many rumours have spread that we civilians scarcely know what to believe." Did she imagine a shadow cross his face? Did he know more than he admitted? A frisson of fear made its way down her spine.

Before her bridegroom could reply, a trumpet sounded. He saluted. In response to the light touch of the spurs, his charger galloped away.

Yet, in spite of her brave words, while drinking pink champagne after the manoeuvres, and listening to Cousin Tarrant reassure her sister, Helen remained anxious. Were the allegations true? Was Wellington on the brink of giving orders to invade France?

* * * *

At the house in Rue Royale, Helen made sure her sister reclined on a chaise longue before she went to her apartment. A sound from her bridegroom's dressing room disturbed her. She opened the door to the room in which a servant, presumably her husband's man, was folding shirts.

"Jarvis, at your service, madam. Don't you worry. The captain's sword's now sharp enough to cut off a Frenchie's head. Is there anything I can be doing for you?"

"No, thank you, Jarvis." Helen clutched the door frame. Futile to be squeamish. She knew war was a bloody business.

"No need to be fretting, madam, I've bought plenty of bandages from the apothecary. I'll be looking after the captain, taking care of his billet, providing whatever he and his horses need."

Dalrymple might be wounded or worse. No, it would be unlucky to think of death. Her throat too choked for her to speak, she nodded at the man before retreating to her bedchamber. What were Wellington's plans? Her jaw clenched. The Duke always appeared so carefree no one would think he had anything more to do than attend cricket matches, dance and enjoy festivities.

She crossed the floor and looked out of the window at Parc Royale, in which Belgians and British promenaded in lively groups, and superbly accoutred officers escorted well-dressed ladies. How could Brussels, protected by England's wealth and the allied army, be at risk? Faced with immediate danger, would her aristocratic countrymen still be here lavishly spending money, and enjoying the fun and military displays? Yet, what if claims, that imminent orders for the army to prepare to check Napoleon's advance, were true? Helen shook her head. If so, by now, surely the Duchess of Richmond would have cancelled her ball.

Helen turned around. She would walk in the park to enjoy the sunshine while Georgianne rested.

She clapped her hands to her ears. The noise must be thunder not gunfire!

A knock on her dressing room door preceded Pringle, who bustled into the bedroom with Helen's wedding gown in her arms.

"Ah, you are back, Miss. Oh, I beg your pardon, I should have said Madam. I've removed the mud from the hem. Have you changed your mind about wearing it to the Duchess' ball?"

"No, and I shall also wear the jewellery which Mister Barnet gave me." She sighed. "I shall miss him." Her hands tensed. If fate were cruel, the loss of Dalrymple, Cousin Tarrant and Langley would be unbearable.

Pringle opened the door. She spoke a few words then turned around. "Someone is waiting to speak to you in the library, madam."

When she entered the room, a solemn-faced gentleman, neatly attired in sombre black, which was relieved only by his white shirt and neck cloth, bowed. "Please allow me to introduce myself, madam. I am Mister Coombe. The late Mister Barnet summoned me to Brussels a few days prior to his death."

Helen sat behind Cousin Tarrant's desk. She indicated the pair of chairs placed opposite her. "Please be seated."

"Thank you. I presume you're Mrs Dalrymple, wife of Marcus, Captain Dalrymple, of The Glory Boys?"

Somewhat surprised she nodded.

Mister Coombe rubbed his hands together. "I am here to follow my late client's instructions. However, after I have dealt with immediate business, I shall return to London. He withdrew some papers, tied with pink ribbon, from a folder. These are for you. I have a copy of them also signed by Mister Barnet."

She frowned. "I don't understand."

"Didn't Mister Barnet tell you? Apart from a number of bequests, you are his sole heir."

She shook her head. Was her inheritance the memento the nabob mentioned in his letter? Speechless with surprise, for the moment, she could not imagine the change in her circumstances.

"You are fortunate. Mister Barnet, a gentleman of great wealth, left everything to you. However, his last will and testament ensures it remains under your control—although your husband is to benefit from certain incomes." He cleared his throat. "I am not prepared to remain in Belgium at the risk of my life. Please inform me when you return to England, where we may deal with the necessary legal matters."

"No need to flee," Helen responded, her voice tart. "The Duke of Wellington will not fail us."

"I hope not, but Napoleon might triumph. Now, if you would be good enough to sign this." He put a paper on the desk.

"What is it?"

"It gives me your permission to pay your staff and attend to your property, prior to your return to England. In accordance with my late client's instructions in his will, I have already paid the servants at the house in Brussels. It is now at your disposal." He placed a card on the desk.

Helen read the paper, dipped the quill into the inkpot and signed.

Mister Coombe stood. "Here is a copy." He added it to the other papers. "Good day, madam."

"Good day."

He lingered for a moment. "Listen. Gunfire! I suggest you return to England without delay."

Gunfire? Did he really think she would desert Dalrymple! She nodded at Coombe.

She had prayed to be independent of Cousin Tarrant, to have her own establishment, be married and have a child. Apart from her bridegroom's refusal to father a son or daughter at this time, God had answered her prayers in a manner she had never anticipated. Indeed, she could not imagine being mistress of such wealth. The news seemed unreal. Until she became accustomed to it, she would not confide in anyone, not even Georgianne. She frowned. Perhaps it would be wrong of her to keep such news from Dalrymple. Excitement flooded her. Due to Mister Barnet's incredible generosity, her future would be quite different from the one she had previously anticipated. She and her husband would enjoy a life of elegance. But first, the outcome of confrontation with Napoleon's army must be faced.

What should she do? Go to the attic to sketch and paint the subjects she dwelt on in her mind? No, she would stroll in the park. When she returned, she would make her first entry in the blank journal, one of the wedding gifts Cousin Tarrant and her sister had given her. She would not write that if Langley had won the lottery or if she had come into her inheritance earlier, they might have married. To do so would be to wish Mister Barnet had died at an earlier date, and seem as if she begrudged him his last days on earth.

* * * *

Helen fidgeted while she waited for Dalrymple to escort her downstairs. Did he know whether or not Napoleon had crossed the border? By now she should know better than to pay attention to rumour.

Nervous, she fiddled with her diamond and pearl earring. What would her husband's reaction to her inheritance be?

A tap on the bedchamber door. Helen opened it. Dalrymple's medals glittered. All too soon he would wield his sword in life or death combat. Maybe he would earn another medal. Yet what did she care about one more decoration on his broad chest? His survival was more important than anything else.

"Dalry—" she commenced. "I beg your pardon. Marcus, I have something important to tell you. A gentleman from London, called Mister Coombe, visited me today."

Her husband put a finger to her lips. "You may tell me later. There are more important matters. The Duke has given permission for those officers, invited to the Duchess of Richmond's ball, to attend, provided they join their regiments when it ends."

"Why?"

"I don't know." His arms encircled her. "My dear love, I have arranged for you to go to Antwerp in the morning."

"Impossible! My sister is in a delicate condition. I cannot leave her."

"I daresay Tarrant has made arrangements for her to leave Brussels. If Mrs Tarrant wishes, you may travel with her and share accommodation."

Helen withdrew from his arms. "Some time ago, Cousin Tarrant asked her to leave. She refused. Don't be misled by my sister's appearance. She appears fragile but she has a will like hard-tempered steel."

"You must leave. Nothing is certain but, for all we know, Napoleon might have reached Charleroi. He might be on the way to the crossroads at Quatre Bras, which is little more than ten miles away. If he defeats us there, he will march to Brussels." He captured her with his arms. His medals pressed painfully into her. "Don't you understand what might happen if he allows his soldiers to sack Brussels? No, I suppose you don't." He sighed. "I will not frighten you with a detailed explanation. It is enough for me to say, no woman will be safe."

Helen straightened her back. "Georgianne and I are not in danger. Wellington will triumph. How could he not, with officers of your calibre and Cousin Tarrant's? When the battle is over, I shall be here waiting for you."

A good Christian woman should obey her husband, but, in spite of the vows Helen made yesterday, she would not flee, leaving her husband behind to ride into danger. She traced the outline of his cheek with her forefinger. Dalrymple opened his mouth to speak, but this time she pressed her finger against his mouth. "Whatever happens, I shall be here," she repeated. "Shall we go to the salon?"

He released her. "Yes, madam wife, I understand my only option is to obey you."

She curtsied. "That is correct, Captain. After all, I remember you saying you are my obedient servant." She glanced down at her gown. "'Pon my word, you have used me ill. Look at my gown. It is crushed."

As she intended, Dalrymple's expression softened. "I would enjoy crushing more than your gown but this is not the moment."

* * * *

In the salon, the British officers seemed so impassive that it appeared they did not believe they might face Napoleon's troops on the following day. Yet although they made light-hearted conversation, Helen's sharp eyes recorded tense mouths, tightly gripped hands and wary eyes. Later, she would add tiny sketches to the entries in her journal.

At dinner, no one mentioned unpleasant subjects, although Cousin Tarrant seemed preoccupied and frowned frequently at Georgianne. No doubt he had tried to persuade her to retreat to Antwerp and she had refused, but not until the ladies retired to leave the gentleman to enjoy their port, did Helen have the opportunity to snatch a few words with her sister.

"Yes, Tarrant tried to make a coward of me," Georgianne snapped, the colour in her cheeks rising. "I refused. Were I not," she lowered her voice, "with child, I would ride by his side to his billet and stay there." She broke

398

off for a second or two. "By God, I swear that if the worst befalls Tarrant, I shall have no reason to live."

Shocked, Helen stared at her sister and caught her breath. "Yes, you will."

"You are mistaken. Now you are married, you understand the true nature of a wife's intimate love for her husband."

No, she did not. Helen forced herself to reply. "But your child?"

Georgianne laughed somewhat wildly. "I would not harm myself."

Helen patted her sister's shoulder. "Shush. You don't want your guests to realise how agitated you are."

* * * *

Helen, together with Dalrymple, Georgianne, and Cousin Tarrant, did not bid goodbye to the guests until ten o'clock. By the time they left the house, they were half an hour late for the Duchess of Richmond's ball. During the drive to the Rue de la Blanchisserie in the lower part of town, they heard bugles and drums sounding the assembly. From the window, Helen glimpsed columns of soldiers.

She sighed. At Georgianne's dinner table a murmur circulated that Prince Bernard of Saxe-Weimar's infantry had made a stance at Quatre Bras and chased away French skirmishers. "Yet," Cousin Tarrant had said, "earlier in the day, the Prince of Orange told the duke the Nivelles-Namur chausée was quiet."

From the corner of her eye, Helen saw Georgianne scrutinise Cousin Tarrant's calm face. "You have not received orders from Makelyn?"

"No, I shall report to him in The Wash House."

"I beg your pardon."

Cousin Tarrant chuckled. "Have you not heard that is what Wellington named the Richmond's villa? He thinks the nick name is amusing. I can only imagine the Duchess's chagrin."

Helen laughed, but, after the coach slowed behind several wagons that blocked the road, her amusement ended at the sight of a woman with a baby strapped to her back, a toddler in her arms, and a young boy who clutched her skirts. The mother clung with both hands to a soldier's arms. He freed himself, but, regardless of the small child, the woman flung her arms around him. He kissed her, pulled away from her and patted his children's heads. When he joined a column of soldiers formed up at the side of the road, he looked back at his loved ones again and again.

Grabbed by fear, Helen held Dalrymple's hand. "So, the army has been ordered to stand at arms?"

Chapter Thirty-one

15th June and early morning 16th June, 1815

Helen eyed the glittering throng in the ballroom at the Richmond's villa. Although no-one appeared to have anything more in mind than enjoyment, she sensed an underlying tension which matched her own. Everywhere she looked, she saw Dutch and Belgian royalty—including Major General Prince Frederick of Orange—British civilians, diplomats, army officers, and aristocrats, amongst whom was the Duke of Brunswick in his black dress uniform. Such sang-froid. Helen struggled not to reveal her ever-present anxiety.

While Dalrymple spoke to Captain Thomas Wildman, one of the Duke of Uxbridge's aide de camps, she admired the rose-trellised wallpaper. In her opinion, the décor, which included pillars entwined with ribbons, leaves and flowers, was not as spectacular as the carefully planned oriental theme of her ball on the previous day. Nevertheless, the Duchess' decorations were impressive beneath the blaze of light from chandeliers which illuminated the House of Orange's colours—crimson, black and gold—featured on hangings and tent-like drapery.

Dalrymple turned to her. "May I introduce Captain Wildman?"

She inclined her head toward the officer. "No need, we were introduced at one of my sister's Sunday luncheons."

The captain bowed. "I have been offering your husband my best wishes. May I congratulate you on your marriage?"

"Indeed, you may. Thank you." Helen decided it was more likely Dalrymple had been asking Wildman for the latest news. She pointed her fan upward at a group of cavalry officers in the gallery "Can you hint at Lord Uxbridge's plans?"

"All I may say, ma'am, is there is no need for alarm. As you must know, the Duke of Wellington's headquarters are here in Brussels and Blucher's headquarters are forty-eight miles away at Namur. Our army and the Prussian army are divided by the chausée which stretches from Charleroi to Brussels. In the unlikely event of Napoleon choosing to proceed along it, I assume the Duke will give orders for our cavalry and infantry to move eastward to close the distance between the two armies." With a handkerchief, Wildman dabbed the perspiration on his forehead. Perhaps it was no more than the result of the crowded ballroom and the heat from the chandeliers.

Helen formed a mental picture of the terrain. "I don't understand why orders have not been given already to close the gap between the armies."

"Unless Blucher warns Wellington of an attack, the duke will neither move troops away from Ghent—where the French court is still in residence—nor away from other strategic towns such as Mons and Tournai." He bowed. "You must excuse me; Lord Uxbridge might have orders for me."

After Wildman retreated, Dalrymple appeared amused. "Did you think he would betray military secrets?"

Helen visualised the possibility of troops marching along the paved chausée from Charleroi toward the capital. "No, not secrets."

"Outside, gunfire can be heard. To be safe, please agree to go north."

She shook her head. "To do so would be lily-livered. It would also imply I don't believe Wellington will triumph over the French."

Dalrymple sighed. "Very well. We are unable to enjoy a wedding trip so let us take pleasure in the ball."

Yes, they should seize the opportunity to have fun, for heaven alone knew when they would have another chance to do so. Nevertheless, she should snatch a moment to tell Dalrymple about her inheritance. Where could they have a word in private? In future, she did not want him to accuse her of deceit.

The band played the first notes of a waltz. Helen followed Dalrymple's lead until Wellington arrived. She scrutinised his face. As usual he seemed unruffled. The Richmonds' daughter, Lady Georgiana, who danced near them, rushed toward the duke. Curious, Helen followed her with Dalrymple.

"Are the rumours that the French are on the move correct?" Lady Georgianna asked.

"Yes." Wellington looked down at the nineteen year-old's frightened face. "They are true; we are off at dawn."

Helen clutched Dalrymple's sleeve. The day she and her sister feared, for so long, had arrived. Who would survive—her husband, Cousin Tarrant, Langley? Although she had married Dalrymple, it did not mean she could not be deeply concerned about the viscount.

Despite her mind being filled with ghastly possibilities, she completed the dance as though she were a carefree young girl. Afterward, all the guests stepped back to the sides of the ballroom in response to the thrilling sound of bagpipes.

Of course, the Duchess of Richmond is the eldest daughter of the Duke of Gordon. Her mother is besotted by everything Scottish—the clothing, the pipes and the dancing. Papa told me her parents, the fourth duke and duchess, raised the 92nd Foot, or as they are commonly known, The Gordon Highlanders.

"Mamma thinks the foreigners will enjoy seeing highland reels," Lady Louisa—another of the Richmond's daughters, who stood nearby Helen and Dalrymple—explained to her partner. "Pipe Major Alexander Cameron will lead the Scots dancers into the ballroom while playing the bagpipes." She laughed. "Did you hear that at the battle of Fuentes d'Onoro a bullet punctured the bag of his pipes? Infuriated,

Cameron fired at the sniper, drew his sword, joined the fight and yelled in Gaelic, 'We'll give them a different type of music!'"

Helen stared in awe at famous Alexander, of the Cameron clan. "Those highlanders are fine fellows and fierce fighting men," Dalrymple commented. "They will acquit themselves well, even if they fall to the last man."

At the vision of them sprawled in death, Helen pressed her hand to her mouth.

"I beg your pardon," Dalrymple apologized, his voice gruff. "Please forgive my plain speaking."

Her hand strayed to his cheek. "You will take care. Please don't perform unnecessary heroic deeds."

Dalrymple's eyes blazed! "You do care for me." Her hand captured by his, he guided her to a pillar. Behind it, he held her so close that their bodies pressed together. She tilted her head toward him. "Helen!" With delicacy, he ran his tongue along the seam formed by her lips.

A spark—of what?—burned deep within her. She wanted more, much more. In turmoil, she turned her face away from him.

"I apologize," Dalyrymple commenced, shame-faced, "no matter how much I want to make love, it is not an excuse for kissing you in public."

A lieutenant approached and saluted Dalrymple. "General Makelyn's compliments Captain; he wants a word with you."

"How tiresome," her husband drawled. "Duty calls. I shall leave you with Mrs. Tarrant while I obey Makelyn's summons.

After he escorted her to Georgianne, he saluted her. "If I don't have an opportunity to bid you farewell, please forgive me."

Helen observed him make his way to Makelyn, who was watching another highland reel from the opposite side of the ballroom. Dear God, I might never see my husband again. Georgianne's hand on her arm prevented her from running after him.

"Dearest, you must allow your husband to obey orders and not distract him. Tarrant has already slipped away to join the regiment."

Helen realized her sister's face was wax-pale.

Georgianne caressed her stomach. For the first time, Helen truly understood why her own husband did not want to risk having a posthumous child. She should have reassured Dalrymple. Told him she loved him even if she fibbed.

"Dearest?"

Georgianne's soft voice drew her from her self-recriminations. "Yes?"

"Hold your head high. Don't give way to fear."

To the skirl of bagpipes, the highlanders marched out of the ballroom in perfect rhythm.

"Shall we go home?" Georgianne inquired.

Distraught, Helen shook her head. "Not yet, Dalrymple might have time for a word with me. Shall we have supper?"

"You may, but I am not hungry."

She put an arm around her sister's waist. "For your child's sake, you should eat."

They walked around the edge of the ballroom and saw the Duchess of Richmond, her hand on the Prince of Orange's arm, and the Duke of Wellington with Lady Charlotte Greville's hand on his arm, on their way back from the supper. A mud spattered courier gave a note to the Prince who handed it to the Duke.

Within moments, word spread that Wellington had received confirmation of the French advance, and that, with the help of Napoleon's Imperial Guard, at eleven o'clock in the morning, the Prussians had been defeated and chased out of Charleroi. Every officer must return to his regiment.

The band stopped playing. The dancers halted. Lord Uxbridge ordered the cavalry officers to join their regiments.

Surrounded by ladies making tender farewells, Helen searched for Dalrymple to wish him Godspeed, beg him to return safely, assure him she would be waiting for him and, that one day, they would have a happy home and children.

From behind, a hand grasped her wrist. Helen winced. Dalrymple? No, he was always gentle. She turned around. Not Dalrymple, Langley. They stared at each other. Candlelight flickered over the harsh lines of his face and taut jawline.

"One kiss for me to remember you by."

He had no right to make such a demand. Like an animal threatened by a predator, she wanted to run away, yet something stirred deep within her. She could not move.

Langley pulled her to him. She should voice a protest. A sharp sensation, half pain, half excitement, gripped her. One hand squeezed her buttock. Outraged, she tried to pull away from him. He held her too tight. His other hand cupped the back of her head. Their bodies pressed together.

"You are no longer an ignorant girl unaware of a man's way with a virgin." He spoke in a harsh, unfamiliar voice. "You and Dalrymple—Curse him!—have shared a night of passion, but I believe you love me, so you will forgive me for this."

Judging by the odour of his breath, the viscount was inebriated. His mouth plundered her lips. His tongue forced its way between them. Their teeth ground together. Shocked by his violent hold, her mouth opened. Langley's tongue thrust deep into her. With her fists, she pounded her protest against his chest. Langley's hand kneaded her buttock. She slapped him across the cheek as hard as she could.

"Methinks the lady doth protest," an ice-cold voice intervened.

Langley released her with such abruptness that she staggered. She became aware of Lord

Uxbridge when he steadied her with a firm hand. Heat scalded her cheeks.

"Sober up; then join your general, Langley," Uxbridge ordered.

"Sir." Langley saluted his lordship then bowed to Helen. "My apologies, I mistook your sentiments and—"

"Please say nothing more."

"As you wish, ma'am."

"There you are." Georgianne put her hand on Helen's arm. "Is Langley ready to slip away?"

"Indeed he is," Lord Uxbridge bowed. "Please excuse me ladies, I have much to do."

"Shall we leave?" Georgianne's voice seemed loud in the quiet following the officers' departures.

Furious with Langley, Helen walked beside her sister to the door, where the Duchess stood.

"Will you not stay for a little longer," Her Grace pleaded. "If everyone leaves, my ball will be ruined."

Helen stared at her hostess. Faced with imminent battle, how could the Duchess be so shallow? Outside, drums beat. The cobbles seemed to shake while bugles summoned both the infantry and the cavalry to assemble. The tramp of the soldiers on the march sounded together with the clip-clop of cavalry horses' hooves and the rumble of the iron-rimmed wheels of the wagons.

Georgianne wrapped her arms around her waist. A troop of scarlet-coated infantry, knapsacks on their backs, marched past them. They broke into song. "Over the hills and far away, King George commands and we obey." But insane King George was locked up, incapable of commanding his army. The scene before her seemed unreal. She could hardly believe Napoleon, in command of the French army, might reach Brussels in a few hours.

Later, much later, she would learn Wellington had declared, "Napoleon has humbugged me, by God; he has gained twenty-four hours march on me." The Duke of Richmond had asked him what he would do. "I have ordered the army to concentrate at Quatre-Bras," Wellington had replied, "but we shall not stop him there, and, if so, I must fight him here." With the tip of his thumbnail he had touched Waterloo on the map.

* * * *

16th June

"No, madam, neither Major Tarrant nor Captain Dalrymple have returned to the house since they left with you and Mrs Dalrymple for the ball."

Her sister's face was very pale and her shoulders drooped. She must be worn to a rag. Helen cupped Georgianne's elbow with her hand to guide her upstairs.

"Shall I send for camomile tea to help you sleep?" Helen asked when they entered the bedroom.

Georgianne shook her head. "Dawson, fetch a carriage dress, hat, gloves and a pelisse." The dresser hesitated. "Don't dawdle."

"I'm not, madam, but I've laid out your nightgown and—please forgive my boldness—I think you need your sleep."

"I think you should get ready for bed," Helen said to her sister, no less concerned than Dawson.

"I am going out," Georgianne snapped. "Please don't argue with me. I shall go to the Namur Gate to watch the divisions set out. You may come with me or stay here, but nothing you can say will dissuade me."

"Why are you going?"

"Do you need to ask? Tarrant left the ball wearing his slippers. He has not returned here to collect either his boots or his medicine case. Tarrant must not—" almost in tears, her voice broke, but she recovered herself. "Tarrant must not leave without them."

Georgianne dabbed her eyes with a handkerchief. "I cannot bear the idea of him going to battle wearing his ballroom slippers. If The Glory Boys have not yet left, I shall give my husband his boots."

Helen stared at her tiny sister, a beauty who could command every luxury, now standing in the centre of the pretty bedchamber decorated in shades of blue and gold, determined to leave the safety of the house. How could she prevent her? "Jarvis!" she exclaimed. "Dalrymple's man can take everything necessary." She looked at Dawkins, who had returned with her arms full of clothes. "Dawkins, find out if Jarvis is still here."

"Whether he is or not, I shall go." Georgianne's tone of voice defied Helen arguing.

"But why?"

"Surely you know! We cannot miss the opportunity…to bid farewell."

No they should not. The possibility of never seeing Dalrymple again tore at her heart. "I will come with you, Georgianne."

"I expected you would. I shall order the carriage."

Helen fled to her bedroom to change her gown. She shuddered. Little more than a schoolroom miss when Langley and Cousin Tarrant rescued her from the Earl of Pennington, with a head filled with romantic dreams that had little to do with reality, she had idolised Langley. She had mistaken his charisma and her gratitude for love. A handsome cavalry officer distinguished in battle, who she believed had fallen in love with her. Yet, had he been equally mistaken? If he had truly loved her, nothing would have prevented him from marrying her— or at least asking her to wait for him to be in a position to do so.

Why, she asked herself, while Pringle helped her to change her clothes, had she not realised love could come gently, softly, wrapping her in a warm cloud? If only she had realised it before they parted, she could have told her husband she loved him. "Dear God, please let Dalrymple return to me," she prayed, then realised she had spoken aloud.

Pringle bowed her head. "Amen," Pringle said.

As keen to reach the city gate as Georgianne, Helen pulled on her gloves.

* * * *

By moon and lantern light, column after column—the infantry in scarlet jackets, the Brunswickers in black, kilted Scots with huge sporrans and folded plaids over their shoulders, riflemen in their distinctive green, and Belgians wearing blue jackets—marched down the road to Charleroi, accompanied by fife and drum.

Helen watched them from the security of the carriage. "They seem in good spirits. So do those soldiers' wives who are marching with their men."

Georgianne pointed at a young lady mounted on the chestnut filly riding beside a heavy dragoon officer. "I envy her. Were I not increasing, I would ride with Tarrant. I cannot bear this separation. Suppose he never sees his child."

"At least he knows how much you love him. Oh, there's Picton."

Top hat secure on his head, she watched the seasoned campaigner, who commanded the British 5th Division, ride past carts filled with produce. He must be on his way to Ninoves, where the light and heavy cavalry had been ordered to assemble under Lord Uxbridge's command.

Helen poked her head out of the window and shouted, "Sir Thomas, what news of The Glory Boys? Are they still in Brussels?"

Picton—interrupted while he greeted friends and giving the impression he had nothing more in his mind than a pleasant ride in the sunshine—looked around. When he saw her, he reined in his horse. "Mrs Dalrymple, are you not? Someone pointed you out at the ball. Fine affair until news of Boney interrupted us. Don't you worry, we'll soon have him on the run."

"The Glory Boys, Sir Thomas, have they left Brussels?"

"Yes, they were among the first to leave. He touched his hat. "Good day to you."

She inclined her head toward him. "May God bless you."

For the first time in her life, she resented Georgianne. If Cousin Tarrant had not made her promise to stay and look after her sister, she would ride to Ninove. Tears in her eyes, she watched the last infantry column disappear in the early morning mist.

Chapter Thirty-Two

16th June, 1815

Helen woke after noon, dressed in haste, and then joined Georgianne in the dining room to partake of a late nuncheon.

Fearful of what the day would bring, Helen ate little. Her sister nibbled a bread roll and spoke only of mundane matters such as instructions she would give the housekeeper.

After the meal, quill in hand, Helen sat at a desk in the salon. She made entries, accompanied by thumbnail sketches, in her journal.

"Mrs Hamilton," the butler announced.

Dread had replaced good-natured Mrs Hamilton's usually cheerful expression.

Helen covered the tiny sketch, of three young ladies smiling at a handsome officer, with a sheet of paper. Only yesterday, before the news of Napoleon's invasion, everyone's spirits were high.

"Good day," Georgianne greeted her guest, mother of a cornet in the Glory Boy's regiment."

"Good day, Mrs Tarrant. Good day, Miss Whitley. I beg your pardon. I should have said Mrs Dalrymple." She sighed. "My mind is on— well you can imagine what."

"Please be seated, Mrs Hamilton," Georgianne said. "A glass of wine?"

"No thank you. I will only take up a few moments of your time. Please tell me if you have news of the regiment," she gabbled.

By contrast, Georgianne seemed incapable of speech so Helen spoke, "No, I regret we have not."

"Shocking, quite shocking," the matron muttered.

Georgianne, her face a mask of apprehension, raised her eyebrows but made no comment.

"Indeed, Mrs Hamilton," Helen began, "in the early hours of this morning, the sight of our men riding out of Brussels shocked us. I don't know why. All of us knew the day would come."

"We hoped it would not." Mrs Hamilton's double chin wobbled. "But, when I said shocking, I referred to those people who regard the French invasion as little more than an excuse for an excursion. Mister Hamilton says they are following the troops in their carriages to view the proceedings. When I think of the danger my son will face. Lud, I beg your pardon, both of you must be worried about your husbands. Oh, it is horrid in the streets which are so quiet with the army gone, and those who have not fled remaining indoors. Mister Hamilton wanted me to leave for Antwerp but I refused. I must be here to greet my boy when he returns." The unspoken words—if he returns—seemed to echo. She stood. "I must bid you good day. Mrs Leigh expects me to join her. She has formed a group of ladies who are preparing bandages."

Helen walked with her to the door of the salon.

When will there be news of Dalrymple? If only she could do something for him. Well, perhaps she could.

After the visitor left, she could hardly bear to sit down again in comfort in the beautiful salon, while, at this very moment, his life might be in danger.

Georgianne opened her sewing basket, took out a tiny, pin-tucked cambric smock and held it against her cheek.

"Mister Tomlinson," the butler announced.

Dressed in a blue coat, canary-yellow pantaloons, and a flamboyant blue and yellow striped waistcoat, Tomlinson bowed. Somewhat red in the face, he straightened up. "Daresay you're surprised to see me?" Unlike Mrs Hamilton, he radiated nervous good humour. "It's my girl, you see."

Helen did not understand, and to judge by the expression on Georgianne's face, neither did she.

He sat opposite them on the sofa. "A sad business brought me back to Brussels. My son-in-law bought a commission in the 30th. Maria insisted on following him, so I accompanied her. I couldn't allow her to travel alone." He leaned forward and drew his hand back at the last moment instead of patting Georgianne's knee. "She's very frightened, Mrs Dalrymple. I hope you'll visit her."

Helen exchanged a glance with her sister. Did the man not understand that although fear for their husbands tortured them, they were doing their utmost to control their sensibilities? She sighed. "I would prefer her to visit me."

Mister Tomlinson lowered his voice to a loud whisper. "I am to be a grandfather so she's in no condition to do so."

Helen sighed. "Congratulations. Tell me where you are putting up. I will try to find time to see her?"

"Thank you. We have rooms at the Hotel Angleterre. If you wish, I can send my carriage to take you there."

"Thank you, but it is unnecessary."

Helen's jaw tightened. There were more important matters on her mind than Maria's understandable distress.

Mister Tomlinson cleared his throat. "I'll take my leave of you." He regarded them somewhat anxiously. "Don't hesitate to call on me if you need my services. If there's danger of the French reaching Brussels, I'll insist on Maria retreating to Antwerp or Ghent. If you wish, I would be pleased to take both of you."

"Thank you." Georgianne stood. "Good day."

"He means well," Helen said after the door closed behind him.

"I know."

"Georgianne?"

"Yes."

"I cannot stay here without news. Would you care to take the air with me?

Her sister shook her head. "No, Tarrant might send a message, or there might be one from Dalrymple. I shall stay here. Go if you wish, but take Pringle and a footman with you."

"Not Pringle," Helen remarked dryly, "she is on the verge of hysterics, but I shall take a footman." She cast a glance at Georgianne. Should she reveal her plan? She would visit the house she inherited from Mister Barnet, to give orders for it to be prepared to receive wounded soldiers. What would be necessary? Food! She would instruct the cook to make large quantities of bread and soup, and she would send for bandages and other supplies from the pharmacies.

She shied away from the thought that Dalrymple, Tarrant, or even Langley and so many friends might die. No! She must not think of death. It was unlucky. She stood. "I must call on some of our friends."

Georgianne raised her eyebrows. "At such a time, dearest?"

"Yes, to find out what is happening." When she returned she would tell Georgianne about the will, with the hope her sister would not upbraid her for failing to mention it earlier.

* * * *

After months filled with crowds of civilians and soldiers in colourful uniforms, Mrs Hamilton's description of the quiet streets was accurate. Most people Helen knew remained behind closed doors and shutters. The few people she met were disinclined to talk, although some claimed Napoleon suffered defeat at the cost of enormous British and French casualties. All the more reason to put her house to good use. Those she called upon had no news. Helen clamped her lower lip between her teeth.

A few steps away from Helen's front door, a lady ran toward her and came to a halt. "The French have triumphed," she blabbered, without an exchange of the usual courtesies. "Even now they are marching to Brussels." She ran on down the street, skirts held high above her ankles, heedless of an impertinent man who ogled her pantalets.

Helen shook her head. Her faith in Field Marshall Wellington was too great to believe the battle was lost and, even now, the French marched toward Brussels. Her head ached. She imagined that whatever the outcome, a finger of doom pressed down on all those remaining in the city.

After repeated knocking on the door of her house, Thomas opened it a little. He peered out. "Miss Whitley!" A broad smile on his face, he opened the door wider.

"Mrs Dalrymple," she corrected him.

"I beg your pardon, madam."

She stepped inside. The house smelled stale. Perhaps the windows and doors had not been opened since Mister Barnet's death only three days ago.

"Where is Greaves?"

"He left along with my poor master's steward and some of the other servants."

"I see. Why did you stay?"

"Because I hope you'll keep me on in your service."

"If Captain Dalrymple agrees, I shall." What should be done first? "Thomas, the house is to be made ready for the wounded; beds, blankets pillows, mattresses on the floor and whatever else is required. Did the cook leave?" Thomas shook his head. "Good. I shall write a letter to Sister Imelda, which I wish you to deliver. I hope she and some other sisters will come here to nurse the wounded." She paused to eye Thomas, who stood straight, his eyes grave. "Assemble the remaining servants while I pen my letter. For the time being, you may act as my butler."

* * * *

Satisfied with her arrangements, Helen, followed by James—Georgianne's watchful footman—made her way back toward Cousin Tarrant's house to the tune of distant thunder in streets suddenly alive with anxious people.

"Lawks!" the hitherto silent young man exclaimed. "What's that noise?"

Thunder? Helen looked up at the clear blue sky from which the sun blazed down. Not thunder, something else. She stood still listening to a sound she could only compare to the repeated thud of a woodcutter's axe against a tree trunk. "I think it is canon fire."

"You are right," a man agreed, then forged his way ahead into the park.

"Mrs Dalrymple, this is no place for a lady. I'll take you home," a shocked voice protested.

She recognised the familiar voice. "No, no, Mister Tomlinson, I must find out what is happening."

His face creased with anxiety, the manufacturer clutched her elbow. "You've been such a good friend to my Maria, please let me be of service. When there's accurate news of where the battle's taking place and how it goes, I promise to bring it to you."

Faint from the heat and fear, for the first time in her life Helen wished she had sal volatile in her reticule. The pungent smelling salts would have revived her. "Thank you. However, there is no need to escort me. My sister's footman will follow me."

Mister Tomlinson touched the brim of his hat. "If you insist, I'll see you later."

* * * *

The front door closed behind Helen.

Georgianne rushed downstairs. "It is past six o'clock. Where have you been? I have been almost out of my senses with worry for the past hour! What is more, Cook is grumbling because the soufflé has fallen." Georgianne's eyes rounded and her hands momentarily shook. Another distant boom reverberated. "But, what does the soufflé matter when I can hear cannonades?"

Helen's stomach rumbled with hunger. "I will change my gown."

"No need to do so on today of all days." Georgianne spoke slowly. "Remove your hat and gloves and come to the dining room. I fear Cook will resign if we don't eat before something else is spoiled."

"I have a lot to tell you."

Georgianne trembled. "Bad news?"

Helen shook her head. She accompanied Georgianne to the dining room where she took her place and stared at the blood red wallpaper. She did not speak until she had emptied her soup bowl. While the second course was served, she spoke. "Georgianne, there is something you should know. Mister Barnet left me his entire fortune and property, with the exception of a few bequests."

Georgianne's glass slipped from her hand. The wine spread across the pristine white tablecloth. "How clumsy of me." She glared at the stain. "Helen, look what you made me do. I never imagined you could be so sly."

"Not sly. Never that. I wanted to tell Dalrymple before I spoke of it to you or Cousin Tarrant, only he rode out before I could." Helen wondered if there would ever be an opportunity to tell him. She pushed some creamed potato onto her fork with her knife. "Please forgive me for returning so late. I have been busy with arrangements for my house to—"

"You won't move into it, will you?" Georgianne interrupted. "I could not bear to be separated from you at such a time."

"Of course I won't."

"Besides," Georgianne rushed on, "Tarrant told me he would ask you to promise to look after me. Not that it is necessary, for I am your older sister, but you know how he worries because I am increasing."

"He did ask, and I promised him I would, so of course, I shall take care of you." She sipped some wine. "But I am busy. At Mister Barnet's…I mean my house…I have organised preparations to receive the wounded—beds, blankets, pillows, mattresses on the floors, soup and bread, bandages and medication." Exhausted, she smoothed the frown from her forehead with the tips of her fingers. "What else… A nun nursed Mister Barnet during his last days. I have requested her to return with more nuns to nurse the men."

A long silence followed before her sister broke it. "I don't know what to say." Shame-faced, Georgiana stared at her across the length of the table. "Dearest, my mind has been full of apprehensions while you think of others. You shall have all my spare bed linens and—"

"Mister Tomlinson," Fletcher announced. "I beg your pardon madam, but he would not be denied entrance."

The manufacturer crashed into the room. "I'm sorry to intrude but I promised Mrs Dalrymple to bring news."

"What is it?" Helen demanded.

"Wagons and carts, filled with those suffering from the most serious wounds, have arrived. Those who were able to walk limped back through the Namur Gate. Fierce fighting took place at Quatre Bras. Those who fought in the Peninsular said the engagement's worse than any other they've known." He sighed. "They can't imagine the outcome. But you have no cause for alarm. The Glory Boys haven't been engaged."

"The 30th?" Georgianne asked gently.

Mister Tomlinson shrugged. "According to a private shot in his right arm, their musket fire peppered Kellerman's brigade. He knows my son-in-law and said he was safe when he left."

"That is good news," Helen murmured.

"Yes indeed." Georgianne commented. "But please sit down, Mister Tomlinson, you look tired." She indicated a chair halfway between herself and Helen.

"Thank you." He sank onto the seat. "Yes, I hope the information will comfort my poor girl, who is feverish with anxiety. Ah well, it can't be helped, for she's of a nervous disposition."

"Have you dined, Mister Tomlinson?" Georgianne asked. He shook his head. "Then you must do so before you leave." She turned her attention to the butler. "Fletcher, a place for my guest. Send for some more soup."

"I'll fill my carriage with hampers of food and kegs of brandy, for wounded men making their way back to Brussels," Mister Tomlinson explained. "Of course, I shall drive as many of them as possible back to town."

Georgianne looked at him approvingly. "How good you are."

"It's no more than my Christian duty; one which I'm glad to perform."

"Mr Tomlinson, you must take the wounded to my house which is ready to receive them." Helen gave him the address. "After I have dined, I shall return there to make sure all is in order."

The manufacturer thumped the table so hard the cutlery clinked. "No, no, Mrs Dalrymple, no lady should see sights not fitting for her."

Disinclined to contradict him, there seemed little more to say. Helen glanced at her sister.

A footman, supervised by Fletcher, served soup to Mister Tomlinson, who spooned some into his mouth, and then took a hearty bite of bread and butter.

After they finished the meal, the manufacturer left, but not before he again asked Helen to call on Maria.

* * * *

Soon after midnight, a foot guard, soaked by continuous rain which had replaced the earlier, almost unbearable heat of the day, staggered through the door of Helen's house, a drummer boy over his shoulder. "All the way from Quatre Bras," he gasped. "Took a cart, then a carriage, until the horses could go no further."

"Let me help you." Helen rushed forward, her apron long since bloodied by those she had nursed, the hem of her pretty gown dirtied. "Put your hand on my shoulder. Come, you can lay him down on a mattress in the salon."

A nun came forward to assist them. She loosened the bloodied stock from the youngster's neck with deft hands. "Il est mort."

The foot guard sank to the floor. He bent his bandaged head. "Poor lad." Tears rolled down his smoke-blackened face. "I couldn't save him." He pulled two pennies out of his pocket, closed the boy's eyes and placed the coins on them.

Chapter Thirty-Three

17th June, 1815

Her eyes blurry with tears, Helen stared down at the body of the drummer boy, and the bloodied foot guard on his knees beside him.

How could she ever forget the agonised mumblings and screams of the first wounded men who had arrived on a cart? Until now, she had never treated more than a graze or some equally minor mishap.

At first sight of the soldiers' hideous wounds, horror held her motionless, until Sister Imelda took her gently by the arm and asked her to write a letter for one of the few Gordon Highlanders who had survived, but looked unlikely to last the night.

Her throat tightened at the memory of the magnificent men who had danced to the tune of the bagpipe at the Duchess of Richmond's ball. After she wrote his last words, which asked his wife to kiss their bairns for him, he thanked her, closed his eyes and, he too, died. Ashamed, because, until now, she was only aware of her own reaction to the carnage, she found the strength to assist the doctor, a surgeon, nuns, and other women who came to help. Time and again, she reminded herself, a soldier's daughter must not flinch.

Helen noticed the life guard mutter something which might have been a prayer; she stooped over him, a hand on his shoulder. Her revulsion turned to pity. She stared at the filthy, blood-stained bandage around his head. "Please get up. Your wound needs to be examined. Don't reproach yourself; you did your best for the boy."

He stared up at her from blood-shot eyes. "There are men in greater need. I can wait."

She straightened. The boy's body must be removed. There were not enough mattresses. Some men lay in rough lines on the floor in the hall, others on the landing in the first storey. The air filled with the sound of many who wept, and screamed.

Close by, a delirious soldier, whose left arm had been amputated, called. "Mam, Mam, where are you?"

Helen knelt by his side to hold his hand. "Hush, my poor boy."

"Mam, I knew you'd come to your Jamie." His pale lips formed a smile. He clutched her hand so hard that it seemed as if her bones would break before his grip loosened. Dead! He might have been amongst those whom she watched marching out of Brussels. Beyond tears, Helen bent her head and prayed. A hand on her shoulder startled her. Despite her fatigue she must find the strength to rise and tend another unfortunate. She looked up. "Dalrymple!" A hallucination formed by her exhausted brain? He stooped over to help her stand. She flung herself into his arms. "Thank

God you are safe. But what are you doing here?"

* * * *

"I should ask you the same question," Dalrymple responded, his voice husky.

"I am helping in any way I can, but there is so little I can do."

Dalrymple smoothed his wife's untidy hair back from her forehead. He kissed her flushed cheek then held her a little away from him. Unbelievable! His hitherto elegant bride's apron, forearms and hands, were bloody. In spite of her pale face with a smear of dried blood on her chin, she stood before him as straight as a lance. Guilt surged through him because he had not been able to protect her from the aftermath of a bloody battle. Yet he was proud of her, so would he have objected to her helping to take care of incapacitated soldiers?

"Did Jarvis deliver your cavalry boots?"

A soldier tugged Helen's skirt. "A drink, ma'am, if it's not too much trouble."

Helen looked down. "Lieutenant Calverly!" she exclaimed. "Of course, I will fetch some water. Oh, it seems so long since you untied my apron strings."

"A world away." Calverly closed his eyes.

Dalrymple's eyes narrowed at the mental picture of the handsome young man untying the knots, but this was not the moment to ask his wife why Calverly had done so.

430

"Some water for the lieutenant," Dalrymple said to one of the footmen, who were helping to look after the patients. An arm around his wife's waist, he guided her to the door. "Time for you to go home."

"But—"

"You have done enough. Your sister told me where you were, so I came to fetch you in a carriage. Don't argue. You are so tired you can hardly stand." There was scarcely room to walk between the mattresses, so he swept her up into his arms and carried her out to the carriage.

On the short journey to the Tarrant's house, she fell asleep with her head on his shoulder.

"Wake up, Helen." He spoke softly into his wife's ear, after the horses drew to a halt. When she did not stir, he smiled down at her, although he had not recovered from the shock of finding her in the midst of such an appalling scene. He smoothed her hair back. "Helen, wake up."

"I shall never forget those poor men and boys," she murmured, no more than half awake.

"I know, but please come indoors; you need to bathe, eat and sleep."

Dalrymple sighed. Although he admired her courage, she would have been spared those gruesome sights if he had insisted she retreat to Ghent or Antwerp.

Helen sat up and looked at him. "You have not answered my question. Why are you here?" Her eyes widened in her pale face. "What of Cousin Tarrant? Is he—?"

431

"No need to fear for him," he interrupted, his voice husky. "The Glory Boys did not take part in the conflict at Quatre Bras, where, you must have heard, the French were defeated at great cost."

"It doesn't explain what you are doing here," Helen repeated as he helped her out of the carriage.

"Uxbridge has brought the cavalry to Genappe where Wellington and his senior officers are putting up. Makelyn, with Tarrant in attendance, is among them. The Glory Boys have bivouacked nearby, so I took the opportunity to come here and fetch an umbrella," he explained, for he did not wish to mention military matters.

"What?"

He laughed at her astonishment. "If the rain continues, I shall be glad of an umbrella."

As they went up the steps to the front door, a flash of lightning illuminated his bride's indignant expression. "I hoped you came to see me."

"What do you think? Of course I did. Yesterday, I wanted to be with you more than anything else in the world. I could not stop thinking of you." In spite of the dried blood and her dishevelled hair, he found his bride adorable. "I am sorry for teasing you about an umbrella. "He would wait until later to ask her who gave her permission to turn the late Mister Barnet's house into a hospital.

* * * *

Her husband guided Helen into the house. Frightened servants, alerted by his tattoo on the front door, ran downstairs to answer the summons. Fletcher in a red dressing gown, maids in nightgowns—shawls around their shoulders—and footmen, who had pulled on whichever clothes came to hand.

Georgianne followed them. Her candlestick wavered.

Helen looked at her sister by the light of the sweet-smelling beeswax candle, in pleasant contrast to the stink of blood and urine which filled her own house.

Georgianne slipped an arm around her waist. "What have you been doing? Are you hurt? Is that your blood on your apron?" She sank down onto the stairs.

Helen shook her head while Pringle, who had reached the hall, screeched at the sight of her. "Stop that noise," Helen ordered. "Georgianne, don't be shocked. I was helping to nurse the soldiers." She looked at the huddle of servants. "Captain Dalrymple is hungry. Fletcher, arrange for food and drink to be brought to my parlour. Pringle, fetch water for me to wash."

"Lawks, Boney will get us," the page boy snivelled.

"Not if our army can prevent him," Dalrymple reassured the young man. "Wellington defeated the French at Quatre Bras,

433

so there is no need for alarm." A few long steps took him to his sister-in-law. "You should be proud of my wife. She is a merciful angel."

"Yes, Captain, I know she is. Come, you shall wash and prepare for bed."

"No, Pringle will look after me. I insist you take care of yourself. If I were not in such a state, I would tuck you up in bed."

"There is no need, dearest; we shall speak in the morning."

"How selfish of me not to ask how you are, Dalrymple," Helen commenced when they entered their apartment. "I cannot imagine how many hours you have ridden today; you must be worn to the bone."

Dalrymple put his hand in front of his mouth to conceal a yawn. "Only a little. After food and some sleep, I shall be ready to re-join Makelyn. Do you think your sister could spare a few bottles of wine for him? If I'm lucky, he will offer me a glass."

"How can you speak as if you are going to a picnic?"

The laughter in his eyes quenched, he sighed.

A knock on the door. Pringle opened it. "There is hot water in your dressing room, madam." She looked at the stubble on Dalrymple's chin. "And there is some in yours, Captain."

* * * *

Her face and hands clean, and her soiled clothes exchanged for a lace trimmed nightgown and a robe de chambre made for her trousseau, Helen returned to their parlour.

Dalrymple joined her. His chin was shaved and he was dressed in a nightshirt worn beneath a banyan made of gold-coloured, heavy silk. He smiled at her. "You are so beautiful."

"And you look splendid," Helen replied, surprised by her unexpected shyness. She gestured to a small table laden with bread, butter, cold cuts of roast meats and ham, cheese, pickles and a decanter of wine. "Shall we eat? I daresay you are as hungry as I am."

After they sat, he served her before he piled his plate with food, and poured wine for both of them.

She finished her meal first, then watched him sympathetically while he demolished everything on his plate. "You were hungry," she remarked, after he declared he could not manage another mouthful.

He nodded and yawned yet again, his hand once more across his mouth. "With your permission, I would like to snatch some sleep." He stood, came around the table and held out his arm.

A quiver ran through her. Would he kiss her? Hold her close?

After they settled in bed, he propped himself up on one elbow, bent forward and kissed her forehead. "Forgive me."

"For what?"

He hesitated before he spoke. "For being so sleepy, I promise to be more attentive in the future."

She stared up at him.

"Don't look so worried, sweetheart. I doubt battle will commence tomorrow."

"Why?"

"Wellington and Boney will need to deploy their troops. But don't fret, I shall enjoy the chase when Makelyn orders The Glory Boys to advance against the enemy."

"The chase?"

He raised an eyebrow. "Yes, I look forward to pursuing the French. It is much more satisfactory than hunting a fox. Can you imagine the fun when The Glory Boys charge?"

"Fun!" Helen scowled. How could he speak with such insouciance? Did he have no fears? "All I want is for the nightmare to be over, and for you to return safely to me."

"My love, do you think that is not what I wish for?" Her husband's dear face swooped down toward her. His kiss lingered in her memory, long after he snuffed out the candle. When she woke in the morning, Dalrymple had left without giving her the opportunity to say goodbye. She trembled. She could only pray for him with the hope it would not have been a final one.

* * * *

.

New arrivals swelled the number of soldiers bedded down at Helen's house, where, after a hasty breakfast, she helped to attend to the soldiers' needs.

Once again, oppressive heat added to the men's discomfort. The servants refilled bucket after bucket of water from the pump in the courtyard.

Helen helped a captain take off his scarlet wool coat.

"It is as hot as the devil's forge. Puts me in mind of India, where we sweltered day after day," he recounted.

India! A picture of her ball, at which the blue boy presided over all the other decorations, entered her mind.

She looked around. All of the unfortunate patients had tales to tell. She dipped a cloth into a bucket of water, squeezed out the excess, and bathed the captain's face. "Perhaps the windows should be opened to let in some air." She spoke more to herself than to her patient.

"I think not, madam."

Puzzled, she looked down at him.

"The flies, there are swarms of them outside; enough of the little devils are buzzing around in here without inviting more."

Although Helen was very busy, the morning seemed to pass slowly, while news trickled in with tortuous tardiness. At some time after noon, Thomas took a trip to the only nearby pharmacy still stocked with supplies. When he returned, he came straight to her, his stained coat long since discarded. Sweat-dampened shirt sleeves clung to his arms. "Good and bad news, Mrs Dalrymple. Yesterday, Wellington defeated the French troops commanded by Marshall Ney, but the Frenchies beat the Prussians at Ligny. It's said our army's marching toward Brussels."

"Don't be frightened, Hookey won't let the French come 'ere," said a wounded private, as Helen removed the makeshift bandage from his mangled foot.

"It would take more than them to scare me," she lied, and handed the soldier a mug of rum to take the edge off his agony.

During the afternoon, the influx of new arrivals lessened, but there was no more news. Fear for Dalrymple, Cousin Tarrant, and her many friends and acquaintances, stalked Helen

A gentle hand clasped her arm. "You have done enough for today, my child." Sister Imelda spoke quietly in her ear. "I have sent for your carriage. If anyone tries to steal it, the coachman and two grooms—whom I have armed with whips—will beat them off."

The nun's mention of whips astonished Helen. "Surely that won't be necessary."

"I hope not, but many of your countrymen and women have panicked, and seek any means to escape from Brussels. They are so desperate to leave that one does not know what they might do."

* * * *

438

Startled, Helen opened her eyes. What was that noise? Where was she? Of course, after she had returned to her sister's house, and washed—prior to changing into an evening gown—she had dined with Georgianne, and must have fallen asleep on the chaise longue. "Canon fire!" she exclaimed, her sensibilities shredded.

"No, no dearest, thunder." Georgianne put her book down. "Don't you remember the storm broke soon after you came home?"

Helen rubbed her eyes. "Of course, how foolish of me to forget." Wind still drove torrents of rain against the windows. A streak of lightning lit up the salon. Chaotic thoughts rushed through her mind. She hoped Dalrymple's umbrella would protect him. Heaven help the troops who bivouacked in such weather. "Some news at last?" she asked, when the double doors swung open.

Large drops fell onto the exquisite carpet from Langley's cape and waterlogged uniform. As he strode toward them, his boots left muddy footprints. But what did some dirt matter? Helen and Georgianne sprang to their feet.

"Have you news of Tarrant?" Her voice reached fever pitch as she pressed her hands pressed against her throat.

"I brought him here. Fletcher, and one of your footmen have already helped me to carry him to his bedchamber and he is being stripped of his uniform. He is injured, and unconscious, but not, I think, fatally."

Georgianne fled toward the door. At the threshold, she turned. "How can I ever thank you?"

"No need, I fear I might have done you a disservice. The ride from Genappe to Brussels has not done him any good. At one point, it seemed my horse would flounder in the mud and I would lose my grip on Rupes."

Georgianne looked at him wide-eyed. "You rode all the way with him before you on the saddle? You are a saint! Helen, look after Langley. Some dry clothes. I think he and Tarrant are the same size. And food." She whirled round and ran out of the salon.

Helen eyed his lordship warily, although she could not deny he was a good friend to her family. Fletcher entered the room carrying a tray with a glass on it. "Brandy, my lord?"

"Good man; nothing like spirits to warm one. The troops breakfasted on beef washed down with rum before Wellington gave them the order to withdraw to Mont St Jean." He downed the drink. "My apologies, Mrs Dalrymple." He removed his cape and handed it to Fletcher. "My baggage did not catch up with me, so I am not a sight for a lady." He gestured to the torn gold lace on his dress uniform, a missing epaulette and the ripped sleeve on the left side of his coat.

"You are shivering, Langley. Fletcher, have a fire lit. Some hot food for his lordship. You may serve it here." She turned around. "Would you prefer to change your clothes or eat first?"

she asked Langley, too frightened to press for news of her own husband. In case it was bad, she would delay questioning the viscount for as long possible.

"Food first." Langley waited to be alone with her before he spoke again.

Chapter Thirty-Four

17th June, 1815

Helen looked around the elegant salon furnished in salmon pink and gold, the scene of so many convivial Sunday gatherings. She breathed unevenly, too anxious to question Langley, who stood, his face stark, with his back to the fireplace.

Two footmen, who carried buckets of small logs, entered the room. After they lit a fire, they withdrew. Alone with Langley, Helen was too scared to question him about Dalrymple for fear the answer would break her heart.

His lordship crossed the width of the large carpet to the fireplace and held his hands out toward the heat. "Ah," he said, after a few moments, "Much better. We were chilled to the bone out there. With your permission, I shall remove my wet coat."

"Please do," she responded, through stiff lips, "but perhaps you should change all your wet clothes before food is served."

Langley shook his head. "There is something I must tell you," he explained, his tone hollow.

If her husband had been wounded or worse, she could not face it. "Is - is Cousin Tarrant badly wounded?"

"Yes," Langley said gently, "his leg is damaged by cannon shot and he has lost a lot of blood, but I wanted to say something else."

"Someone told me The Glory Boys did not participate in the action at Quatre Bras."

"You are right, but allow me to explain what happened afterward?"

Good. For the moment, her words diverted him from whatever news he might have of her husband.

Langley shrugged himself out of his coat.

She stared at the blood which stained the left sleeve of his shirt. "You are wounded!"

"A musket ball grazed my arm."

While the question of Dalrymple's fate filled her mind, Helen summoned servants and ordered them to bring hot water and bandages.

"No need to concern yourself, it's only a scratch," Langley reassured her.

"Nonsense, I have helped to nurse the casualties since the first ones arrived in Brussels." She took a pair of scissors from Georgianne's sewing box. "These will do to cut your shirt sleeve."

"No, no, please don't inconvenience yourself. One of the footmen can attend to me. Although the wound is trivial, an ugly sight is not fit for your eyes."

After hot water, bandages and other necessities were brought, Helen ignored

Langley's repeated protests. Again and again he tried to distract her from her task. Relentless, she cut his shirt sleeve from wrist to shoulder.

"You have ruined a good shirt," he teased.

"I shall buy you another one." She winced at the sight of blood soaked linen stuck to his skin.

Langley's fingers enclosed her wrist. "Thank you for your help but, as I said—"

"Do be quiet unless you are too frightened to allow me to treat you?"

"Frightened! If only I could make you listen—"

"Yes, yes, I daresay you would challenge me to a duel," she ribbed him as if he were a peevish invalid. "This might hurt, but don't be afraid, my lord."

Langley's arm stiffened. "I am not a weakling."

Helen clamped her lips between her teeth. Afraid of conversation, because it would force her to question him about Dalrymple, she admitted her cowardice.

She applied a sponge soaked in water to free Langley's wound from the linen which adhered to it. "When were you and Cousin Tarrant injured?"

"After Wellington received news of Blucher retreating from Ligny—in order to maintain communication with him—he commanded the army to withdraw to Waterloo. We were fortunate because Napoleon did not return to Quatre Bras until the afternoon, so our troops had time to retreat, protected from the French lancers by our cavalry."

Helen peeled the wet linen away from Langley's deep flesh wound. "You have not answered my question."

"We fell afoul of the French at Genappe." He caught his breath as she removed shreds of linen and wool with tweezers.

"I am trying not to hurt you, my lord, but your wound is ugly. I must clean it so it will not fester." She teased out another scrap of black thread. "What happened at Genappe?"

"Keen to engage the French, Uxbridge led the rear guard in a charge against Ney's French lancers, along the village high street."

Although blood oozed after she removed a deeply embedded strand of linen, Langley bore the pain without complaint. "Did you defeat them?" she asked, with the hope he would speak about Dalrymple, although she dreaded bad news.

"Of course, the Glory Boys did not disappoint Uxbridge." He sighed. "A nasty business, not made easier by torrential rain which turned the ground into a quagmire. After a fierce encounter, they were forced to retreat and reform. The lancers did not follow, allowing the wounded to be saved. I beg your pardon; you cannot be interested in this. You will think I am an insensitive brute, but I must tell you—" he broke off.

Her hands trembled. Her stomach clenched. "Tell me what?"

"While I tried to deliver a message from Makelyn, Uxbridge ordered the cavalry to retreat." He spoke carefully, causing her to sense that he intended to say something else. "The rain increased, lightning streaked across the sky and thunder rolled. Neither horse nor man could see ahead of them. Yet The Glory Boys charged against those damned French who blocked the street with their lances pointed at us. A bullet winged me while I took a message to Makelyn, and a lance pierced Rupes and— well, never mind that for now.

"Lady Luck favoured us because the lancers did not pursue, so we took our wounded, including Rupes, to safety. Now, please bandage my arm. After I eat, I must change my clothes and report to Makelyn."

She frowned. Had he been about to give her some entirely different news? "Your arm is injured. How can you ride? Surely you will not be expected to return? You have already done your duty."

"I've suffered worse than this and fought on."

"If you say so." She pulled the bell rope.

The butler, who must have been waiting near the door, entered the salon, his steps less stately than usual.

"Fletcher," Helen began, "please bring a bottle of brandy."

Langley smiled. "Aha, at last, something more to fortify me."

"I am sorry to disappoint you, the brandy is to cleanse your wound." She frowned. "Fletcher, after you have brought it, send for a doctor. I think the gash should be stitched."

The butler inclined his head. "There is no need to do so, madam. Doctor Longspring is with Major Tarrant. Before he leaves, I shall ask him to attend to his lordship."

Langley straightened his back. "How is the major?"

"There is talk of amputation, my lord." Fletcher replied. His eyes moist, he went out of the salon.

"Confound it!" Langley exclaimed. "After Rupes was wounded in the Peninsular, the sawbones saved his leg; please God don't let another one hack if off now." With a groan, he sank against the back of his chair.

Helen pressed her hand against his forehead. "Feverish, I am not surprised. You were soaked bringing Cousin Tarrant here. We must take care of you."

His eyes blazed when he looked up at her. "My poor girl, what do I matter? Even now, most of my men are hungry and cold, bivouacked in this damnable rain."

Accidentally, perhaps, his finger brushed hers. The atmosphere stilled, broken only by the ticking of the clock on the mantel piece.

Why had he called her his 'poor girl'? For a moment she imagined her heart would stop beating. Motionless, she stared at him. She summoned her reluctant courage. "Langley, is there something I should know?"

"Yes—" before he could complete the sentence, Fletcher brought the brandy.

"Thank you. Open the bottle and give it to me, then please steady his lordship's arm while I pour the spirit onto his wound."

"I don't need anyone to hold me," Langley muttered. "I am not a milksop."

"I know you are not, my lord, but the sting is sure to make you jerk."

Fletcher stood behind the viscount's chair, leaned forward and imprisoned his arm with both hands.

Helen poured the brandy into the ugly laceration. Although Langley clamped his lips together, a groan escaped him.

"You are fortunate, my lord, the bullet passed through your flesh without penetrating the bone." She bandaged his arm.

Langley whispered a curse before he raised his right hand to wipe the sweat from his forehead.

She ignored the expletive. "Thank you for your assistance, Fletcher. Please bring a shirt for his lordship before food is served. While he eats make sure fresh clothes are laid out for him. Lord Langley and Major Tarrant's sizes are similar. I think my cousin's spare uniform will fit his lordship."

Her heart raged with fear as Helen crossed the room to gaze into the heart of the fire. A few hours ago she sat with her husband while he ate.

She must, really must, ask Langley a question no young bride should have to voice. Yet, in the depths of her being, she did not want to hear the answer, for her sixth sense told her the news could not be worse.

Even if Dalrymple had been injured, no matter how seriously, surely Langley would have told her when he arrived instead of calling her 'his poor girl'. Well, she could not avoid the truth forever. "Is there any news of Dalrymple?" she asked, her back toward him.

In a dreamlike state she heard the viscount's firm footsteps cross the salon.

* * * *

Langley stood so close behind Helen that he could smell the faint fragrance of her perfume. Accustomed to the sight of injured men and death, he would have given almost anything not to be the one to confront Helen with the truth. Ladies should always be protected from anything unpleasant, but he could not shield this admirable young bride. He wished she could have been spared the sights of injured and dying men. It required no imagination to visualise the harrowing scenes she had witnessed. Moreover, he admired the way she had tended his wound.

"Helen," he ventured, to delay the moment when he must confront her with the truth, "for the sake of our friendship, I hope you will not object to my addressing you by your Christian name. I apologise for the unpardonable kiss I forced on you at the Duchess of Richmond's ball."

"I don't know if I can forgive you and I don't understand why—"

"Why I kissed you?"

She nodded, adorable wisps of hair dancing on the nape of her neck.

"Out of insane jealousy because you married Dalrymple."

"Why? After all, you did not love me enough to marry me."

Did he hear a tinge of regret in her voice? "I loved you too much to marry you without the means to support you in comfort. The sale at Christies would only have paid off the mortgage and Father's creditors. My own money merely paid for my sister Charlotte's London Season. Although Mamma wrote to tell me she is to marry well. Papa is almost penniless. As the future Earl, I accept responsibility for my younger brothers and sisters. The truth is, much as I love you, I could not bear to subject you, as my wife, to the same privations I would have had to tolerate."

"Love me?"

"Yes, please forgive me for saying this, one more time, before I leave you to return to Makelyn. I shall love you until the day I die."

Helen turned around. Her glorious green eyes gazed into his. "Perhaps; but I think you will fall in love with and marry a lady more suited to you than I." She bowed her head. "Langley, I am sorry for having been a silly schoolroom miss with a head stuffed with romantic novels. When you rescued me, you fitted my image of a hero, so I imagined I loved you. Please forgive me."

"There is nothing to forgive." He guided her to a chair and knelt beside her. "If you loved Dalrymple, he might have made you happier than I ever could."

Helen swayed. "If I loved him?" Her eyes widened. "What do you mean by 'might have made me happier'?" She shuddered. "You cannot mean——. No, I will not, indeed cannot voice the question."

"I am sorrier than I can say. From the moment I arrived, I tried to decide how to frame the words to tell you of his fate, but could not find the right ones."

Helen's forehead wrinkled in a deep frown. Her eyes glittered by firelight with unshed tears. "You are sure?" She pressed her hand above her heart like a soldier who had received a death blow.

"Yes, I am certain. I can only repeat how sorry I am."

"Coward! You should have told me when you arrived."

"Please forgive me. You are right, but I did not know how to break the news gently."

Her lips quivered. "How——"

"I am so sorry to be the one to tell you that a French soldier thrust his lance at Dalrymple's chest. Your husband toppled to the ground. No man could have survived such an injury."

He admired her more than ever. Another lady would have given way to copious tears. In keeping with her supremely calm character, Helen had herself well in hand. He wanted to draw her close and comfort her but feared she would push him away. Instead, he inclined his head. His heart overflowed with pity. "Please believe me when I say I will always be at your service. Never hesitate to ask me if I can be of assistance to you." He refrained from adding the words 'If I survive taking messages to and fro during the next battle.'

"There is something you can do for me." Her voice wavered.

"Anything, within my power."

"Send Dalrymple's body here for a decent burial. I-I cannot bear to think of him lying forever in a mud-sodden foreign land."

He clasped both of her hands. "I am sorry. It is impossible. Don't you know most English warriors are buried where they fall? By now, the majority of those who perished will already be underground."

Helen squared her shoulders like one who had assumed a heavy burden. Her dignity touched his heart as little else could have done. He sighed. Only seventeen years old when they first met, her tranquil nature coupled with her beauty and intelligence won his love.

Fletcher entered the salon with several footmen who carried trays of food.

"Excuse me, my lord, I must – must attend to my sister."

A footman closed the door behind her. Langley cleared his throat before he addressed the servants. "I am sorry to tell you that Major Dalrymple forfeited his life during a recent battle."

* * * *

Helen paused on the landing. A French lancer had cheated her of love. Her happy future now dead, her husband's mutilated body buried in the mud in an alien land. A howl rose in her throat. She choked it back. All the tears in the world would not return Dalrymple. How could she bear it?

"A glass of brandy for the shock, madam," Fletcher suggested sympathetically.

Startled, for she had not heard him come out of the salon, she shook her head. For the first time she understood why her mother drank to excess.

"No thank you," she whispered, although it would be easy to down several glasses of brandy to numb her pain.

From upstairs the sound of a woman crying filtered down. Georgianne! Her sister would need her if Cousin Tarrant's leg was amputated.

Tears filled her eyes. According to Langley, her own husband had been fatally wounded. How could he be certain Dalrymple died immediately? Helen hoped he had. She could not bear the idea of him lying in agony in heavy rain and mud without a word of consolation before he died.

How long had she been standing at the foot of the stairs her mind tortured by her thoughts? Each step an effort, she made her way to the second floor. Georgianne hurtled along the corridor. Tears cascaded from her swollen eyes. Helen reached out to stop her headlong flight. Her sister struggled for a moment. "Georgianne?"

"Tarrant's poor leg. Doctor Longspring says the shin bone is shattered. His leg must be amputated below the knee. I cannot bear it."

"You must, for his sake."

Georgianne shook uncontrollably. Helen gripped her upper arms and held her firm.

"How can you be so composed?" The words burst from between Georgianne's lips. "Have you no sensibilities? Can you not imagine how much I am suffering?" She wrenched herself away from Helen's clutch.

"Think of Tarrant, not of yourself."

"I am. I would prefer to have my leg cut off to spare him pain."

How well she understood. She would prefer her own death to Dalrymple's. She slipped her arm around Georgianne's waist and shepherded her into her bedroom. "Wash your face, Georgie, and tidy your hair. When it is over you must not allow Cousin Tarrant to see how distressed you are."

She walked toward the door. "Where are you going?" Georgianne demanded.

Helen hesitated. She took a deep breath, in order to calm her shaking hands. If she told Georgianne that Dalrymple was dead, her sister's sympathy would open the floodgates of uncontrollable grief. She could not bear inaction, particularly at this time. Either she could stay here to mourn or she could serve the living and ease the dying. "I am returning to my house to help those in need."

Chapter Thirty-Five

18th June, 1815

Sister Imelda walked toward Helen between two rows of men lying on pallets spread on the carpet of the salon. "My dear child, it is past midnight. You should be in bed."

Helen shook her head. She gestured to the soldiers with both hands. "I could not sleep, so I prefer to make myself useful."

The nun's shrewd eyes narrowed. "Why?"

Helen looked away from her. "Is there more to say other than, your patients need me?"

"Not if you don't wish to confide in me. Please talk to the men, give them rum to diminish their pain, and write letters to their loved ones."

For as long as she lived, Helen would never forget the sound of relentless rain lashing the windows, mingled with the groans and sobs of men in agony. The pathos of soldiers, grateful to her for listening to them, for her gentle touch and soft words, brought tears to her eyes. She wished she could do more to ease the suffering of those who would either die in the night or be crippled. Helen did not know who touched her heart most—youngsters who wanted their mothers, married men fearful for their wives and children, or veterans with skin tanned like leather, who endured torment in silence.

Regardless of rank or fortune, all of them were bound by agony, and her own anguish connected her to them.

In every pair of pain-driven eyes, she imagined Dalrymple's at the moment of death when he lay mortally wounded in glutinous mud. No matter how often she told herself he most probably died before he reached the ground, she could not dismiss the image which tore at her heartstrings.

At long last, daylight arrived but rain continued to sheet down from a grim sky. She pushed her sweat-dampened hair back from her forehead. June should be a month of sunshine with sweetly perfumed flowers. She wanted to be a carefree child playing with Georgianne at Whitley Manor, her parents' home.

While she held a mug of rum to a young subaltern's mouth, she remembered Georgianne's declaration that she would never marry a soldier for fear he would be maimed or killed in battle. In spite of those words Georgianne tied the matrimonial knot with Cousin Tarrant and had paid the price for it. Yet she envied Georgianne because Tarrant lived. Her hand wobbled. Some rum spilled from the mug down the subaltern's neck. "I am sorry."

"Nothing to apologise for, madam. I'm not a sight for a lady's eyes. I can't imagine what Papa would say if he could see me now. He always insisted on his sons being clean and tidy." He made an obvious attempt to be light-hearted despite the fear revealed in his eyes.

Helen looked down at the youngster whose right hand had been amputated. "I am sure he would be proud of you. King George commands and you obeyed." Her throat choked with emotion. She helped him to finish the rest of the rum. When she stood, her body ached as much with grief as fatigue.

Halos of candlelight dazzled her eyes. She blinked. After several deep breaths, she poured more rum for another helpless soldier.

Sister Imelda tapped her arm. "Enough, child. Helen opened her mouth to protest. The nun sighed before she continued. "I fear the number of wounded will double or quadruple tomorrow. If you wish to help them, you must go home to sleep."

Exhausted, Helen tottered from the room, barely able to keep her balance. Her tired brain told her she should take the nun's advice, and also find out how Cousin Tarrant fared. Yet she dreaded Georgianne's sympathy for she did not want to converse about Dalrymple's death.

"Ah," Sister Imelda said, "here is Thomas. He will escort you home. Where is your cloak?"

"Should I fetch the carriage, madam?" Thomas asked.

"No, it is not far to my cousin's house."

Bundled up in her cloak, the hood pulled over her head, ribbons fastened beneath her chin, Helen made her way through quiet streets, head bowed against the onslaught of the rain. What time was it? But what did time matter now that she would live bereft of Dalrymple? Yet suppose, only suppose Langley was mistaken and her husband lived. Even now, perhaps he waited for her. No, she must not allow her weary brain to deceive her. Ah, they had reached the house. She glanced at the footman who had draped a blanket around his shoulders in an attempt to ward off the worst of the rain. "Thomas, I shall tell Fletcher to see to your needs. Dry clothes and food, I think, and some rest before you return to my house. Thank you for all you have done."

"If I may say so, madam, helping those poor bas—beg your pardon—those poor men, made me feel guilty."

"Why?"

"I should have taken the king's shilling and fought the French."

Before she could comment, a footman opened the door and stared at them. She ignored his horrified expression at the sight of them, and sent for Fletcher.

"Mrs Dalrymple!" the butler exclaimed, obviously shocked by her bedraggled appearance. Almost immediately he resumed his usual impassive expression. "Please allow me to express my condolences, on behalf of myself and the rest of the servants, on the death of Captain Dalrymple."

"Thank you." She wanted to scream her grief aloud at the sound of her husband's name. "Major Tarrant?"

"I regret to say his leg has been amputated, but his life is not in immediate danger. The biggest fear is that the stump might become gangrenous."

Almost asleep where she stood, Helen issued instructions, and requested Fletcher to tell her sister she would be in her apartment. "And," she ended, "make sure Thomas is well taken care of, and send Pringle to my apartment."

Weary beyond words, she forced herself to go upstairs.

"You're wet, madam," Pringle said, when she bustled into the bedchamber, "and doubtless chilled to the bone. A bath will warm you."

While a maid lit a fire in the dressing room, to ward off the cold of the unseasonable weather, more maids fetched cans of hot and cold water to fill the bath, Georgianne burst into the bedroom. "My poor, poor sister," she crooned, as she held Helen in her arms.

Helen tensed. She feared a storm of tears. "Please don't say anything. I am cold, hungry and tired. If you want to help me send for something hot – soup or stew, if there is any. No, don't look at me so – so reproachfully. Fletcher told me Cousin Tarrant is as well as can be expected."

"Yes, thank God he is."

Helen looked at Georgianne's rounded stomach. "You must take care of yourself."

Pringle bobbed a curtsey to Georgianne but looked at Helen. "Your bath is ready, madam."

* * * *

A flurry of loud, argumentative voices woke Helen. She rubbed her eyes and then squinted through the half-light at the clock on the mantelpiece. Seven o'clock. It seemed wrong for a heart-broken widow to have slept for so long.

"Mrs Tarrant, I assure you, Mrs Dalrymple will thank me for my news."

She stared at the open door of her bedroom. Mister Tomlinson!

"If you will tell me what it is, I—" Georgianne protested.

"No I shall not."

"I insist you observe propriety. Wait downstairs while I wake my sister and she gets dressed."

"Propriety be damned! Beg your pardon, Mrs Tarrant, but I'm a plain spoken man."

"It is outrageous of you to force your way upstairs and insist on entry to my sister's bedchamber. Give me one good reason why my men servants should not throw you out of my house."

"Because I don't fight like a gentleman. I use my fists, feet and teeth."

Helen sat up. What did the manufacturer want? To reproach her for not visiting his daughter?

"Mrs Tarrant, please listen to me. You cannot imagine the sights I have seen. This afternoon, after the rain stopped, when I rode out of the Namur gate in my carriage to bring

461

more wounded to Mrs Dalrymple's house, I could scarcely believe my eyes when I saw folk from Brussels behaving as though we are not on the verge of another battle. Those native to this country sat at tables, swigging beer and smoking pipes."

"Mister Tomlinson, I fail to understand what this has to do with my sister," Georgianne addressed him in a steel-hard tone.

Helen pulled the bedclothes up to her neck. "Allow him to speak to me, Georgianne," she called. "If you don't, he will not go. Besides, it will relieve his mind to consult me about Maria, after which he might leave us in peace."

Georgianne preceded Mister Tomlinson into the bedroom. "This is improper."

Helen ignored the objection. "Is Maria having a hysterical fit, Mister Tomlinson? Do you need me to calm her?"

Mister Tomlinson's ruddy face split into a wide smile. "I have not forced my way into your bedchamber to speak of my daughter. I am here to tell you I have taken your husband to your house where he is being treated for what must have been a severe blow to his head. My carriage is outside. If you wish me to, I shall take you to him."

Helen stared at the manufacturer. Faint, she imagined as if the blood had drained from her body. She had never swooned and would not do so now. "But he is dead…" she faltered.

Mister Tomlinson laughed. "Nay, lass, he is alive. He is unconscious but with a strong heartbeat."

All consideration of decorum gone, Helen thrust back the bedcovers. "How is he? Has he any other wounds?" She swung her legs over the edge of the bed.

Mister Tomlinson looked away from her. "A couple of broken ribs the sawbones has strapped up and says will mend."

"Why didn't you bring him here?"

"I supposed you would still be with the wounded at your house."

"How can I ever thank you? You are all goodness! Your heart is pure gold!"

To judge by his grin, Mister Tomlinson was exceptionally pleased with himself.

"Pringle!" Helen yelled as loudly as a vulgar hawker. "Come here! I must dress!"

* * * *

25th June, 1815

Helen smiled again and again. She sat on the edge of the bed and gazed into her husband's eyes. With relief, she noted they now focussed on her. He seemed aware of his surroundings. "At last, you are awake. How are you?" She continued to observe him, her heart filled with gratitude to God for sparing his life.

"For how long did I sleep?" He touched the large lump at the back of his head. "I have a fiendish headache and my right side hurts, but apart from that I don't think I have any injuries." He winced. "I don't understand why I am here. The last thing I remember is when I swung to the side on my horse a brute of a lancer almost skewered me."

"Mister Tomlinson brought you here in his carriage, long after Langley saw you tumble to the ground. He believed you were dead."

"That was good of Tomlinson." Dalrymple frowned as though he tried to make sense of her words. "I don't blame Langley. The rain was falling like a curtain. I could only see a foot or so ahead. The lancer who charged at me seemed to come from nowhere." He grimaced, obviously in pain, but managed to smile, his eyes scrutinising her face. "I hope you are glad to see me."

Throughout the anxiety of recent days, including those when, due to Doctor Longspring's grave verdict, she feared Dalrymple would not regain his wits, his words broke her calm. Hands across her face, she wept as she had not since her father died.

"My heart's love, please don't cry." Dalrymple leaned forward from the bank of pillows behind him. Despite his broken ribs, he drew her into his strong arms.

Although she rested her head against the smooth linen covering his broad chest, it took her a long time before she regained control of her sensibilities. "What must you think of me?" She wiped her eyes with the back of her hands.

"I am sure you don't want a watering pot for a wife."

His dimples revealed themselves when he smiled. "Watering pot or not, you are the only wife I want. Thank you for marrying me." He explored the bump of his head. "Forgive me, I am a little dizzy, not to mention my sore side." He lay back against the pillows.

"Dizzy or not, you are the only husband I shall ever want."

"I should hope so." He studied her face. His eyes gleamed. "I promise you that when I recover, my arms shall be your haven and we will share the delights of marriage in our bed."

She trusted him and looked forward to becoming his wife in more than name. Unfamiliar but not unpleasant tension coiled deep within her.

The expression in his eyes sharpened. "The battle?" he asked. "Trapped by my pleasure at being with you, I forgot to ask. What sort of an officer am I to forget my men's welfare? What of Langley and Makelyn?"

"Langley has no more than a wounded arm. Makelyn died leading a charge. I am told a bullet went through his head so he did not suffer for more than a moment. She looked down at the quilt. She could not bear to speak of more losses which The Glory Boys had suffered. "The final battle was fought and won at a Waterloo, although I hear Wellington said, 'It was a near run thing.' If the Prussians had not arrived in time to take part, who knows whether he would have triumphed."

"Your cousin?"

"Has lost his leg, but my sister says, it is a small price to pay for his life. I don't know if Cousin Tarrant agrees. However, he says only having one leg will not prevent him from riding with his son or daughter. Now, what may I do for you?"

"Love me for so long as we live."

"I shall." A long, happy sigh escaped her. She leaned forward to kiss him. "I love you, Marcus."

The End

Rosemary Morris books published by Books We Love

Historical 18th Century
The Captain and the Countess
Far Above Rubies

Regency
False Pretences
Sunday's Child
Monday's Child

About the Author

Rosemary Morris was born in 1940 in Sidcup Kent. As a child, when she was not making up stories, her head was 'always in a book.'

While working in a travel agency, Rosemary met her Indian husband. He encouraged her to continue her education at Westminster College.

In 1961 Rosemary and her husband, now a barrister, moved to his birthplace, Kenya, where she lived from 1961 until 1982. After an attempted coup d'état, she and four of her children lived in an ashram in France.

Back in England, Rosemary wrote historical fiction. She is now a member of the

Romantic Novelists' Association, Historical Novel Society and Watford Writers.

Apart from writing, Rosemary enjoys classical Indian literature, reading, visiting places of historical interest, vegetarian cooking, growing organic fruit, herbs and vegetables and creative crafts.

Time spent with her five children and their families, most of whom live near her, is precious.

www.bookswelove.net